EVA ETZIONI-HALEVY is professor emeritus of political sociology at Bar-Ilan University in Israel. She has published fourteen academic books and numerous articles, as well as two previous biblical novels. Born in Vienna, she spent World War II as a child in Italy, then moved to Palestine in 1945. She also lived in the United States and spent time in Australia before taking up her position at Bar-Ilan. Eva lives in Tel Aviv with her husband; she has three grown children.

Praise for *The Garden of Ruth*

"Etzioni-Halevy's choice to fashion the novel as a bit of a mystery helps provoke the reader's curiosity. . . . [I]t is satisfying to compare the ancient struggles of women to those of today."
—*Forward*

"*The Garden of Ruth* is a delightful explicit look at the plight of women in ancient times."
—*Midwest Book Review*

"Etzioni-Halevy . . . returns to the ancient Middle East for an imaginative second novel riffing on the story of the biblical Ruth. . . . [T]he mystery is intriguing and Etzioni-Halevy depicts ancient women chafing at limited choices with verve."
—*Publishers Weekly*

"Etzioni-Halevy . . . offers a beautifully sensitive, lustily feminist romance inspired by the Book of Ruth . . . a brazen rendering of the biblical material breathes fire into a ripping good saga."
—*Kirkus Reviews* (starred review)

"[This] fictional telling of the story of Ruth leaves the reader eagerly waiting for the author's next work. . . . *The Garden of Ruth* is an enthralling, sensual work that carries the reader to biblical times."
—*The Jewish Tribune* (Canada)

"[*The Garden of Ruth*] offers dramatic new perspective on an ancient tale."   —*Detroit Jewish News*

Praise for *The Song of Hannah*

"A thought-provoking look at an old Bible story."
                                                      —*The Dallas Morning News*

"This dramatic retelling of Samuel's story reminds the reader that even God's beloved servants are susceptible to temptation."   —*Booklist*

"A work of biblical fiction that speaks in two women's voices weaving the whole into one tale of sorrow, revenge, and redemption through feminine strength and love."   —*Wisconsin Jewish Chronicle*

"*The Song of Hannah* gets top marks for its sheer delight and will surely sweep you off your feet, keeping you enthralled until the last word."
                                                      —Bookpleasures.com

"*The Song of Hannah* does not disappoint. It is engrossing without being preachy, spiritual without being overly religious."   —Curledup.com

The Triumph of Deborah

Eva Etzioni-Halevy

A PLUME BOOK

PLUME
Published by Penguin Group
Penguin Group (USA) Inc., 375 Hudson Street, New York, New York 10014, U.S.A.
• Penguin Group (Canada), 90 Eglinton Avenue East, Suite 700, Toronto, Ontario,
Canada M4P 2Y3 (a division of Pearson Penguin Canada Inc.) • Penguin Books Ltd.,
80 Strand, London WC2R 0RL, England • Penguin Ireland, 25 St. Stephen's Green,
Dublin 2, Ireland (a division of Penguin Books Ltd.) • Penguin Group (Australia),
250 Camberwell Road, Camberwell, Victoria 3124, Australia (a division of Pearson
Australia Group Pty. Ltd.) • Penguin Books India Pvt. Ltd., 11 Community Centre,
Panchsheel Park, New Delhi – 110 017, India • Penguin Group (NZ), 67 Apollo Drive,
Rosedale, North Shore 0632, New Zealand (a division of Pearson New Zealand Ltd.)
• Penguin Books (South Africa) (Pty.) Ltd., 24 Sturdee Avenue, Rosebank, Johannes-
burg 2196, South Africa

Penguin Books Ltd., Registered Offices: 80 Strand, London WC2R 0RL, England

First published by Plume, a member of Penguin Group (USA) Inc.

First Printing, March 2008
10 9 8 7 6 5 4 3 2 1

℗ REGISTERED TRADEMARK—MARCA REGISTRADA

LIBRARY OF CONGRESS CATALOGING-IN-PUBLICATION DATA

Etzioni-Halevy, Eva.
    The triumph of Deborah / Eva Etzioni-Halevy.
      p. cm.
    ISBN 978-0-452-28906-2 (trade pbk.)
    1. Deborah (Biblical judge)—Fiction. 2. Bible. O.T.—History of Biblical events—
Fiction. 3. Women in the Bible—Fiction. I. Title.
    PR9510.9E89T75 2008
    823'.92—dc22   2007038716

Printed in the United States of America
Set in Horley Old Style and Dalliance

PUBLISHER'S NOTE
This is a work of fiction. Names, characters, places, and incidents are either the product
of the author's imagination or are used fictitiously, and any resemblance to actual persons, living or dead, business establishments, events, or locales is entirely coincidental.

Deborah, a Prophetess, the wife of Lapidoth, was judging Israel at that time. She would sit under the palm tree of Deborah . . . in the hill country of Efraim, and the Israelites came up to her for judgment.

Judges 1.4–5

Part One

An Embattled Prophetess

Chapter One

Two women were standing on high places, shielding their eyes from the blazing sun with their hands, peering into the distance in search of messengers from the battlefield. Each knew that her life depended on the outcome of the battle; but their lives depended on opposite results.

✻

On the rooftop of the royal castle in Hazor, in the north of the land of Canaan, stood the youngest daughter of King Jabin, the mightiest of all the kings of Canaan. Asherah, an arrestingly beautiful young woman seventeen years of age, had long, straight hair the color of ripe wheat. Her large eyes, slightly tilted at the corners, were a blue-green color and endowed with the sparkle of precious stones. The skin of her face and body was the shade of pure white milk, with pink roses of Sharon gracing her cheeks.

She had inherited these features from her father, whose mother had been brought by his own father, the previous king, from the land of the Hittites. In this land, far to the north and west of Canaan, people's skin was as white as the snow that covered the face of the earth in the winter, and their eyes were almost as light. Because of Asherah's rare coloring, her delicate, small nose, and her finely chiseled mouth, she was renowned for her beauty in her father's kingdom.

The princess was the new wife of the chief commander of the army, Sisra. Their marriage had barely been consummated when he had been compelled to interrupt their brief spell of love and passion and lead her father's army into war against the Israelites.

Now, four days later, she was anxiously awaiting news of him. Yesterday a torrential rain had battered the castle, but now the sky had cleared. She stood with her windblown hair swirling about her like a cloud, braving the relentless autumn sun that was scorching her light skin.

The imposing structure on whose rooftop she stood was built on a high hill. From this lofty vantage point she had a clear view of the rolling hills beyond carpeted with lush green meadows, and of the plain below dotted by cultivated fields, vineyards, and fruit trees. Among those, she saw several men on horseback riding toward her. Her eyes were moist with the strain of her effort to ascertain whether these riders, still at a fair distance from the castle, were those she had been waiting for. Her heart was thudding as wildly as the approaching horses' hoofbeats, in anticipation and fear.

Before climbing up onto the rooftop, she had bowed down to the goddess Asherah, the goddess of passion and fertility, for whom she had been named. Her mother, the queen, had called her by that name, because even as a newborn infant she had been as fair as a goddess. She had always felt close to the deity whose name she bore, and kept a beautifully crafted golden statue of her on a sideboard in her room. Weeping in agitation before this image, she had prayed that Asherah would send her beloved husband back safely to her arms and save her family from destruction.

Yet the prayer had not laid to rest her fear of defeat, which could spell death not only for Sisra, but for herself and her family. For if the Canaanite army had been destroyed and was no longer able to protect them, the Israelites would soon conquer the town of Hazor and overrun the castle. It was well known that they were a brutal, murderous lot. They would show no mercy toward their enemies, not even toward women, no matter how delicately nurtured they were. If they came charging in, her fate would be sealed. It would be death by the sword; or even worse: rape, capture, and slavery.

🐾

Some way to the south, on the top of Mount Tabor in the heart of the land of Israel, another woman stood: the Israelite prophetess and judge

Deborah. Unlike the Canaanite king's daughter, she was not a young bride, but a mature thirty-five-year-old woman. One who had been married to her husband, Lapidoth, for sixteen years, when, disregarding their many years of happiness together, he had sent her away.

Unlike Asherah, she was not beautiful, but overpoweringly magnificent: unusually tall, her face expressive, her body voluptuous, her raven black eyes compelling. Her hair burst forth from her head in riotous black curls, with just a hint of reddish highlights in them. Because her curls were wild and easily tangled, she wore her hair shorter than Asherah. Yet, at this moment, there were marked similarities between her and the Canaanite beauty. Deborah's hair, too, was blown by the wind, and her eyes were strained from staring into the distance.

From the crest of the mountain, which rose in solitary splendor in the Valley of Jezreel, she had a commanding view of the vale below, laid out at her feet like a richly patterned rug. She spotted neatly tended fields, on which the wheat had been sown already. Orchards of plentiful olive trees spread to the distant hills beyond, on whose gentle green slopes woolly fleeced sheep and goats grazed contentedly; their occasional bleating could be heard at a distance. Like Asherah, Deborah was wondering whether the men she saw riding toward her were the bearers of tidings from the battlefield.

Deborah, too, was torn between hope and fear. She had long been blessed with an unfathomable closeness to the Lord, the God of Israel. She had never been privy to visions of herself bowing before his golden throne amid angels and stars. Nonetheless, at times she had felt her soul soar high to touch his infinity. But during the last few days, she had sensed that his very holiness had put him out of reach of her prayers, and that the gates of heaven had been shut to them. Although she would never have admitted this to anyone, her heart, too, was pounding at a mad pace in a hell of uncertainty.

She was the one who had dispatched the Israelite sword bearers to war against King Jabin's army. She was responsible for the lives of the young men she had sent out, and for the life of the young commander Barak, who was leading them at her behest.

An Israelite defeat would spell death for them and for her. Leaving their chariots at the foot of the mountain, the enemy's soldiers would soon overrun her hastily pitched tent at its summit. Their commander, Sisra, who had seen her before and hated her on sight, would easily recognize her. She expected no mercy at his hands. She could flee, but it would be dishonorable for her to abandon her warriors. She would remain where she was to meet her fate. After that, Sisra would follow up his feat by devastating the entire land of Israel and destroying its people, and so also her own sons and family.

As she faced this harrowing possibility, Deborah tried to banish her doubts about sending Barak to confront the Canaanites. She had not done so lightly; she had been convinced that there was no other choice.

The people of Israel had been facing increasing hardship at the hands of Jabin and Sisra. Their soldiers raided peaceful Israelite villages. They killed men and children and captured other men and women and turned them into slaves for themselves and the priests and noblemen of Canaan. They plundered the farmers' flocks and cattle and the produce that was stocked up in their storerooms and burned down their houses and fields.

This persecution had been going on unceasingly for twenty years, worsening by the day. Over time, matters had become so dire that most people were afraid to travel on the roads or live in the countryside or in villages. Many deserted their properties and farms to seek protection in fortified towns, surrounded by walls. These were often far removed from their fields so that they were cut off from their sources of livelihood and suffered the pangs of hunger. But at least they could sleep peacefully, without fear of being slaughtered in their sleep.

During this time, Deborah had become renowned for her divine gift of prophecy, and had also established herself as the most widely acclaimed leader and judge in Israel. She had never been anointed. But she was endowed with that intangible spark that, by the grace of God, sets leaders apart from ordinary men and women. So she had gradually drifted into her position, and no one had ever disputed her leadership.

She judged the people in the mountains of Efraim, and litigants from all parts of the land of Israel flocked to her for judgment there. Those who were troubled in their souls also came to seek her advice, and she was able to lift even the most downcast of spirits. Thus, when the yoke of the Canaanites was heavy upon the Israelites' necks, they turned to her with their complaints. As they groaned under the heel of oppression, they expected her to bring them relief.

Deborah was quick to perceive that their patience had run short. More and more men were willing to bear swords and come out in defense of their people. Yet they required a leader who could steer them to victory. The battle that had raged the day before had been the result of her reluctant willingness to assume this wartime leadership.

The favorable outcome she fervently prayed for would compel her to confront Barak, who would expect the reward he had insisted on in return for carrying out her orders to become commander of the army. She had always been unfailingly faithful to the man who had been her husband for so many years. Even now that he had divorced her on an unfathomable whim, she was still bound to him with the bonds of a love that had not waned. But in the days that had passed since then, she had relegated it to the nether regions of her soul, as she gradually came to harbor a lust for Barak that was as unexpected as it was compelling. Now, if he returned safely and victoriously, it would be difficult for her to turn him back from his design. Nor did she any longer wish to do so.

Chapter Two

Asherah, being not a judge but a closely protected princess, knew little about the antecedents of the war. But although she was unaware of it, her father had not dispatched Sisra and the Canaanite army into war wantonly either. Like Deborah, he had been convinced that there was no other way.

He was sure that the Israelites, those creeping insects who had already conquered and destroyed a large part of the land of Canaan, were out to demolish and establish their rule over the rest of it. He was determined to prevent this by raiding their land without respite, by stripping their fields bare and laying them to waste, by harassing and decimating them until he could inflict on them a final defeat. Thereby he would rid Canaan of this scourge, so that his people could live peacefully off the fat of the earth, as they deserved.

King Jabin had long made a practice of sending out spies into the land of the Israelites, to be his eyes and his ears, and apprise him of what was going forth in their midst. Through those, he had lately become aware of the winds of war that were blowing among them. Thus he was convinced that an all-out war was inevitable, and the sooner it was waged, the more confident could he be of a favorable result.

So he sent for Sisra, the young officer from the nearby town of Harosheth, whom he had recently appointed as supreme commander of his army. Even while he was still a lower-ranking officer, Sisra had staged daring raids on the Israelites. Hence Jabin pinned his hopes on him. It was time for the young man to demonstrate that these hopes had not been misplaced.

It was Sisra's first visit to the castle. When he passed through its sturdy iron gate, the guards advised him that the king was awaiting him in his throne room, where he was accustomed to receiving those who came before him, noble and poor alike. Sisra walked over the cobblestones that paved the ground in the large courtyard, inhaling the smell of moss that hung about the thick wall encircling the castle. Standing among the large oak and fig trees that shaded the yard, the building itself, whitewashed, was constructed of burned bricks interspersed at short intervals with stout cedar beams.

As he ascended the wide stairway leading up to the elegant hall in which the king waited, Sisra was struck by the sheen of the white marble floor and the magnificent bronze statues of Jabin's ancestors that lined the walls. He found the king seated on his elevated throne, a richly decorated, gold-carved chair flanked on both sides by cherubim carved of gold, who, facing each other, were leaning forward, as if intent on guarding the king.

Jabin was a tall, slim man, and the splendor of his royal purple attire made him look even taller than he was. He was rightly known as "the handsome king," no less for his light hair than for the brilliance of his blue-green eyes. There was an uncommon dignity in his bearing: He was immaculately gracious, and every one of his gestures bespoke his elevated stature.

The young man faced the throne and bowed down. Then he stood with his head bent, as was the custom, waiting to hear what the king had to say to him.

Jabin was used to pandering to the vanity of the dignitaries who came before him. He would inquire about them, their families, and their properties and listen with unfailing patience to their lengthy replies. But Sisra was his employee, and he saw no need to humor him. Instead, he came straight to the matter at hand. "The barbarian Israelites are about to mount an invasion on us. It is incumbent on you to ready the army for battle immediately and preempt their attack with one of your own," he ordered Sisra. "You must inflict a crushing defeat on them, from which they will never recover."

After some hesitation, Sisra replied in an ingratiating manner, "I am but dust under my lord the king's feet, and the king's will is holy to me." But he added, "Yet I must point out that I have but recently assumed my post and I have not had the opportunity to train the army properly for what lies ahead."

The king was displeased. "Even before your appointment," he retorted frostily, "the army was being built up. You have no less than nine hundred chariots, and fearsome horses to draw them, at your disposal, while the Israelites have none. It should not be difficult for you to trample them under your wheels as grass is trampled under a herd of cattle."

"My lord king," said Sisra, "the horses and chariots are very well. But as my nocturnal raids on the Israelites have always been on foot, the charioteers are not properly versed in the art of war. I need time to drill them."

"We have no time," countered the king irritably. "It is blatantly clear that the Israelites are preparing for war; it would be foolhardy to hold back. I have worked toward this end for years. If we don't attack now we will be like a woman who has carried an infant in her womb until her days are full to give birth, yet has no strength to bring it forth."

"I hope that my lord the king will bear with me for a few days, so that I may consult my officers," replied Sisra.

Jabin took this as a sign of the young man's insubordination, which he resented. But he realized that there was no sense in pressing him any further, and with a dark look in his eyes and a grim mouth, he curtly dismissed him.

On that same evening, he invited a few noblemen and the old priests who presided over the temple that stood adjacent to the castle to a small banquet in Sisra's honor. In the castle's elegant eating room, they partook of a meal of choice veal cooked in fresh butter to delicious tenderness, and a delicately spiced red lentil and onion stew, washed down by a golden-colored wine. This meal was set before them by slave women garbed in gray robes, gliding by as silently as the spirits of the dead. While they ate, the king presented Sisra to his guests and his family.

At this moment, it was as if the king's youngest daughter emerged out of a deep slumber and, for the first time in her life, became truly and vibrantly alive.

🜚

From the day of her birth, Asherah had been wrapped in comfort and luxury. But this was nothing to her, because she had never known anything else. From an early age she had been aware that she outshone the king's other daughters in her beauty, and that she was among them like a rose among thorns. Yet she did not bask in her looks, either, because there was no man nearby whom she would have wished to savor them. There were only her father's underlings: his courtiers and officers and guards. They gaped at her in slavish admiration, but it left her untouched. She paid no more heed to men than she did to the air she breathed.

Until the evening on which her eyes first alighted on Sisra. As they sat opposite each other at the meal, she was attracted to his sandy hair, gray eyes, and rugged face as a moth was drawn to the flickering light of an oil lamp. She could only stare at him with open lips in stunned silence.

Sisra soon returned Asherah's gaze. Though she was clad in a fine linen dress of a violet color, with a delicately crafted gold belt encircling her slender waist, he did not notice her garment. He merely drowned his eyes in hers, shimmering like the water of the Great Sea, and they smiled at each other. Then they continued to exchange furtive glances and fleeting smiles throughout the entire meal.

The next morning, Asherah arranged matters so that she had the opportunity to meet Sisra. She was strictly guarded and knew that she would not be permitted to meet him alone. But with her nurse trotting behind her, she stepped out into the landscaped garden, a profusion of trees and bushes that had been planted around the castle's wall. There she found a stone, sheltered from the sun by the shade of an elm tree, and sat down to await him.

As she had hoped, he did not delay and went out to search for her in the grounds surrounding the castle. He soon discovered her and was overwhelmed by her beauty, as dazzling as the sunshine that was strengthening by the moment. He stared at her in rapt contemplation, then sat down beside her and talked to her tenderly.

After that, he sought her out whenever he was not conferring with his officers. They sat on the same spot every day. He plucked thin little branches off the bushes and wove them into her hair, pleating it into tresses that hung charmingly over her temples. Each time they met, their talks and their looks became more intimate.

Every fiber of Asherah's being responded to him. To his stocky frame, his legs as powerful and well shaped as pillars carved of marble; to his features, as harsh as a wolf's, which stood in glaring contrast to his smile, as soft as a barely weaned lamb; and to the gentle manner in which he treated her. Although at first she had been attracted to his manly ruggedness, it was the contrast between hardness and softness that awakened her love for him. Through this love she unfurled her petals, as did the flowers that grew in the garden in the light of the sun.

Sisra soon declared his love for her and clasped a golden necklace studded with pearls around her neck, whispering his hope that the king would accept his offer to make her his wife.

The princess had known since childhood that her father had designated her to be the wife of one of the other kings of Canaan. Ever since she could remember, it had been understood that in the fullness of time she would become a queen, and she had regarded this exalted position as her due. But out of the depth of her love for Sisra she abandoned this prospect without regret, and although there was no certainty that her father would do so as well, she told Sisra exuberantly that she shared his hope.

🦂

When eight days since Sisra had requested time to think over the king's order had elapsed, Jabin called him once again to his throne room. As he had done before, so now, too, he quickly broached the matter that troubled him.

"The king's words are as a fountain of wisdom for me," responded Sisra, and a smug smile spread on the king's face. Then things took a different turn from what Jabin expected. To his utter surprise, the young man announced: "I have a request: that my lord the king give me his daughter, Asherah, in marriage, as I have come to love her with all my heart."

The king, who had no inkling of what had been going forth stealthily in the castle's garden, was taken aback. He knew the army commander to be an ambitious young man whose aspirations knew no limits. He evidently harbored a secret desire to succeed the king. His sons would be first in line for the succession, but occasionally, if a defunct king's sons were dead or unfit to rule, other members of his close family became claimants to the throne. Apart from two sons, the king had four married daughters. Sisra apparently believed himself to outrank their husbands in talent, so that when the time came, his claim would take precedence over theirs in the eyes of the noblemen. It was for that reason, thought Jabin, that he was keen to marry his daughter.

This ambition was not to the king's liking. But because he was desperate for the attack on the Israelites to go forward, he decided to use it in his own favor. He erased the hurt expression from his face, cleared his throat, and spoke to him solemnly: "Sisra, I have had my eye on you for some time now. You have been going from strength to strength in every way. Hence I will accede to your entreaty and bestow on you my daughter."

Jabin did not do anything as crude as to link Sisra's marriage to Asherah with the young commander's acceptance of his decree concerning the war. But he trusted that Sisra was sharp-witted enough to understand the connection implicit in the king's promise. Thus he now expected him to roll up his sleeves and get down to the task that awaited him.

Sisra, against his better judgment, but because he had no wish to jeopardize the king's consent to the marriage, caved in to him. Yet he was deeply troubled because the king was pushing him into battle prematurely, before his own preparations for it had been completed.

🌸

When Sisra, once again sitting with Asherah in the garden, reported to her the result of his talk with her father, he hinted only indistinctly that a conflict with the Israelites was brewing. He did not think this a fit topic for discussion with a woman, especially such a refined young lady. Thus, when she learned that her father had consented to give her to Sisra, her joy knew no bounds.

"It is a gift from my own special goddess," she whispered. "The holy deity has answered my most fervent prayers."

"She must have been in league with the other gods," replied Sisra.

"Happiness such as ours can come about only when all the gods and goddesses are of one mind. May they smile upon our love forever."

"Since I awoke this morning, I sensed in my bones that they would. A white dove rested on my windowsill. It was a most auspicious omen."

"The best," he concurred, "for the same dove sat on my window as well."

"No wonder. I sent her to you, bearing a message of my love," she said with laughter in her eyes. In her exultation, she foresaw that her life with her beloved would be one of heavenly bliss until a ripe old age.

Suddenly a black raven flew by, so close it almost brushed her hair. It was known as the worst of portents. Asherah saw it but said nothing to Sisra, nor he to her. But she was rattled to the depth of her soul. She could not make up her mind whether it was the good omen that she was to trust, or the bad one that she was to fear.

Now, as the riders came nearer, she could only hope that, like the black raven that had briefly disconcerted her on that day, his parting from her so soon afterward had also been but a short interruption of their happiness.

Asherah realized from the men's dusty clothing that they had traveled from the distant battlefield. She saw that Sisra was not among them, but she had not expected that he would be.

She had said as much to Sisra's mother, an ailing lady of great refinement, who was visiting the castle when the war broke out. Leaning out of a castle window that faced its gate, the elderly woman had been wailing out her fear: "Why does his chariot tarry? Why is it so long in coming?"

"Even if all has gone well, as we all hope it has," Asherah had explained to her, "your son will not come back immediately. There will be much for him and his men to do in collecting the booty and sharing it among themselves, and taking one or two of the enemy's women for each, to become their slaves. At first he will send word to apprise us of the glad tidings, and only later will he follow."

As Asherah stood on the roof, she reckoned that if Sisra had been victorious, by now he would have completed all that needed to be done and would have set out from the enemy territory on his way back to her.

But if the battle had ended in defeat . . . she was not going to dwell on that now. It was unthinkable.

Chapter Three

As she waited for the riders, Asherah also recalled that her marriage with Sisra had taken place thirteen days after her father had consented to it.

She did not know, though, that the king had been reluctant for it to be arranged with such unseemly haste, as if Asherah were already carrying the fruit of Sisra's love in her womb. But his future son-in-law pointed out to him that the battle he was to lead was fraught with danger, and that he might never come back. He insisted on consummating his love for his betrothed beforehand. Because Sisra was so adamant, and the king was eager to mount the attack at the greatest possible speed, he gave in to him on this as well.

After the day of the wedding was set, Asherah continued to sit with Sisra each morning in the garden. Sisra would bring his head close to hers, until their foreheads touched and brushed against each other. This enabled them to murmur ever more ardent words of love into each other's ears, under her nurse's slack supervision.

But each day, after they had sat together for a while, he would rise to his feet and mysteriously disappear. When once she asked him about this, he merely smiled darkly and wrapped himself in silence.

Sisra's reticence enhanced his stature even further in her eyes. She envisioned him surrounded by his charioteers, issuing commands to them, eliciting their obedience. Then she conjured him up in her mind riding out at their head into the distance. Thereupon her imagination gave out, and she merely saw him fading into a nebulous landscape, into which her gaze could no longer follow him.

On the day before the wedding, as they once more met in the garden, Asherah whispered shyly, "Will you enlighten me in the ways of love? For they are like an alien land to me."

He looked deep into her eyes. "I have been eager to do so since the evening on which I first met you."

"One of my older married sisters warned me that there would be blood. Will our blood mingle?"

He laughed. "No, my beloved. Men and women both shed blood, but on different occasions. Women bring forth blood during their monthly courses and their initiation into the act of love. Men spill blood in the battlefield. Women tenderly generate blood required for the creation of life. Men's cruel bloodshed leads to its extinction."

"Can men never let off from warfare?" she protested.

"Once we have expelled those savage Israelites from our land, we will do so and peace will reign."

"When will this come about?"

"Soon, I trust," he replied, his voice imbued with a confidence he did not feel.

By speaking these words, Sisra now for the first time admitted that war was imminent. Thereupon he clammed up and all her anxious inquiries went unanswered. Asherah felt that he drew back from her like a turtle retreating into its shell. A tremor ran through her limbs.

🐾

The wedding was held with great pomp, befitting the stature of the king's daughter. Her two brothers, who at the time were engaged in collecting tribute of wheat and oil from the peasants for the king's storerooms, were called home, along with the rest of the king's large family. Sisra no longer had a father, but his mother and three brothers and all his relatives assembled at the castle. So, too, did the noblemen and women from all parts of Jabin's domain.

The ceremony that made them husband and wife took place in the temple that stood next to the castle. In its honor, the bridegroom wore a shimmering golden tunic. The bride wore a dress of the finest silk, imported from a distant land. It had alternating white and crimson stripes—white as a sign of her purity; crimson as a mark of the act of love that was to follow the celebration.

When Sisra and Asherah entered the sanctuary, their eyes were blinded by the light of the countless candles that shone inside it. And they were overcome with awe at the sight of the huge statues of the gods and goddesses of Canaan—Baal, Asherah, Ashtoreth, and others—that were perched up there.

In the presence of only their families and the priests of the temple, Sisra and Asherah both burned sweet-smelling incense on the altars that stood before the deities. Then they paid homage to them by kneeling and resting their foreheads at their feet. They recited humble supplications for each of the gods and goddesses to bestow blessings on their life together and on Sisra's seed and the fruit of Asherah's womb.

Thereupon the head priest of the temple collected the ashes left by the substance burned on the altars and put them into a bowl into which he poured the purest of olive oils. After stirring the mixture with a wooden stick, he dipped his right finger into it and sprinkled some of it over Sisra and Asherah. This he repeated seven times, after which he proclaimed ceremoniously that all the heavenly beings had sanctified their union and that their prayers were sure to be fulfilled.

And the king blessed them with these words:

May your descendants be plentiful and may
they disinherit their enemies.

At the conclusion of the ceremony, a solemn procession set out from the temple to the castle. It was headed by the king, who was followed by the queen. Behind them strode Sisra's mother with the bridal couple in her wake, trailed by the others who had witnessed the wedding.

The rest of the guests were already seated in the banquet hall, awaiting them. The enormous hall was decorated with purple hangings fastened to the top of the windows with shining copper rings and bands of fine white linen, and cascading down their sides. The tables were lit with the trembling light of myriad candles in artfully crafted silver candlesticks and set with multitudes of burnished red bowls, which reflected their light.

The guests were robed in their most festive apparel. When the king made his entrance with the queen at his heels, the guests rose to their feet and bowed low, until their faces almost touched their knees. And when the bride and bridegroom appeared, they gasped at the bride's beauty and the glow of happiness in her face.

The feast that followed was as splendorous as any princess could wish for. Poems in honor of the bridal couple were recited, singers appeared and lifted their voices, and the sound of violins, flutes, and drums floated through the air, to gladden the guests' hearts. Colorfully attired female dancers whirled to their sounds.

Sumptuous dishes, too numerous to count, were set on the table. Succulent pork baked in saffron, brought by caravans from distant lands, was served side by side with roasted fish from the Great Sea flavored with the fruit of the citron tree and figs dunked in cinnamon. Sweet red wine, poured into golden goblets, was lavished freely to show off the king's bounty. The guests ate and drank and became merry and broke into singing and dancing.

Asherah, oblivious to the babble of voices around her, noted that her father and Sisra and their advisers from time to time withdrew into a corner of the hall. There they huddled together, and even from a distance she could perceive the grave expressions on their faces.

When the bride and bridegroom finally repaired to the bridal chamber, Sisra seemed preoccupied. "Pray, share your worry with me," Asherah begged him.

"It has to do with those murderous Israelites, but it need not concern you, for I have everything well in hand."

Then he put his arms around her, kissed her gently, and led her to the bed. What she experienced with him there was so totally unknown, and so wholly delightful, that it made her forget the Israelites. It lifted her out of her placid maidenhood into passionate womanhood. It was branded in her memory all the days of her life.

Yet early in the morning, when Asherah rubbed the sleep from her eyes, she was perturbed to find Sisra already dressed, on the verge of leaving. She had hoped that their session of love and passion would continue throughout the day. But her bridegroom told her that war was looming in a matter of days, and that he had to busy himself with preparations. Thus he left her filled with fear for his fate.

The wedding celebration was scheduled to go on for seven days, as was the custom for royal weddings. That evening, another huge banquet was held. And the festivities for the guests were followed by their own.

Asherah was determined not to let her anxiety for Sisra's safety detract from their joy in each other, and even sought for a way of enhancing it. In between their lovemaking, she played for him on the harp, and sang soft melodies and voiced words for his ears alone.

A few weeks before, when she had been about to meet her father in the scroll room and he was delayed, she had absentmindedly browsed among the scrolls. Inadvertently, she discovered a most unusual one, which lay on a high shelf, concealed behind another book. It contained poems written by one of Jabin's ancestors, who, besides being a king, had also been a poet. To her surprise, the poems' words were lascivious, and she blushed at the mere sight of them.

When she heard the king's footsteps approaching, she hastily rolled the scroll up again and restored it to its previous hiding place. She would not have thought that such lewd words would ever cross her chaste lips.

Yet after her and Sisra's first night of love, she went to fetch the scroll and stealthily abstracted it from its hiding place and memorized those words before placing it in its remote corner again. Then she set melodies to them. And at night, in Sisra's presence, they spilled from her mouth as readily as wine from a tilted jar. Sisra drank them, and they were sweet and strong to his palate. They spurred him on to renewed feats of love.

This was repeated on the next night, and on the one after that. But each morning Sisra softly closed the chamber door behind him and did not return until nightfall.

On the fifth evening, the celebrations were brought to an end prematurely. Midway through the banquet, two strangers appeared. They turned to the king, who arose and led them to his office. Then Sisra and the king's advisers and sons were called in, and there was the scraping of chairs on the floor as they arose and followed the king.

An ominous hush fell over those at the tables, merriment gave way to worry, and what had been a cheerful feast became a somber meal. It was not long before Sisra emerged from the office, tossed down a goblet of wine, and prepared to take hasty leave of Asherah. She would not let him. With tears in her eyes, she followed him to the castle's entrance hall.

There he took her in his arms and kissed her with great fervor, and promised that he would return to her embrace with the speed of a wild stallion. She knew that he had to leave, and stood back with a heavy heart.

Only on the following day, when she asked her father, did she find out what had actually occurred. To his dismay, he had been advised that the Israelites were on their way to Mount Tabor in preparation for the battle. His plan to surprise them before they were ready had been foiled. But the plan of the Israelite commander to take the Canaanites unawares had also come to naught. Sisra had immediately called out all the men under his command, with their horses and chariots, and they were now on their way to the Valley of Jezreel.

"The Canaanite army enjoys vast superiority over that of our enemy," added Jabin, "for it is made up of hastily assembled foot soldiers who are not properly trained."

But Asherah had the feeling that the king's words were merely designed to soothe her, and that he did not truly believe them.

As she remembered this, she saw that the runners were now close to the castle. She gathered up the skirt of her long dress and, with the agility of a gazelle, ran down the stairway that led from the castle's roof to its courtyard. There she met the men as they dismounted their horses.

Chapter Four

As she stood on top of the mountain, Deborah recalled that before calling on Barak to assemble the army, she had attempted to seek a covenant of peace with the Canaanites, such as those the fathers of the people, Abraham and Isaac, had forged with local kings in their time. She was aware that the Torah imposed a stringent prohibition on alliances with the inhabitants of the land. But after consulting her husband, the elders of her tribe, and her own heart, she decided that this prohibition, valid at the time of the conquest of Canaan by the Israelites, was now superseded by the requirement to save the young men of Israel from a cruel death that might result from the otherwise inevitable war.

She sent a little rolled-up scroll, containing a missive, to King Jabin, offering to meet him on whatever day and at whatever location he should nominate, to negotiate a peaceful settlement of their dispute. Jabin deemed it below his dignity to come himself, but he sent Sisra to convene with her. He might as well have refrained, for during their brief encounter there had been nothing but cold malice in his bearing toward her. The meeting not only failed to prevent war, it brought it even closer.

Deborah and her retinue had ridden their donkeys all the way from the hill country of Efraim, in the central part of the land where she judged the people, to the borderline of Jabin's kingdom to the north, where she was to meet Sisra. She had a large tent pitched at the designated spot and decorated with colorful curtains and rugs. She had bags of myrrh mingled with sage concealed in its corners so that when Sisra entered, his nostrils would be suffused with a pleasing fragrance, which would put him in a receptive mood.

She arrayed herself in her finest dress. It was of a richly patterned scarlet color, overlaid with a yellow shift. On her right shoulder she wore a large, shimmering jewel of emerald set in gold. Thus did she hope to impress him with her regal appearance. It was all to no avail.

As soon as Sisra entered her tent, Deborah saw that his face did nothing to conceal his disgust for her. The Canaanite and Hebrew tongues were similar to each other in the manner in which they were written, but different in their sound, so that Israelites and Canaanites could not speak to each other. But Deborah was familiar with the Canaanite tongue, in which she addressed him, forcing herself to recite the words of welcome she deemed proper for the occasion. He flatly disregarded her words and merely nodded curtly.

Then she attempted to mellow him by offering him a goblet of spiced, sweet wine. He declined the wine and pointedly ignored the elaborate chair her people had brought along, which she now offered him. Then he favored her with a hard-edged look and chilling words: "It was not wise of your leaders to appoint a woman to speak to me."

The prophetess would not allow him to slight her, but she had no wish to enrage him either. So she said in an appeasing voice: "I am the leader myself, even though I am a woman."

He glared at her and gave a snort of sneering laughter. "A woman leader? A woman should extend a helping hand to her husband, which is what you should be doing now, instead of interfering in men's affairs."

Deborah had never hesitated to interfere in whatever she deemed important. She had never shirked any task or considered any matter beyond her. "Why?" she challenged him.

He regarded her ample bosom and said coarsely, "Women's attributes lie in other domains. They lack the ability to understand such affairs."

By that time, Deborah had formed an exceedingly poor opinion of Sisra's own ability to understand anything at all. In his short, shimmering, green tunic, he strongly reminded her of a slimy frog that had leapt out of a marsh. She would have gladly chased him out of her tent with a stick. Her mission, though, was too crucial for her to give free rein to her disdain.

In a further attempt to placate him, she said, "Men have the wisdom of the mind, but women have the wisdom of the heart. They are mothers of sons; therefore, they understand how crucial it is to reach peace. We offer you peace. If you do not wish to talk to me yourself, send one of the women of your royal palace to meet me, and we will negotiate with each other and overcome the differences between us."

"Our women don't negotiate," he retorted in a cutting tone. "They are true women. They are delicate and soft like fluttering sparrows, not coarse and presumptuous and domineering like hawks, as you are."

Sisra had spoken to Deborah as no man had ever dared speak to her before and his words struck her like a slap in the face. Her anger flared up, and this time she retaliated with sharp words of her own. "I have no wish to learn your opinion of me. I want only to attain peace with your king and with your people."

"You should not have invaded our country. Your murderous leader, Joshua, and his rabble attacked our peaceful cities. They burned down Hazor and reduced it to a pile of ruins. It was a more splendid city than any other in these parts, and they burned it to the ground. Even though over a hundred years have passed, the town and the castle compare to those that stood there before as copper compares to gold. If you wanted peace, you should not have waged war against us."

"Our God has commanded us to come here."

"And *our* gods have commanded us to throw you out."

"Let us live side by side, without killing and plundering each other, and we will all enjoy the abundance of the land."

"If you want to prosper you will have to go elsewhere. You will not do so here."

By now, their hatred for each other was flowing over like boiling water from a full kettle and could no longer be held back. Deborah felt a strong urge to strangle him. Her voice trembled in fury as she said, "Then it will be war to the death between us."

He responded in kind. "It truly will be. And since you act like a man, you may expect no leniency from me in this war because you are a woman."

Sisra turned on his heels and prepared to go, and she called after him, her eyes shooting arrows of fire, her whole body shaking with rage, "You deserve to be killed by a woman."

He whirled around and hissed, "And you—by a man. Me, perhaps." With these words he turned once again and left.

She continued standing in the deserted tent and waited for her shaking body to calm down. Then she gathered her entourage around her, and they returned to the domain of Efraim.

The memory of this scene made her knees tremble. She was sure that Sisra, too, remembered it. If the Israelites had been defeated, he would soon find her and carry out his threat.

🜚

After her disastrous meeting with Sisra, Deborah had felt at a loss. She sensed that the trouble that had befallen the Israelites was the rotten fruit from the tree of their own misdeeds. For years, many had fallen into the degrading practice of bowing down to graven images of the gods and goddesses of Canaan. They profaned the Sabbath; and well-off people closed their hands to the poor, thus forsaking the Lord, who was forsaking them in return. As long as sixteen years ago, when she was still young and unmarried, she had admonished them to change their ways. She would go out to wherever people were assembled and roar at them:

> You have defiled yourself through idol worship
> and oppressing the poor.
> Hence the Lord will bring destruction to our land:
> blood and fire and pillars of smoke.
> Put away the foreign gods. Observe mercy.
> Remember the Sabbath to keep it holy.
> Return to the Lord that he may return to you.

She was awesome in her wrath. Her black eyes, whose color always mirrored her feelings, would blaze like glowing red embers and her voice was like the sound of the Lord's vengeance itself. She could intimidate them for a while, but as soon as her back was turned they reverted to their depravity. Her words were as chaff scattered into the wind.

Nonetheless, Deborah's heart went out to her people. Over the years, she perceived the beginning of a change of heart as, one by one, men and women began to return to the One who reigns in the heavens and the earth. She was determined to show them that their penitence had not gone unheeded.

At first, she could not think of any way in which she might bring them relief. Although she had nothing but disdain for Sisra's loathsome words to her, she had to admit to herself that as a woman she could not assume all the tasks of a leader. She knew next to nothing about the art of waging war, which was as a sealed scroll to her. She could hardly envision herself striding into the battlefield at the head of an army, and she could not conjure up the name of anyone else capable of doing it.

The foremost military commander was Shamgar, the son of Anath, a man distantly related to her husband. He had inflicted an overwhelming defeat on another of Israel's enemies, the Philistines; but that had been years ago. Since then, he had dismally failed whenever he battled the Canaanites. Defeat had become his constant companion. He was elderly now, as well, and the times had passed him by. He knew little of the manner in which wars were waged these days. There could be no battle against the Canaanites unless she could find a man more fit than he was to lead it. For a while she was at a standstill.

Then word reached her of one, Barak, the son of Abinoam, from the tribe of Nafthali in the north. A young man who was like his name: a flash of lightning, who had been battling Jabin's raiders successfully for several years. He was the man she required, and she resolved to have him come to her. But she was wary of sending for him without first talking the matter over with her husband, Lapidoth. She had been used to doing so with weighty decisions all throughout the years of their life together, and she did not foresee how disastrous the consultation would prove to be.

🦁

The mountain in the hill country of Efraim on which Deborah judged the people towered over the others around it. Apart from her maids and aides and their dwellings there was nothing on it, and at sunset she always mounted her donkey and returned to her home. It was the house Lapidoth had built shortly before their wedding sixteen years ago, which also housed the five sons she had borne him, who now ranged from thirteen to six years in age.

It stood at a distance of only a short ride away from her hill, in a hamlet so small it did not even bear a name. One through which the scent of stews on the cooking stones, and tidings of new loves and quarrels, instantly spread from one end to the other. Almost the only cluster of houses still inhabited outside walled towns, it was heavily guarded from sundown to sunrise.

That evening, when their boys were in slumber and all had calmed for the night, Deborah remained with Lapidoth in the front room. It was autumn, when the gathering in of the grapes and olives on Lapidoth's property had barely been completed. The days were still hot, but the evenings had cooled, and Deborah sat with her husband at the oblong table that stood in the room's center, in the light of the oil lamps on it, and of the fire aglow in the hearth. She told him of her conviction that a war with the Canaanites could no longer be postponed.

Her husband readily concurred. But when she further advised him of her search for a man to lead the battle, he surprised her by saying, "Search no further, for the man you are looking for is close at hand. He is of our own family: the widely renowned Shamgar."

Lapidoth was a man of Deborah's own height, whose kind and candid features, no less than his solid build, inspired trust. She had always set great store by his counsel, but this time he disappointed her. She had hoped for a better notion, or preferably for none at all, as she had already made her choice.

She shook her head determinedly. "He is your kinsman," she conceded, "and as such I honor him deeply. But his manner of waging battle is outmoded; he is not the one I need. I have already singled out a man for the task. He is Barak, the son of Abinoam, from the town of Kedesh in the tribe of Nafthali."

Lapidoth was dismissive of what she told him and cupped his hands over his ears to indicate that he had no wish to listen to her any further. "I have heard of the man you are keen on selecting. I assure you that our relative is seven times as trustworthy as he is. He always lays the most careful plans for battle."

To her mind, her husband's words were senseless. "But they inevitably come to naught, for he is outwitted by the enemy. I will not let him plunge us into disaster."

Waving his arm in the air as if shooing away a fly, Lapidoth continued to dispense his irksome advice. "Appoint him as commander confidently, for he is much more astute than the man you have in your mind. The son of Abinoam has never been in charge of a true battle in all his brief life. He has learned only how to waylay an enemy stealthily but not how to confront him on the open battlefield."

Lapidoth's reasoning eluded her. She said, "With a devious enemy such as the one we are facing, we must be shrewd. A proverb advises,

By ruses shall you make war,

and rightly so. I require a man who can devise the proper ruse at the proper time, so as to confound the enemy, who is much superior to us."

"His men are an ill-assorted lot," Lapidoth persisted.

Deborah was stubborn as well. "But heroes who never hesitate to put their lives at risk for the sake of the people."

"He has an unsavory reputation with regard to women."

Deborah had been puzzled as to the true reason for Lapidoth's strong aversion to Barak. At last she fathomed it, and it was not good in her eyes. It was as if he suspected her of being ready to fall victim to the wiles of another man, which he well knew had never happened before.

She retorted vehemently, "You are finding fault with him for the paltriest of reasons. As he will be called upon to battle men and not women, his bad name in this regard has no bearing on the matter."

His only response was a derisive laugh, which left Deborah furious and speechless.

That night they were not united, and slept away from each other. The spirit of peace that had always permeated their home had stealthily fled.

🐾

The next evening, when Deborah came home, she was surprised to find a visitor there. He was none other than Shamgar, whom her husband had brought in without advising her of it ahead of time.

She bowed to him, as befitted his advanced years, and invited him to share their evening meal.

While they ate, Shamgar expressed his approval of her intent to go to war against Sisra. Then he added, "Great lady, it has been brought to my attention that you require a military commander to lead our men into battle. I offer myself willingly for this task."

Wary of hurting his feelings, Deborah retorted as gently as she could, "It is valiant of you, esteemed sir, and I wish with all my heart that I could accept your offer. But the mission has already been laid upon another."

"Barak, the son of Abinoam," he said scornfully. "The milk from his mother's breasts has barely dried on his lips. Surely he is not equal to the task!"

When Deborah made no reply, his aged face puckered and the deep wrinkles that were already there deepened even further. All her attempts to coax him out of the sullens remained unsuccessful. He ate the rest of his meal without uttering another sound.

Later in the evening, when Deborah and Lapidoth were alone, he complained, "You have shamed my kinsman."

"It was ill done of you to bring him here, where nothing but disappointment awaited him," she retorted reproachfully.

"I was hoping that he could sway you."

"Though he could not, I have shown him unfailing courtesy."

He scoffed at her. "You have haughtily spurned him, and thereby you have also humiliated me. You believe yourself to be above error. You have ascended high into the sky and set your dwelling among the stars. Your very conceit will bring you down."

Following this altercation, and for the second time since their wedding, they spent the night apart.

It was the beginning of the dire quarrel that would tear them asunder. For in spite of Lapidoth's decree to the contrary, Deborah sent out her summons to Barak to come before her, and Lapidoth did not take kindly to that brazen defiance.

Chapter Five

On the crest of Deborah's hill there stood a palm tree that had grown to gigantic proportions, apparently with the express purpose of shielding her from the scalding sun. It had sprouted profuse long branches that curved gently outward and downward and provided her a cool, shady spot. There she'd had an elaborately carved judge's chair set up for herself, on which she would sit donned in her judge's robe, of deep blue linen, with twelve white stripes—the number of the tribes of Israel—running down its front.

There were two stone benches facing her, set up for the contenders who came before her. Some fifty paces behind it, wedged between two terebinth trees at the edge of an olive grove, stood a tent, where she took respite in the heat of the day, when the justice seekers thinned.

Eight days after she had sent out her summons to Barak, when she had barely returned to her judge's chair from her noontime rest in her tent, the young warrior made his first appearance before her. He was flanked by six of his men, all on horseback. Since the Israelites bred no horses, those animals must have been looted from the Canaanites. Riding them, they looked like fierce heroes in her eyes.

Barak stood out even among such men. When they dismounted their snorting stallions and the stable boys in Deborah's employ took charge of them, she saw that he was the tallest of them. He had large, dark eyes under bushy eyebrows, set in an even-featured, sun-scorched, and dust-covered face.

As was customary among warriors, he wore a sleeveless garment that reached down no farther than his thighs. She saw that he had muscular arms and legs, and that his body, which was narrow at the hips and widened into broad shoulders, was as sturdy as a wall.

His shirt was of a light brown color. Its lower corners displayed the fringe laced by a blue string, which, by Torah law, was the obligatory attire of all Israelite men. But his garment was creased and his fringe's threads were sloppily entangled with each other. His profuse, curly dark hair was unruly and uncombed, and it protruded on all sides from under his head covering. Barak's curly beard, which badly needed a trimming, had white dust lodging in it as well. And when Deborah bent her gaze to his feet, she saw that they were shod in boots plastered with dry mud that had not been washed off for many days.

There was an air of wild power about him, which, she thought, was enhanced by his untidy appearance. Yet she also perceived something touchingly youthful in his demeanor. He stepped up to her and bowed deeply. Then he stood there, regarding her with frank admiration.

After he and his men sat down on the stone benches in front of her and were offered cool cinnamon-spiced water to drink and savory cakes to eat, she spoke to him solemnly. "Barak, the son of Abinoam, you are still young, but already you have made a name for yourself. I have heard it said that you are a man of great deeds, but so far you have shown your might in your own tribe only. The time has come to show it to all of Israel. You must fight Sisra and inflict on him an irrevocable defeat."

Barak raked his hand through the hair at the sides of his head, leaving it even more disheveled than it was already, and mulled over her words in silence for a while. Then he replied uneasily, "Sisra has got a multitude of chariots of iron. He is a well-trained and cruel warrior. I have been successful in laying traps for his men in the dark of night. But if I wage an open battle with him, he may be the one to bring a devastating defeat on me."

"The evil Canaanites breed nothing but evil. We cannot sit with our arms folded across our chests and let them perpetrate their atrocities on us with impunity. The God of Israel commands you to assemble ten thousand men around you at Mount Tabor and to go forth in his name. He will draw Sisra there and give him into your hands."

"How do you know?" he queried dubiously.

"I cannot explain this to you. I know it as I sense the radiance of the sun on my skin and taste the sweetness of honey on my palate and smell the scent of aloe with my nostrils."

Barak regarded her thoughtfully. Finally, he surprised her by saying, "If you come with me I will go, but otherwise I will not go."

She could not imagine why such a hardened warrior, a commander of fighting men, should show such a childish dependence on her. "Why do you need me? You know how to wage a war, and I am merely a woman, entirely ignorant of this craft."

"I can muster warriors from my own tribe of Nafthali and from the neighboring tribe of Zebulun. But I have no influence here and in other tribes. You are the leader in all of them. If we want the people of Israel to stand united, you must join me in leading them."

Deborah was not convinced. She suspected that he needed her presence to bolster his own confidence, rather than for any other purpose. Numerous men had previously fallen under her spell, developing such a filial dependence on her. They adored her not merely as a judge who abhorred injustice but also as a motherly woman. One to whom they could pour out their troubles, whose ears were ever attentive to the aches and pains in their hearts, which they readily opened to her gaze.

She knew Barak to be ten years younger than she was, and that his mother had died when he was still a small child. Thus she understood that he regarded her in some vague way as a woman who resembled the mother he had hardly known. He certainly looked like a boy who badly needed a mother's care, the kind she lavished on her own sons.

Yet what she needed was not another son who was keen to lean on her strength, but a skillful military officer. She let him glean her displeasure. "If you insist, I will surely go with you. Nevertheless, the path you are treading will not lead you to glory . . ." Suddenly she felt a prophecy she did not know had been stored up inside her spewing out of her mouth, as if of its own volition. "For the Lord will give Sisra into the hands of a woman. She and not you will snuff out his life."

"It does not bother me. I need no glory. But there is something else."

He motioned to the men who had come with him to leave them alone.

Then he looked at Deborah's aides sharply, until they scurried away as well. When they had all gone, he sat there for a while, regarding her boldly from under his half-lowered lids and thick eyebrows. Finally he said, "I demand a reward from you for my obedience to your high-handed command," and his gleaming eyes clearly indicated the reward he had in mind.

She was startled by his audacity, could hardly believe what her ears had just heard. She knew her body to be sensuous, but so far it had commanded young men's awe, not their passion. As she had been sure that Barak regarded her as a mother, it had not occurred to her that he would even notice.

She felt a responsive quiver run through her body, which vanished as suddenly as it had appeared. She remained adamant. "I am a man's wife," she pointed out, "and the reward you are seeking would make us both guilty of a flagrant breach of the seventh of the Ten Commandments, which sets out that

You shall not commit adultery.

Barak looked at her unflinchingly. "True," he retorted, "yet there is no commandment that obliges me to bow to your decree. Find another man to carry out your design."

Deborah gasped in indignation. "Are your people nothing to you? Will you stake the fate of Israel on this whim?"

His gaze became chilly and he frowned at her. "I do not need you to teach me the love of Israel. My heart is wrung for my people. All its twelve tribes are engraved on it, as they are on the high priest's breast piece and on the stripes of your robe. I have put my life in peril for their sake for years. Even now, if this venture goes forward, I will be among the first volunteers who answer the call for the army. But I will not be its commander. Let someone else do his share."

With these words he rose up from his seat and bowed to her and was about to turn away.

Deborah was seized by panic; she knew no other man she could call upon who would be as capable as Barak. She resolved not to give in to his sinful proposition, but neither did she intend to jeopardize the outcome of the war by rejecting it out of hand.

So she cast about in her mind for another solution. She lowered her eyes demurely. "First, you must show me what you can achieve on the battlefield. When you come back victorious, I will consider granting you a reward."

With what seemed to her the petulance of a child whose mother had denied him a toy he craved, he grumbled, "I want it now."

So, though his reputed skills in warfare compelled her respect, she spoke to him as she would to a child. "You cannot have it now." Then she added, "Without a battle there can be no chance of gathering the spoils."

For a moment she feared that she had overstepped the limits, for she sensed that below his childish demeanor there lurked a ruthless side to his nature. He looked like one accustomed to having others defer to his wishes, not the sort of man who was used to being thwarted.

Yet, to her surprise, he accepted her temporary rebuff. "The prospect will spur me to victory," he said as he bowed to her again and rejoined his men.

Standing at her Tabor high spot, as she watched the riders and their horses approaching, Deborah recalled that after Barak had left, she had continued sitting under the palm tree, searching her soul.

🌺

Curiously, Deborah had been endowed with a quality of motherly leadership since she had been a little girl. This elusive attribute deeply affected those she dealt with. As far back as she could remember, she had instructed other children playing in the fields as to what they must do. And they, boys and girls alike, had invariably carried out her orders without questioning them.

Whenever they fell into a quarrel, they would come to her to settle it, and they accepted her verdicts. No matter how bitter their fights, she always succeeded in effecting reconciliation between them.

Girls were not obligated to learn the Torah, but neither were they prohibited from doing so. Her father, a scribe and a scholar, was adamant that his only daughter be as learned as his three sons. Along with them, he in-

structed her in reading and writing and in the stories and laws of the Holy
Scripture. Although she was much younger than they were, she had no difficulty in following the lessons. Her being the only girl in the hill country
of Efraim who had acquired that much knowledge did not disturb him. He
took inordinate pride in the brilliance of her mind, and her mother followed his lead.

Gradually her reputation as a scholarly judge grew, and men and women
from near and far began swarming to her, charging her to settle their disputes according to the law handed down to Moses on Mount Sinai, and demanding advice from her as to how to go about their lives. She was only
fourteen when adults first came to see her, and she understood little of their
troubles. But for some inscrutable reason they were convinced that she could
set everything right for them. As she matured, she acquired wisdom and the
incisiveness to see through deception as one sees through clear water.

Her ears were ever attentive to the voices of people's hearts, their cries
of distress and their pleas for help. She never spoke harshly to anyone and
could be counted on to voice the right words of comfort. No matter how
heavy the burdens they dragged with them when they came, they invariably left satisfied, with the sorrow inside them eased.

Soon she left her childhood; her body ripened and she looked and acted
like a grown woman. There was no dearth of young men wishful to take her
for their wife. But they did not dare approach her father, nor did they lure
her to secluded spots to steal kisses from her, as young men were wont to
do with other girls.

Instead, they were slavishly devoted to her and held themselves in
readiness to run errands for her and do her bidding. She would issue direc-
tives and they would carry them out. Gaining her praise for doing whatever she had charged them with seemed all they dared to hope for. She
believed them to be worthy men, but she had no respect for them. She
could not imagine becoming the wife of someone she did not honor.

Her tall stature stood her in good stead as a judge, for people were almost always compelled to look up to her. But it put her at a disadvantage
when it came to searching for a man with whom to share her life. For she
could not imagine linking her fate with one whose forehead reached no
farther than her cheeks.

By the time she was nineteen and had almost despaired of finding a man who was to her taste in both demeanor and stature, she encountered Lapidoth. He was six years her senior, and their eyes were level with each other's.

He was also the first man of her acquaintance who did not treat her as an earthly substitute for the Almighty. He made it clear that he would not join the throng of her followers but, on the contrary, expected her to follow him to his home as his wife.

Deborah remembered the day, some sixteen years ago, when she had first met him. As now so then, she had remained sitting on her chair pensively after the completion of her work. It had been a summer day of overwhelming heat, with no breeze to move the branches of her palm tree, to make them fan her and lighten the burden.

Suddenly the noise of heavy footsteps approaching jolted her out of her lethargy. It seemed that a man had been so inconsiderate as to come before her, just when the sun was about to set. The man was young, an intent gaze in his brown eyes.

"Have you come to lodge a claim?" she addressed him sharply, to indicate her displeasure at his late arrival.

This called forth a smile in his eyes, which did not brand him as one who bore a grudge against another. "I am Lapidoth, the son of Joel. I came neither to seek judgment nor to be judged, but to observe. You have made a reputation for yourself from Dan to Beer Sheba, and I came to see the woman behind the name."

In surprise at this unanticipated response, her irritation evaporated and she asked, "And what do you see?"

He regarded her appraisingly, and it was a while before he replied. "An entrancing girl," he finally said, "who is guiding others, yet in need of guidance herself."

"Which you are willing to provide," she offered laughingly.

"If you will let me."

"Only if you lead me in the paths of righteousness," she continued to jest.

"No other thought would ever dare to cross my mind," he retorted in the same spirit. "And if it did, I would instantly banish it."

Lapidoth paused for a moment, then said, "I will ride with you to your home."

Deborah bent her head in acceptance of his offer.

She stepped down from her judge's chair. They both mounted their donkeys, which a stable boy had tethered to a nearby tree. The two men and a woman who served as Deborah's guards, and who always accompanied her from and to her home, followed at a distance.

Lapidoth pointed in an easterly direction. "My own home and property lie across those hills, not far removed from here."

"Strangely, our ways have never crossed before," Deborah mused.

"They have, now, and so also our hearts. Today you may show me the way to your home. In time I will guide you to mine."

In the following weeks, Lapidoth fell into the habit of seeing her home almost every day, and each day their love for each other gained strength. Deborah began to rely on his escort not only through the hills and valleys they traversed, but through life. She saw him as a steadfast man whose strength would constantly sustain her, as hers would nourish him.

When he became her husband, he also became her skilled lover, and she welcomed him with all the passion that had built up in her and found no release since the way of women had first been upon her, seven years before.

Despite the quarrel they'd had a few days ago, she still loved Lapidoth to the depth of her being, as he loved her. Throughout the years, none of the many men who came before her had ever dared to demand more than justice or motherly advice from her, and she had never yearned for any one of them. Apart from one brief moment, neither had she felt any craving for Barak. But he puzzled her. And she reclined on her chair, wondering about him.

Chapter Six

Although Barak was only twenty-five years old, he had been on his own for ten years. During those years he had led a wild life, dividing his time between battling the Canaanites and savoring the favors of the string of lovely maidens who admired his muscular body no less than his courage against the enemy. But those who knew Barak more closely than Deborah did found little to puzzle them. For his restless life was the aftermath of what had overcome him before.

The young warrior was born on the night of a thunderstorm. His father, Abinoam, intended to call him "Thunder," but his mother decided in favor of "Lightning." For she said that he had made a violent, tearing exit from her womb, emerging as quickly as the lightning that appeared in the sky at that very moment.

When the relatives and friends who attended the celebration of the boy's circumcision learned what his name was to be, they raised their eyebrows in disapproval. They thought it strange that a boy be named so, in preference to any of the names that already existed in the time-honored Israelite tradition. But they were polite and did not say so; instead they blessed the mother upon her speedy delivery.

It was to be not only her first but also her last. Her womb closed up for four years, and then she died of a mysterious illness that was rife in the town at the time. Abinoam mourned her in his heart for two years. But finally he decided that, as indicated in the Torah, it was not good for a man to be alone, and he took a new wife.

The six-year-old Barak was told that this woman was his mother, but he knew better. For in his mind there loomed the memory of another woman. One with dark curls like his, and large dark eyes, and a caring look in them that was reserved for him alone. A woman who spoke to him the way a man talked to his friend, as if he were big, and clever, and important. One who stood next to him when other boys threw stones at him, who infused him with the courage to stand up to them, and whose lap was his refuge when he failed.

His father's new wife did not resemble this woman at all. She was devoted to him but found no pathway to his heart. It was not long before she began bearing his father one little son and daughter after another. Then she was busy from morning to nightfall with the babies that filled the house with their laughter, their chatter, and their wails, and hardly paid any heed to him anymore. As the number of his little brothers and sisters grew, and so also the number of his years, it became clear to him that he had to fend for himself.

This suited Barak well, because it gave him the freedom to grow up in his own manner. His father loved him, but he was overburdened with the work of his farm and his need to provide sustenance for his six new children. So Abinoam heeded the Torah commandment

You shall teach them to your sons

by sending Barak three times a week to a scribe, who taught him reading and writing and the Torah. He was proud of his firstborn, who could make sense of the strange signs engraved on stones and on scrolls of parchment and even put up signs of his own on them, something that Abinoam and most of his friends had never learned to do. And he derived pleasure in knowing that his son was well versed in the laws of the Torah, even more so than he was himself. But apart from that he left him to do what was right in his eyes.

Thus the boy grew up without any restraint. When he was not at his teacher's house or at his father's side in the fields, he went his own way. He gathered a group of boys, as restless as himself, and they began teaching themselves the use of the sword. Although they were still youngsters, they nursed dark designs against the Canaanites, whose raids on villages and farms were becoming more and more devastating.

This went on until Barak was fifteen years of age, when the Canaanites attacked his father's farm, his home. As it stood in isolation outside the town of Kedesh, it was Abinoam's practice to set two men to guard it at night. But either the guards had fallen asleep at their posts or the attackers had come upon them by stealth. Whichever it was, the guards were killed before they could raise the alarm, and the raid took the family entirely unawares.

Barak was in the habit of sleeping with his sword on his thigh; but he had been heavily asleep. He did not wake up until he heard his little siblings' piteous squeals as they were being assaulted. He drew his sword and ran to their room. He was in time to see his father's wife trying to fend off the attackers. He thrust his sword into the backs of two of them, but he could not get to them all, and the others slashed and killed the children and their mother.

When Barak saw that they were past saving, he rushed out to rescue his father. But as soon as he entered his room he saw that Abinoam was already dead, wallowing in his own blood; the Canaanite sword bearers were now closing in on him. He took hold of a chair, which he used as a shield to keep them at bay. He retreated to the window, climbed out of it, and shuttered it from the outside.

Dense bushes clung to the house. Since the night was moonless, and the sky was overhung with dark clouds and starless as well, he managed to hide in the thick of the shrubs. He succeeded in crawling from one to another without being spotted, and then made good his escape onto the nearest hill.

From there he looked down onto his father's house. After the Canaanites had ransacked the house and emptied it of all the produce that had been laid by in its storerooms, and of the sheep and goats in its pen, they set fire to it. It went up in flames before his eyes, together with the bodies of those he loved. His world collapsed around him.

🐾

After that, one of Barak's kinsmen and his wife, who lived within the walls of Kedesh, took the boy into their home. Having torn his garments,

Barak donned sackcloth and strewed ashes on his head. He sat down on the ground in his relatives' home, and he mourned his father and his brothers and sisters for thirty days.

When the days of his mourning were over, he was more determined than ever to lead the people of his tribe in defending themselves against the continuing attacks. In addition to his previous gang, he brought together a band of fierce young men, the rough and tough of the earth. With them, he would sleep during the day and lie in wait for the attackers at night.

They were not always successful, but frequently they anticipated which way the fiends would come. They would ambush the intruders and kill most of them. Those who fled in panic they would chase back to their own territory, where they ruthlessly avenged the attacks on his tribe by rampaging through the land and looting the Canaanites' grains and flocks and cattle. He could not stop the Canaanite incursions, but his feats led the attackers to seek out other tribes instead of his for their continued invasions.

Barak's success in those ventures brought him an unexpected windfall. He and his men would bring the booty they had collected from the Canaanites to the tribe's elders to distribute. Those elders bestowed the lion's share of the spoils on Barak, and smaller shares on his men. The farmers whose farms he had preserved from destruction brought him part of their produce as tokens of their gratitude. He shared those offerings with his men, but there was enough left for him to sell, and he accumulated large amounts of silver shekels in his coffers.

By the time Barak was twenty-five and had been summoned by Deborah, he had been able to use the silver he had saved over the years to buy himself extensive lands, in addition to those he had inherited from his father. He cultivated them with the aid of hired workers, and in this, too, his path was paved with success. He had become a man of substance.

Since he knew that the Canaanites detested him and that he was a prime target for their attacks, he sought a way to enhance his safety. Kedesh was a thriving town, protected by a high wall. It contained a neighborhood of simple people, a multitude of tiny mud huts nestling against each other. There was also a neighborhood of the wealthy, where the houses were large and constructed of heavy stones, where the air was suffused with the zesty smell of the flourishing plants and the blooming hedges around them. But neither of these suited Barak.

He bought a large lot on top of the steep hill that overlooked the town, and had a spacious mansion built up on it. As he accumulated more silver, and as he deemed the protection provided by the town walls insufficient, he surrounded his house with a high, thick wall of its own. Visible from afar, it became the best-fortified stronghold in Kedesh.

Barak knew that it was incumbent upon him to take a wife and sire sons and daughters so as to fulfill the first commandment set out in the Torah:

Be fruitful and multiply and fill the earth.

Had his father and mother still been alive, they would have enjoined him to do so and he would have honored their wish. But they were not. And while his kinsmen and kinswomen frequently reminded him of his duty, Barak politely disregarded them.

He recognized his obligation of fulfilling the injunction. There would be time for that later, though. Right now, he had no wish to drink tasteless water from his own well when he had stolen water, as sweet as date nectar to his palate, from several springs at his disposal.

The Torah also set out that

*If a man seduces a virgin who has not been
betrothed and lies with her he must speedily
take her for his wife.*

This was another injunction Barak felt himself compelled to disregard for the time being, although he had every intention of heeding it when the time was ripe. But as he was meticulous in fulfilling all other commandments, he hoped that the Almighty would forgive him his two temporary transgressions.

He had to engage a number of maids to clean and tidy the house, grind flour and knead dough and bake bread in the furnace, cook his meals on the cooking stones, and launder his garments. He soon found that several of these maids were available to him.

Most of them were young and pretty and boasted well-shaped bodies, which their tight dresses purposely accentuated for his inspection. So he gradually fell into the habit of spending the evenings on which he was not fighting the enemy at home, enjoying the company of one or another of them. Thus Barak's sudden lust for Deborah, who in her royal bearing was as different from a maid as a rose in the garden was from a wildflower in the field, was entirely unusual for him.

When his eyes rested on her for the first time, a vague memory stirred up in him. Or perhaps it was the memory of a tale he had heard. Or of a dream he had dreamed. But for a moment he recognized in her the mother whose image had long paled inside him. One with whom at his side, he would be able to march forward and defeat his enemies. The memory evaporated almost instantly, and he saw before him a woman who was nobody's mother; a woman whose tantalizing body was a pleasure to behold and ripe for his touch, which she forced him to delay.

Deborah's memory, too, continued to dwell on that same meeting, as she watched the messengers glide off their horses at the foot of the mountain. At this inopportune moment she felt a soaring of passion for Barak, even a momentary regret for not having acceded to the wish he had voiced then. For the men below might well be fugitives from the battlefield, bearing a message of defeat. It might be too late, and if so, she would never forgive herself.

Chapter Seven

On the day on which Barak had made his sinful demand, and after he accepted the uncertainty of its fulfilment, Deborah rode home. There she apprised her husband of the approaching war, which was set to take place on Mount Tabor in the Valley of Jezreel, and of her intent to accompany Barak there.

At first Lapidoth would not hear of her going anywhere near the battlefield.

She explained that the commander was unwilling to go to war unless she was there to oversee the call-up of sword bearers from all the tribes and to raise their spirits once they arrived at the designated place of assembly.

"I knew that nothing but a curse could emanate from summoning this infamous man," objected Lapidoth with a snort. "Whoever heard of demanding the presence of a woman on the battlefield?"

Although she did not believe in her own words, Deborah reassured him by saying, "I will not be on the battlefield itself, but on the peak of the mountain. My guards and my aides will surround me like an impregnable wall. They will see to it that I come to no harm."

Lapidoth was not mollified. "Send this man back to wherever he came from, and appoint a worthier man to be in charge of the army," he ordered.

"Men like Barak are as rare as sunshine at midnight," Deborah objected.

"Or as darkness at noon," he retorted determinedly.

"Either way, unearthing him was nothing short of a miracle."

"One we could well have forgone."

When Lapidoth perceived that he could not turn his wife back from her misguided purpose, he insisted on accompanying her.

"If the war ends in defeat," Deborah reminded him, "it will not be long before the Canaanites invade the mountains of Efraim. Our sons cannot be left to the mercy of these marauders on their own. Much as I long to have you at my side, it is necessary for you to stay behind in order to protect them." She concluded her argument by saying, "You will not abandon our sons to their fate."

Reluctantly, Lapidoth relented. "You speak rightly. I will remain here and defend them with all my might. And so will the men who work for us in the fields. If indeed you must go, I will see to it that your three brothers accompany you."

Deborah balked at the notion. "They are too old to do battle. If the worst happens and the Canaanites climb the mountain where I and they will be, they are apt to go forward and be the first to fall victims to the fiends' swords."

By that time the tension had mounted, and shouts were flying back and forth between husband and wife. "You cannot be a sole woman amid an entire army of men without anyone from your own family to uphold your virtue. It would cast doubt on your honor and shame on your husband."

"I will have my maids as my guardians."

"Their servility to you is well known. And so is it known that they would form no barrier to whatever wrongdoing you may be contemplating, and neither would they squeal on you afterward. They will do your reputation no good."

"They are as sharp-eyed as hawks and nothing escapes their notice. They will jealously safeguard my good name."

He said nothing, but his eyes spoke his rancor, which she perceived but saw no way of warding off.

※

On the next day, Deborah sat with Barak to plan the call-up for the army. He told her that they would go to his hometown, Kedesh, first and send out the summons, and assemble the army there, before they made their way to Mount Tabor together. Indeed, it seemed to be the most expedient plan, so she consented. It was decided between them that they would set out the next morning at the break of dawn.

At twilight, she again rode to her home. She had not deemed it wise to withhold from her sons the knowledge that she was about to take part in the forthcoming confrontation with the Canaanites. Hence they crowded one of the house's front windows, anxiously watching out for her.

Lapidoth intercepted her as she was about to enter the house. Since she seemed harassed, he looked at her questioningly.

She answered his unasked question by saying, "I came to take leave of you and the boys, for I will be leaving for Kedesh with the fading of the stars."

He was taken aback, and a shadow was cast on his face. "I had it in my mind that you were to go to Mount Tabor," he said sternly, "and now it transpires that your destination is Kedesh."

"It is necessary to go there first to summon the men to the ranks of the army."

He rounded on her, his face darkening even further. "Are you out of your mind? Have you thought of where you are to sojourn there? Surely you will not lodge in this wild ruffian's house, for whom the debauchery of women is—is—his daily fare. He will not hesitate to trample your honor, and thereby mine, under his feet."

Deborah did not divulge that he had already made some such suggestion. Instead she protested, "This is merely slander based on gossip."

Her husband flew into a rage, and though their sons were within earshot, he raised his voice at her. "However that may be, I forbid you to avail yourself of his hospitality for even one night."

"Where else can I put up in Kedesh?" she asked mildly.

Lapidoth disregarded her question. "If I stood by and let my wife spend her nights in this debaucher's house, I would be as small as a grasshopper on the meadow in my eyes. And so would I be in the eyes of others."

"Set your mind at rest," she tried to placate him. "I will not be there with him alone. He is a man of great riches and his house is a vast fortress. I will insist on having an entire part of it for myself and my maids and my people, and he will not set foot there."

Lapidoth's eyes were ablaze with wrath. "You may be an illustrious judge and prophetess, but as a wife you rank poorly. Even an eminent woman must bend her will to her husband's."

His words rankled, for they echoed those Sisra had spoken to her before. "Have I not always deferred to you as the moon gives way before the sun when it rises in the morning in all its glory?" she said, attempting to justify herself.

"On the contrary," he objected. "It is you who have always been the sun, while I have been the moon, basking in your dazzling light, overshadowed by your greatness. At first, I was content for it to be so, for I took pride in your luster. But more and more I have been forced to efface myself before you. And now you are blatantly overreaching yourself. I will not bow my head in submission to this new humiliation."

Deborah, who had always looked into the soul of strangers, had failed to do so properly with her own husband. At times she had felt that there was some animosity stored up in him, and she had tried to assuage him by letting his views prevail whenever she could. But she'd had no notion that it had reached such gigantic dimensions. It must have been gathering force inside him for years.

Still, she could not give in to him this time. "The fate of the people of Israel is at stake. The burden of seeing to its welfare is heavy, but I alone have been entrusted with it. It is a charge I have not chosen to assume; it has been imposed upon me. Yet neither can I relegate it to anyone else. Not even to my deeply revered husband. If I refrain from going to Kedesh, I will be unable to steer the people toward this war and thus fulfill the mission that has been laid upon me."

"Go, then," he said with seeming resignation, with only the sagging corners of his mouth attesting to the weight burdening his heart. "But you will not leave empty-handed, for I will give you something to take with you."

Her baffled eyes flew to his. But he showed her his back and abruptly left for his room.

For a moment she was perplexed over what his announcement might entail. Then she slipped away into her sons' quarters, and the boys took her mind off her husband. There were a hundred questions in their mouths, and in their anxious eyes, about the forthcoming war. It took a long time, but she finally succeeded in allaying their fears about its outcome and her fate in it. After crushing them lovingly in her arms, she returned to the yard.

There Lapidoth stood waiting for her, with two of his workingmen at his side and a rolled-up scroll in his hand.

"You have scorned my advice and defied me no less than three times," he lashed out at her. "Your disobedience exceeds what is permissible. You bear the mark of a rebellious wife, and I shall not keep such a one in my home."

She waited in agitation for his next words, which did not fail to come. "Here is your book of divorcement, the book that sets you free for any other man. It has been written by my own hand and sealed with my own ring; I am handing it to you in the sight of two witnesses," he growled, holding the scroll out to her.

These words bore down on her, heavy as an immense stone on an olive press, almost crushing her. "I have done no wrong. No man but you has ever known me. I have committed no sin."

He smiled sourly. "But you are on the verge of doing so."

Her voice trembled. "No one can be held culpable for a misdeed he has not perpetrated. And I swear to you, as the Lord lives, that I will never do anything I cannot reconcile with my conscience, or with Torah law. I will not accept this dismal book."

Both her hands were balled into fists at her sides. But he stepped forward, took hold of her right hand, and attempted to press the book into it. "Take it, for you cannot remain my wife against my will."

Seething with wrath, she protested, "You cannot discard me, as if I were nothing but a pile of trash."

"It is rather you who are dealing with me as if I were garbage," he retorted, his voice rising as he spoke, and continued to push the book into her hand.

She had no choice but to open her hand slowly and take possession of it.

"Go forth from my house and make your abode elsewhere, for from this moment onward you are no longer my wife, nor am I your husband," he declared solemnly.

She did not deign to reply. Unwilling to show how devastated she was, she turned from him and mounted her donkey, which a stable boy held ready for her, and returned to her palm tree.

Deborah spent a sleepless night in her tent, while Barak and his men slept under the open sky, some distance away.

The next morning, somewhat later than planned, when the treetops captured the first rays of the sun, together with Barak and his six companions, all as disheveled as he was, they took the road to the north, to Kedesh.

Chapter Eight

It was Deborah's custom, when she rode out of her domain, to be escorted by a small but impressive cavalcade of people, all mounted on donkeys. At its head was a man bearing Deborah's banner. It consisted of a pole to which a large white sheet of cloth was tied with strings, and it had these words inscribed on it in dark blue on both sides:

The Lord is One

When it fluttered in the wind, it was like the flap of angels' wings.

The banner was customarily followed by three men with torches, which were affixed to their donkeys' saddles and lit at night so as to show them the way. Behind them rode three guards, watching out for possible marauders. Then came Deborah, mounted on her flawlessly white she-donkey, a sure-footed animal for whom she had a great fondness. The rest of her guards and clerks and maids, trailed by two carts laden with her tent and belongings, brought up the rear.

This time the cavalcade included, besides Deborah and the people who worked for her, Barak and his men. One of those had relinquished his horse to her in exchange for her white she-ass, and Barak himself rode at her side. Deborah had never ridden a horse before, and she felt insecure on its back. But because they had to adjust their pace to that of the donkeys, their progress was labored and slow. This made her feel safe on the unfamiliar animal, enabling her to look inward, rather than forward, and immerse herself in melancholy thoughts.

There were tears in her heart, though not in her eyes. That year the first rains had come early, long before the harvest of grapes in the vineyards was completed. But since then, several weeks had passed, during which the sun had been bearing down with all its strength and the soil had dried out again. If her eyes were rimmed with red it was because of the burning sun and the dust of the road, and not, she told herself, because of the unshed tears in them.

Uncannily perceptive, Barak asked, "What is troubling you? Your spirit seems to have fallen. Are you no longer confident of our victory?"

She was vigorous in dispelling his doubts. "My faith in the Rock of Israel has never wavered."

Since she had not explained her dejection, his eyes held a mute question in them. She wanted to tell him her trouble, but her chest was tight, there was a lump in her throat, and the words she intended to utter would not cross her lips. Instead, she reached into her bag and rummaged in it, as Barak took hold of her horse's reins. She brought forth the scroll, her book of divorcement, and held it up before him.

He required no lengthy explanations to understand. Being one of the few men she had encountered who was taller than she was, he had to tilt his head down to talk to her. "Was it because of my demand from you?"

She did not wish to reveal what had come to pass between her and Lapidoth, nor yet the turmoil in her soul, and merely shook her head and took refuge in silence. But somewhat later the words tumbled out of her, and she could not hold them back. "I am a lone woman now."

"Be of good cheer," responded Barak, "for I am entirely willing to dispel your loneliness as soon as you give me leave to do so. As you are no longer a man's wife, this will not be a transgression of the commandment prohibiting adultery either for you or for me. Indeed, it will not be an infraction of any Torah law at all."

She shook her head again, for she was not keen for what he offered. He had spoken truly, for the Torah did not forbid a divorced woman knowing a man, nor did it prohibit a man from coming to a divorced woman. But although there were no longer any shackles tying her to Lapidoth, she still felt herself wedded to him, bone of his bone, flesh of his flesh, as she had been for almost as long as she could remember.

Barak handed her horse's reins back to her. For the rest of the way she immersed herself in her hurt, and he, sensitive to her mood, respected her reticence. He became taciturn and spoke to her no more than was necessary.

As all those in the cavalcade were united in their wish to reach Kedesh as soon as possible, they stopped only to replenish their water skins from nearby wells and for a short break at noontime. But they could not do without rest at night, when a tent was pitched for Deborah and her maids. The men slept under the open sky in a circle around it, taking turns at keeping vigil, so as to protect the women from marauders.

※

Three days later, as the daylight petered out, they reached Kedesh. It was not necessary for Barak to offer Deborah and her people hospitality in his home, for it had been understood as a matter of course that they would all be his guests.

He placed them in a part of the house that was separate from the rest. Contrary to Deborah's promise to Lapidoth, after the evening meal, he did set foot there. But it was only to ensure that a bath had been prepared for her, and that she had all she needed for the night.

Deborah fully expected him to renew his advances. She had prepared herself to rebuff him if he did, but it proved unnecessary. He stood in awe of her and seemed to have submitted to her temporary rejection of him.

He merely ran his eyes over her body and waited for an indication that she'd had a change of heart. When none came, he bowed, withdrew, and left her. There was little doubt in her mind that, unlike her, he would not spend the night in solitude.

During the following days they were fully occupied, sending out envoys to the elders of the tribes and towns and villages around the land of Israel, with edicts instructing all young men aged twenty and above—who by Torah law were eligible for army service—to assemble in Kedesh. And they welcomed those who arrived. But when night fell, Barak took his evening meals in his mansion's front room alone with her. Afterward, they spent the evenings together, devising and revising plans for the upcoming confrontation with the enemy.

Although this gave him all the opportunity he could have wished for to seduce her, he made no further attempt to do so. It seemed to Deborah that during the days they spent in his home, his hunger for her had abated. She was relieved, yet wondered which of the pretty maids he kept in his service was responsible for stilling it.

Not all tribes heeded their call. But Barak was well respected in his tribe of Nafthali and the neighboring tribe of Zebulun. And Deborah was widely revered in the tribes of Efraim, Menasheh, Benjamin, and Issachar. Thus, within two weeks, they were able to call ten thousand men from these tribes to the banner, as indeed Deborah had predicted on her first meeting with Barak. They considered that this number sufficed for their purpose, so once this task was complete, leaving the horses behind, they all saddled their donkeys and headed for Mount Tabor.

⚘

It was the twentieth day of the eighth month, a cool autumn day in which the earth, having dried from the previous rains, was parched again, but the sky was watery gray, holding the promise of an impending downpour.

When they approached their destination, they gazed in silent wonder at the majestic mountain rising steeply from the ground, almost as high as the Tower of Babel, with its crest in the sky. Then they all, men and women and beasts, climbed up and encamped on its upper slopes. There they rested, let the donkeys graze, and refreshed themselves with the provisions they had brought with them. Soon they were advised that Sisra's army had been sighted on the northern end of the Valley of Jezreel, and they understood that the time of reckoning was near.

Deborah stepped on an elevated stone as they rallied around her. In her fiery, clear voice that rolled out into the distance, a special gift with which the Lord had endowed her, and with a flame smoldering in her eyes, she proclaimed this prophecy to Barak and the soldiers assembled there:

Arise, Barak, and stand up, you heroes of Israel.
　Go out into battle and be fearless.
　Sisra and his men have chariots and horses, but
you have the Lord our God, who goes out before
you. He will give Sisra and his warriors into your hands.

Her speech imbued the warriors with confidence, which had been flagging before. They cheered with great zest, believing in the Lord and in Deborah his prophetess and in the promised victory. And so, thought Barak, did she. Having spoken, she seemed to be at peace with herself and, together with her maids, withdrew contentedly into the tent that had been pitched for her.

Barak remained standing silently in front of it and became pensive. Although Deborah and the soldiers were confident of a favorable outcome, his assurance wavered. What if she mistook the Lord's design? It was easy for her to speak of God's giving Sisra into his hands, when all she had to do was survey the proceedings from her lofty post. It was more difficult for him to believe in that promise, when he was the one who had to make it come true.

Soon his eyes met clouds of dust swirling up from the ground, like flour released from a copper sieve. It was raised by a huge column of chariots traversing the valley at a breakneck pace, heading toward them. It looked as if the horses drawing them were treading not the ground but the air, as if their manes had turned into wings and they were flying, swifter than eagles in the sky.

When Barak saw them charging forward in their multitudes, he was overcome with certitude that Deborah had made a grave error. He saw no way in which his foot soldiers, armed only with paltry swords and shields, could overcome this mighty host of chariots. His spirit plummeted like lead in deep water.

Bitterly, he thought that at least she could have let him come to her, as he had ardently desired to do, while he still had the opportunity. But she had preferred to nurse the painful memory of the man who had ruthlessly expelled her from his house just as she was about to endanger her life in the service of her people. She had kept herself aloof from Barak as if she were a queen and he her courtier, and now the chance for him to know her might never come.

🐸

Deborah was not aware of how little dependence Barak had placed on her words before the beginning of the battle. But as she looked down upon the approaching messengers, she recalled that (contrary to Barak's guess) after she had retired to her tent, gradually her own fortitude had given way to fear.

Previously, she had always had an inexplicable sense of how the One who reigns in the heavens and the earth would deal with the people of Israel. When she had voiced her prophecy in the ears of the warriors, she had still believed it to be infallible. But in the face of the fateful event that had loomed before them, her trust in her own prediction had abandoned her, and her spirit had faltered. She had listened for the voice of the Eternal One in her heart—in vain. And the grim stillness had droned in her ears louder than any noise could have been.

Yet there was no time to dwell on this now. The envoys had started to climb from the foot of the mountain to its top. Mount Tabor itself seemed to be holding its breath, awaiting their messages.

Deborah raced down the grass-covered decline as fast as she could. Her legs became entangled in the folds of her long dress, so she raised her skirt with her hands and continued her descent. Her feet now carried her at the speed of a gazelle, until she met the messengers halfway down the slope.

Chapter Nine

A part from Asherah, there was another young woman in Hazor who was anxiously awaiting news of the battle. This was Nogah, who was two months older than the king's youngest daughter. From her room on the second floor of a building that bordered the castle, she overlooked its courtyard and would be able to see anyone who entered it.

Nogah was not dazzlingly beautiful like Asherah, but she was well shaped and pretty. While Asherah had prayed to her goddess, she had prayed to the Lord, the God of Israel. Asherah had prayed for a Canaanite victory, but Nogah's heart was divided and she did not know what to pray for.

Her mother, Reumah, who was an Israelite slave, had told her that if the Israelites won, they would come and set them free. But her father, who was a Canaanite, had told her that if the Israelites achieved victory, they would attack the castle and attempt to kill them all. Nogah loved and trusted both her parents, and she could not decide which one of them she should believe.

🙊

Nogah had been born into wretched slavery in King Jabin's castle. At first, she knew only her mother but not her father. Ever since she was a little girl, she sensed that there was mystery attached to him. But for years her mother would not tell her who he was.

Reumah was from the town of Hamon in the tribe of Nafthali, and she had been captured during one of Jabin's men's incursions. The king's raiders had killed her four brothers before her eyes. And they had hauled her off, tied to the top of a donkey like a bag of corn. Since she was very young and pretty then, with large dark eyes shining in her soft face, she was taken to be a slave in the king's castle.

There she was set to do the heavy work of cleaning, grinding flour, cooking and baking, and serving food to the king's family and his large entourage. She worked from the first gray hint of dawn until dusk shaded over into darkness, and she was frequently at the beck and call of male slave masters. She did her best to hide her comely face and body and concealed her luxurious dark hair by binding it tightly under a kerchief. But this did no good. As happened to so many other female slaves, she soon found herself pregnant. Since swelling bellies were common in the slaves' hall, nobody paid much attention to her and no one asked any questions.

Aided in her delivery by the other female slaves around her, Reumah gave birth to a girl. She called her Nogah because, she said, she had brought the shining light of God into her life. As Nogah grew from infancy into girlhood, Reumah thought that she had chosen a most suitable name for her daughter: She looked as if there were, in fact, a radiance emanating from inside her. She was endowed with rich wavy hair like her mother's, except that it was lighter than Reumah's, the color of tarnished bronze, with golden streaks woven through it. She had a small straight nose, soft full lips, and skin the color of milk and honey, as smooth as alabaster.

Her truly outstanding feature, though, was her large eyes of a blue-green so deep that their gleaming beauty eclipsed the rest of her pretty but unprepossessing appearance. It was by way of those eyes, her mother thought, that the radiance of her soul shone through and was manifest for all to see.

After Nogah was born, Reumah did not regain her shapely body. Jabin embittered the lives of his Hebrew female slaves with hard labor without respite, and whenever they were not serving food at the king's table, they were dressed in torn rags. But the king did not stint where food was concerned. They ate bread at the sweat of their brow, but there was always a surfeit of it, with plenty of oil and vinegar in which to dip it. She ate much, remaining plump from being with child, then grew fat. Her belly was as round as a heap of grain, and her flesh became slack and flabby like that of an old ewe grazing on fat pastures.

This suited her well, because it ensured that none of her supervisors was sufficiently attracted to her to make her pregnant again. She expected that both she and Nogah would spend all the days of their lives in slavery, and she had no wish to bear another fatherless child, who would begin and end his life as a slave.

Nogah's father could have redeemed them from this dreary existence. But when, after Nogah's birth, Reumah told him that the child was his daughter, he scowled at her in disbelief. When she swore to him that no man but he had ever come to her, he glanced at her with a derisive smile on his face and warned her never to approach him babbling this dubious nonsense again, on pain of severe punishment.

At first, Reumah had frantically searched for a way of avoiding her and her child's fate, but she soon realized that there was none. She had weighed the possibility of using the shelter of the night to flee the castle. But the citadel was encircled by a massive, high wall interspersed with even higher turrets, and the only way out was through the gates, which were always heavily guarded. Besides, if they were to be caught outside the castle's walls, they would be put to death immediately, as had happened to some fugitives before. No escapee had ever survived.

So Reumah abandoned all thought of flight and gradually resigned herself to the bitter prospect of interminable drudgery.

🦗

Unlike her mother, the daughter was not aware of the cruelty of her fate, for she had never known anything else. She did not resent it any more than a donkey resents being ridden on, or the floor resents being trodden on. From early childhood she had learned to bear herself submissively, as was proper for a slave. But there was an innate dignity in her bearing, on which the women around her frequently remarked, and which her mother took as a sign that, in her heart, Nogah would never truly be a slave.

Initially, mother and daughter lived in a large hall, on the bottom floor of a building attached to the castle. Together with all the other female slaves and their children, they slept on a thin sheet on the rough ground, herded together like prisoners in a dungeon. The hall was noisy and dirty and full of the smell of unwashed bodies, which Reumah detested.

Then she discovered a torn tent of goatskin that a soldier had discarded on top of a pile of garbage behind the castle. She worked for months washing and mending it. Whenever she was not cooking and cleaning the castle, she busied her deft fingers with the tent.

When it was ready, she obtained permission from the woman who managed the king's household to set it up in a corner near the citadel's rear wall. In it mother and daughter still slept on a thin sheet on the inhospitable ground, but it was quiet and clean.

Sifting through the heap of rubbish in the backyard again, Reumah unearthed a dirty blanket riddled with holes. This she washed and darned, then used to cover them along with the threadbare blanket they already had, in order to fend off the biting chill of the winter nights. The tent became their retreat from misery.

Nogah's resourceful mother also got hold of a discarded old and battered bronze pitcher and basin, which she cleaned and polished. She filled the pitcher with water and poured it into the basin each day, so that they could wash themselves with the fragrant soap she had abstracted from the king's storeroom. Not only their tent but their bodies, too, were clean.

From the age of seven, all the slaves' children were initiated into work. The boys were taken to the stables to serve as grooms for the king's horses, to polish his elegant carriages, and to tend the castle's extensive gardens. The girls were required to work alongside their mothers and toil in the king's household. This was also Nogah's task.

But in the evenings she and Reumah were alone in their tent, and her mother would sit next to her in the dark and recount stories to her. These were wondrous tales about their people, the people of Israel, their forefathers and mothers.

Nogah liked filling her ears with the accounts of their adventures. But as she grew, she began asking questions. When she was ten years old, she wanted to know how it was that the Israelites her mother told her about had both mothers and fathers, when she and all the other slave children in the castle had only mothers. This was a question to which Reumah had no reply.

The child's inability to solve this riddle nagged at her for a long time. She mentioned it to her mother again when she was eleven years old. At that time she wanted to find out how children came to emerge from women's bellies. Her mother explained that a child was a gift from the Lord.

This led Nogah to the conclusion that a father, too, was a gift from the Lord. Apparently he had not seen fit to endow any of the slaves in the castle with this blessing. But when she revealed this conclusion to her mother, Reumah merely smiled in silence.

One evening, about a year later, another woman slave came to visit Reumah. Her mother told Nogah to go to sleep while she sat with her friend in front of the tent.

But Nogah, unable to stifle her curiosity, listened to the two women whispering together. At first she could not make out what they were saying, but after a while she heard her mother's friend whisper, "She has got your skin and your mouth, and her hair is darker than his, but she has got his eyes and his small, straight nose."

Then her mother murmured: "What does it matter?"

"It is of great importance. When he sees her he will know who she is, so at least he will not lie with her."

"I would kill him."

The other woman sniffed her doubt. "Since there is no way you could kill him, it's just as well that he will not try."

"I would find a way."

"The guards and slave masters will not dare to force themselves on her either."

"I would kill them, too."

Nogah puzzled over these words until she was overcome by sleep, and her mind still whirled with questions on the next day. In the evening, when they were alone in their tent, she inquired, "My mother, who is 'he,' whose eyes I have got and whom you are going to kill?"

Reumah, temper on edge, would only say, "You should not have eavesdropped."

Nogah pestered her mother about this for a few days. When she realized that she was distressing her, she ceased; yet her mother's silence only exacerbated her bewilderment.

Eventually, the riddle was solved in a repellent manner; it was then that Nogah came to be truly divided in her heart. Beforehand, she had always regarded herself an Israelite. But when she discovered that her father was a Canaanite, and after he had made her study the Canaanite heritage and had denigrated the barbarity of the Israelites in her ears, she no longer knew who she was.

So when the battle broke out, she could not pray for victory, for she did not know for whose victory to beg. But as she stood at the window, she wept for herself and for both her parents, imploring God to let all three of them survive. And she pleaded for peace between the people of Israel and the people of Canaan.

In the meantime, peace was as distant as honey was from bitter herbs, while war was raging in the land. But not until much later did Nogah become aware of how horrifying it had been.

🦅

Nogah had discovered who her father was two years before the war, through an occurrence that at first boded disaster. In the years before that, her growing body bloomed like a vine in the spring into alluring curves, and she began having the way of women. As her breasts bulged, so did the slave masters' eagerness for her. They began gloating at her and pawing her.

When Reumah noticed this, she finally explained to Nogah what the girl had already vaguely guessed: how fathers were connected to children. She warned her that in order to escape mistreatment at the slave masters' hands, she must always paste a submissive smile to her face. But on no account was she to let any of them know her, lest she become pregnant and bear a child into slavery.

This led Nogah to the sad realization that her father must be one of those uncouth taskmasters whom she detested. But when she asked her mother whether this was so, Reumah merely shook her head, and left her wondering.

By the time she was fifteen, the overseers no longer confined themselves to eying and fondling her, but became more and more determined to have their way with her.

During the day, while she cleaned the rooms in the castle, her supervisor was a woman. But as soon as she left the royal quarters, the male slave masters would harass her, as they did the other slave girls. Prudently, her mother never let her daughter out of her sight, and when the slave masters laid hands on her, she tried to chase them off. This led them to abuse Reumah with words and push her out of their way with coarse hands, but it gave Nogah an opportunity to escape from their hold and conceal herself in one of the castle's countless hidden corners.

One late afternoon, when she was fifteen years old, two of these men trailed Nogah and her mother to their tent. The younger one gripped Nogah's arm so tightly that she winced, shoving her in front of him and pushing her to the ground. He tore off her garment, bore down on her, and forced open her legs. The other hurled Reumah to the ground and held her back to prevent her from rushing to her daughter's aid. Both attackers covered their victims' mouths with their filthy, evil-reeking hands, to stifle their screams.

Nogah's throat went dry with the jolt of fear that shot through her. She struggled to fend off the rapist, but his hold was unbreakable, like iron handcuffs. Suddenly Reumah, with a fortitude born of despair, bit the hand of her tormentor, and while he momentarily removed his hand to nurse his pain, she screamed to the other man, who was on the verge of desecrating her daughter, "Leave her alone! She is the king's daughter. If you abuse her, it will not bode well for you."

The two men merely laughed in disdain, and the one who bore down on Nogah prepared to penetrate her. But while straining to free herself of her own villain, Reumah persisted. There was still some light outside and she cried, "Take her out of the tent and look at her eyes. Then you will not laugh."

The rapist on top of Nogah hesitated. His hold on her slackened, and this gave the girl a chance to pull away from under him and roll out of the tent. Both men lurched after her, dragged her toward them, turned her on her back, and held her down. Then they peered into her eyes.

Several of the castle's guards had light eyes, but they were either gray or pale blue. Only the king and some of his descendants had eyes of a deep blue-green, such as Nogah's. Aware of this, one of the assailants mumbled, "He may have sired her, but he doesn't concern himself with her fate."

"He would concern himself soon enough if he found that she was raped."

The men vacillated, unable to decide whether they should take Reumah's claim seriously. But to be on the safe side, they released Nogah and sauntered away, grumbling into their sticky beards in disgust.

As soon as the women managed to wrap themselves in their torn dresses, Nogah, still trembling in the aftermath of her harrowing experience, clutched her mother's hand. In deep agitation she demanded to know if she had spoken the truth. Reumah could no longer deny it, and Nogah was dazed.

Once she had somewhat calmed down, and considered what had come to pass, she asked her mother, "Did the king force himself on you, as these men tried to do now?"

"He did not attack me. No," replied Reumah soberly. "But he had—still has—the power of life and death over us. Refusing him would have been as unthinkable as halting the sun in its journey through the sky."

Nogah sighed with understanding, but also with relief. At least she had not been the issue of a stark act of violence.

For the rest, she was aware of the king's enslaving her mother and of the atrocities his men had perpetrated on her family. But since as far back as she could remember, she had been overawed by the mere mention of his name. Now that she knew him for her father, her awe deepened and she felt that it was not for her to judge the man who had given her life.

🦁

Two years had passed since that day. Although Nogah knew herself to be the king's daughter, she retained her modest bearing, and she never appeared where she knew she would not be wanted. Looking out of her window, she saw the long-awaited messengers entering the castle gate and Asherah skipping down the stairway, running toward them to hear what they had to say.

She knew a strong urge to do the same. But she held herself back, knowing that she had no right to do so. For after she had discovered her father, she had also learned without being told that he expected her not to embarrass him and to remain quietly in the background. And this was precisely a place where she would not be welcome.

So she attempted to make out from the vague noises that reached her what it was that the messengers were conveying.

Whatever it was, at least their arrival indicated that the collision was now over. But still she did not know how great was the devastation it had left behind.

Chapter Ten

Nogah anticipated that she would be the last of the king's children to be apprised of the tidings, but she did not resent this. What the king had done for her since learning that she was his daughter was beyond what she could have prayed for. She was profoundly grateful and did not expect any more of him. Even this bounty, she knew, had come upon her merely by chance. In the wake of the two slave masters' attack, word of her descent spread among the rest of them. After that, they never accosted her again, and this itself was a great relief. It did not occur to her that there would be any further consequences.

Yet somehow the rumor reached the king. About a month after the assault on her, Nogah was summoned into his presence. She was ashamed to face him in her faded and tattered gray woolen dress, which was not nearly fine enough for his royal eyes to rest on; but she had nothing else to wear, so she came as she was.

She was ushered into the throne room and bowed deeply to the king. Then she stood at the door respectfully, her head modestly bent. Until this day she had only seen him from afar, and she was eager to know what his face looked like. But although she had never been told so, she sensed that to raise her head and look at him would be a grave breach of good manners. She refrained.

The king commanded all the servants and officials who were there to leave, and instructed her to approach him. She came forward and stood at the foot of the stairs that led up to his throne, with her eyes still cast down.

Jabin descended the steps, slung his arm around her shoulders, and led her to a window. There he took her face between his two hands and looked into her eyes for a long time. This gave her the opportunity she had been waiting for to steal a glance at his, and she saw her eyes mirrored in them.

He saw the same in hers. While he ran his heavily ringed fingers along her cheeks, he declared. "Your eyes bear testimony to my lineage on my mother's side." Then he fingered her earlobes, looked at them intently, and said, "Your earlobes have just the slightest cleft at their lower end, the very mark that distinguished my mother—your grandmother and her descendants—from all other dwellers on earth. There can be no doubt. You are my seed, my own flesh and blood."

King Jabin returned to sit on his throne, and she resumed her humble position at the bottom of the stairs. Yet her humility quickly waned. She had expected the king to be haughty, but to her he was not so. From his next words she could tell that he looked kindly upon her, and she took heart from this.

"So your name is Nogah," he mused. "It is not a name I would have chosen for you, but no matter. When your mother told me that I was the father of her infant girl, I did not believe her. Other slaves have come to me with this story, invariably a lie. Your distinctive looks had not yet emerged, and there was no reason to suppose that you were other than the child of one of the lusty slave masters I keep here. So I did not concern myself with the name your mother chose for you, nor with your welfare. It was a mistake."

He was lost in thought for a while. Finally he spoke again. "I cannot recognize you in the sight of my family and my people. But from now on I will provide a good life for you here in the castle, under my supervision. You will no longer clean rooms or sleep in that dilapidated tent I have been told about. I will have a comfortable room prepared for you, and you will have good dresses to wear, instead of the rags that cover you now."

Sensing that his words called for a response, Nogah finally raised her eyes to look at him and spoke for the first time: "Thank you, my lord king. This is very kind of you. I have one request, though: that my mother be allowed to live with me in my new room."

"Your mother is merely a Hebrew slave, like all the others in the castle. She can live in the slaves' hall with the rest of them."

"Sir, she has brought me up with devotion and love. I beg that she be allowed to share my room."

"You are a bold girl. If it is that important to you, she may stay with you."

"Thank you, my lord."

"I will see to it that you learn to play the harp, and whatever else it is that young ladies of refinement learn."

"I have no wish to play the harp, but I would like very much to learn to read and write, so that I can read scrolls with wondrous tales on them and write tales myself."

"You have a mind of your own. I like that. You will learn to read and write, but you will be instructed in the Canaanite writing, and you will learn the tales of our people and of our gods. You will remember that you are a Canaanite and not an Israelite, and you will not let your mother poison your mind if she tells you otherwise."

She inclined her head in acceptance of his decree.

He looked her over and pronounced his verdict on her appearance: "You are pretty. Not a stunning beauty, but quite pretty. This is good. When the time comes, I will find a wealthy and kind husband for you. I will make sure that you are well established in life."

She thanked him once more, and he told her that if she needed anything she was to let him know. Then he raised his hand to indicate that her audience with him was at an end.

"May my lord King Jabin live forever," she said and bowed deeply and, backing out, left the hall.

🐾

The king considered the female slaves his due, but beyond that did not indulge in excess. He was not given over to heavy drinking, and took no other wife besides his queen. He kept his concubines at a distant location, far from her attentive gaze. If he had children from them, no one in the castle knew of it.

Because the queen was jealous and mean-spirited, Jabin was forced to perpetrate his deeds with the slaves in secret. Thus, she was only dimly aware of those exploits. For the slaves, and all others who were employed in the king's household, were left in little doubt as to the manner in which their master would deal with whoever gossiped about them to the queen or his offspring. Once, a slave had done this, and the royal retribution was swift and ominous. On that same day, the tale bearer was forcibly led out of the castle, never to be heard of again. Henceforward, all those in the castle meticulously guarded their tongues. Therefore he had no difficulty in concealing Nogah as well.

He was aided in this by the compound of the castle comprising several buildings with a welter of rooms in them, and a maze of passages leading from one to the other. So he housed her in a side building, in a room that was hidden away at the end of a narrow twisting passage.

Compared with the royal quarters, the room allotted to Nogah was austere, but to her it spelled luxury beyond anything she had ever experienced. It had two beds in it, and it was the first time in her life that she had slept in one. Her mother had slept in a bed before she'd been taken into captivity. But that was so many years ago that she had forgotten the feel of it. They both enjoyed this unexpected comfort.

When Nogah asked the king to release her mother and permit her to return to her own land, he flatly rejected her appeal. Her many entreaties to let her mother go were to no avail: In this he remained as steadfast as a rock. But he became much more lenient toward Reumah, and he acceded to Nogah's petition that she be exempt from toil. She was assigned no duties other than that of standing guard over her daughter.

The king also lavished other luxuries upon Nogah. A seamstress was sent to her, and she was allowed to order as many dresses as she wished. They were not ostentatious, in order not to arouse the queen's suspicion, but they were well fashioned. She was also supplied with shoes so soft and skillfully shaped that she hardly felt them on her feet. She had some dresses and shoes made for her mother as well, and the king did not reprimand her. A large tub and warm water were brought to her room every day for her bath, alongside soap and expensive oils scented with myrrh to pamper her body. Those, too, she shared with her mother.

She spent her days studying with a teacher who had been hired especially for her to instruct her in the writings and the lore that constituted the legacy of the Canaanite people. Once a week, she was summoned into the king's presence. He met her in the scroll room, where she was allowed to sit down next to him; she knew this to be a great honor.

There he would question her, quite rigorously, about her studies. She made a strenuous effort to retain in her memory all she had learned, in order to please him. At times, the king put his arm around her shoulder and instructed Nogah as to the proper conduct expected of a young lady. In particular, he impressed on her the importance of preserving her virginity, dubbing it her most prized possession. He warned her that losing it would destroy the opulent life he was planning for her, as a budding spring flower would be destroyed by the premature advent of the scorching summer heat.

She promised him that she would guard her flower. Since the only men she had ever seen were his guards and slave masters, whom she detested, and her teacher and his clerks and priests, who were old, she had no difficulty adhering to his wish.

But the king did not rely solely on her promise. He charged her mother with the task of ensuring the preservation of her virtue by adhering to her like glue.

Yet he warned Nogah again and again not to let her mother damage her mind by telling her stories about the Israelites and the strange god they worshipped. "The Israelites," he explained, "are an inferior, malicious rabble of wandering tent dwellers. Coming forth from the eastern desert, they have overrun our country like a swarm of locusts and wreaked havoc in it. They are nothing but a festering plague in this land.

"As for their god, he is patent foolishness, because he is invisible. And as any child could tell you, whatever cannot be seen does not exist."

In the evenings, though, Nogah entered a different world, as far removed from her daytime world as was the desert in the east, where the sun rises, from the Great Sea in the west, where it sets. Sitting close to her in the shadowy candlelight, whispering so that she would not be overheard outside their room, Reumah spoke to her in Hebrew. Over and over she told her the tales of the Israelites, who, she stressed, were her real people. Of how the Canaanites had attacked them, killing and raping, capturing and enslaving, pillaging and burning. Of how the king had used her many years ago, and then had cast her off as if she were but a soiled rag to wipe off his shoes.

"Do not let the king persuade you to engage in his people's despicable idol worship," she admonished Nogah. "Bear in mind the second of the Lord s Ten Commandments:

You shall have no other gods beside me. You shall
not bow down to them, nor shall you worship them.

Nogah believed that both her father and her mother were speaking the truth, and she was torn asunder between them.

One day when she was with the king, he advised her that after their meeting a priest would come to lead her to the temple bordering on the castle, where he would instruct her in the proper ways of worshipping the Canaanite gods and goddesses. He also ordered her to adopt Anath, the goddess of war and granter of fertility, as her special deity. She was to supplicate the goddess to make her bear her future husband sons who would grow up to be fierce warriors.

When she came out from the scroll room, not only the priest but also her mother was waiting for her. While they were trailing the old man to the temple, her mother whispered into her ear, ordering her not to set foot in it.

"I dare not defy the king's order," Nogah whispered back.

But her mother replied in a low voice—which was nonetheless like a shouting reprimand to her, "It is preferable for both of us to die than to defy the Lord."

As they made their way through the passages and paths that led from the scroll room to the temple, Nogah vacillated, while all this time her mother's sharp nails dug into the flesh of her arm. When they reached the threshold of the temple, the gods and goddesses in it seemed to beckon her to come forward and bow down to them. She was overcome with horror.

She clasped her stomach, folded her body, and advised the priest that she had been seized with a sudden cramp and must repair to her room immediately and lie down on her bed until she recuperated. Then she grabbed her mother's hand, and they both fled as fast as their legs would carry them.

That night, Nogah's sleep was disturbed by nightmares in which the king let loose his priests on her, and they tortured her with rods of iron and whips and scorpions, until there was no life left in her. She was not surprised when, early next morning, she was summoned to his scroll room again.

This time he did not invite her to sit next to him, and she stood before him with her head down, as she had done the first time she had confronted him. For a long time silence reigned, and he purposely let her stand there, choking with fear. She felt herself shrinking before his eyes, until she became nothing but a tiny ant crawling on the ground, then sensed herself being slowly reduced to nothing, on the verge of vanishing from the face of the earth.

After what seemed an eternity, he spoke to her in an icy voice. "I will not put up with your pranks, and you will do as you have been ordered to do. And your mother, who, as is now evident, is seducing you to follow her evil ways, will be transferred to the slaves' hall, where she can do you no further damage, and she will do household work again. A Canaanite woman will be appointed to guard you."

With tears bursting forth from her eyes, Nogah said, "I assure you, my lord king, that the decision not to enter the temple was mine alone. Let your ears be attentive to my pleading and do not tear my mother from me." Then she raised her head and added, "When I stood before you for the first time, you deigned to say that I had thoughts of my own in my mind, and that this was good in your eyes. Pray, do not punish me now for such thoughts."

"I did not mean thoughts of evil," said the king stiffly, but Nogah could tell that the coldness had vanished from his voice.

She took her courage in her hand, looked straight into his eyes, and asked evenly if he himself believed in the gods and goddesses of Canaan.

For a moment the king was speechless with wrath. But then Nogah noted the merest hint of a smile lurking in his eyes as he replied evasively, "They are of the utmost importance in the Canaanite heritage. It is necessary for the people to believe in them, because a people that worships its deities also adores its king, whom it sees as their representative."

"But I adore my lord king as it is," she said.

The smile that was previously hidden now spread over his face as he said that, for the time being, it would be sufficient for the goddess Anath to be displayed in Nogah's room. Then he waved her out of his presence, and Nogah felt that he had opened his heart to her again.

When the bronze statue of Anath—borne on the priest's raised hands—arrived in her room, Reumah took the abomination from him and, as soon as he left, shoved it as deeply as she could into the case that stood against one of the walls. Mother and daughter smiled at each other, in the knowledge that they were nursing a dark secret between them.

The next time Nogah was summoned to the king's scroll room, she bore with her a large stone tablet, which she set up against one of the walls, on which she had chiseled this inscription:

May King Jabin Live for All Eternity

With the passage of time, she grew fond of him, as he came to be of her. Occasionally he would regale her with presents—a small and blunt, but artfully engraved ivory knife; an intricately crafted gold necklace; a richly embroidered sash for her waist; and more—as tokens of his affection. Before he dismissed her, he would bestow his blessing on her and fold her in his arms and kiss her on her forehead.

Once she felt emboldened enough to embrace him in return. She stood up on the tip of her toes, raised her head, and kissed his cheek. The king was so much moved by this tender gesture that he told her that, since she was a princess, she was no longer to call him "my lord king," but "my father."

This life of luxury and love for both her parents, and the wavering it implanted in her soul, went on for two years; then it was rudely interrupted. At first Nogah was not aware that her life of comfort was drawing to an end. But when she saw the commotion below, as soon as the messengers had arrived, she realized that what was going on there was deeply disconcerting. She had a premonition of doom.

Part Two

In the Throes of War

Chapter One

When Deborah raced down the hill, not knowing the final outcome of the war, she was trembling with anxiety in anticipation of the messengers' report. Yet she had been aware of the confrontation's initial horrors immediately, for its first stage took place close by. She had withdrawn into her tent, but her aides served as her lookouts, and frequently reported to her on its progress.

By their account, at first Barak stood nearby, leaning on a tree. Gradually his officers gathered around him to await his orders.

When Barak's men saw Sisra and his army approaching, their first impulse was to meet them head-on, and they prepared to blow the ram horns as a sign to their soldiers to charge forward. But Barak would not let them.

He told his officers that he knew, with the certainty with which he knew that God's reign spanned the heavens and the earth, that meeting the Canaanites on the plain in the light of day would be disastrous. Their enemies would utilize the superiority of their chariots to the best advantage, and the Israelites would be defeated. Their only hope lay in proceeding with the cunning of a fox.

Since the Canaanites would not be able to clamber up the mountain with their chariots, it would be prudent for the Israelites to remain there for the time being. The officers were afraid of a lengthy siege, in the course of which they would run out of their provisions of food and drink and be forced to surrender; but Barak was the commander and they accepted his decree.

Soon the Canaanites encircled the mountain and halted, pending further orders from their own commander. There were two courses open to them: They could leave their chariots behind and climb the mountain on foot, or they could remain on the plain and lay siege to the mountain. As time went by and nothing happened, Barak concluded that Sisra had decided in favor of the second course.

Posting sentries at appropriate spots to alert him if the Canaanites began an ascent to the top, he ordered his men to take another rest. He hoped that if the Canaanites sent out spies to investigate his intent, this would convince them that no attack on his part was imminent. He stretched out in the shade of the tree himself, and despite his anxiety over the wisdom of his plan he soon fell asleep.

He awoke after nightfall and used the cover of darkness to send down spies of his own to infiltrate the enemy's camp. They returned with the tidings that the Canaanites had unhitched their horses from their chariots, had fed and watered them, and had tethered them to trees, and that all was calm for the night.

Barak knew the Canaanite charioteers to be weary from their long trip from the north, while his own troops were rested; hence he waited until such time as he judged that the Canaanites would be immersed in deep sleep. Then he gave the order for his men to be awakened noiselessly. He aimed for the moment when the weary Canaanite sentries of the first watch would have gone off to awaken those of the second watch, and before the new sentinels had a chance to assume their posts.

Hoping to catch the enemy off guard, Barak gave the signal for his men to descend the mountain on tortuous pathways concealed among trees and bushes, warning them to tread the ground as silently as the dead bodies to which, he hoped, the Canaanites would soon be reduced.

The Canaanites' haphazard camp was engulfed in sleep, and the air was suffused with the smell of horses' dung. The Israelites entered it soundlessly, with their swords drawn. Their first task was to fell the stunned watchmen. In this they succeeded only in part: Several of them remained unharmed and sounded the warning call of their trumpets. But before Sisra's combatants fully realized what had befallen them, Barak's swordsmen were upon them.

This caused rampant confusion among the Canaanites, and the Israelites slew as many as they could by the edge of the sword. Barak, with several of his most trusted men, raced forward in an attempt to lay his hands on Sisra, for the spies had told him where he had set up his command. But when he reached the designated spot, his chief adversary was no longer there. He and his men roamed the area in search of him, but in vain. To his chagrin, Barak realized that Sisra had slipped through the ranks of his warriors.

By now the Canaanites had recovered from the shock of the onslaught. Despite the bloodshed, about three-quarters had survived. While some warded off the Israelites with their long spears, others hastily harnessed their horses to the chariots. They urged the animals forward, and with their hooves noisily pounding the ground, they escaped in a southward and westward direction.

In the first light of dawn, the commander and his officers surveyed their own army. Only a few of their sword bearers had been cut down, and they were encouraged by their success. But they knew that this had been merely the prelude; the decisive part of the endeavor was still to come.

Barak mounted a lone horse, and roared to his soldiers to follow him in pursuit of the Canaanites. They took over the horses of those who had been killed, but as they had no experience in riding them, they fumbled, and in the end they gave up and advanced on foot.

Although Deborah had been apprised of this initial stage of the battle, her aides did not follow the two armies when they left the Tabor. So she knew nothing of what had transpired afterward. Thus, when she met the messengers, she immediately plied them with questions about the subsequent collision, which must have decided the fate of the war. She was eager to listen to them yet dreaded their response, for she did not know what it might herald.

🦁

As Deborah learned in reply to those breathless inquiries, the devastation that had its beginning at the foot of Mount Tabor continued at Taanach, close to the southern border of the Valley of Jezreel.

The Israelites chased the Canaanite chariots on foot, and this gave

Sisra and his men a head start. Once they reached Taanach, they were joined by small contingents of chariots the other Canaanite kings had sent out as tokens of their support. There they also had the leisure to recuperate before the Israelites, trotting heavily on their weary feet, caught up with them.

It was then that the leaden sky, which had been covered with increasingly heavy clouds, kept its promise. An enormous downpour began, which Barak hoped would work in his favor. When his troops reached the Canaanites, he ordered them to position themselves in a half circle to their east and south, with the intent of driving them toward the west and the north, where there was a trap awaiting them.

It was not of Barak's making, but had been set by the Lord himself. Yet it was still too early for him to gauge if it would fulfill his hope of ensnaring the enemy. The engagement there began while the torrential rain, pouring out of the sky like pitchers of water, was still battering the ground. The warriors on both sides had difficulty seeing what lay in front of their eyes. On Barak's orders, the Israelites charged into the rain, aiming for the Canaanites' horses, which, in the poor visibility, were easier to get to than the charioteers behind them.

The horses reared in terror and squealed in pain as they were being stabbed, but undeterred by this furor and their own exhaustion, the Israelites forged ahead and felled large numbers of them. As the horses collapsed in front of them, many Canaanite charioteers tumbled out of their chariots and became foot soldiers. As such, they were inexperienced, and were quickly overrun by the Israelites, who outnumbered them.

The Canaanites held their ground for a while, but then flung back in confusion. When Sisra foresaw that defeat was imminent, he shouted out orders to retreat. As the Israelites were overrunning them from the south and the east, the Canaanites who still had control of their chariots thundered west and north.

This was precisely what Barak had been aiming for, because in that direction lay the trap that he hoped would seal their fate: the River Kishon, which curved its way through the valley.

Sisra knew that the river was there, but he was not aware of its treacherous quality. In clear weather, it was sluggish and little bigger than a brook. But its banks were shallow, and when strong torrents poured down, as happened on that day, it turned into a snare: It swelled and its waters ran over, drenching its banks. The surrounding areas turned to mud and were fast becoming a big swamp—easy to enter but difficult to come out of.

When Sisra and his charioteers approached the river and saw what lay ahead, they stopped in confusion. But the Israelites were behind them, surging forward like a tidal wave in the Great Sea. Overcome with panic, they continued their retreat toward the river, where some of their chariots were swept away by the gushing water, while others were bogged down in the mud.

Once again the Canaanites were thrown into disorder, stumbling over each other and their own dead and wounded, as they were overwhelmed by the charging enemy. Even as hardened a warrior as Barak was aghast at the bloodbath and the enormous number of men who, screaming in mortal agony as they were being pierced, slumped down before his eyes. Soon the earth was covered by heaps of the tangled bodies of men and horses, prey to the swarms of scavenging vultures in the sky.

By that time the rain had ceased and the river had lost some of its fury. The piteously small numbers of Canaanite soldiers who were still alive swam across it and fled to the north. Barak and his army did so as well and gave chase, driving them all the way to Harosheth, where all that was left of Sisra's army fell before Barak and his soldiers.

The Valley of Jezreel had become a vale of slaughter. But the River Kishon subsided, and there was barely a ripple left on its waters to testify to the feat it had accomplished.

※

Of the Canaanite army summarily vanquished at the river, only Sisra did not flee with the rest. While the battle was still raging, he realized that things were past hope, and felt that the gods were battling against him. Like his men, he had been forced to abandon his chariot and swim across the river. With the shrieks of his men echoing in his ears, he cowardly separated from them and fled alone.

With his garment still inundated in water, he reached the thick of some bushes and hid in their ample foliage. As a revered military commander, he had always had his underlings at his beck and call. Now, for the first time, he found himself totally on his own. To survive, he would have to rely solely on his wits and stamina, and he could only pray that, as he was in dire straits, they would not fail him.

Chapter Two

A fter Asherah reached the castle gates, she was joined there by her father and her mother and her two brothers. The messengers, whose bearded faces were dripping with sweat, bowed down before the king. But instead of speaking, as they were ordered to do, they burst into mournful wails. Asherah's cries mingled with theirs.

The king restrained Asherah in his arms and ordered the messengers to present their report of the battle. But Asherah cried out, "The outcome is clear from their sorrow. There is no need to say more. All I want to know is what happened to my husband."

One of the messengers recovered sufficiently to ask, "Lady, who is your husband?"

"He is Sisra. Quick. Tell me his fate."

Before the messenger could reply, whimpers were heard from Sisra's elderly mother, who rushed forward, making for the gate as rapidly as her frail limbs allowed. Soon her sobs were even louder than those of the messengers had been. The queen could not calm her down. And the king ordered the messengers to ignore her and continue.

As soon as they concluded the account of the incredible disaster that had befallen the Canaanite army, Asherah, her face waxen with horror, pulled herself from her father's arms and stepped over to one of the men, shook his shoulders with her hands, and cried, "Where did Sisra go? Where is he now?"

The messenger disregarded her wild behavior and answered, "Lady, we only know that he fled the battle on foot," he replied respectfully. "We don't know what fate has overtaken him. We can only hope that he is safe, and that he returns to you speedily."

🎵

On the day before, this hope had been shared by Sisra, as he crouched, hiding in the brush. His tunic was torn and the sharp-edged branches of the plants around him grazed his bare body until they drew blood. His heart was heavy inside him for having callously abandoned his men to their dire fate, an act of treachery no military commander in Canaanite history had ever committed before. Yet he knew that he could not have saved them from perdition. He himself was merely a piece of smoking wood, left over from the smoldering fire of the battle.

After the sun had set, he was aghast to see the bare outline of Israelite soldiers scanning the area in search of him. A knot of fright balled his stomach, and his eyes bulged with fear, as he plunged still deeper into the bushes' shadows. There he lay low, holding his breath, as the men's footfalls came closer, roaming near him, before fading into the distance. When he looked up, he saw their receding figures blending into what had become the blackness of the night.

But he did not permit himself to feel relief, for he was well aware that his pursuers would soon come back to hunt him down as foxes hunted down a helpless rabbit. The darkness outside penetrated his heart, which yearned for the fragrant garden flower that was his wife. He had hoped to return to her victorious, and now it looked as if he might not come back to her at all. A sword was lying at his throat, yet he was determined to do all he could to stave off his impending doom.

He decided to head north, toward his own hometown, Harosheth, where he would be safe. So he began running in that direction and, with his breathing shallow and rapid, he ran until he was almost too weary to breathe. His legs gave way and he went sprawling down into the mud; but he knew that if he were to live, he must be tenacious.

Summoning the last vestige of his strength, he dragged himself up to his feet and went forward. He continued until he tripped over a stone and staggered and fell down again. This time he was incapable of getting up.

He crawled until he found shelter in between two rocks, and lay down in a daze.

Sisra remained there until his throat was so parched with thirst that he could no longer bear it. He found a large puddle of rainwater. It looked murky, darker even than the night itself. But there being no other water in sight, he cupped the muddy liquid in his hands and drank his fill from it. Then he hid among the stones again and fell into an uneasy sleep. He awoke in the middle of the night, scrambled up, and continued his flight under the mantle of darkness.

When the stars receded into the paling sky of the dawn, Sisra had reached his destination: the outskirts of Harosheth. But even the sun in its eternal motion seemed to be set against him. For when its first rays penetrated the thick foliage in which he was hiding, his brow darkened at the unexpected sight of Israelite swordsmen blocking the entrance to town.

His heart kicked up inside him in terror for his life. He had hauled himself from the jaws of death so far, but he had no breath left in his lungs to continue his flight. Drenched in a mixture of mud and sweat, his feet refused to carry him any farther.

Yet fear for his life drove him to exert himself beyond the limits of human strength, and he dragged himself along the way leading to the Israelite town of Kedesh. He had an acquaintance, Hever the Kenite, who lived on the outskirts of this town, so he decided to seek refuge at his home.

He knew Kedesh to be the hometown of Barak, but with the clear vision that comes from utter despair, he reckoned that this would be the last place his archenemy would look for him.

❦

Hever, his wife, Jael, and their three grown sons, together with a group of other Kenites, had separated from the Kenite people who dwelled in the south, and settled down among the Israelites. They built up their own neighborhood at the edge of Kedesh, where they set themselves up as smiths, mending all manner of tools. Since there was peace between the Kenites and the Canaanites, Hever had frequently visited Harosheth, where Sisra gave him work to do for the army.

Thus, Sisra trusted the man. But when he arrived, Hever and his sons were not at home. Jael came out to greet him. She had not previously met him, but word of the battle between Barak and Sisra had reached her, and it was clear to her that the fugitive who had come to seek shelter under her roof was the defeated Canaanite commander.

Since her hut was small, Jael had a tent standing next to it, and she now invited him inside. "Come, sir, come in, don't be afraid," she called out.

At hearing her reassuring words, Sisra was awash in gratitude to her for offering him safe haven. He felt that a heavy stone had rolled off his chest, and he finally permitted himself to expel the sigh of relief he had been holding back for so long. The image of his beloved Asherah rose up before his eyes, and with it soared the hope that he would soon be able to hold her in his arms again.

He followed Jael into the tent and, overwhelmed with fatigue, stumbled over his own feet and sank down on the woolen rug that covered the ground. His throat was parched with thirst again and, smiling pitifully at her, he begged feebly, "Please give me a little water to drink, for I am thirsty."

She opened a skin of milk and gave him a drink. When he had emptied it, he rose to his full height, but his knees gave way and he collapsed again in a heap at her feet, then lay prostrate on the ground. Jael saw that he was wet and chilled, and she covered him with a blanket.

With renewed hope audible in his voice, he said to her, "Pray, stand at the entrance of the tent. And if any man comes and asks you, 'Is anyone here?' say, 'No.'"

She reassured him once more, and her face hovering over him, wreathed in a friendly smile, was the last thing he saw before he turned on his side and, curled up like an infant in its mother's womb, fell into a deep sleep.

Then Jael stationed herself in front of the tent and agonized over what she should do.

🜚

When Deborah heard the messengers' account of the final part of the battle, she was flooded with relief. She could draw breath freely again. Even the shrubs around her seemed to breathe her relief. Only now did she fully realize how intolerable the strain had been.

Once she had apprised her people of the joyous tidings, she sat with them for a long time, exulting in gratitude to the Lord, offering up prayers of thanks for his redemption.

Her anxiety now laid to rest, Deborah's thoughts reverted to Lapidoth, who had been not only her husband, but her lover and friend and companion since her youth. Sensibly or insensibly, she had been hoping for a missive from him, telling her that he had relented and was eager to welcome her into his home again.

It failed to arrive. Thus, bit by bit, she had begun to feel like a branch felled off a tree. Perhaps, in time, she would be grafted to another tree, but that time was not yet. Now she merely sensed that she had no desire to wither away in the loneliness Lapidoth had unjustly imposed on her.

The acute consciousness of being thrust away by Lapidoth made her thoughts shift to Barak. She wondered what was keeping him, and why he had not come as yet to apprise her in person of what he had accomplished. The messengers had reported that Sisra had fled, but also that nobody knew where he had gone. It did not seem that Barak would set out on a chase of his foe to an entirely unknown destination, which must inevitably prove fruitless. So she began worrying that some mishap had overcome the Israelite commander.

🦗

But Barak did try to track down Sisra. When he saw that all the remaining Canaanite warriors had perished in Harosheth, while most of his own had survived, he was elated. Then an officer told him that Sisra had been sighted near Harosheth a short while ago, and he decided to pursue him.

He surmised that Sisra would not be able to cross into Canaanite territory, since Israelite soldiers were stationed along the border. He knew that the Canaanites were on good terms with the Kenites who had settled in Kedesh. So it might be that Sisra had decided to trick him by lying low there until he could reach his own land. He had no certainty of this, but he decided to follow his guess. With only six of his men, and after the briefest rest, they set out on their horses for Kedesh's Kenite neighborhood.

🦗

At the same time that Barak reached the outskirts of Kedesh, the group of people at the gate of the Hazor castle dispersed silently, and Jabin and his sons went into the king's office. There they sat with a heavy spirit, as the king, his face gray with despair, murmured in disbelief, "How could such mighty warriors have fallen! How could such awesome weapons have been destroyed!"

His two sons urged their father not to succumb to despondency. But Jabin mumbled under his breath that he had been sorely deluded in Sisra. He had entrusted the young man with a glorious army, and the young commander had reduced it to rubble. He had depended on him, yet his son-in-law had proved to be a splintered cane, which breaks as soon as one leans on it.

The two princes told their father to take heart, for better times lay ahead. Although there were no remnants left of their own troops, there were still the other Canaanite kings, who would now come to their aid. Together they would build up an even mightier army, which was sure to crush the Israelites underfoot, as befitted the despicable worms that they were.

The king dejectedly dismissed their notion. "Before the war, those rulers spoke loftily of their staunch alliance with us," responded Jabin in dejection. "But when the time came to prove their mettle, their assistance to us must have been paltry. We could not else have been so thoroughly routed. These other Canaanite kings are nothing but weaklings. They have resigned themselves to the Israelites' presence in our land and given up the battle against them long ago. Trying to enlist their help now would be as useless as digging a well in the dry soil of the desert."

"Even so, not all hope is lost," insisted the elder of the king's sons. "We will refurbish our own force, and this time we will appoint a more skillful commander who will ensure our victory."

But the king was listless and told his sons to do as was good in their eyes. Hence they sent for his advisers, with whom they explored ways of breeding new horses and building new chariots and launching a further attack on the Israelites. The king merely sat by, silently tugging at his beard.

While the men conferred in the king's office, the queen, Asherah, and

Sisra's mother repaired to a parlor that was set aside for their use only. It was one of the most elegant rooms in the castle, its walls covered with fine tapestries embroidered with silver and gold thread and its floor laid over with exquisite rugs. It boasted several softly upholstered couches placed in a circle, on which the ladies could recline in comfort while doing delicate needlework and talking to each other.

The ladies had abandoned hope for a victory, but not for the defeated hero's homecoming. As they awaited him, they felt the weight of time bearing down almost palpably on their chests. All they could do was to sit glumly and stitch their way through the moments that refused to move on.

Female slaves placed bowls of apple nectar, almonds, and dates on small tables that flanked the couches, and withdrew. But the noblewomen were awash in their sorrow and anxiety, and the silence was broken only by sniffs and sighs. The refreshments remained untouched.

The room was located on the castle's top floor, and from its window there was a view of the castle's entrance. When the slaves came in again to replenish the refreshments, they were instructed to place three chairs in front of this window. Sisra's mother sat down on one of them and peered out through its lattice, flanked by the queen and Asherah.

As time went by and still her son was nowhere in sight, she began languishing, her hand clutching her bosom, her eyes a fountain of tears. Asherah, tenderly holding her mother-in-law's other hand in her own, gently reminded her that Sisra had embarked on his flight on foot, so that it would take him longer than previously reckoned to reach them, and there was no case for worry.

More time passed, and as Sisra's mother shrilly lamented his tardiness again, the queen tried to soothe her by suggesting that they offer up prayers for his safe return. This found favor with the other two ladies, who rose to their feet.

In one of the walls there were large alcoves that held statues of the Canaanite goddesses Asherah, Anath, and Ashtoreth. The women now approached these statues and bowed down until their foreheads touched the ground. Then they rose and poured a libation of wine mixed with frankincense into bowls, which they placed before the goddesses. They raised the palms of their hands in devout supplication, while the queen led them in a fervent petition for Sisra's delivery from danger.

Afterward, Sisra's mother stalked to the window. She sat down and gazed out of it again, and her renewed sobs filled the room with despair. Asherah knelt at her feet and laid her head on her mother-in-law's lap and, her hope having fled, sobbed with her.

Much later, when the day had drawn to an end, and just as one of the king's aides had come to invite the ladies to the evening meal, Sisra's mother finally beheld the sight she had been waiting for: A figure was entering the castle gates. She called out, and Asherah arose and she and the queen looked out the window.

Because it was dark, they could not make out whether it was Sisra. Pushing the chairs out of the way, they raced down the stairway.

Chapter Three

Jael, wife of Hever the Kenite, stood at her post in front of the tent where Sisra slept. She had no doubt that this murderer of multitudes of Israelites, the people who had granted her own clan hospitality in their midst, deserved to be put to death. She also had no qualms about her husband's wishes. Although he gladly made part of his living from the chariots he mended for the Canaanite army, his heart was with the Israelites, who had welcomed him and his family into their land.

Yet Jael hesitated. For she was one of Barak's most ardent admirers, and what concerned her most was what *he* would want her to do.

She knew Barak because, like many other Israelites, he visited her husband's workshop to have his tools repaired. While he chatted with the husband, the wife would come in and offer him refreshments. Despite being thirty-seven years of age and the mother of grown sons, she was still good-looking. She had a long, slim body and dark eyes framed by thick but uncommonly light lashes. The seductive glances she shot him through those lashes, and the purposeful wriggling of her hips whenever she strode past him, indicated to Barak that she would be willing to offer him much more than food and drink.

Despite her good looks, she was not to his taste: he found her hardly more enticing than the pruning knives her husband was mending for him. Yet he had always been friendly to her, so she had never given up hope of leading him astray.

Barak, she decided, could not wish for anything but his enemy's death.

She was also certain that he would be following him. He would, no doubt, crave the glory of bringing about Sisra's demise with his own hands. But if Sisra chanced to wake up and flee before Barak arrived, he was sure to blame her bitterly for having failed in her duty to him and his people.

After considerable hedging, she resolved that she could not take that risk. As Barak himself would realize, the deed could not be delayed until he was there to do it himself. When he entered her tent, she would be able to show him a sight that called for a tangible token of his gratitude.

Having reached her decision, she stepped into the tent. Sisra was sound asleep. Resolutely, she took hold of one of the pegs that held the tent to the ground and the sledgehammer that had been used to fasten it. Softly, she crept up to him and slung one foot across him.

Before her courage deserted her, she bent down over him and drove the peg into his temple with the hammer, until it went down into the ground on his other side. His lifeblood spurted out of him, then oozed to the ground, dyeing the sleeve of her garment and the rug around him bright red. His arm went up of its own accord to protect his temple, but before it could reach its destination, his limbs twitched and he died in his sleep, without knowing what had overcome him.

Jael shuddered and averted her eyes from the abhorrent sight in front of her. She wiped her hands on the blanket that covered Sisra. Then, trembling uncontrollably in all her limbs, she went to renew her vigil in front of the tent, to await Barak.

🐦

By the time Barak and his escorts entered Jael's neighborhood, she had calmed down to some extent. She stepped forward to meet them. When they were still some distance away, she called out, "Come in and I will show you the man for whom you are searching."

Leaving his men and his horse behind, he followed her into her tent. When he saw his adversary lying murdered at his feet, every fiber of his mind and body shrank away from the sly manner in which Jael must have perpetrated her deed. With the sweetness of crushed dates on her tongue, but death in her heart, she must have beckoned him to enter her tent, then soothed him, lulling him into a sense of safety, until he fell asleep. Then, in a base betrayal of his trust, such as that of a viper born of a snake, she used his helplessness to kill him.

Jael had expected Barak to be thankful for the sight that met his eyes, but he just stood there, his bushy eyebrows pulled together, almost touching each other, a wrathful look in his eyes. She had been hoping to earn Barak's praise and much more. Instead, she had to face his fury, and she shrunk before him.

After a long silence, he spoke with a chilly note. "What have you done? When he fell asleep you could have removed his sword from its hilt. Unarmed, he would have been harmless. He could have been captured. There was no need to kill him."

The ice in Barak's words cut through her like a knife. "These words are unjust, sir," she replied vehemently. "I was here by myself and I was not strong enough to capture him. If he had awakened before you arrived, I would not have been able to prevent his flight. Had I let him go free, he would have come back to wreak his revenge upon you at some other time. He might have killed you then, so I killed him first. I did it for you. I thought you would be pleased."

"I am excessively displeased. I am a warrior, not a murderer."

Jael quailed at his words, and the color drained from her face. "Neither am I a murderess." These words were followed by many more that she poured out at Barak in self-justification.

Barak had no patience to disentangle her muddled explanation; he preempted whatever else she had to say by declaring, "Your deed is a blemish on our honor. You have desecrated our victory, demeaning us even in our own eyes."

The Kenite woman rebutted his accusation. "He was the hateful tormentor of your people. He killed thousands of you. I merely meted out the death penalty that brought justice upon him."

His mouth tightened. "You had no right to pronounce a verdict and carry it out yourself," he snapped.

Jael was rattled by this reprimand. She threw back her shoulders in defiance and whispered in a trembling voice, "There was no one here to guide me. I acted in your defense and in the defense of your people. You cannot slander me and brand me a murderess."

"It is not for me to say. I will see to it that you are taken to stand trial before our elders. Let them judge you."

Jael took fright. "You will not denounce me to the elders!"

Barak refrained from giving her the assurance she sought. "Your wrongdoing will denounce you, and the blood on your sleeve will bear witness against you."

The Kenite continued to stand before him, her body shaking like a leaf in the wind. Finally she whispered, "I have loved you for years. I could come to your house tonight and teach you the secrets of an art known only to my tribe."

For women, Barak had a spot as soft as butter in his heart, and he was never willfully vicious to any one of them. Hence, even in his wrath, he refrained from telling her that she was as tiresome to him as a persistently buzzing bee, and that he wanted neither her sting nor her honey. Instead, he replied evasively, "It is not the right moment."

He instructed two of his men to bury the ill-fated Sisra at some appropriate spot, and two others to bear the tidings of Sisra's death at Jael's hands to the town elders, before they all joined him at his own home for food and rest. Then he threw a leg over his horse's saddle and rode away.

As Asherah and the other ladies approached the castle gates for the second time, they saw that the man who had just entered was not Sisra, but someone quite different. He was not even a Canaanite. His attire was outlandish, his skin dark, and he spoke in a foreign tongue the likes of which they had never heard before.

He seemed deeply distraught, rocking wildly back and forth like one in a trance. From his wild demeanor they understood that something was sorely amiss, and Asherah's heart was hammering out her foreboding.

The foreigner uttered the word *Sisra* over and over again, but beyond this, they could not make out what he was saying. Only when the king and his sons arrived on the scene could they interpret his words for them.

As they revealed, the man before them was a Kenite who lived near Kedesh, and he had come to convey the most bitter of all tidings: Sisra had sought refuge in the tent of a Kenite woman, and she had murdered him in his sleep by using a hammer to drive a tent peg through his temple.

Upon Ashera's hearing these words, the castle's walls began spinning around her. Together with her mother-in-law, she collapsed to the ground; both women broke into howls that rent the air, such as those of jackals in the night. Then they beat their breasts and tore the skin of their flesh with their nails, until Asherah's two brothers gathered them up in their arms and bore them into the castle.

They drank from the cup of sorrow, loudly bemoaning their fate, and the king's family and all the courtiers and guards and slave masters mourned with them. Before long, Sisra's mother took to her bed, where she remained in unendurable grief for many a day.

Chapter Four

After he left Jael, Barak headed for his home, where he and his men bathed and ate and spent the night. They set out again at the break of dawn and rode almost unceasingly until they reached Mount Tabor.

Deborah, watching out for them, blinked into the setting sun, which had tinged the clouds first in gold, then in grayish pink. It had almost slid behind the rolling hills in the distance when she spotted them.

The road, drenched with the previous day's rain, was still full of puddles of mud, which the cantering horses' hooves stirred up. When Barak arrived, he was dirty again, even more disheveled than usual, and his eyes were bloodshot with fatigue.

He and his men ate and drank with Deborah in front of her temporary abode. Their hearts wept for their friends, fortunately only few, who had fallen in battle. Yet they flowed over with jubilance as Deborah recited a hymn of gratitude for the Lord's salvation and blessed him for allowing them to survive and reach this time.

When Barak's men dispersed into the night, Deborah led him to the tent that had been erected and made ready for him, and prepared to return to her own. But Barak opened the flaps of his tent and ushered Deborah inside. Staring with undisguised intent at the heavy breasts that strained out of her dress, he announced: "I've come to collect my reward."

The need having built up in her during the last weeks, Deborah felt the stirrings of a responsive lust and a strong urge to yield to him. But no man other than Lapidoth had ever so much as lifted a finger to stroke her cheek; thus, she continued to be reticent. She wished to stall Barak for a while longer, until she felt truly ready for him. In the hope that sweetness might yet emerge from bitterness, she intimated that she expected further achievements from him before she did his bidding.

Barak could no longer comprehend the hurdles Deborah was strewing on his path. She was shying away from the act, assuming the demeanor of an innocent young maiden, rather than that of the mature woman she was. "Is it possible that you are reneging on your promise?" he asked, raising his eyebrows in disbelief.

"No. I always keep my word. But I have not promised to grant your wish, only to consider it," she said. "In any case, I did not promise it instantly. There is much that we need to discuss. You have performed a great feat, but this battle has not spelled the end of the war."

Then she blurted out what had been simmering at the back of her mind since she had sent Barak on his mission: "Unless you follow it up by charging into Hazor, it will all have been in vain."

Deborah's words hit him like thunder on a clear day, but he was too exhausted to ponder them now. "We will talk this over tomorrow, after I've had a rest. Right now I am tired. I want to come to you then go to sleep."

Continuing to hedge, Deborah retorted, "If you feel so, there will not be much pleasure in it. I prefer to wait until you are rested."

Barak, who since his arrival no longer seemed to stand in awe of her, became impatient. "Deborah, so far I have held back, for I felt for you in your distress over the man who was your husband. But now you are teasing me, and being teased is not my favorite pastime. I have waited for this moment long enough. Let me come to you now, or not at all."

Without waiting for her response, he let down the tent's curtains and tied them closed. Then he strode up to her and undressed her, and they lay down on the soft blankets piled up in a rear corner.

For a brief moment, Deborah felt that her body was no longer hers. She herself was hovering above, watching two strangers about to come together. Then she and her body became one again. With deep misgivings, yet also eager and greedy for life, she accepted for the first time ever a man who was not her husband.

Barak prepared to bear down on her, but with new strength coursing through her veins, she resolved to establish her mastery over him. She straddled him and rode him throughout their battle. With her body bent forward and her face tilted backward, her riotous curls tumbling over her neck to the rhythm of his thrusts, his mouth claimed the ripeness of her breasts until the moment came and she reached victory.

When he had followed her into triumph, she eased herself off him, preparing to rise up; but he detained her. He drew her down to him, and this time he established his dominance over her. She yielded to his sword stabbing into her, and she enjoyed her surrender even more than she had enjoyed her victory before.

After that, weariness overcame Barak and before long he plunged into a deep sleep from which, Deborah surmised, nothing short of the blast of ram horns—like those that had toppled the walls of Jericho—would raise him. She returned stealthily to her own tent.

🦌

As Deborah and Barak sat eating their meal in front of her tent in the next morning's breeze, she once more broached the topic of the battle that, she believed, still remained to be fought. "We must now rain down fire and brimstone on Hazor, and render to it the fate of Sodom and Gomorrah."

"We?"

"I mean you, naturally. I am merely a woman, as weak as a newborn kid."

Barak laughed in delight. "You were as weak as a lioness when we lay with each other last night."

"That is another matter," said Deborah, abandoning her stance. "But if the burden is too cumbersome for you to shoulder on your own, I will grasp a sword in my hand, and we will climb the castle's wall side by side and vanquish our enemies together."

Barak grinned in appreciation of the image conjured up by her words. "That would be fascinating, yet I think that I will have to decline this enticing offer. If I engage in this attack at all, I will do it without holding on to your dress. But I am not yet convinced that I should."

"Why are you hesitating?"

"Our strength must be guided by prudence. Carrying off the attack you envision will be a most difficult task. We won this time because we fought in our own land, familiar to us but not to the Canaanites. If we invade theirs, they will have an insuperable advantage over us, since we know nothing of the terrain. Even if we reach Jabin's castle without mishap, we are ignorant of its layout. We could be ambushed within its walls, and felled to the last man."

"What other course is open to us?"

"To sit with our hands folded in our laps. The Canaanite vandals have suffered a lasting defeat. They will not stick out their tongues at us for years to come. In the meantime, our land and our people will flourish."

"Are you not eager for the reward that will follow your new feat of bravery?"

Barak was not swayed. "It is alluring, of course. But to survive is even more tempting."

"Lift your eyes and see what lies before you. The Canaanites are like a troubled sea that constantly casts up filth. Before we are aware of what is before us, they will be upon us again."

The warrior raked his fingers through his wind-tossed hair, as he was wont to do when he was immersed in thought. Weighing Deborah's words in his mind, he realized that he would have to find out what was going forth in the enemy's camp, and that the hazard of a new attack on Jabin might be inevitable.

Finally he replied, "I will send out spies to investigate the Canaanites. If it transpires that they are indeed refurbishing their army, I will forestall their attack and destroy Jabin's bastion before they destroy us. But first I will have to send out more spies to investigate its layout, and this cannot be accomplished hastily. In the meantime, I want another sign that you appreciate my being so meek as to give serious consideration to your new orders."

"We have established a rule. I will grant your wish when you come back victorious."

"The new venture I may have to wage at your behest will be fraught with greater peril than the previous one. I may not come back at all, and then your offer will be of no use to me. This time I will exact double the previous price for my obedience. I insist on two rewards: one before I go and one after I return."

"You are inciting me to pile shame upon shame," she demurred, "without even knowing whether you will do what needs to be done."

Barak, having finished his meal, rose from his seat. He stretched himself contentedly and said, "Deborah, if you feel that what we have been doing is shameful, henceforward you may cast your shame into the depth of the sea. Banish it from your mind as if it never was and be as meticulously virtuous as a virgin. And may the Lord be with you." He bowed to her, then turned on his heels and walked away in search of his men.

She felt that she had no choice but to accede to his demand, and realized that she was not averse to doing so. With a newborn turbulence raking her soul, she jumped up and followed him and placed her hand on his shoulder. Barak turned around and led her to her tent.

This time, Deborah was unable to conceal her doings from her retinue. Her people had served her for years, and they were fiercely loyal to her. Though they were uncommonly vigilant where her safety was concerned, she knew that if she wished for it, they would be as totally blind and deaf and mute as Canaanite idols. No word about this would ever escape their mouths.

She was only a little embarrassed before them, for she knew their secrets, too, many of them the kind that would best be concealed from the glare of daylight. So she entered the tent with Barak without qualm, and there they reveled in each other's passion until the midday meal was brought around.

They ate it in a daze of weariness in front of the tent. Then, plans for Barak's coming actions having been laid, he prepared to depart. When he had walked a few steps, she called after him, "Barak!"

He turned back and bowed his head, and Deborah said with tears in her eyes:

May the Lord bless you and keep you.
    May the Lord lift his countenance upon you
and be gracious to you.
    May the Lord make his countenance shine
upon you and grant you peace.

The tidings of the victorious outcome of the war had spread all over the land of Israel, as if they had been carried from one place to another on birds' wings. Thus, in the scores of towns and villages Deborah and her retinue passed on the way home, multitudes of men and women came out to welcome her. Overwhelmed by the glory of the Lord and his prophetess, they would burst into song and dance accompanied by tambourines and flutes in her honor. In response, she would descend from her white donkey and dance with them. Then she would raise her arms and reach out to heaven and chant a hymn of praise in her resounding voice:

O Lord, when you came forth . . .
the earth trembled . . . heaven quaked . . .
Bless the Lord!

And the people would cheer and leap up and down in ecstasy, until she remounted her donkey, waved to them, and rode out of sight. Thus was she detained in each of the villages she passed, and she did not reach the hill country of Efraim until eight days after she had set out from Mount Tabor.

Since Lapidoth had divorced her and sent her away from his home, Deborah could no longer dwell in it. But it was the house in which her sons resided, and she craved most urgently to see them.

So her first destination in the mountains of Efraim was the hamlet in which Lapidoth's house stood, the little village she had called home for such a large part of her life. As there was no longer any danger of Canaanite marauders, she dispensed with her guards and made her way there on her own. When she arrived, its three hundred inhabitants, young and old, came out as one man to greet her, raising a big shout and enfolding her in loving arms.

Lapidoth was not among them, and she had not expected that he would be. But neither had she expected the frosty reception he accorded her. He was nowhere in sight when she entered his yard, where a stable boy took charge of her donkey while her sons tumbled into her embrace. Neither was he inside the house, where her sons dragged her, unabashedly lifting their voices and weeping with relief at her safe return.

Then they drew her into their quarters, and they spent a long and bliss-ful time together. But when later she came out into the front room, Lapidoth stood there, favoring her with a less than affable speech.

"The war has spared you, and us," he said, "and I am gladdened in the Lord's salvation." But she could perceive no signs of gladness in his face, as he looked at her with narrowed eyes and continued. "Before you left, you assured me that no one but me has ever touched you. Can you still give me that same assurance today?"

And she, who had never lowered her eyes before any man, cast them down before Lapidoth.

He did not let off, looking at her insistently while she continued to avoid his gaze. At long last she pursed her lips and raised her head and replied, "I am a divorced woman, who by Torah law is not barred from doing what is right in her eyes. I can still say that I have done nothing I cannot reconcile with my conscience, or with the Torah commandments."

Lapidoth was disconcerted. "This is merely a subterfuge," he ranted. "You are quite devoid of a conscience. Not only did you defy me three times, but now you have added a grievous sin to your rebellion by letting yourself be defiled by that uncouth man. No matter how much fragrant soap you use to wash yourself, you are tainted in my eyes."

His voice, in which pain and wrath and humiliation at her hands bat-tled each other, resounded through the still air. It was so loud and shrill that their sons came and looked at them in hurt astonishment. Deborah's cheeks were aflame, and she felt a hot red color wrapping itself around her body like a shroud.

A shiver of indignation ran through her. When Lapidoth had handed her the book of divorcement, he had expressly declared it to be the book that granted her freedom, as indeed was the law. But now, although he had retracted from his commitment to her as her husband, he was holding her to her obligation to him as his wife, and unjustly declared her to have sinned. She was not accustomed to such volatility on his part. As she was stained in his eyes, so was he tarnished in hers.

"You have been tested and found wanting," Lapidoth continued, re-buking her further.

Anger throbbed through her and hot words rushed to her mouth. Yet she swallowed them and kept her lips pressed to each other, for she had no wish to remonstrate with him before their sons. Nor would a sharp reply from her serve to mollify him and mend the rift between them. So she suppressed her annoyance, and what she had to say remained trapped inside her.

As Lapidoth said no more and merely stood there with a sneer on his face, she stepped into the chamber that had been hers, to collect her belongings. She found them neatly packed into cloth bags, piled up in a corner. The large case that stood against one of the walls, in which they had been stored before, had its doors closed. She did not open them to find out what it contained now, but a feminine scent hung in the air, and it was not hers.

The man with whom she had shared her life for sixteen years had evidently not waited for her confession before deciding to make it as clear as the sunlight that permeated the room at this moment that he did not want her back in it. Had he foreseen her admission, or had he wished for it as justification for his own deeds? Or was he simply so jealous as no longer to be guided by reason? As she had no intent of asking him these questions, they would have to remain unanswered.

Deborah had repeatedly taught her sons the Torah injunction

You shall not bear tales among your people.

Hence she was not surprised that they had failed to mention the woman who had apparently sojourned in her room, even though she was not there now. They stood by watching her helplessly for a moment. As she bent to lift the bags to her shoulder, they rushed forward and took them from her hands and out into the yard. When the stable boy brought out her donkey, they affixed the bags to hooks attached to its saddle, which she mounted.

She returned to her palm tree and to the tent that still awaited her behind it. This, she reckoned, would henceforward serve as her abode. From that day onward, she was careful to visit her sons only during the day, when Lapidoth was out in the fields.

Chapter Five

The two women who mourned Sisra spent their days together in his mother's room, convinced that there was nothing, not even the passage of time, that would ever ease their pain. Out of the depth of her sorrow, the bereaved mother, who was keeping to her bed, began whispering dire words into her daughter-in-law's ears. Her firstborn's blood ought to be avenged. His murderer and the murderess, the one who had carried out his design, must not remain unscathed.

Eight days after they had been apprised of his death, when the king came to visit Sisra's mother, she shook an accusing finger into his face and shouted her wrath. "Both the woman who sent out her hand to kill Sisra and the villainous commander at whose behest she perpetrated the deed must die like dogs. Each day in which their hearts still beat in their chests is a slight on my son's memory."

The king, who was still in a deep oppression of spirit, retorted half-heartedly that the day of reckoning was sure to come.

Asherah listened but did not believe her father. As she lay on her bed at night, with the place where her beloved husband should have lain beside her empty, she began to spin visions of revenge. In those, she herself would visit on both the assassins the punishment they deserved. In the light of day, she was forced to admit to herself that these notions were only childish foolishness. But in the loneliness of the night they came back to haunt her stubbornly. And when she fell asleep, they wove themselves into her dreams.

Then the rumor reached her that the barbarians, not content with the destruction they had brought down upon them already, were intent upon demolishing their home and all its inhabitants with it. Her father assured her that he had appointed his best men to guard them. But when she looked at the pallor of his face, and his trembling hands, she understood that he had little confidence in his officers.

Once again, Asherah put her faith in her adored goddess. She pleaded with her, saying that if it was her destiny to die at the hands of those ferocious animals of prey, at least let it not be at the time of their incursion, so that first she might be granted the opportunity to avenge her husband's death.

🐉

The king's slave masters apprised the Israelite slaves and their offspring neither of the Canaanite defeat nor of Sisra's death. They found out about these events in devious ways, and when they did, they rejoiced. But they took care not to let their delight be apparent on their faces or in their hooded eyes, and they continued to perform their menial tasks as submissively as they had done before. Soon, though, their secret ecstasy was marred by grave misgivings, for the castle came alive with rumor.

In almost inaudible whispers, the word passed from mouth to mouth that the Israelite warriors were about to mount an assault on the fortress. This opened the prospect of their redemption from slavery and a return to their own land, where good days would lie in store for them. Yet they also feared that when the attack came, the Israelite swordsmen might not recognize them as their own people. They could only pray to the Lord that in the heat of battle their own warriors would not kill them along with their enemies.

When Nogah learned of what had come to pass, her heart rejoiced for her mother and for Israel, and bled for her father and for Canaan.

She had never spoken to Asherah, or to Sisra, so his death meant little to her. But she grieved for her father, who had become a different man overnight. His proud regal bearing and dignified assurance had vanished. His strength had been sapped away as the juice of blossoms is sucked out by bees. In a matter of weeks his hair had turned gray and the skin of his face had assumed a sallow shade. Whenever she embraced him, he would hold her to his chest convulsively and shed tears into her hair.

At first she thought that this would be the end of it, and she cherished the hope that her father would soon recover his spirits. Then the whispers reached her that the Israelites were to attack the stronghold, and she saw them reflected in her father's fallen face. Her mother, though, had a sense of suppressed excitement about her. Nogah herself was thrown into a greater confusion than she had ever known before.

For despite all the rapturous tales Reumah had told her, she had no notion of what to expect of the Israelites, of whom she had heard much but seen little. Apart from the female slaves and their offspring, she had never met any of them; she did not even know what Israelite men looked like, much less could she imagine what they would do when they overran them.

※

Deborah's sons were used to accompanying their father to the fields in the morning, to work there, each according to his age and capability. At noontime Lapidoth would bring them home and leave them with a teacher he had hired for them. Deborah fell into the habit of visiting them on the second and fifth days of each week, when the shadows barely became visible in the east, thus giving their teacher a respite.

Lapidoth's house stood halfway up a steep incline and looked as if it were about to tumble down into the valley. But it was, in fact, solidly built, its foundations carved deeply into the rocks of the hill on whose slope it was perched

As Deborah approached it on her second visit there, she raised her eyes to it, to the house where she had known so many years of happiness. Where every corner held recollections of caring words spoken, soft melodies sung, hugs bestowed and received. Where every sight and sound and smell had been as familiar to her as her own self. The house to which, now and henceforward, she would only come as a visitor.

She was not a woman to give voice or tears to her sorrow. It sat heavy as a lump of copper inside her, but its only outward sign was her dry, cracked lips. She saw her boys, all five of them, standing on the rooftop, leaning against its fence, waving her in, their calls of welcome jumbling together.

Soon she held them in her arms, covering their heads with kisses, tucking sweet cakes of barley and crushed dates from her palm tree into their pockets. And in her boundless love for them, her sadness was eased.

Later, when their teacher had taken charge of them again, she stepped out into the yard. There she was met with the sight of a scantily dressed girl, no more than fifteen years old, quietly being sick at its edge.

Deborah approached and waited. After her sickness had left off, the girl turned to face her.

She had woolly black hair and skin to match its color, and eyes the shape of almonds and the color of ripe dates. She bowed deeply but clumsily to Deborah. "Lady, don't look at me askance for being black," she said apologetically, "for I have been scorched by the sun."

Deborah regarded her wordlessly.

"I have been working in the fields, and now I am out in the sun all day tending the garden in the rear of the house," added the young one, by way of explanation.

As she was nearly as black as granite, Deborah was sure that the shade of her skin had been bestowed on her at birth and had little to do with working in the sun. This made her eager to put the girl at her ease. "The Lord has endowed the children of Adam with different colors. We have all been created in his image. One is no better or worse than another."

"Yes," said the girl doubtfully, yet with a glimmer of pride in her eyes.

"Who are you?"

"I am a slave girl."

"Have you no name?"

"After I was rent from my mother, no one called me by the name she gave me. I was merely called Kushite, 'the Black One.' But the master, he said that I was black but fair, hence he called me Naavah, 'the Fair One'; so now that is who I am."

"And what are you doing here, Naavah?"

"The master, he bought me at the marketplace in Bethel, where my previous master had put me up for sale."

"What is ailing you that made you so sick before?"

The girl dipped her head and shuffled her bare feet in confusion, and a light went on in Deborah's mind.

"Lady," the girl stuttered with a guilty pleading in her voice, "it was the master—he—I could not refuse—he—he said that I was no longer a slave, that the entire country was before me and I was free to go wherever my whims might lead me. That is what he said. But my family dwells in a distant land in the south, where the sun sizzles and beats down relentlessly on the earth and the sand burns under the soles of your feet all year round. I would not be able to get there on my own. There was nowhere for me to go. I could not but stay here, and so I had to yield to him. And now, as you see . . . Pray don't judge me harshly, and grant me forgiveness," she apologized profusely, "for it was not my fault."

There was a captivating lack of guile about Naavah, and Deborah could not help but feel for her, nor could she entirely blame Lapidoth for having taken a fancy to her. So she took pains to reassure her. "It is nothing to me. I am no longer his wife, nor is he my husband," she said with feigned indifference. "I merely came to visit my sons."

"Your garments and oils and scents," continued the girl lamely, "it was the master who ordered me to pack them into bags. There was nothing I could do about that, either."

"It is of no consequence."

At that moment, Lapidoth, returning from the fields, entered the yard. Deborah weighed in her mind the notion of holding him to account for his deeds with Naavah, as he had done to her with respect to Barak, but she knew it would be useless. Neither of them could retract what they had done, even had they wished to do so.

She regarded him with as kind a look as she could muster. Then she turned from him and rode back to her palm tree and her tent.

Before darkness descended, she sat at its entrance. Her hands, which morning and evening had never lain idle in her lap, now had nothing to occupy them. For other hands, those of maids, mended the tears in her sons' clothing when they went to sleep, and combed out their knotted hair when they rose up. Thus she was left to her reflections and to spending the night on her own.

The rumors of an impending attack on the Hazor castle were not immediately realized: It took more than three and a half months for Barak to reach a decision, complete the preparations for it, and bring it to fruition.

It was not easy for him to locate spies who were willing and able to infiltrate the castle in the guise of vendors who came to deliver their merchandise, and there to befriend the courtiers and learn from them the king's actions and plans. Eventually he gathered the knowledge he had sought on the rebuilding of Jabin's army for a renewed attack, and he learned the layout of the castle. Then he selected the best men available to take with him on the assault. Even after that, he still waited for a rainy night, in which the moon would be hidden by clouds, as dark as Egypt during the ninth plague.

On the night Barak had chosen for his invasion, black clouds had rolled in and hung heavily in the sky. Just as they were about to set out, those clouds burst into a thunderstorm, which Barak counted as a blessing.

He gathered his men in front of his home, and raising his voice over the noise of the storm, he spoke to them. "Hear me, warriors. Tonight we are going out again to face our enemies for the sake of our people and our land and our God. Our goal is to conquer the Hazor castle, and then the town itself."

He explained to them that they would have to walk silently, so that the rain and thunder would drown out the noise of their steps. He showed them four ladders he'd had built, which they would have to carry with them. They would lean those against the castle's wall and climb them silently. On a night such as this, the guards stationed on the wall were apt to seek cover in the rooms within its watchtowers. Barak's men would sneak into those rooms and fell them before the sentinels realized what had overcome them. After that, they would slay the warriors who defended the stronghold from the inside.

"Then," he continued, "we will destroy the temple that stands close to the castle and pull down its altars and crush all its graven images, as the Torah commands us to do. We will also ransack the castle and lay our hands on vaults containing treasures of gold and silver ornaments, jewels, and precious stones.

"But we will not raise our swords to women and children and unarmed men. If it should chance that Jabin and his sons are not armed, we will not kill them but capture them. There are Israelite slaves and their children in the castle. We will be extremely careful not to harm them. We will remove all unarmed people from the place before we consign it to the fire.

"Once our handiwork is completed the castle will be reduced to rubble, soon to become a haunt of wolves. Then we will do the same to Hazor, a town made up of simple huts and tents, which we will turn to ashes.

"And now hear this! There will be no raping, which is an abomination before the Lord. And there will be no slipping of spoils into your own pockets. They will be brought before the elders, who will distribute them as they see fit."

The men nodded their heads, and a few of them called out, "Whatever you command us, we will do."

The rest of the way was made in silence. Barak was overcome with grave misgivings. For despite the confidence he had displayed before his men, he was far from certain of their success, knowing that much could go right but even more could go wrong. The outcome of the looming hazardous mission was as unpredictable as the drift of the wind. He prayed to the Lord for victory. Following his prayer, he silently took a vow:

God of Israel. If you will be with us and deliver
our enemies into our hands, and if there should
chance to be a beautiful woman among the
captives whom I desire, I will deal with her as
you have set out in the Holy Torah: I will not
come to her immediately, but keep her in my
house for a full month, so that she may mourn all
she has lost. Only then will I know her and take
her to be my wife.

His prayer and vow imbued him with a measure of relief and a new confidence in the success of his mission.

Chapter Six

The day that preceded Barak's attack had been a tiring one for Deborah, with numerous complainants shrilly voicing their claims. She had succeeded in appeasing them all, and they had left in contentment. But now, at dusk, after the last litigants had dispersed, she remained on her judge's chair, her mind a void of exhaustion.

Distant memories began washing over her as they had not done for a long time.

They were of the weeks that led up to her wedding with Lapidoth. It was a time of distress for her, because the Israelites' idolatry had assumed staggering dimensions previously unheard of. She took to appearing at the sites of their worship and reprimanding them for their transgressions. Lapidoth was always at her side, imbuing her with strength and standing guard over her so that she would come to no harm.

On one of those occasions, their donkeys brought them to the foot of a hill, where many other asses, and the boys in charge of them, were waiting. They found a boy to take charge of theirs in return for silver they weighed into his hand.

Then Deborah covered her face with a veil so that she would not be recognized, and they climbed to the top of the hill. There a shrine with two pedestals set up under a large, leafy tree held glittering bronze statues of a Baal and an Ashtoreth. Each had a clay jar of wine in front of it and from time to time a man or a woman would approach to fill their cups. An altar to the right of those statues held a sacrificial lamb. A priest chanted incantations and poured a libation of wine over the altar.

Facing the shrine were scores of people, some of whom Deborah recognized. She was appalled. They bowed down, their heads touching the ground. Then they lifted their heads and raised their hands in supplication, offering up prayers for abundant rains and plentiful crops and the blessing of the womb. Other men and women sang and swayed, their eyes closed as if in a trance. Still others were beating drums in ever-growing exuberance.

Having adopted the prevailing unbridled licentiousness of idol worship, some of the women were in various states of undress. Priests and other men were playing with them in utter abandon, and Deborah caught a glimpse of one couple disappearing behind the bushes. A few men hailed Lapidoth and her and beckoned them to join in.

She cast off her veil, and with her eyes shooting sparks of fire, she blasted at them:

Hear me, Israelites. You are transgressing against
the Lord, hence his anger is unleashed against you.
  Though you have built houses, you will not dwell
in them.
  Though you have sown fields, you will not reap them.
  Though you have planted vineyards, you will not drink
their wine, for aliens will devour them.

The priests and worshippers recoiled and stepped back from her in momentary fear.

The prophetess took hold of a heavy stick that, fortuitously, was lying on the ground, and with hitherto unknown strength in her arm she used it to hack the idols' heads off. When they fell at the sides of their bodies, she kicked them with her shoe and watched them roll slowly down the slope of the hill. Then she rattled the idols until they fell flat on the ground.

By then the priests had recuperated from their initial shock. The one who was their leader stepped forward and shouted, "You are a false prophetess. The Canaanite gods and goddesses are benevolent and merciful. They will bless our houses and our fields and our vineyards."

Deborah continued to thunder:

They are but lifeless pieces of bronze.
    Repent, and love the Lord your God with all your
hearts and all your souls and all your might.

The head priest was not intimidated. "You may be able to remove the gods from their pedestals, but you cannot extract them from our hearts. Go forth and disseminate your evil prophecies of doom elsewhere, lest the Baal wreak vengeance on you, and we will be his holy tools."

"The Lord is my shield from adversity," she declared. "What can you do to me?"

Lapidoth now intervened at the top of his voice. "If you as much as cause one hair from her head to fall to the ground, I will come back here with my men and make you share the fate of your beheaded idols."

Yet neither of them felt as confident as they strove to appear. So when Lapidoth grasped Deborah's hand and drew her away from her adversaries, she did not resist.

Sadly, she had to admit to herself that her prophecy had been no more than a voice calling in the wilderness.

After they descended the hill and calmed down and mounted their donkeys, Lapidoth brought his close to hers. "As you are so astoundingly familiar with the Lord's intentions," he queried with a touch of gentle mockery in his eyes, "tell me this: How many sons and daughters will he grant us?"

She felt elation pervade her being, for she yearned to bring his sons and daughters into the world. Yet she had no reply to his question. "I can foresee only what lies ahead for the people, not for me—for us," she corrected herself, thus indicating that his wish to take her for his wife was also hers.

"How is this?"

"In my own life I am like everyone else," she admitted shamefacedly. "There is nothing to mark me off from other young women of my age."

"I would not want it to be otherwise," he consoled her. He took her left hand off the donkey's rein, and felt it fluttering in his. "Then you cannot prophesy whether your father will be willing to bestow you on me?"

It had not escaped Deborah that both her father and her mother had been anxious for some time over her ability to find a suitable husband. Hence she stated without hesitation, "He will."

"Will he also permit me and my men to come and guard your house from these vile men until I have you safely ensconced in mine?"

"He may."

And so it was. After having obtained her father's consent on both counts, Lapidoth came back with his men, all bearing arms, each day at sunset, in readiness for what the night might bring.

For six nights, nothing untoward happened. But on the seventh evening, the head priest of the Baal, the one who had rebuked Deborah, and six of his underlings appeared in front of her house.

Lapidoth and his men went out to meet them, with their swords drawn from their hilts.

But the one who was their head announced, "Sheath your swords, for we have come in peace."

"What is your request?" asked Lapidoth suspiciously.

"We request to have speech with the prophetess."

"After the manner in which you have insulted her, she will not see you."

"She may, if you tell her that we repent our sins and want to return to the Lord," he said humbly.

Deborah came out and invited them into her home and welcomed them at her table with bread and wine and blessings. "You know the Torah commandments, so there should be no difficulty in your upholding them again," she said.

"True, but the difficulty lies elsewhere. Be aware, illustrious lady," the head priest pointed out, "that we are giving up not only our faith but also our livelihood. Without our share of the sacrifices to the Baal, which worshippers have been used to bring to us, how will we sustain ourselves?"

"You are Cohanite priests. Don the priestly garbs you must still have in your possession. Go to the temple in Shiloh and there perform the duties that appertain to you by your birthright. Then you may obtain your share of the sacrifices, as the other priests do."

"They will not accept us into their ranks."

"They most certainly will, once they are advised that"—Deborah hesitated and looked at Lapidoth; he nodded his head, and she proceeded—"that your head has officiated at our wedding, which is to come about shortly, that two of you have served as witnesses to our ceremony, and that the rest have aided the head priest in performing the ritual by holding up the poles of our canopy."

So it came about that Deborah and Lapidoth's wedding was celebrated by the erstwhile priests of the Baal, though with meticulous adherence to the laws and customs of Israel.

Afterward, Deborah remained indefatigable. At her request, Lapidoth shepherded her to many similar sites of idol worship, there to proclaim the word of the Lord. Some two years later, when her first pregnancy began, she left off traveling. But she continued to send out dispatches to the elders of all the tribes and towns and villages, bearing the prophecies she had previously delivered by mouth.

In the event, the Lord had not seen fit to endow them with any daughters at all, but he had blessed them with five sons, who had inundated their house with joy. All had boded so well for their life together, and it had fulfilled all the hopes she had pinned on it, and more. The years had fled speedily, like passing shadows, and they had seemed no more than a few months to them because of their love for each other. She could not fathom how things had gone awry between them to such an extent that Lapidoth had banned her from his life and turned to another woman, while she had welcomed the advances of another man.

This deflected her thoughts to Barak. Although she had not rested her eyes on him for more than three and a half months, he had been much on her mind and she was not averse to seeing him again.

No, she had to admit to herself that it was more than that. She had been, and still was, longing for him, for his touch on her flesh, for an opportunity to have his deeds upon her repeated.

By that time, the sun had set and darkness was slowly creeping in. She repaired to her tent, where she consumed the evening meal her maids had prepared for her. Then she sat in front of her abode to contemplate the sky of the night, which had come to be overhung with clouds.

Although she had not been apprised of it, Deborah had an inner certitude that this was the night that Barak had settled upon for his attack, the one that would decide the fate of Israel for many years to come.

Setting aside the vicissitudes of her own life, Deborah prostrated herself on the ground and prayed to the Guardian of Israel to crown the commander's endeavor, in which he would be engaged at her instigation, with success. She sensed that her pleading would not remain unheeded. As she lay down on her couch, this confidence eased her into sleep, until the rising sun summoned her to face a new day.

Chapter Seven

E ven though everyone in Jabin's castle knew that an Israelite attack was imminent, no one, least of all the king, had any notion of when it would eventuate. Hence, though anxiety was rife, life proceeded much as usual. Thus, when the attack came about, all were taken unawares.

On the evening before, a heavy thunderstorm had begun. As Nogah lay in her bed, she could hear the wind rushing through the nearby trees, their branches creaking and beating against her window. Flashes of lightning slid through the sky, and thunder broke over her head.

She remembered the thunderstorms she had braved when she and her mother had lived in the tent. Those had occasionally borne down with great might on their vulnerable abode, toppling it and forcing them to seek refuge in the slaves' hall until it could be repaired and set up again. Because of those recollections, Nogah dreaded a thunderstorm even now, inside the castle. She tried to shut out its sights and sounds from her mind by covering her head with her blanket. Even so, it was a long time before she fell asleep.

Soon after, she and Reumah were roughly awakened to the awareness of hasty footsteps approaching and the frantic rattling of their door. This commotion was followed by the voice of a guard, muffled by the thick barrier of the door, from which they surmised that the sword had descended: The Israelites were upon them.

A jolt of alarm shot through Nogah. She jerked upright and jumped out of her bed as one bitten by a snake. She and her mother wrapped themselves in their tunics and pulled open the door. The guard bade them follow him to a room where the women of the house of Jabin were being brought for their protection, and they staggered forward in his wake.

After winding their way through a succession of lengthy passages, they reached a large hall where the Hebrew slaves were being assembled. Little of their previous pleasurable anticipation was discernible in their faces now. They sat on the floor in numb terror, too scared of both their Canaanite masters and the Israelite attackers to utter a sound.

Reumah and Nogah prepared to sit down with them, but the guard said that the king's orders were that they be brought into a room tucked away at the rear, where they could be better guarded. In front of it some fifty guards were stationed, entrusted with defending the royal women. The guard propelled them inside and closed the door behind them.

Inside the room, the queen and her youngest daughter and Sisra's mother were sitting huddled together, visibly trembling, stricken with fear. Since they did not know Nogah and her mother, they looked at them briefly with raised eyebrows; but they were too scared for their own lives to pay any heed to them.

Nogah and her mother sat down in a corner of the room, hunched forward, and paid no attention to the other women in the room either. They, too, were paralyzed by their own fright. Cold shivers ran down their spines, yet they perspired. In their need for warmth, they pulled their tunics close around them, but tangled wisps of sweat-dampened hair hung limply over their temples.

At first they heard nothing. The castle was frozen in silence, as if it were inhabited solely by statues. As time passed and this did not change, the queen's perplexed gaze came to rest upon Nogah, and she began muttering to herself. After a while, setting her dread of the attack aside, this ominous lady raised her voice to the girl: "What are you doing here? This room has been set aside for the king's family. You should not be in it."

Nogah straightened herself but, as good manners dictated, kept her eyes downcast as she responded soothingly, "My lady the queen, we have been brought here by the king's orders."

"Why?"

"For our protection."

"Why does he want to protect you?" The queen's suspicion reared its head, and she began to quiz Nogah with wrathful eyes. The room was lit by only sparse, shadowy candlelight, so the queen was not aware of the blue-green color of Nogah's eyes. But even in the dim light she could see that the young one was pretty, so she leveled an accusation at her. "You must be the latest slave to share his bed."

"My lady queen," Nogah replied in a soothing voice, "I assure you that I am not sharing his bed."

Asherah, her head resting listlessly on the table, showed little interest in what was going on around her. But now she whispered into her mother's ear, "Please leave this. We have more important matters to worry about."

The queen disregarded her, and glancing at Nogah in disdain, she continued, her voice as sharp as a dagger, "I think that you *are* sharing his bed. One day I passed by his scroll room when its door was being opened, and there you were, sitting next to him, while he was hugging you."

Reumah intervened. "If she were sharing his bed, she would not be sitting with him in his *scroll* room."

This reasonable comment did nothing to appease the queen, who demanded harshly, "Then who are you, the two of you?"

"I am one, Nogah, and this is my mother, Reumah."

"I still think that he protects you because he likes you in his bed. Get out of here, both of you," she fairly shouted at them, her voice now trembling not with fear, but wrath.

Asherah, who had been squirming uncomfortably, once again spoke, this time more boldly. "My mother, they are doing no harm. Please leave them alone."

Nogah and her mother, having exchanged a silent glance, rose up and walked to the door. They tried to open it but found it to be locked from the outside.

They returned to their seats. For a while the queen rambled on, muttering inaudibly to herself. But eventually her voice petered out, and thereafter all the women sat in hostile and increasingly anxious silence.

There was an eerie stillness outside their room as well, broken only by the lament of the wind and by thunderbolts that followed each other in rapid succession. Time moved sluggishly, in a blur of flickering candlelight and flickering alarm. They had no knowledge of what was going forth in all other parts of the castle. Looking at her mother's pale face, Nogah knew that she no longer held firm to her belief that they were being liberated.

Nogah herself became increasingly doubtful that they would still be alive to welcome the rising sun in the morning. Terror slid through her in mind-numbing waves, as she sensed the shadows of death closing in on them. She whispered a silent supplication to the Lord, to send them succor at this time of their affliction.

After a while the women, pricking their ears, heard some unfamiliar sounds. At first, the noises emanated from a distance and were indistinct. But soon they grew louder, clearer, and more terrifying, drowning out Nogah's prayer.

🐾

The Canaanite officers were shouting out orders to their men, and these were interspersed by orders in Hebrew. Before long the Hebrew commands drowned out the others, as the men calling them out approached their room.

Then the air was suffused with the blood-chilling death screams of agonized men, as they were being slit by their enemies' swords. Nogah shook in horror and felt her mother's sweat-bathed body against hers as the older woman hugged her protectively, as if she could thereby shield her from danger.

Before long the door to their room was unlocked and several Israelite warriors burst in. Thus Nogah had her first glimpse of the men who her mother had told her were of her own people.

It was not a pleasant sight. The Israelites, who had felled the guards in front of the royal women's room, were soaked from the rain and splattered with a mixture of mud and their enemies' blood. They were drunk with triumph, wild-eyed and crazed with a murderous rage, brandishing their blood-stained swords in the air.

Fright widened Nogah's eyes as she saw them turning their fury toward the women. Ignoring their anguished pleading, they slammed them down to the floor, old and young alike, and savagely tore off their robes and dresses.

Reumah, addressing them in Hebrew, admonished them to stop, but the men were in no mood to listen. Her words were soon blotted out by the screams of the royal women. Nogah heard whimpers escape her own mouth, as one of the invaders bore down on her, planting his knees on her thighs, forcing them apart. Like the other women in the room, she desperately tried to free herself, but she had little hope of success.

Until another Israelite burst in, at whose sight Nogah's attacker slackened his hold on her. As her eyes flung upward to him, she noted that his garment, too, was dripping with rain, plastered with mud, and spattered with blood, and his hair clung in wet strands to his face. He, too, was in an ill-contained rage, and fury boiled over in his dark eyes. But his wrath was aimed at the men.

His loud voice overbore all others, as he ordered, "Halt at once. Whoever transgresses this order will be put to death. Instantly."

This brought the men to their senses. Reluctantly, they released their victims and rose to their feet, leaving behind only their offensive odor of sweat and blood. Nogah, still prostrate on the floor, drew in a deep breath of relief and raised herself on her elbows. She stared wide-eyed at the Israelite commander.

Ignoring the women's gazes upon him, he set three of his warriors to guard them and bore the would-be rapists off with him. The women dragged themselves up from the floor and covered themselves with their torn clothing as best they could. After that, they sat down on their chairs again, still shaking in panic, as the shouts and screams invading the room from outside slowly abated.

The air in the chamber was stifling, and one of their guards stepped over to the shuttered window and opened it to let some fresh air in. When he moved back, Nogah, who sat close by, looked out into the yard at the back of the castle. But the dimness of the night prevented her from seeing anything but a black void.

By that time the rain had long ceased, but lightning still parted the sky. A flash lit the scene, and for a brief moment that seemed to last an eternity, she glimpsed the horror below.

Large numbers of slashed bodies were sprawled on the ground, their faces contorted in agony, blood still seeping from them. The gruesome sight was overwhelming, and she groaned as her stomach coiled in pity and disgust. Her insides churned and she was overcome with nausea. She bent over, with her head almost touching her knees. When she straightened herself, her sickness lurched upward inside her, and she darted to the window and leaned out.

The Israelite commander returned in time to witness her retching convulsions as she vomited into the yard. When she turned back from the window her gaze swung to his, while he scanned her ashen face.

Nogah saw a fleeting look of compassion steal over his face, before it clammed up. She cringed in resentment of his condescending pity, and her chin went up a little, a gesture of defiance he failed to notice. Then, swaying on her feet as the room began to reel around her, she returned to her chair.

The commander surveyed the other women in the room. Then he addressed them in the Canaanite language, which he apparently had mastered fairly well. "All has come to an end. King Jabin and his two sons have fallen on their swords, and the castle's guards and slave masters are all dead as well. The women and children have been spared. You will be taken into captivity. My men will escort you to your rooms, where you will gather up a few of your belongings. From there you will hurry to the courtyard, so that we can take you out of here before we pour the oil from the king's storerooms into the castle and set fire to it."

He appointed several men to accompany the women to their quarters. Then he stepped out of the room before he could be detracted from his purpose by their cries.

🦁

Only when he had shut the door behind him did Nogah become conscious of his appearance: his unusually large proportions, the muscles that corded his legs and chest and his broad shoulders, his fierce dark eyes, and his fatigue-strained face.

He did not look like a killer, yet he had just stabbed the men in the castle to death, or at least he had been in command of those who had done it. Even if, as he had claimed, her father and brothers had killed themselves, they must have done so in hopeless despair, driven to it by his onslaught.

Was she to curse him for causing the death of her beloved father? Or was she to bless him as a savior redeeming her beloved mother from the slavery she had been doomed to under her father's rule? For years, her mother had lavished praise on the Israelites in her ears. Had he acted as an Israelite should have? For a moment, her throat was tight with the agony of doubt.

Then she forgot the commander, and her thoughts reverted to her father. It struck her that one of the last thoughts he'd had in his mind was seeing to it that she was brought to a place of safety. For that reason more than for any other, her soul screamed in anguish, as the tears streamed out of her eyes.

Despite the abrasive manner in which the queen had addressed her, Nogah suddenly felt close to her and to her daughter, who were huddling sobbing wildly in grief for the man who was her father, and for the men who were her brothers, even though she had only ever seen them from afar.

She and the wailing women had nothing to tie them to each other except their mourning for the same men, but at that moment it was all that mattered. She felt an impulse to walk over to them and embrace them, but she knew that if she did they would scornfully repel her, so she refrained.

Instead, her tears blinding her, she stepped out of the door with her mother, who was stroking the desolate girl's hair soothingly.

Nogah was revulsed by the pierced dead bodies piled up around them. She sidestepped them while averting her eyes from them, as she trailed Reumah to their room to collect their belongings.

Reumah, who had foreseen that they would have to leave the castle, had sewn up some large cloth bags for their garments. She and Nogah pushed as many of those as they could into the bags. In between her clothing, Nogah placed the presents her father had given her, which now were doubly precious to her, both as signs of his affection and as tokens by which to remember him. Then they pulled on their goatskin cloaks to protect them from the cold, took hold of the bags, and followed their Israelite guard outside.

The black, cloudy night rushed at them. But as their eyes became used to the dark, it could not conceal the bodies strewn across the cobblestones or the rivers of bloodstained rainwater flowing down the slope in front of them. Soon the other survivors lumbered out into the courtyard. Shoving aside the bodies on the ground to form a path for them, the Israelite warriors led them out of the castle.

There they were given saddled donkeys to ride. They attached their cloth bags to hooks on the saddles. Mustering all the remnants of her courage, Nogah mounted hers. Barak's men took them on a slippery path down the hill and through the town of Hazor. Now they no longer kept company with the royal women, but unwittingly mingled with the slaves and their offspring, as some of those preceded them, while others followed in their wake.

By then the clouds had dispersed, leaving behind a sky feebly lit by the pale moon and the stars. As they crossed the town, wrapped in the ominous silence of death, Nogah saw that the town's people had not fared better than the inhabitants of the castle. Hazor's streets were paved with the bodies of those fallen in battle, a sight to which, she realized with disbelief, she was becoming inured.

🦎

They had barely left the town behind when Nogah heard voices calling out to them to turn around. She did so and was transfixed by the sight of the castle going up in flames, clearly outlined against the night sky. Tongues of fire licked its walls, devouring some of them while the rest fell in on themselves. She heard the crash of its ceilings as they toppled, their beams swallowed up by the fire.

The blaze spread to the town of Hazor. Balls of fire rolled swiftly from one hut to another, leaving none intact. Nogah's eyes slid closed, and she clamped her hand over her mouth to keep from screaming at the heartrending sight.

The sky began to pale as dawn arose, but a huge pillar of smoke rising from the town darkened it again. It became murky, as if it were clothed in mourning. The wind blew the smoke at them, and Nogah felt herself engulfed in it, forced to inhale its suffocating thickness into her lungs.

At first she was awash with relief at having escaped the smoldering fire. A moment later it dawned upon her that her father's body must have been consumed by it. Her heart cried out for him, of whom there was nothing left, not even a body for burial, and for herself, abandoned by him. Now that he was no longer here to protect her, her sheltered life had irrevocably come to an end; she was but a leaf adrift in the wind. Her mind was numbed, refusing to grapple with the enormity of her loss.

She was on the threshold of the unknown. Her future was shrouded in a mist as thick as that now rising from the damp ground. She brought her donkey close to her mother's and tugged at her sleeve, wanting to gain reassurance from her. But Reumah's forehead was creased and her face was drawn and weary and pale. Her mother, too, was visibly in deep concern about what lay ahead.

Nogah resolved not to pester her, and nursed her trepidation in silence.

Part Three

In the Power of Lightning

Chapter One

Giving silent thanks to the Lord for the result of their mission and the small number of those fallen in battle, Barak and his warriors left Hazor shortly after the break of dawn. With them were the nearly fifty Israelite women slaves and their children they had liberated, and the royal ladies and other Canaanite women and their children from the town of Hazor they had captured. They had the gold, silver, and precious stones, and the goats, sheep, and cattle they had looted. They also brought with them the horses and donkeys they had confiscated for their own and the captives' transport.

In the light of the rising sun, Barak saw that the air was heavy with soot from the fire. Therefore, and also because there was still a danger that swordsmen from other Canaanite domains would come forth to attack them, he was eager to be gone. He spurred his men to advance as quickly as they could, but the women and children and the goods they were bearing hampered their progress to a maddeningly slow pace, a sore trial to Barak's patience.

After they had put some distance between themselves and the town, Barak, put in mind of it by his officers, allowed them to halt for a rest. By then they had reached an open plain, where they could see into the distance and get early warning if anyone was pursuing them.

Barak assembled all the women and children and, as the sun was beginning to beat down on their heads, made them sit in the shade of a grove of olive trees. There was a brook running at its edge, and he instructed his men to draw water for them from it.

He also ordered them to ensure that the Israelites were kept separate from the captives. There was no difficulty about that, since they spoke Hebrew, while the Canaanites did not. Reumah made a great show of speaking to the Israelite men in their own tongue; hence they made her and her daughter sit with the Israelites.

This done, Barak approached the Israelites, and as all eyes swung to him, he proclaimed himself to them and spoke thus: "Hear me, Israelite women and youngsters. We have not captured you, but redeemed you from captivity. You are free to do whatever you wish. But you will be safer if you stay with us until we cross the border of our land."

The commander waited to see if they had anything to say. One, who seemed to be the oldest, spoke in their name: "Barak, we bless you for what you have done for us. But we were taken to be slaves many years ago. Since then we've had no tidings from our families, and we don't know what has become of them. What can we do?"

"You can accompany me to my town, Kedesh, where you will be most welcome in my home. We will discuss the rest when we arrive there. In the meantime, rest assured that I will not abandon you."

If the women failed to be calmed by his words, they did not show it and he was unaware of it.

The pungent smell of the smoke in the doomed town still in her nostrils, Nogah called up memories of her father; of his tenderness; of what he had said to her and of what she had said to him; and of what she should have said about her love for him but did not, and now would never be able to say.

She still agonized over whether to condemn Barak or praise him, yet she was also intensely curious about him and the other Israelite warriors. Struck by their attire, which was still filthy from last night's battle, she asked Reumah, "My mother, why are these warriors wearing such strange habits?"

Reumah, having more pressing matters to worry about, retorted distractedly, "What is strange about them?"

"They have got fringes laced with blue threads at their edges. I have never seen anything like it."

"This is what all Israelite men are obliged to wear by Torah law."

"Why?"

"I don't know."

"I want to understand those laws."

"In time, you will."

Presently Nogah forgot about the garments and the men who wore them, in her anxiety over the unknown fate that loomed before them.

🜨

Having spoken, Barak turned from the Israelites to survey the captives. He decided to appropriate the royal women for himself, and went to search for them.

It was not difficult to tell them apart from the Canaanite women of Hazor, since they were clad in finely woven, well-crafted, and richly embroidered linen dresses, which stood out from the coarse woolen tunics the poorer women wore. With the water from the brook, they had washed off the soot that had streaked their faces. Hence he could see that their skin was delicate and soft, unlike that of the others, which was as tough as the skin of goats. Besides, they sat in a separate group, and the others regarded them with awe in their submissive eyes.

There were three of them: two old and one young. Barak did not heed the old ones, but turned to the girl and found himself staring at a divine apparition, descended from heaven expressly for his eyes to feed on. This he did for a long time, unable to take them off her countenance. He believed only in the Lord, the God of Israel, but this maiden looked as he imagined a goddess would look, had there been any such goddesses in existence.

Barak was enthralled. Weary from battle, he was resuscitated by the sight of her. He approached, and extended his hands to help her rise. She pointedly ignored his friendly gesture and drew her hands back, out of his reach. With a sigh of exasperation, he bent down and grasped her waist instead and hauled her up to her feet. Then he asked softly, "Who are you?"

"I am Asherah," she replied with a sullen face.

"Your name suits you. You look like a goddess." She was unimpressed by his praise and her face remained surly.

Undeterred, he proceeded, "Whose daughter are you?"

With a limp finger she pointed to one of the women sitting on the ground beside her and replied, "That is my mother." Then she pointed to the other woman and added, "And this is my mother-in-law."

"And your father?"

"You have just killed him," she retorted.

"You are King Jabin's daughter," he stated.

She made no reply.

"As I told you before, he and your brothers put an end to their own lives. Our swords did not touch them."

"You must have been upon them," she said, "to drive them to such despair that they preferred to meet death at their own hands, rather than being tortured to death by you."

"We have never done so. We promised them safety if they laid down their weapons, and we would have kept our promise."

"But you would have crushed their pride and dignity under your coarse feet."

The beauty's voice was colorless. But when Barak looked into her eyes, he saw a flash of dark hatred in them that strangely inflamed him. At that moment, he decided to take this girl for his wife, as by Torah law he was entitled to do.

He promised himself that in time he would school her into submission and transform the glint of loathing in her eyes into the gleam of love. He did not doubt his ability to achieve these goals, and he anticipated the prospect of taming her with relish. Ignoring her last words, he said, "I will take you to my home, where you will live from now on."

A cajoling note now invaded her voice. "Sir, you are widely renowned for your kindness," she lied without compunction. "Pray, take pity on us and let me and the other royal women go."

When he made no reply and she saw refusal in his eyes, she bit her lip in disappointment and her voice assumed a more adamant tone. "You have done enough harm by causing the death of our men. Is that not enough for you?"

"No," he replied with conviction. "Look at what you have done to our women." He spread his arms to take in the Israelites. "You deserve no better."

"I have done nothing."

He laughed scornfully. "Don't talk such nonsense. You have used our women as slaves for years. Do you call this nothing?"

She was about to reply, but he raised his hand to cut her short and said, "We will talk later. Right now I am setting my men to guard you."

The soft note crept back into her voice as she beseeched him again. "At least let my mother and my mother-in-law go. They are old women and you have no need of them."

Barak ran his eyes over the two women, on whose skin the years had plowed deep creases. Indeed, he could not see what use they would be to him, or to any of his men. So he told them that they were free to go wherever they wished.

So far, the older women had been silent. But now they broke into piteous wails and declared themselves unwilling to be so callous as to abandon the young one to the cruel fate of captivity.

Barak reassured them, promising that she would be treated with all the consideration called for by her noble descent, and that she would be allowed to write them letters. After Asherah added her entreaties to his, and Barak arranged for donkeys to carry them and two men to escort them to the closeby town of Harosheth, the two matrons finally left.

Abandoning Asherah with difficulty, he instructed two of his aides to take charge of her. The newly appointed guards, too, seemed to be ensnared by her beauty. Their eyes were irresistibly drawn to her, like ants to a bowl of honey. They remained on her for as long as she was in their charge.

He himself went to the remaining Canaanites. There were several hundred of them. The men of Hazor had been armed and met their death in the night's battle, but there were still the women and children. He passed among them and told the old ones that they were free to leave.

The young women and their children he commanded to stay, for he had promised his men that if they achieved what they had set out to do, he would allow each of them to select a few female captives to work for him. Now was the time to redeem his promise.

Before he did so, he reminded them of their obligations. "Hear this, Israelite warriors. You have acquitted yourselves well in this battle, you have done great deeds for Israel, and each of you is a hero. You deserve the reward you have been promised. You may now pass among the Canaanite captives, and choose three women each to be your slaves.

"But remember that even slaves are human beings. There will be no killing or raping, either now or later. If anything like that happens, I will know of it and arrange to have you brought before our tribe's elders for trial. And you know well what your punishment will be. Also, you will not separate children from their mothers. He who takes a mother must take her children, too, and care for them.

"And if you have desire of one of these women, you must follow the Torah precept and allow her thirty days to mourn all she has lost, and only then may you come to her, whereupon you must take her for your wife."

Barak waited for the men's reply. As was their practice, they called out in unison, "All you have said, we will do."

He did not place much dependence on their keeping their promise, but he did not see what he could do to ensure that they did. So he went off to look for Asherah.

🦂

The king's daughter was sitting under a tree, her knees drawn up, gazing pensively at the ground in front of her. Her two guards stood at either side of her, their gazes still glued to her; but they left when Barak approached.

She ventured to raise her eyes at him inquiringly, while he stood there silently drinking in her flawless beauty.

After a while, he called out to his men to prepare for departure and to bring him two of the looted horses. When they arrived, he lifted her to her feet, hoisted her onto the saddle of one of the horses, and handed her the reins. Then he swung up onto the other.

Since she was a king's daughter, he was confident of her ability to ride a horse properly. Soon he saw that she sat on the mare's back proudly erect. He raised his hand, the sign for the cavalcade to move forward.

Barak no longer minded the painstaking pace, which the women on donkeys and the flock and cattle forced him to assume. For it gave him leisure to feast his eyes on Asherah again. His gaze almost constantly strayed in her direction. He could not drag it away.

He remembered that she had spoken of her mother-in-law; hence she must be a married woman. This did not deter him, for he had no less of a right to capture a man's wife than a virgin girl. But he had not asked her who her husband was. He did so now, and was not surprised when he saw fury flaring up in her eyes again, as she replied, "You have butchered him, too."

"Who was he?"

"Sisra." Suddenly the image of him with a tent peg piercing his temple, his blood spurting out of him, arose in Asherah's mind as it had never done before. Her abomination of Barak assumed previously unknown, ominous proportions.

For his part, Barak felt some unease, which showed in a flicker of his eyelids. "I assure you that I did not kill him, any more than I killed your father. My hands did not perpetrate this despicable deed."

Her eyes glittered with the loathing inside her. "You have his blood on your hands," she hissed like a snake.

Barak scoffed at this notion. "You are mistaken. By the time I trailed him to the tent of the Kenite woman with whom he had sought refuge, she had his blood on her sleeve already. I was deeply disgusted by this."

"You were the commander in charge of the whole."

Barak glanced at her and was struck by the even fiercer look of unmitigated hatred in her brilliantly sparkling eyes. He was prepared to take this in stride because of his undeniable pleasure in her company. He still did not doubt his ability to eradicate the look he had seen on her face and replace it with one of tenderness, but he realized that it would be more difficult to achieve this goal than he had first anticipated. He was also aware that arguing with her at this point would be useless. He decided to speak to her no more for the time being.

The ensuing silence gave Asherah the opportunity to concentrate her entire being on her grief for the husband and father and brothers she had loved, and on how ferociously she detested the fiend who, despite his words to the contrary, had murdered them—the man whose clothes were still crusted with their blood.

She was not oblivious of the fact that her captor was handsome and had a commanding height and bearing. But she did not find him attractive. Her mind now conjured up the image of Sisra while he was still alive, of his sharp features, which remained dearer to her than the most handsome ones in the world. There was no such sharpness in Barak's face, and she thought it unremarkable.

Although he had captured her, he would never capture her heart; hence she had nothing to look forward to in his house but a life of unalloyed misery. She had no doubt that Barak was spellbound by her and would soon come to her. Perhaps even that night. She could not think of any way to hold him off. No matter how wildly she struggled, he would overpower her. The prospect of being raped by him made her tremble with revulsion.

Plans for revenge, which previously had prevailed only vaguely in her fantasy, now began taking clearer shape in her mind. She had no qualms of conscience. It would be nothing but justice if, like Sisra, the man responsible for his death were to be killed in his sleep by a woman.

The only question was how she would accomplish this. Unlike the Kenite murderess, who had used a hammer and a tent peg as her weapons, she herself was unlikely to be housed in a tent. She would have no such implements to hand. It was also not feasible that she would be able to put her hand on a sword or a dagger. If Barak kept such weapons in his house, they would be locked away.

But if she could make her way into the cooking room, she would no doubt find a knife there. She might be able to slip it into her sleeve before anyone noticed. At night, after Barak had had his way with her, he would fall into a deep sleep, as Sisra had done after their feats of love.

Then . . . but here her thoughts broke off abruptly. For despite her previous fantasies, she could not envision herself as one thrusting a knife into another human being, even her husband's cruel assassin. Perhaps if she were subjected to sufficient humiliation at his hand, it would bolster her determination.

Her heart also screamed for vengeance upon the woman who had spilled Sisra's blood with her own hands. Her beloved had told her that women only brought forth blood tenderly for the creation of life. How wrong he had been! She knew that the Kenite dwelled in Kedesh, and if she did find the courage to bring about Barak's demise, she would next head for her tent and deal with her as she deserved.

Her thoughts taking a more sober turn, she realized that if she did kill Barak, she would be found out and put to death long before she could leave his house and make off for the woman's abode. She was strongly attached to life. But was a life at the mercy of a detested killer worth living?

While those thoughts floated through Asherah's mind, Barak regarded her and he did not find it difficult to guess what they were. He would have to ensure that she was heavily guarded every moment of the day and night, until he could be sure that she had surrendered to him in her heart.

Chapter Two

In this manner, with dread on her side and suspicion on his, captive and captor continued to travel in silence, the sun blazing down on them and the wind fluttering strands of Asherah's long hair against her cheeks, until they reached Kedesh. On their arrival, they made their way to the town square. There, the elders and the masses of Israel had assembled to welcome the heroes and raise cheers in their honor.

Barak presented the elders with the spoils of war. After taking stock of the looted goods, the elders bestowed the lion's share—most of the gold, silver, and precious stones they had unearthed in the castle—on Barak, and smaller portions on his soldiers. The rest they distributed among those who had been impoverished by the Canaanites' attacks on their properties, who were waiting at one corner of the square to obtain their share.

Then the warriors took leave of Barak. They blessed each other with peace, took charge of their captives and their booty, and dispersed. Barak, too, gathered his share, and Asherah. He renewed his invitation for the Israelite women and children to come to his home, and they accompanied him there.

They entered its gates before sundown. He bade the Israelites sit down in his courtyard. He instructed his maids to bring them bread to eat and milk to drink, while he wrapped his arm around Asherah and led her into the house.

By that time, Nogah had pushed the terror of the previous night to the back of her mind. Sitting with the other Israelite women, she was overwhelmed with the novelty of the sights around her and gazed at them with wide-eyed curiosity.

She liked Barak's house and was surprised that although it was smaller and less splendid than her father's castle, it was not much different. It was encircled by the same kind of thick wall with turrets along it, and it had the same type of large courtyard in front, shaded by fig and oak trees. Like the castle, it was a two-story building with a stairway leading from the yard directly to the upper floor. It seemed even sturdier, for it was built of heavy hewn stones from its base to its rooftop.

When Barak and Asherah passed by, Nogah turned her gaze from the house to its owner. Her eyes followed him and her sister, daughter of her father, across the yard. She craned her neck, her gaze trailing them until they climbed the stairway and disappeared from view. She was not surprised at Barak having singled out Asherah from all the other women, nor by the utmost reverence with which he treated her, for she was enchanting beyond compare. She noted that Barak formed a suitable counterpart to Asherah. With his large dark eyes, and the even features of his swarthy countenance, he was no less handsome than she was beautiful. Thus they seemed to belong together.

Still, Nogah knew that Asherah had loved Sisra with all the strength of her youthful soul. She could not imagine her yielding to the man she must regard as his murderer, and the killer of her nearest relatives. What, then, she pondered idly, would be the outcome of his fascination with her?

She did not participate in the chatter of her mother and the other freed slaves, but leaned against a tree, with her legs crossed before her, frowning. Her new life would not be paved with roses. She and her mother were free, but destitute. They would have to work hard for their sustenance, and where would they find work?

Barak came back and, sensing their worry, addressed them once more. "Hear me again, Israelites. We have reached our land, and you are free to go wherever you wish to go, whenever you wish to do so."

The same woman who had spoken up before told him, "We have nowhere to go."

Running his hand through his hair thoughtfully, Barak responded, "You may wish to return to your former homes or visit the homes of your relatives, or those of your erstwhile friends, and seek shelter with them. If you find that they are no longer alive, or that there is no place for you there, you may come back here. Until you settle elsewhere, my home is your home."

"Can we not stay and work for you?"

"I will hire twenty of you to work in my fields and stables and household. Those I hire will earn good wages. But I cannot hire you all. There is not enough work to be done. The rest of you can consider this house as your own until you find other homes, or for as long as you like. Is that good in your eyes?"

They all called out, "Yes," and nodded their heads.

It struck Nogah that Barak would have some thirty women and children living in his house, possibly for years, eating his food and drinking his drink, without rendering any service in return. She marveled at his generosity.

Oblivious of her or anyone else's admiration, Barak continued, "I will now pass among you and select those most suitable to do the work that needs to be done. My clerk will register their names, and the overseer of my household will show them to their rooms. Those I cannot hire will be accommodated in other rooms that are standing empty. I also have a large hall that I will set aside for the bigger boys who can no longer share their mothers' rooms."

He then came by to select twenty young people to work for him. When he passed Nogah, their eyes locked briefly, dark ones with liquid blue-green ones. To her shame, the heat mounted in her face. But if he was aware of this, he showed no sign of it and after the briefest of pauses went on to survey the other women.

To her relief, Nogah was among the ones he selected to work in his household. But her mother was not. In the evening they sat in front of the mansion's wall together, attempting to settle on what was best for Reumah to do.

In front of them, the silvery light of the moon and the stars, together with that from torches at the head of Barak's house, glittered on the dew-dampened grass.

In the distance they saw the houses of Kedesh, and an aura of peace seemed to have descended on the town. Nogah was cheered by the lights that shone through the cracks in their shutters, behind which she imagined husbands and wives and children enjoying the calm of the evening together.

"The small town in which my family lived before I was captured, Hamon," Reumah explained, "is only a few hills removed from Kedesh. As I have told you before, eighteen years ago, on the day Jabin's soldiers captured me and killed my brothers, my mother and father were away from home. Though they survived the attack, by now they are probably no longer alive."

"Then stay here, as Barak has invited all women to do, so that at least we may be together."

"Am I to live on a stranger's charity then?"

"What else can you do?"

"I believe that it will be best for me to walk to Hamon tomorrow morning to find out who is still alive in my family, and who has taken over my father's house and property. Though I would not dislodge whoever has inherited it, at least I have some claim on dwelling in it again."

Nogah found nothing to say in return and thus, for the first time in their lives, mother and daughter were about to part. But when Nogah hugged her mother and clung to her, Reumah promised to be back soon to apprise Nogah of the results of her mission.

🦗

While Nogah and her mother sat outside the castle, Asherah sat inside. The chamber into which Barak had ushered her was situated one flight of stairs up from the ground floor and it was well furnished. It could not compare to her room in the castle, but it was better than she would have expected these coarse Israelites to supply.

Its walls were hung with colorful rugs, as was its floor. Against one of the walls stood a carved sideboard designed for the storage of feminine apparel. At the foot of the bed was a table flanked by two chairs. Several lit oil lamps cast a soft light over the room.

After Asherah had eaten the bread and cheese and dried figs and drunk the milk that had been brought to her on a tray, and the tray had been removed, she stayed at the table, familiarizing herself with her surroundings. Eventually, she rose and opened the door of her room a little way. It led out into a long passage with many doors. She met with the unpalatable sight of two guards, with swords at their thighs, stationed at her door.

She quickly retreated into her room again and decided to lock the door. But here she met with another unpleasant surprise: The key that should have been in the lock had been removed. To her chagrin she realized that Barak, who was now her master, had removed it so that he could enter her room whenever he wished to do so. She would be at his mercy at any time of the day or night.

Asherah went to the window and found it latticed with ironwork. She opened another door at the rear of her room. It led into a bathing room, with a large stone bathtub and basin, like the one she'd had in her own home. This time she was pleased. But when she approached its window to see if it offered a way out, she found it latticed as well. She realized that she was locked up like an animal in a cage.

Still dazed from all that had happened to her, she leaned aimlessly against one of the walls. Then, since there was nothing else for her to do, she unpacked her bag, placing her few belongings on the shelves in the sideboard.

Among those, there were some gifts from Sisra and her father: several precious jewels and an elaborately carved ivory knife, which the king had given her in commemoration of his most successful attack on the Israelites.

For a moment, Asherah considered whether she might not use it as a weapon, with the aid of which she could take revenge on Barak for her loved ones' deaths. But though it had been shaped as a knife so as to bring alive the memory of the battle, it was pitifully blunt. It was designed for decoration rather than cutting. Regretfully, she realized that it could not serve her purpose, and that she would have to acquire a sharp knife from elsewhere. So she bestowed it in the sideboard with the rest of what she had brought with her.

Upon completion of this task, she sat down at the table again and gazed unseeingly in front of her. Her loneliness did nothing to dispel the memory of her beloved husband, whose strong arms would never encircle her again, and she felt the void of his absence inside her.

Fortunately, she'd had the presence of mind to bring her small, beautifully carved golden statue of the goddess Asherah with her. She had already placed it atop the sideboard, and now rose up from her chair and prostrated herself before her. As she did, the numbness inside her melted and gave way to grief. She prayed to her special goddess, begging her to mourn with her the destruction of her life, and to deliver her from her humiliating captivity. The tears streaming down her cheeks brought her some measure of relief.

Her despair alleviated through prayer, she became conscious of what was around her again. She fixed her eyes on the small metal mirror she had previously placed on the sideboard, and realized that the woman reflected in it was dirty, in dire need of a bath.

Pitchers of hot water had already been placed near the tub. They had not cooled off yet, so she poured them out and set the empty pitchers back on the floor. She was on edge, afraid that Barak would take it into his head to come in just when she was reclining in the bath. Time and again she glanced at the door in apprehension. Still, she saw no choice but to shed the dirt from her body. So she undressed, stepped into the bath, and, with a weary sigh, sank down into it.

After she had washed herself, she sensed the soothing effect of the water upon her. She leaned against the back of the tub, soaking in its slowly diminishing warmth when, just as she had feared, the door was jerked open and Barak stepped in. Overcome with panic, she frantically reached for her dress and covered her body with it.

Barak laughed, wrenched the wet dress from her hand, and tossed it to the floor. Then he sat down on a low stool next to the tub, while she did her best to cover her nakedness with her hands. With a swift move, he grasped her wrists and pulled her arms above her head. She struggled wildly to twist free from his hold, but this only made him tighten his grip. He stared with blazing eyes at the translucent whiteness of her limbs, and of her breasts, and at the rosy buds that protruded from them, the like of which he had never seen before.

Asherah felt herself cringing before him, inwardly recoiling from his impending touch. It did not come.

"Don't be alarmed," he reassured her. "I will not touch you now. I merely want to look at you."

She found his gaze upon her rude and disgusting. "Get out of here," she lashed out.

He laughed again, and she perceived that he was getting more and more aroused, and that he was breathing heavily and checking himself with difficulty. "Your beauty outshines the lily of the valley," he panted, "and not only the beauty of your face."

"What do you want?" She snapped with indignation.

"Just to regale myself with the sight of you."

Asherah was baffled. "Is that all?" she exclaimed doubtfully.

"It is all I am allowed to do with you at the moment."

The young woman's lips parted in surprise. But before she could gather her wits sufficiently to inquire what he meant, she met with an even greater shock. With the heat of his desire still blazing in his eyes, Barak abruptly rose up and, without sparing her another glance, strode to the door and vanished behind it.

Asherah remained in the bath, relief sliding through her. Yet she was also puzzled. Barak's dealing with her defied reason. She could not make out why, obviously transfixed by her, he had so suddenly bolted from her presence. She had braced herself to fight off his expected rape. And when he failed to make the attempt, she did not know if she was glad to have escaped a repulsive fate, or disappointed at having been deprived of the opportunity to give vent to her loathing by repelling him.

Barak rushed to his own bathing room, where one of his maids stood ready to pour pitchers of water into his bath. Without looking at her to ascertain that she pleased him, he led her into the bedroom and flung her onto his bed and came to her, until he found release.

❦

Nogah, too, had been allotted a room. Unlike Asherah's, hers was a simple one, which she had to share with two other maids. There were no beds or ornaments in it, only plain pallets to sleep on and coarse blankets with which to cover their bodies. Nogah had become used to sleeping on a soft bed, and she found lying on the hard floor exceedingly uncomfortable.

As she lay in the dark, memories of the horrific events of the night before floated back to the front of her mind. She wanted to stretch out her hand to touch her mother to gain comfort from her, as she had done so many times in her childhood, but Reumah was not there. In all the seventeen years of her life, she had never spent even one night with her mother out of reach, and she missed her sorely. But what she had lately gone through had left her so exhausted that she fell into a dreamless sleep.

The next morning, as soon as she arose, she went in search of Reumah but found that she had already left.

She was set to clean rooms, precisely the same work she had been doing when she was still a slave. It occurred to her that she was hardly better off now than she had been then. She was free to abandon her post at any time. But if she did, she would have to leave Barak's house, and where would she find shelter?

She did not place much hope on her mother's exploration. Even if Reumah unearthed some relatives who were willing to take her in, it was unlikely that they would wish to be saddled with her daughter as well. Even if they did, she would probably be expected to work in their household no less than she was working here. So going there would not improve her lot.

Still, she was anxious for her mother to come back, and to learn what had come to pass. Perhaps a miracle had happened and Reumah had found a way to redeem her daughter from her new life of drudgery.

Chapter Three

While Nogah worked, Asherah spent her day in idleness, with nothing to occupy her. Apart from the maids who cleaned her room and brought her meals and the water for her to wash and bathe in, she saw no one. All that was left for her to do was to sit at the window and peer into the courtyard. There was a constant commotion of people moving back and forth in it. But Asherah's eyes were blind to what was going on before them; they were gazing at the memories inside her.

She recalled her wedding celebration, and her bliss in Sisra's arms. She remembered her elevating talks with her father and the pleasant afternoons she spent with her mother in the ladies' parlor, chatting or playing the harp. The companionable family meals they partook of together. The days on which people from all over her father's domain came to be judged by him. The occasions on which noblemen and women arrived to pay homage to her father and his family. All this had collapsed, leaving only her sorrow—so strong, it felt as if the very stones of her room's walls were crying out with it.

Once more, she bowed down before her goddess. She summoned her to witness her suffering, and begged her to move heaven and earth to bring her succor in whatever way she could. She also begged her to grant her the opportunity to wreak vengeance on the Israelite man and the Kenite woman who, each in his own way, had destroyed her life. As before, her prayer brought tears, which gave her some relief.

After that, time moved at an excruciatingly slow pace. Asherah became so restless that she mindlessly paced the floor. As the evening fell, she was so heartily bored that she could have scratched the white paint off the walls.

When Barak finally appeared and invited her to join him for the evening meal, she welcomed him with a sense of heartfelt relief. After her day of pain and loneliness, even the company of the man she abhorred and despised was preferable to being left on her own.

Barak led her to the front room, in the center of which stood a table for eating. It was large and brick-shaped and surrounded by numerous chairs, in anticipation of the wife and sons and daughters that, he hoped, would one day grace it with their presence. For the time being, he was used to taking his meals there on his own.

To his smiling admiration, the princess sailed into the room on the whisper of her swishing, skillfully fashioned, brick-colored silk dress that enhanced the transparent whiteness of her skin. While they ate a meal of baked meat garnished with almonds and apples, she prepared to question him about his behavior the night before.

He made it unnecessary. "You may have wondered why I did not come to you last night," he said. "It is because of a commandment in the Torah, the book that sets out our laws. It forbids us to come to a captive woman before her month of mourning for all she has lost is over. I have taken a vow to keep this commandment. But I am eagerly counting the days, and when the thirty days are past I will make you mine."

After a brief pause he added teasingly, "Until then, you will have to be patient."

She laughed with withering scorn. "If you believe me to be keen for you, you are greatly mistaken."

Nettled by her disdain, he retorted in kind. "If you believe yourself to be the only woman who can satisfy my needs, you are greatly in error as well."

"So you left abruptly last night in order to come to another woman?" she called out sneeringly.

"There was no choice."

"What will be my fate if I don't want you to come to me when the thirty days are over?"

"I will make you want it."

"And if I still don't?"

"I will not rape you. But you will remain confined to your room."

"For how long?"

"For as long as it suits me."

Asherah made no response. Her hatred was thinly veiled behind a mask of cold indifference, and he was not sure which he preferred.

The next day, the emptiness of Asherah's new existence led her to demean herself by trying to talk to the maids who served her. Since they did not know the Canaanite tongue, and she did not know the Hebrew one, these attempts led nowhere.

But she found that the maids were friendly and did their best to please her. At her instruction, expressed through the gesture of leading her cupped hands to her mouth, they brought her decanters of grape juice and milk to drink. And, out of sheer boredom, she drank even when she was not thirsty.

In the evening, Barak once more led her to the front room to share his meal. Before the food was brought to the table, with his dark eyes on her face, he reminded her that two out of the thirty days of her mourning had passed.

Asherah shot him a derisive glance. "Are you so careful to keep all the commandments in that Torah of yours?"

"As best I can."

"Then how is it that you infringed what I have been advised is the most important of your commandments: the prohibition of murder? My father told me that the Israelites had this prohibition yet totally disregarded it, and he was right."

"I have never committed murder in my life."

She laughed an embittered laugh. "Except when you killed the men in our castle."

"Defending ourselves from those who are about to kill us is not murder. There is no commandment to let ourselves be led like lambs to the slaughter."

"Those men would not have killed you had you not invaded their stronghold."

"They have been killing us for years. And following their defeat at the Valley of Jezreel they were rebuilding their army and preparing for a renewed attack on us."

"This is a lie," she railed at him. "My father and my brothers were not planning any attacks."

"Do you believe that they would have apprised you of their plans?"

"Then how did it come about that they advised *you?*"

"I found out through my spies."

By that time, their voices were raised in anger, and neither of them had any desire to eat the food that had been placed on the table.

Barak shoved back his chair, grasped Asherah under her elbows, and said, "I will take you to your room and have your meal brought to you there."

When they reached her room, he noticed the golden statue of the goddess Asherah on the sideboard. He took it and tossed it to the floor. When it failed to break, he lifted it up and shoved it under his arm.

Asherah yelled, "Don't dare to touch my goddess. Give her back to me."

"In this house knees will bend and tongues will swear only to the Lord. There will be no shameful idols in it. I will give her back to you once I have melted her down."

Asherah struggled with Barak in an attempt to wring the statue from his grasp. He laughed and said, "You will not get far with me in this manner." With these words he tossed her down onto the bed, extricated her breasts from her dress, kissed them hungrily, then left with the statue in his hand.

She rose up from the bed, opened the door, and slammed it noisily. She was left standing there, seething in a helpless fury, the likes of which she had never known before.

Two days after her departure, Nogah's mother returned. She had been able to find her erstwhile home in Hamon. It was now inhabited by her cousin and his family. He had inherited the house and the property that was attached to it from his father, who had inherited it from Reumah's father—his brother—upon his death.

"My cousin has invited me to come and make his home mine, and I have accepted the invitation," she told Nogah. "Naturally I will not be able to sit and eat the bread of idleness in his house; I will have to work hard to earn my keep. But there is nowhere else for me to go."

Nogah could not deny her mother's statement and sadly nodded her head.

"My cousin and his wife have enjoined me to bring you to live with them as well."

But the girl knew that this would mean exchanging one type of toil for another. "My mother, for the time being I prefer to stay where I am. Here, at least, I earn wages for my work. If I lay by all the silver I earn, I may be able to use it in a few years' time to buy a small cottage for both of us, and we may begin a new life in it together."

"I would rather have you with me now at all times."

"So would I prefer it, but it is not to be. At least we have each other close at hand."

Since Reumah did not know what reception her daughter would meet with in her cousin's house, she reluctantly gave in to her. Mother and daughter parted again, but they promised to visit each other as often as they could.

🦂

As she performed her work during the next days, Nogah occasionally looked out of a window and gained brief glimpses of Barak going about his various tasks. Sometimes she watched him talk with his friends, or kinsmen, or workingmen. In his tall stature and manly build, he was among them as a cedar among thorn bushes. The more she saw him, the more she admired him. She was still divided inside herself about the evil he had done to her father and the good he had done to her mother. But she became more fully conscious than she had been before of the manly attraction he held for her.

Despite the brief meeting of their eyes on the day of her arrival at his house, she did not expect him to be aware of her existence, and so it was. She was merely one of the thirty or so serving maids he employed in his large household. Most of them adored their master, most of them were pretty, and she did not stand out in any way from the others.

There were rumors that Barak frequently selected one or another of the maids and summoned her to his room. But also that it meant nothing to him, and that after he demanded the presence of a maid in his bed for a few nights, he easily forgot her. Nogah had no wish to be one of them, yet she found herself craving him and was powerless to stave off the upheaval he caused in her heart.

According to the whispers of the maids, at present his attention was riveted on Asherah, who had blinded him like strong sunlight. But he still used the maids to tide him over until he was allowed, under Torah law, to come to the princess.

Once again Nogah was entangled in feelings that clashed with each other. She could not make up her mind whether she adored Barak for his prowess with women no less than on the battlefield, or despised him for treating them as if they were garments that he could use and discard at will.

Her father had done much the same with the slaves, and she had never held it against him. Barak was not a king, so he could claim no royal prerogative. On the other hand, he was a warrior, a commander of multitudes. Perhaps that justified his acting as one.

Nogah's mother and father, each one in turn, had cautioned her to preserve her virginity. But neither of them had warned her of the tumultuous, jumbled feelings that now overtook her: of recoiling from a man, yet being lured by him. Each night, as she lay under her blanket, she was overcome by reticence clashing with eagerness, doubts wrestling with her newly awakened desires. She was suddenly aware of secret spots in her body to which she had paid only scant attention before; their nagging hunger tugged at her, and she tossed back and forth restlessly.

As the images of the night of the battle in the Hazor castle began to recede in her mind, other images came to the fore: Barak's untamed power; how it would feel to be enfolded in his arms, in his strength. She attempted to chase them away, yet they came back to taunt her. For a long time, she lay in the darkness of her room, the fever inside her mounting, spinning such images in her mind.

Chapter Four

Deborah was not much given over to dreams, at least not such that she could later remember. Yet four nights after Barak's attack on the Hazor castle, she did have one. In it there appeared a Canaanite king, who, surprisingly, looked much like Sisra, sitting on a throne in his castle. The huge hall in which he sat was illuminated by an odd, bluish light.

Before him stood his wife, the queen, paying homage to him by handing him a large sunflower. Behind her was another woman, possibly a princess, playing the harp. The hall was filled to capacity with Canaanite noblemen and women, swirling around to the sound of the harp's melodies. In one corner of the hall there stood a soldier, with two Israelite prisoners behind him.

It was clearly a celebration of victory by the Canaanite king and his court over the Israelites. She could not ascertain what victory it was, for she woke up and beheld that it had been a dream.

A dream that did not make sense, for Sisra had been dead for four months. Moreover, barely five days before, she had sensed, with all the certainty that the Lord's voice inside her had granted her, that the turn of events had been precisely the opposite: Having stormed the king's stronghold, Barak and the Israelites had been victorious, and the Canaanites had been so thoroughly devastated that they would have been unable to attack or celebrate anything.

Yet the dream was strong and vivid, and when she fell asleep again, it was repeated. It discomfited her, and in the morning she resolved to send a runner to Barak to inquire about his attack.

Before she could convert her thought into deed, a messenger bearing a dispatch from Barak arrived. It confirmed what she had been sure of already: Against all odds, his attack had been a resounding success. Jabin's castle and the town of Hazor had been razed to the ground, all arms-bearing men had been killed—while the Israelites' casualties had been few—and the gold and silver and precious stones in the castle's treasury had been looted.

Sighing with renewed relief, she sent the commander a return message, blessing him profusely for his accomplishment. Alone in her tent in the evening, she once more prostrated herself to the ground and recited prayers, extolling the Lord for his salvation.

Nonetheless, she could not banish the dream from her mind. Why would the Lord make her privy to a scene that marked a defeat for Israel such a short time after he had granted the people such a glorious victory?

It struck her that despite the hymns of praise she had chanted on Mount Tabor and on the way back from it, and the prayers of gratitude she had offered up in solitude, still she had not thanked the Eternal One sufficiently for his deliverance from their enemy. She resolved to hallow his name before all of Israel. After that, perhaps he would be merciful and not allow the Canaanites to be resuscitated to the extent of mounting a new attack on them, let alone a victorious one.

This resolution did not allay her discomfiture about the dream, however, and she continued puzzling over it. After a while, the solution to the riddle occurred to her: Sisra must have a brother who looked much like him, one who was still alive. He was evidently the man she had envisioned in her dream. His appearance in it must have been in the nature of a warning. The Almighty was indeed merciful. His mercy lay not in preventing a new Canaanite attack, but in alerting her to its possibility, so that she might forestall it. But how was she to do that?

Since the dream had not elucidated this, she would have to figure it out herself. This would not be easy, for the Israelites could not well attack an army that was no longer in existence. And neither could she seek a meeting with the Canaanite king who was to replace Jabin, for none had yet been appointed.

Besides, her disastrous meeting with Sisra was still painfully branded in her memory. She had no wish to instigate anything that remotely resembled it by offering to meet his sibling. What, then, could she do? She racked her brain for a long time, but nothing came to mind.

In the meantime she busied herself with planning the celebration of thanksgiving to the Lord. She composed a poem acclaiming him for his deliverance, which she would chant in the hearing of the people. This would be followed by singing and dancing, much in the manner in which Moses and Miriam had glorified the Lord in their time, when, after the exodus from Egypt, Pharaoh and his chariots had chased after the children of Israel to the Sea of Reeds, and the Holy One had parted the sea for the Israelites to cross and hurled the Egyptian Pharaoh's horses and chariots into its depths. As he had risen in triumph then, so had he done now at the River Kishon, and it would be proper to exalt him in a similar manner.

Only then all of Israel had been assembled already, which was not so now. She would have to summon the people to a holy convocation. In order to make it worth their while to travel from afar, it would have to be followed by a feast in which the masses of Israel would eat and drink their fill and be satisfied.

Next, she considered where it should be held. At first, Mount Tabor and the River Kishon sprang to her mind. But she dismissed both spots, since there were no sufficiently large towns in their vicinity from which supplies of food and drink for the multitudes could be procured. Failing those, the most proper location was Kedesh, the town in which the Israelite army had been assembled, and from which it had set out for its triumphant war.

Honesty compelled her to admit that Barak's house being situated there also weighed with her. He would probably make an appearance in response to her summons at whatever place she nominated, as he had done when she sent for him the first time. But she was not loath to spending some days in his mansion again.

Besides, coming to Kedesh would afford her an opportunity to aid Jael, the wife of Hever the Kenite, she who had fulfilled Deborah's prophecy that the Lord would deliver Sisra into the hands of a woman.

Jael had been imprisoned by the Kedesh elders. Despite more than

three and a half months having passed since then, seized by strange inde-
cisiveness, they were still agonizing about what to do with her.

To Deborah's mind, it would have been preferable if Sisra could have
been meted out justice properly by means of a judicial verdict. Yet he had
spurned the peace she had offered him, opting for a massacre instead. Had
Jael not dealt with him as she did, he might have escaped. Then he would
have been like a bereaved bear, ferociously seeking vengeance on those
who had brought about his downfall. Many more would have been killed.

This Jael had prevented, wherefore Deborah felt nothing but kindness
for the Kenite woman, and she cast about in her mind for a way to bring
her succor.

She decided that it would be best if, when she came to Kedesh, she
made her reflections known to the town's elders by voicing them in the
hearing of all of Israel.

So she sent word advising Barak of her impending visit in a week's time,
adding that she would explain its purpose when she arrived.

🦁

As there was no king in Israel, Deborah was revered as the greatest
leader, as the only man or woman who could forge a connection with the
One who reigns in the heavens and the earth. But in matters pertaining to
daily life, each of the twelve tribes was under the slack and erratic rule of
a group of elders, with the one they considered the worthiest among them
at its head.

The next day, as Deborah sat in judgment of the people under her palm
tree, a delegation of six of these elders came to see her. They were the head
elders of the tribes that had not responded to Deborah and Barak's call-up
to the army before the war.

As was the elders' custom, they wore long, flowing mantles of a white
color, the color of wisdom, and their long hair was of a matching shade.
After they bowed to her until their garments touched the ground, and sat
and were served refreshment, they asked her politely if she was well.

Then the head elder of Reuben, whom they had appointed as their spokesman, announced the matter that had led them to come from afar to seek her
out. "Illustrious judge and prophetess, we have come to plead the cause of

our tribes. Since the war a vermin has been devastating our grain. At first it was hardly noticeable, but now it has reached ominous proportions. And our cows and goats and ewes have been aborting the young in their wombs."

The head elder of the tribe of Dan, whose dwelling was at the shore of the Great Sea, added, "Since we have insufficient land at our disposal for growing wheat and the grazing of sheep, trading and fishing are our main sources of livelihood. Yet the sea has been stormy for weeks, so that our merchant ships and fishing boats have been prevented from going out to it, to provide us with sustenance."

Deborah was not surprised. "The Lord is righteous in all his ways. He is rendering you what you deserve," she chastened them. "When I followed Barak to Kedesh there to arrange the call-up to the army, we sent out a summons to all the tribes' elders and so also to you."

She rummaged in a box, which, at her request, one of her aides had brought and was holding out to her. "I will read you some of the letters we received in reply, whose content may have escaped your memory. Here is one that is particularly edifying," she said, her eyes burning with the fire inside her.

Hear us, illustrious commander and prophetess. We, the elders of Reuben, are giving your missive all due consideration. But we own a multitude of cattle and flock. If our young men go out to war, who will tend to them?

Thus, there is much heart searching in our midst. We are divided into factions, and there is heated argument among us. We will write to you again, as soon as we reach unanimity.

"Your next missive arrived after the war was over, and I threw it into the refuse without even looking at it. And here is the letter from the elders of Dan":

Hear us, exalted leaders. Just now we, in the domain of Dan, are engaged in building merchant ships and fishing boats. It is a most inconvenient moment to go to war, for if our young men leave in the midst of this urgent task, where will our livelihood derive from?

"We have not forgotten the shameful content of our letters," they admitted humbly, the palms of their hands turned up in an apology.

She went on relentlessly. "Can you permit your brethren of the other tribes to go out to war in your stead, and endanger their lives for your sake, while you stay hidden away in your houses and remain unscathed?"

"Exalted lady, your words are true, like silver purified in a furnace. But what has been done cannot be undone. We beg that you intercede with the Lord on our behalf, so that we may not die of hunger but live."

Deborah let her grim glance sweep slowly over the elders. "You have sinned against your brethren. You must first gain their forgiveness by making restitution to them. You are obliged to cede a tenth of last year's crops and other earnings to them. Convert those to silver. Divide it among the tribes that went to war in your stead, and bring to the elders of each of them the share owed to it as a guilt offering."

"We will carry out the command you have laid upon us. Only we beg you to pray for us immediately, before it is too late."

"It would be useless," she said with strong determination. "The Lord would not lend ear to my prayer. You must first fulfill your duty to your brethren. Only then will I plead your cause before him, in the hope that he may eradicate the pestilence from your land and calm down the sea."

After the elders left, a man came to consult Deborah, as so many men and women were wont to do. She knew him vaguely, for he resided in a nearby village. He had been widowed some four months before, and since then she had often observed him loitering about aimlessly on the hill on which her palm tree stood.

Deborah made him sit on one of the stone benches facing her and waited patiently for what he had to say. But for a while he was fidgety and embarrassed and had difficulty in coming forward with his request. Deborah had date nectar brought for his refreshment and spoke soothingly to him.

Finally he spilled out the question that had been weighing on his mind for some time. "Exalted judge, what does the Torah decree: How long after his wife's demise is it permissible for a widower to take a new wife?"

"If this matter has been burdening you, you did well to come to me with it, for I have good tidings for you: The Torah does not lay down any injunction at all in this respect. All you need to do is to consult the dictates of your own heart. And since I surmise that by now you are hankering after a new woman," she added shrewdly, "you would do well to consult her, too."

To this the man had a rather astounding reply. "It is precisely what I am doing at this moment."

It was only then that Deborah looked measuringly at his appearance. He was no longer young, but still of a good build and a pleasing countenance. Also, there was much kindness in his eyes and an open smile on his face. Even more important, there was something steady and reliable in his bearing. He was undoubtedly a man on whom a woman could lean and in whose arms she would be shielded from the storms of life.

Yet she felt no tug in her heart that might draw her to him. Thus she smiled at him benignly but shook her head. "You are aiming for the wrong woman. I can never take your wife's place."

"My name is Menahem, which means 'the Comforter,' " he retorted. "I am like my name. I came to comfort you and myself at the same time."

"It is considerate of you," she said, "but I have no need of comfort."

She knew this statement to be somewhat at odds with the truth, for she could well have done with a man's consolation. But she spoke as she did for she had no wish to hurt him. Yet just as sure as she was of the Lord's bringing in morning and evening at the proper times, she was sure that Menahem was not the man who could supply what was lacking in her life.

"Are you still keeping faith with the one who has basely supplanted you with a young concubine?" he queried.

"I am keeping faith only with my own self," she averred.

But he did not let off so easily. "I swear, as the Lord lives, that if you become my wife, I will never send you away or take another woman, either wife or concubine." Bashfully, he added, "Although I cannot read and write, I promise to master the art and also learn the Torah, so that you will not be ashamed of me."

He concluded by telling her that he owned a large property, and that if she became his wife and brought her sons along, they would all live with him in prosperity.

She shook her head again, this time with finality. "It can never come to be."

Menahem looked disgruntled and she quickly went on, "But let me bring some comfort to you: The woman you yearn for will make her appearance shortly."

"How can you be sure?"

"Your heart is clearly receptive to a new love, and it will not be long delayed."

As soon as the widower left, Deborah stepped up the preparations for her visit to Kedesh. She was eager to go there not only to hold the planned assembly to hallow the name of the Lord. No less was she eager for the comfort that, as a divorced woman—there being no Torah prohibition against it—she had every right to seek. The comfort she wished for from Barak, and which she was unable to accept from Menahem.

Chapter Five

After Barak had confiscated Asherah's goddess, he did not come back to see her for two days. During that time, her pain was overwhelming. Now that she had been deprived of her goddess, she was also bereft of her ability to pray and weep. She felt totally deserted.

On the third evening, Barak came in bearing a lump of gold, which he handed to her. She cried out in rage and hurled it at his head.

He intercepted it with his hand and decreed, "This piece of gold is not safe in your hands. I will keep it until you have calmed down sufficiently to receive it."

With these words he left her boiling in indignation and did not return for two more days. This time he did not invite her, but ordered her to come and eat her evening meal with him.

She sat in stony silence, but eventually Barak broke through it with considerate words. "I realize that you are in grief. I would like to ease it for you, but I don't know how I may do so."

"You could let me go."

"I will not, because I want you for myself. But I am aware that you also suffer vast boredom and this, at least, I can alleviate. What would you like to do? Tell me, and if I can I will help you."

At this, Asherah became suspiciously amiable, and she flashed him what Barak thought was an amazingly ingratiating smile, which immediately alerted him to danger. "I would like to be free to walk around by myself inside your fortress. Since it is encircled by a high wall, with guards stationed at its gates, you need not fear that I will escape."

Barak was exasperated and amused all at once, and a wry smile crept onto his face. "Since you try this ruse, you must think me singularly stupid. It has not escaped me how much you abhor me, and what you wish to do to me, if only you get the opportunity. In time, I will tame you and turn your aspiration for revenge into subservience and love. Until then, I cannot grant you the freedom to roam around my house that you desire. But I will let you walk around for a bit every day, accompanied by the guards. Have you any further wishes?"

By that time Asherah had virtually despaired of gaining an opportunity to put the Kenite murderess of her husband to death with her own hands. Hence she said, "I want the woman who had my husband's blood on her sleeve to be executed."

"I have had Jael incarcerated, pending her trial before the elders."

It was the first she had heard of this, but it merely increased her disgruntlement. "Why has it been so long delayed?"

"The elders have not been able to reach agreement on how to deal with her."

"Could you not prompt them?"

"No. They do what is right in their own eyes. They heed no outside advice, unless they are the ones to seek it."

"You are strong in causing death, but weak in seeking justice," she exclaimed contemptuously. "Could you not approach them, at least, and let them know your thoughts?"

He was unperturbed. "I would be a fool in their eyes. They would merely laugh at me, and so would all those who heard of my appearance before them."

After a brief pause he asked, "What else would you like?"

Realizing that she would have to let some time elapse before she brought up her concern about the murderess again, she moved on to a different matter. "In my father's castle I was accustomed to playing the harp."

"I will procure a harp for you as soon as I can put my hands on one. I also have a notion for you. I promised your mother and mother-in-law that you would be writing them letters. There is a scroll room in my home, and an old scribe who is in charge of it. I will ask him to give you some scrolls on which you can write. When you have done so he will pass them on to a messenger, who will find the two ladies wherever they may be at present, and deliver them."

"Thank you," she replied in a subdued voice.

"While you are there," he continued, "my scribe will teach you the Hebrew language and writing."

"I have no wish for this."

"Since you are to live among Hebrew-speaking people, you will be better off if you know their language. Most of them cannot speak the Canaanite tongue as I do. You will spend part of every day on those studies."

After the meal, Barak escorted Asherah to her room. He closed the door, took her into his arms, and kissed her. She tried to push him away, but he held her hands behind her back and gripped them in one of his. With the other, he lifted her chin so that her mouth faced his and continued to kiss her.

Unlike his mouth on her breasts, which had been wild and hungry, his lips on hers were soft and gentle. They remained there for a while and, despite herself, they caused her to feel a strange sensation. It was not the tender passion she had felt for Sisra; but neither was it the disgust that had overcome her when he had touched her before. It troubled her, and she managed to free herself from his hold and spin away from him.

🦂

Thereafter, Asherah's state became more bearable. The very next day, she availed herself of Barak's permission to leave her room. Her guards, stealing longing sidewise glances at her, escorted her for a walk around the front and back of the mansion. One of them knew a few words of the Canaanite language, so she could explain her wishes to him. At her request, they showed her the house's reception hall and the large hall at the rear, in which the people who worked for Barak took their meals.

Asherah weighed the merits of the house, noting that it was well kept, its walls painted in soothing light colors, though much could be improved. She had hoped to use this excursion to extract a knife from the cooking room. But when she asked to be shown that room, her guards told her that their orders were not to admit her into it, and she was greatly annoyed.

The men then led her to the scroll room, where the old scribe was waiting for her. He told her his name, Uriel, the son of Nathan, and that Barak had instructed him to give her some scrolls for her letters.

While she wrote, Asherah looked around her. Although the scroll room was inferior to the one at the Hazor castle, it was spacious, its walls lined with heavy bookshelves that were crammed with multitudes of scrolls.

Then her gaze fell on the front door, and to her disgust, she saw that one of her minders was stationed there. She looked in the opposite direction and found a back door, with the second one leaning against it. Once again, she was dispirited.

She finished writing reassuring letters to her mother and mother-in-law. Uriel took them from her and promised to have them dispatched. Asherah thanked him, rose to her feet, and prepared to leave. But the scribe intercepted her and told her that Barak had ordered him to teach her the Hebrew language and writing.

Asherah now looked at him more particularly, and she did not like what met her eyes. He was, without doubt, the oldest man she had ever seen. His hair was white and thin, his face was as wrinkled as a sheet that had been slept on and, in her eyes, exceedingly ugly. But what disturbed her most was his mouth, from which most of the teeth were missing, giving it a sunken look. When he opened his lips, it became a gaping pink hole in his thin white beard. Her distaste for him was enhanced by the censure of herself that she perceived in his faded eyes.

The queen had taught her to be gracious to the noble and the humble alike, so she made a great effort not to show her distaste. But she did not look at Uriel's face more than was necessary. Since she had nothing better to do, she reclaimed her seat and, keeping her eyes on the scroll he had placed before her, began her first attempts to decipher the Hebrew letters.

Henceforward, she took a stride through the courtyard every day except on the Sabbath, before she settled down for her lesson with Uriel. She was far from keen, but the differences between the Hebrew and Canaanite letters were small, and she was bright, so she and Uriel could pride themselves on their success.

❦

During those days, the only light that penetrated Nogah's life was the new friendship she had forged with old Uriel, the clerk who had registered their names on the day of her arrival. A few days later when she found out that he was also a scribe and had a scroll room for his office, she went to visit him. Unlike her sister, she paid no heed to his crumpled face and sunken mouth, but cherished his kindness for her, which was clearly perceptible in his voice and his gaze.

Nogah did not delude herself that in Uriel she had found a substitute for her father, for he was much different from what the king had been. He was also much too old to have begotten her. But with him she, who had never known either of her grandfathers, came as close as she ever would to enjoying a grandfatherly love. An affection that she hoarded as bees hoard honey, and warmly reciprocated.

On her first visit he beckoned her in, and after she had bowed to him by way of greeting, she told him that she was eager to learn to read and write in Hebrew and asked if he would be willing to teach her. She offered to pay him for his efforts out of her wages, in proof of which she extracted from her belt a pouch containing the first silver shekels she had earned through her labor.

He told her that he would teach her, but added laughingly that it was he who would pay her. For, as his wife and his friends had died years before, and his daughters and their children lived some distance away, he was as lonely as a lamb that had been orphaned from its mother. Spending time with her would be balm for his soul, for which he would not exact but pay a fee. So they reached a compromise whereby neither would pay the other.

Nogah came to the scroll room every day after work, except for the days on which Uriel was summoned to Barak's room to confer with him there, and except for the Sabbath, on which they all rested. She stayed there until the evening meal, and soon she and Uriel fell into the habit of telling each other about their hopes and their worries.

Uriel recounted that he had etched out a meager living by copying scrolls to fill the scroll rooms of rich men. This he had done until Barak had hired him to be his clerk and had also put him in charge of his scroll room. He paid him good wages and allotted him a room next to the scroll room for his abode. And as there was not much work for him to do, he lived in lazy comfort and was deeply indebted to his master.

After eliciting an oath of secrecy from him, Nogah revealed that she was King Jabin's daughter and Asherah's sister; and he kept the knowledge in his heart. She intimated that despite all the evil her father had done, she had still loved him very deeply. She was grieved by his death and wanted to mourn him in the proper fashion.

The scribe approved of her intent. He taught Nogah the Israelite customs of mourning, which entailed tearing one's apparel, donning sackcloth, strewing earth or ashes on one's head, leaving one's hair untrimmed, and sitting on the ground for thirty days. He helped her to tear the front of her dress. Sadly, though, she realized that as a maid who had to work for her sustenance, she would not be able to follow the rest of these precepts.

Apart from talking together, Nogah's time with Uriel was devoted to studying. Since she was keen to learn and no less bright than her sister, it did not take her long to master the Hebrew letters. Soon she could read and write as fluently as if she had been doing so since childhood, and Uriel's gaze upon her was aglow with praise.

But when she wanted to break off her lessons with him, he would not allow it. He said that henceforward he would be teaching her the Torah. She smiled at him and kissed his cheek in gratitude.

Indeed, Uriel opened a new world for her. She had heard all the Torah stories many times over from her mother. But now, for the first time, she saw them in writing and she was elated. In addition, he taught her the laws and explained them to her. He also read with her some other scrolls that related the trials and tribulations of the people of Israel in later days, after the Torah had been completed.

🦁

One day, as Nogah sat with Uriel, she made him privy to her soul searching. She wondered aloud why it should have been necessary for Barak to destroy the Hazor castle after he had already inflicted such a crushing defeat on the Canaanites on the Kishon River.

Uriel explained that Barak had learned from his spies that Jabin's sons had gone into a frenzy of rebuilding the Canaanite army, preparing for a surprise assault on Israel. They had left Barak little choice but to attack first.

When he perceived a question in Nogah's eyes, he told her that he would show her an unusual scroll. He stepped over to one of the walls, reached up to a high shelf, and pulled down a scroll that was of a lighter shade, and therefore newer, than the other ones he had stocked up there. He bade her read it.

To her astonishment, she found that it had been written by Barak. It unraveled the tale of the war, beginning with the destruction the Canaanites had wrought in the land of Israel for more than twenty years and confirming what Uriel had just told her about the spies' reports.

It set out in detail how the invasion of the castle had been planned and executed. At the very end it laid bare an event of which Nogah had previously been ignorant. Barak and ten of his men had headed for the room in which, they had been apprised, the king and his sons were concealed. Standing in front of its door, they called to them to lay down their weapons, and promised that if they came out stripped of their swords, no harm would befall them.

While they were waiting for a response, they were taken unawares by another door opening behind their backs. The king and his sons and a score of their soldiers burst out of it and attacked them from the rear. In the ensuing battle, five of the Israelites and most of the king's swordsmen were killed, while Jabin and his sons and the remaining ones retreated into the room from which they had come, locking the door behind them.

Barak and his surviving men had hurled themselves against the door, but it was heavy and it had taken them a while to break it down. When they finally did, they found the king and his sons and the rest of the Canaanites lying dead on the floor, their swords' handles protruding from their hearts.

After she finished reading, Nogah sat in dazed silence, for the first time able to visualize the ghastly manner in which her father and her brothers had met their end. In his scroll, Barak berated the king for acting as treacherously as the Egyptian Pharaoh who, having let the Israelites go, then followed and fell over them from behind.

Nogah could not share this view, but neither could she judge Barak and his men harshly for defending themselves from her father's onslaught, driving him and his men back into their room, there to seek the refuge of death rather than fall into their enemies' hands. When she realized that Barak could not have acted other than he did, she was relieved.

The scroll was precious to her also because it shed a new light on Barak, who, as it now transpired, was not merely a warrior but also a man fluent in writing.

She begged for Uriel's permission to copy the scroll for herself. He handed her a large empty scroll, for which he refused to accept payment. After she completed the task of painstakingly copying the scroll word by word, Uriel permitted her to take the copy she had made with her as a keepsake. Since then she had sat each evening at a small table in her room and by the light of the oil lamp perused what she had copied, over and over again, obsessed with it, though still unaware of how it was about to shape her life.

The more she read, the more a matter she had not thought of before became apparent to her. Although he depicted the war in great detail, Barak failed to mention any wish on his part to seek peace. He seemed to rely on the second defeat he had inflicted on the Canaanites to keep them at bay, subservient forever. Peace, he seemed to believe, would ensue of its own accord.

Yet Nogah, who had studied the Canaanite heritage, knew that this would not come to pass. Inside her there lodged the certitude that soon their smiths would be toiling like ants, constructing new chariots to replace those that had been destroyed. And their horse breeders would be investing all their skill in breeding noble young stallions, in readiness for the day they would be sent into battle in which, once again, thousands of young men would be felled.

She wondered why Barak had not set out a vision of forging a covenant with whoever would be the next Canaanite king. Deborah, the exalted judge and leader, she learned from the scroll, had tried but failed in this purpose before the war. But Nogah herself, being familiar with the Canaanites, could have shown him how to go about such an endeavor.

Thus would she ponder Barak's words until the oil ran low in the lamp. Then she would lie down on her pallet and forget the scroll, and think of the man who had written it, and yearn for him in the manner a gazelle in the desert longs for water, until she was overcome by slumber.

Chapter Six

During one of their lessons, Nogah asked Uriel about the fringes on the Israelite men's garments, which puzzled her. He showed her the passage in the Torah that commanded Israelite men to wear them so that they would be reminded of the Lord's commandments and obey them, and not be led astray by their roving eyes and wanton hearts. Then he added that, sadly, some men who were meticulous in keeping the commandment of the fringe were not thereby kept from foul purposes. He looked at her meaningfully, leaving her in no doubt as to whom he had in mind.

Although Nogah had told Uriel much about herself, she had not revealed her tangled but increasingly strong feelings for Barak. But he seemed to have guessed what was in her heart, for he began to speak ostensibly in praise of their master, but in truth voicing a blistering tirade against him.

"My child," he began, "since your father is no longer alive, and you don't have your mother here to advise you, it is my duty to do so. Barak is a man of many fine qualities. He has an incisive mind and unequaled talent as a military commander. Yet he never boasts about his heroic deeds. He is not haughty or conceited. He is honest and unfailingly generous toward the people who work for him. I myself have much cause to be grateful to him for his magnanimity. But where straying with girls is concerned . . ."

Nogah had no inclination to hear more. "There is no need to warn me," she interrupted defiantly. "I am aware."

"I don't believe you know the whole."

As she was not keen to gain any further knowledge about Barak's misdeeds, she said that they must go to the hall, where the servants were already seated for the evening meal. With the forgetfulness of old age, Uriel was momentarily distracted from the warning he had been about to deliver. But she had no doubt that he would come back to it another time.

🐞

Before he had an opportunity to do so, when Nogah finished her work on the next day, her mother came for a visit. They hugged and kissed each other, and Nogah was astounded to see how much her mother had changed in such a short time.

During her slavery she had looked old beyond her years. She had never shed the fat her body had accumulated during her pregnancy, and in time she had even added to it. But now she had slimmed, and she looked much younger than her age of thirty-three. Her brown curls had been skillfully trimmed, and her dark eyes were framed by a subtle blue paint that made them look large and seductive. She wore a green and yellow striped linen dress and looked radiant and, in Nogah's eyes, very pretty.

After Nogah advised Uriel of her mother's arrival, she returned to her and they sat down at the far end of the grounds to talk.

"My cousin and his family are being unexpectedly friendly to me," she recounted. "They have even invited to their house a good-looking and kindly widower, Yair, who is no more than forty years of age."

"Naturally he must have been attracted to you immediately," said Nogah affectionately.

Reumah nodded her head gravely. "I hope that he will soon offer to make me his wife."

"Are you content for it to be so?" Nogah inquired.

"I will eagerly welcome my life with him."

"I rejoice with you in your good fortune," said Nogah, with tears glistening in her eyes.

"The widower has four children for whom I will have to care," continued Reumah, "but I do not mind this, because he owns a considerable property and thus is well off, so there will be maids to help me. My workload will not be heavy."

Once she had poured out all these glad tidings into her daughter's ears, she regarded her, and spoke words of censure. "Why are you wearing this old dress which is torn at the front? You have brought several fine dresses with you from Hazor. Why are you not wearing any one of them? And why have you not trimmed your hair, as I bade you do on my last visit?"

"My mother, my work is that of cleaning rooms. What would be the sense of wearing a fine dress to do that?"

"You have finished your work for the day, yet you have not changed your apparel. And your hair looks wild and untidy. Why do you not take better care of yourself, in the manner of other girls, as you used to do at the castle?"

"I am still in mourning for my father. It is not even thirty days since he died. If I cannot wear sackcloth and sit on the ground and mourn him properly, at least I can wear a torn garment as a sign of my mourning. And I will not dress up and trim my hair until this period is over."

"Who taught you these injunctions?"

Nogah told her mother about Uriel and the lessons she was taking with him.

Reumah approved of the lessons but was doubtful about the mourning. "Your father was not an Israelite. Are you obliged to mourn him in accordance with our customs?"

"Uriel says that I am. In any case, I am grieving for him in my heart also, so I cannot make myself look pretty such a short time after his death. Besides, what would be the purpose? There is nobody here to look at me."

When she spoke those words, she realized how true they were. Despite her doubts about Barak, she wanted very much to be noticed by him. But she knew that it was unlikely to happen: The rooms she cleaned were in a remote part of the house. The woman in charge never appointed her to work in proximity to him, and she saw him from a distance only. There was no sense in her dressing up to attract him.

Unaware of her daughter's reflections, Reumah replied, "Could you not go into the town after you finish your work, to meet the people of the land?"

"Where would I go? I know nobody."

"But the other maids do. Could you not go with them?"

"After the thirty days of mourning are over," Nogah replied, "I may."

Shifting her thoughts back to her own life, Reumah said, "Soon I hope to be able to invite you to my wedding; and after I settle in Yair's house, I will come and take you to live with us. I will see to it that you cross the path of young men who are suitable for you. If you don't encounter anyone here, I will make sure that there will be someone for you there."

"Thank you, my mother, this is kind of you. But the truth is that I don't want to meet anyone."

"Why is that?"

"I don't feel eager for it."

"Why?"

"I don't know, myself . . ." Her voice trailed off unhappily.

Reumah looked at her daughter, and she was puzzled and worried.

After her mother left, while Nogah was eating her evening meal, she reflected that despite what she had told her mother, she did know why she had no wish to cross the path of any young man. So far she had not faced the truth of what was in her heart. She had tried to convince herself that it was divided, but realized that it no longer was. She simply harbored feelings that had no hope attached to them, which could do her no good, but only destroy her life. The sooner she rid herself of them, the better off she would be.

🜚

The next evening when Nogah visited Uriel, the scroll spread out in front of them remained unread, as he broached the topic of Barak's wrongdoings again. "The Torah forbids bearing tales. Yet alerting of danger is permitted, and there is no one here to do so but me."

Nogah was loath to listen, but it was too early to go for the evening meal, and she could think of no other excuse to stem the tide of his words, which now spewed forth. "Barak is fascinated with your sister and is determined to take her for his wife. But he has no notion of being faithful to her. From new moon to new moon he lies with a fifth as many women as there are days in the month, and he will continue to do so when she is his wife."

"I know this, sir. It is not necessary to waste your words telling me," Nogah replied dejectedly.

"By Torah law, when a man desecrates a maiden, it is incumbent on him to take her for his wife, a law many men disregard and Barak does so with special zest. As set out in the Scripture, it is a grievous sin for a girl to come to her bridal bed no longer a virgin, an injunction which, to their shame, some girls disregard as well. But that is not what I wish to speak to you about."

She looked at him with a question in her eyes.

"Barak comes to many young women. So it is not to be wondered at that occasionally one becomes pregnant."

"Are there now ways to . . . to avoid . . ."

Nogah was too shy to continue, but Uriel, gleaning what she had in mind, said, "They are not of great value. Far from foolproof. So there have been a few pregnancies. What do you think happens then?"

"What?" Nogah asked, trying to speak in an offhand manner.

The answer made her prick her ears in astonishment. "He locates a destitute man who owns nothing and bestows a small property on him in exchange for marrying the girl he has made pregnant."

Nogah was taken aback. "Wherefrom does he take the property?"

"He buys it. He is so rich that he can afford to do so. But the girl who is in dire straits because of him has no voice in the matter. She has to accept whatever husband he provides for her, or else she would be left to bemoan her fate and suffer shame and dishonor. You would not want such a disaster to overtake you."

"No," Nogah replied with strong conviction.

"The maids worship him as if he were the golden calf to which the Israelites bowed down in the desert. You must not be of their number. If he summons you to his room you must refuse him," he prodded, waving a bony finger at her face.

"He will never summon me to his room, because he never sees me," said Nogah evasively.

"He may still spot you somewhere," he persisted.

"Would he not send me away from his house if I repulsed him?"

"No. If a maid rejects him, he is annoyed, but he does not punish her in any way. Nor does he take her by force. He is not malevolent," Uriel admitted, "only thoughtless, like a child whose own urges are foremost in his mind."

Uriel's thoughts seemed to be momentarily diverted to other paths. But after a while he resumed the thread of his argument. "I love you as if you were my own granddaughter, and I don't want you to be hurt."

"So do I love you as if you were my grandfather. But you must know that he does not bestow his ... his favors ... on all the maids. He will probably never notice me at all," said Nogah mournfully.

Chapter Seven

Barely two days later, when Nogah was sitting with Uriel in the scroll room, Barak came in. They both rose in his honor and bowed to him.

He ignored this and, looking Nogah over from her head downward, asked, "Who are you?"

Barak always summoned Uriel to his room to confer with him there, and it had not occurred to Nogah that he would visit the scroll room. Hence she was taken unawares and thrown into confusion by his presence, and more so, even, by the torn and faded dress that she was wearing. But she reminded herself that she had not quaked before the king when she had first been brought into his presence, and there was no reason why she should be childishly bashful now before a man who was not even of royal descent.

Meeting his gaze head-on, she spoke with a voice that she hoped concealed her trepidation. She told him her name and added, "I am one of the girls you liberated from the palace in Hazor. I am now working in your house as a maid."

A vague memory flicked up in him. "Yes, I remember you now. You were one of the slaves in attendance on the queen in that back room. You are the one who . . ."

Nogah blushed and dropped her eyes in shame at his remembering her vomiting in his presence. He realized this and stopped midway through his words. Instead of going on with what he was about to say, he added, "I also saw you the day you arrived here. You had just been redeemed from slavery. Yet you were sad, as if you were in mourning. Why was that?"

He did not seem to remember the locking of their eyes. Or perhaps it had all been a figment of her imagination. She was surprised that he recalled anything at all. "It was nothing worthy of your attention," she said bashfully.

Barak did not persist. "What are you doing here?" he asked.

"Uriel has been very kind to me. He is teaching me the Torah laws."

"That is admirable. But if this is right in your eyes, I would like to confer with him now."

Nogah bowed and strode off to her quarters.

On the next evening, the woman in charge of the household came to her room and ordered her to prepare Barak's bath. Putting aside her mourning, she quickly changed into her blue dress, the best she owned, and hurried to his room.

Having gained permission to enter, she opened the door and stepped over its threshold, the threshold of her fate.

🜊

Barak stood gazing out of the window. He turned and let his eyes roam over her body. He noticed her dress, which enticingly outlined the fullness of her breasts by nipping in at her narrow waist, and, not being overly long, afforded him a view of her shapely legs. "Did I cause you to miss your lesson with Uriel?" he asked.

"No, sir. I sat with him before the evening meal."

"And what did you learn?"

"The laws of captivity."

"Which one?"

"That the Torah forbids the Israelites intermarrying with the peoples of the land lest they be drawn by them into idol worship, but that this prohibition does not extend to female captives."

"And what are the precepts with respect to those?"

She recited what she had learned:

> *When . . . you see among the captives a beautiful*
> *woman and you have desire for her . . . she . . . shall*
> *remain in your house and bewail her father and*
> *her mother for a month; after that you may*
> *come to her . . . and she will be your wife.*

"True. I have been suffering under this law myself," he conceded. "Fortunately you are not a captive," he added, and a shot of satisfaction ran through his face.

These words threw Nogah into disarray, for they made it obvious what his design with her was. Her face came to be suffused by a pink color, that of the sky at sunset, the color of shame. She stood before him, intently regarding the floor.

He alleviated her discomfort by ordering her to fetch pitchers of hot water for his bath. But when she brought in the first one, he noticed that it was heavy for her. Although he could not fathom why she should find it hard to lift the pitchers that were easy for other maids to carry, he went with her and helped her bring the rest.

They poured the water into the tub in his bathing room, and he began to shed his garments in her presence. She prepared to leave, but he called her back. Without the least embarrassment, he removed the last piece of concealing clothing, then eased his large body into the tub and ordered her to wash him.

She had never seen a man's nakedness before, and her rosy color turned into flaming red. "Sir," she objected breathlessly, "could you not wash yourself?"

"I could, of course," he said, mocking her gently, "but it will be much more enjoyable if you do it."

"Do the maids usually perform this task?"

"Only rarely. Come, have no fear. It won't hurt you."

She tensed, yet approached reluctantly, then rolled up her sleeves and did as she was bid. She knelt down on the floor, removed a stray wisp of hair from her eye, and began running her soapy fingers over his sun-scorched swarthy chest and over the muscles that stretched across his shoulders. He reveled in the feeling of her hands moving smoothly over his body, and while he savored this pleasure he regarded her body appraisingly, as if he were gauging its price.

After a while she swung back on her heels and lifted her dripping hands from the water, signifying that she had completed her task. Quite unabashed, he pointed out that there were parts of him that still required washing.

When she hesitated, he was patient with her at first. But finally he ordered her to proceed. Overwhelmed by his commanding voice, she did so, while averting her face, now darkened into the crimson of sin, from his body. She drew air and it grew as hot as fumes from a furnace inside her. Her fingers fumbled on his body under the water, but she barely felt his arousal when he quickly stepped out of the bath, splashing water on her face and the floor and her best dress.

He handed her a cloth, and as she crouched down to dry his thighs and his legs and his feet, he inserted his hands into the front of her dress and fondled her breasts. He heard her gasp of pleasure, as he reveled in their round softness and in his mounting need.

Once she was done, he lifted her up and carried her to his room, where he lowered her down onto the bed and stripped off her dress. She voiced a feeble protest, to which he paid no heed at all. In the dim light of the moon slanting in through the window, he saw the mass of her thick, bronze-colored hair cascading in waves over the pillow underneath him. And he observed her big eyes, her pupils dilated with shock, with the turmoil in the recesses of her being.

Anger at his intent of using her battled with her need. For a moment she thought of breaking away from under him and fleeing to her room. Then reticence evaporated like dew in the sunshine, in her uncontrollable urge to yield to him. Her parents' warnings to preserve her virginity, no less than Uriel's advice to reject Barak, were now as far removed from her mind as was the Lebanon from the Sea of Salt.

Neither her mother nor her father nor Uriel had enlightened her about the pain slicing through her with the rupture of her barrier, receding as the heat unleashed itself in her, seeking an as yet unknown summit, mounting it, erupting into fire and a call of love for him, bringing forth the breaking of his own peak.

Afterward, he held her in his arms and asked, "Did you mean what you just said?"

"Yes. But you must have heard those words many times before."

"Not at this particular moment. They greatly enhanced my enjoyment."

Before she had an inkling of what he intended to do he was inside her again. Her senses swam, and only when her delight had once more soared and burst into shudders did she realize that they were both stained with blood.

Nogah was frightened, for neither her mother nor anyone else had warned her about the blood either. On a sharp intake of breath she pointed it out to Barak. But he reassured her. "It is always so the first time," he explained.

By then the water from the bathtub had drained into a pipe that made its way into the earth's entrails. They filled it again from the water still left in the pitchers, and bathed in it together. And when later they reached their shuddering pleasure for the third time, he immediately drifted into sleep. She dressed and slipped back into the maids' quarters, walking on the tips of her toes so that her roommates did not notice her when she came in.

The next day when she sat with Uriel, her guilt plainly written on her features, she was reluctant to raise her eyes and face the expected censure in his. But he was a wise old man who had seen much in his life. So although he was well aware of what had come to pass, he stroked her hair fondly. When she finally gathered the courage to look into his eyes, she discerned nothing in them but a deep worry for her welfare.

Three days after Asherah had taken up her lessons with Uriel, she returned to her room to find a magnificent harp awaiting her. There was no doubt in her mind that its price was beyond rubies, and for a short while she was touched by Barak's generosity. Soon her enmity toward him revived. Still, she was eager for the tunes it could produce and dreamingly sat playing those she favored.

Vivid pictures rose up in the eyes of her mind. Of her mother listening to her play, correcting her errors. Of her father's pride in her talent glowing in the brilliant eyes that she had inherited from him. Of Sisra in their bridal chamber, watching her as she strung tunes accompanied by lewd songs of love from her lips.

She was sure that even from the depth of his grave he still remembered those songs. For the first time since Barak had destroyed the statue of her goddess, the tears came streaming from her eyes, easing her grief.

When Barak came to fetch her for the evening meal, he found her eyes still sparkling as with dew. He pulled her to her feet and kissed her and said, "Asherah, I love you. I regret that we met in war and not in peace. I have no wish to be your captor. I want to be your husband."

Despite his gentle words, to Asherah he was still the vicious one who had killed the men she loved. He would never be able to touch the strings of the harp in her soul.

On the way to the front room, she apprised him of this. "I cannot return your love. Had we met in peace, you would have found me to be a married woman, and not a widow as I am now. Then I certainly would not have loved you."

Her words galled him and he retorted, "It would have been easier to win you away from a live husband than it is to erase from your heart the memory of a dead one."

The Canaanite laughed with what, to his chagrin, Barak recognized as pity. "If you think that, you don't know how desperately I loved him. No one would have been able to pry me from him."

Barak scowled at her. "Unfortunately, we will never be able to ascertain if that is so. In time I will make you love me."

They had reached the front room, and as they sat down, Asherah said quietly, "You will never make me love you. If you truly cared for me, you would let me go back to my land and to my people, to make a new life for myself there."

"I will not release you. But I will do all I can to make your life here more pleasant. Is there anything more that you would like?"

"I would like a maid who can speak my language, so that I have someone to talk to."

"I can give you one, of course. But I must warn you that these women, who have been your slaves, probably hate you. You will not feel comfortable in their company."

"You seem to feel at ease in *my* company."

He laughed. "You are not only beautiful, Asherah, but also clever. I will do as you wish. What else do you desire?"

"I walk with your guards every day. They are nearly as mute as the fish in the Great Sea. It is crushingly boring. I would like to walk with you instead, so that you can show me the house and explain to me what its various rooms are used for."

"It's a great felicity to me that you take an interest in my house, since it will be yours, also."

Asherah veiled her eyes. "Perhaps we could stroll outside its walls, as well?"

There was a glimmer of amused understanding in his eyes. "If you think that this will bring you closer to your goal, you are mistaken. But it will be as you say. We will walk outside the walls on the Sabbath, when I have the leisure for it."

Barak's house was perched on a hill, with the town of Kedesh below it on the one side, and a slope leading to a narrow valley with meadows and cultivated fields on the other. The morning on which Barak kept his promise, the grazing ewes, heavy with lamb, announced the approaching spring. A gentle breeze was moving the branches of the blooming pomegranate trees and mandrakes, whose fragrances it bore into the distance. A multitude of colorful wildflowers had sprouted; they glistened like precious stones from the dew of the night that still clung to their petals.

Asherah was not blind to the charm of the land spread out at her feet. But it was not hers and she felt no joy in it. Her own country was not far away, and she cherished its memory and yearned for it.

The expression on her face remained carefully aloof, but in her mind she harbored wild thoughts of escape. She toyed with the notion of breaking away from Barak and running and running until she reached her own people, who would offer her safe haven.

Barak regarded her, fascination for her mingling with amusement, as he said, "I would not advise you to try it. I am quicker than you are. And I would have to confine you to your room again for a long time."

Asherah knew that he was right, and that she could not achieve her purpose without a weapon. She continued to grapple with the question of how to obtain one.

Chapter Eight

After her first encounter with Barak, Nogah was summoned to his room each evening. At first she still considered rejecting him, but her love for him was swelling inside her by the day, and she knew that she could not.

In bed with him, she would stroke his body, feeling his powerful muscles bulging under her roving fingers. One evening she overcame her shyness and began kissing the length and breath of him, adoring each part with her lips, begging for his invasion, which was not long delayed.

One day Barak came home earlier than usual. While Nogah sat with Uriel in the scroll room after her usual fashion, the woman in charge of the household came in and ordered her to abandon whatever she was doing and head for the master's room immediately. Nogah looked at her teacher in distress, and he smiled at her sadly but forgivingly.

As soon as Nogah entered Barak's room, his eyes swung to her body. "An odd thing has happened," he said in a churlish tone, as if he were voicing a complaint. "While I was out in the fields I had a sudden yearning for you, which forced me home early."

It was the first time he had come to her during the day. Even after their first encounter, the room was still lit by sunshine. As she lay at his side, he leaned on his elbows and scrutinized her. "I have not noticed before how pretty you are," he said. "Not a stunning beauty, but quite pretty."

Nogah was dispirited at this tepid appraisal, and laughed in embarrassment.

"Why are you laughing?" he asked.

"Someone else has spoken these same words to me before."

"Who was it?"

"My father."

"Who is your father?" he probed.

Her eyes clouding over briefly in memory, she replied: "He was a Canaanite."

Barak remembered that several of the officers he had confronted in battle had light eyes. He had never observed the difference between their pale color and the distinctive blue-green color of the king's eyes, which he had passed down to Nogah. Hence he thought that her father must have been one of those warriors, who were in charge of guarding the castle. "It is evident by the color of your eyes," he said. "But who was he?"

"He is no longer alive and it is painful for me to speak of him."

By that time he had lost interest in her sire, and he took her in his arms again and she lost herself in her love for him.

But when Nogah returned to her room, she remembered his adoration for her sister, and all the other women he was taking to his bed, and was cast down again.

🐉

The next day, at sunset, Nogah's mother arrived. Glowing with happiness, Reumah announced that she had come to summon Nogah to her wedding, which was set to take place in ten days' time.

Then she regarded her daughter, and saw that the luster had drained from her eyes, so her own happiness waned. "My daughter," she said, "there is something very wrong with you. What is it?"

"I am well."

"I know you since the day of your birth. You cannot fool me. Tell me your trouble."

"My mother, please leave this," she demurred. "I don't want to talk of it."

"Is it this Barak, who is your master? Rumor has it that he comes to any girl in sight."

Nogah bristled in his defense. "It is not so. I know several girls to whom he did not come."

"But were they in his sight?"

"They were, and he passed them over."

"So now you think it a great honor that he did not reject you. But by honoring you, he has also exploited you. And he has inflicted pain on you, because you are only one in a long string of those he has taken before you and those who will come after you."

Nogah flushed but made no reply.

"If you think you are important to him, you are sorely mistaken. If you were, he would not expose you to the peril of pregnancy. I wish I had warned you about him before. But word of his exploits has reached me only recently."

With a weary sigh, Nogah replied, "Don't distress yourself, my mother."

"As soon as I am settled in my husband's house I will come and take you with me. In the meantime, you must promise me that you will not let him know you any more. If you become pregnant, your life will be destroyed. I only pray that it may not have happened already. I owe Barak my freedom and my newfound happiness. But this does not lend him the right to wreak havoc on my daughter's life, and I will not let him do so if I can prevent it."

When Nogah made no response and wore a stubborn expression on her face, her mother dispensed a different piece of advice. "I have heard it said that it is beneficial for a woman who wants to prevent pregnancy to insert a rolled-up strip of linen, coated with an ointment of beeswax mixed with olive oil, into the mouth of her womb to bar the seed from penetrating it. She must leave it there until the next day, when she is to wash it. At least do this, if not for your sake, then for mine."

With these words Reumah handed her a cloth bag she had with her, which contained several strips of linen and a bowl full of the ointment she had mentioned. Nogah took it from her hands with words of gratitude.

From then onward she used one of the scraps of linen with the ointment her mother had given her. But she was never sure whether she had positioned it the way it should be, and she feared that in the heat of the moment it might be dislodged. She did not place her trust in it.

That night, Barak did not summon Nogah to his room. Later, when she lay on her pallet in her own room, her longing for him was so overwhelming that the next evening, when he did send for her, she hurried to him with the speed of a lizard.

🪰

On the day after that, Barak, unlike his usual custom, came home before the midday meal. Nogah was ordered to prepare his bath, but he hardly noticed her. He washed and dried himself quickly, put on clean clothes, ordered her to tidy his rooms, and left.

As she stood at his window, she watched him standing in front of the house, as if waiting for a visitor. Soon a group of people astride donkeys entered the gate. Nogah saw a proud and magnificent woman at their head, riding a white she-donkey. And she knew her to be the prophetess and judge Deborah.

Barak bowed to her and assisted her in dismounting her animal. He issued instructions for the escorts' refreshment and accommodation. Then he invited Deborah to join him for the midday meal.

Deborah's host did not ask her why she had come, but waited for her to tell him. After quenching her thirst, Deborah divulged that she had been moved to write a hymn in praise of the One who had given Sisra and Jabin into their hands. She had come to hold an assembly to mark the victory and to read her poem before the people.

Barak did not see the necessity of this, but he had no wish to argue with Deborah. So he said that her poem was no doubt of great beauty, and he remained silent about the assembly.

When they finished eating their bread and cheese and olives, she complained, "This time you did not come to obtain your reward."

"I was busy with my property. Did you come all the way here to offer it to me?"

"If you still want it."

After Barak had demolished Hazor and sent Deborah a lengthy missive apprising her of the event, she had virtually faded from his mind. But now his desire for her was revived and he said, "I want it. And I want it now."

"I am tired from my long ride. I prefer to bathe and rest first."

"Don't tease me again, Deborah. You may do that afterward."

Without waiting for her response, he led her to the room he'd had prepared for her. And Deborah relished even in his impatience, in the hasty, inconsiderate manner in which he took her.

After he had repeated his deed, he rose out of the bed and apologized for having much that needed to be done in the fields right now. This would give her the opportunity to bathe and rest; then he would be back.

He closed the door behind him and summoned Nogah to prepare Deborah's bath.

When Nogah entered her room, Deborah noted that the maid was young, pretty, and silent. Since Deborah's room did not have a bathing room attached to it, Nogah brought a copper tub into the bedroom. It was too big for her to carry, and Deborah helped her. Then she carried in pitchers of hot and cold water, which were also too heavy for her to lift, and Deborah assisted her with those, too. They filled the tub together, and Deborah undressed and sat down in the tepid water, which dissolved the fatigue of her journey.

Nogah brought fragrant soap and a large towel, placed both on little stools at the side of the tub, and prepared to leave.

The judge detained her. She was used to chatting with all manner of people, also with her own maids, and she intended to do the same with Barak's maid. Upon her inquiry, the girl told her that she was one of the Israelites Barak had brought over from Jabin's castle.

When Deborah wished to know more about her, Nogah revealed that she was, in fact, an Israelite only in part. This made Deborah curious, and she would have pelted Nogah with a welter of further questions, but she could tell that the girl was reticent and eager to leave. Still, she could not keep herself from making one last inquiry. "Is Barak kind to you?"

The girl flushed, and her voice was tinged with humiliation. "He is as kind as I have any right to hope for." With these words she bowed and withdrew.

And Deborah, who had much experience in interpreting the hidden messages enfolded in words, drew her own conclusion.

🙗

As Barak came to Deborah's room at dusk, he was eager to continue where they had left off. Yet afterward he seemed distracted. He told her that he had other matters to attend to but would come to fetch her for the evening meal.

Deborah held him back, saying that they needed a little time together to talk. He had no wish for this, but he resigned himself to the inevitable. He sat down on the edge of the bed, facing her, and waited for her to speak.

"During the months in which we have been away from each other," she said, "my flesh was eager for you. It is as if a serpent has invaded my body and is seducing me to eat from the fruit of the tree of knowledge with you."

He laughed. "Your serpent is my pleasure."

"You don't seem to be as eager for me as you were when you first demanded a reward from me."

"Deborah, I admire you, and I always will. But we must beware, so that this snake of yours does not cause us to be expelled from the Garden of Eden."

"If I were your wife," she said with a mellow voice, "we could gorge ourselves in the Garden of Eden together all the days of our lives."

He had no wish to nourish her illusions and did not mince telling her the truth. "You know well that it is not possible. If you came here to be my wife, you would not find contentment. You have your own domain, where you are a renowned judge. Here the people have the elders for their judges, who would not relinquish their posts in your favor. There would be a struggle, and I am not sure how the people would respond. They revere you as an exalted leader; but when it comes to litigation, they feel comfortable with their own elders."

Deborah could not envision abandoning her mission as a judge, nor yet living at a distance from her sons, hence she tacitly agreed with Barak. "What is to be done?" she asked.

"Let me live my life," he said bluntly. "There is peace in the land, and I want to enjoy it."

"Is this young maid who prepared my bath part of what you want to enjoy?"

"What are your words aimed at?" he asked sharply.

"She said nothing, but I gained the impression that she was more to you than a mere maid."

"She is no more than that."

"Have you not come to her?"

"Naturally I have. It is what I do with several maids."

"Even if she is no more than a maid to you, you are certainly more than a master to her."

Barak smiled contentedly. "Do you think so?"

"I am sure of it. Does this not worry you? Are maids not human beings with feelings of their own, which you hurt with your thoughtlessness?"

"They are. Wherefore I never impose myself on any maid who is unwilling, and I never take anyone by force. But if they agree, why not?"

"Since you are their master, they can hardly refuse."

"You are mistaken. Some have refused, and I have left them alone." Barak was becoming impatient. "What has it got to do with you?"

"I sense that there is a new woman in your life. If it is not this one, who is it?"

Barak seemed embarrassed. "It's not your concern," he said tersely, then rose to his feet and left.

Later on, when Deborah stepped out of her room, her eyes alighted on two swordsmen standing farther down the passage, guarding a door. She waited, hoping to learn why they were posted there. Presently the door was flung open, and a young beauty with wheat-colored hair spread over her slim shoulders emerged. She stood briefly in the doorway, then she quickly pulled the door closed and disappeared behind it.

Since King Jabin had been known as the light-haired king, Deborah had no doubt that she must be his daughter. She was sharp-witted enough to realize that her presence in Barak's house supplied the reason for the cold wind that was blowing from him to her.

🦎

During the next day, Deborah and Barak busily prepared for the assembly of acclaim to the Lord that was to be held with great fanfare in the town square. Barak had no taste for pompous ceremonies, and he would have gladly forgone the whole. But since Deborah had set her heart on it, he let her have her way.

With Uriel's help, they sent out messengers bearing missives enjoining the elders of all tribes, and in all parts of the land of Israel, to assemble the people in Kedesh within a week. The people responded, and thousands began to stream into the town, which came to be in an uproar such as it had never known before.

On the appointed day, when the heat had passed, an impressive procession set out from Barak's mansion in the direction of the square. It was led by Deborah and Barak, riding proud black horses that had their origins in Jabin's stables. Barak wore his usual untidy clothing; but Deborah was donned in her festive scarlet dress, overlaid with a yellow shift, her short black curls with the reddish highlights in them spilling over her head like unruly children. And the crowd that poured into the streets hailed Barak for his victory in battle and Deborah as the prophetess and leader she was.

Barak and Deborah were followed by her aides and his warriors, all mounted on looted horses as well. The people who worked for Barak, and so also Nogah, followed on donkeys.

Asherah, who was still confined to her room, was unable to come to the square. Nor had she any wish to witness an assembly celebrating the victory of her people's enemies over her loved ones. But she watched from her room's window as the cavalcade assembled in the courtyard, and from this vantage point gained her first glimpse of the judge and prophetess Deborah.

She was clearly a highly unusual woman, the likes of which could not be found in Canaan. From the looks the bystanders cast at her, Asherah concluded that she was highly revered. But from the glances Deborah herself stole at Barak, Asherah deduced that holding the assembly was not the woman's only purpose in visiting Kedesh. So this would not be her last visit, and they would see more of her in the future. Her captor was clearly attractive to other women, as he was not to her, and she turned this over in her mind long after the procession had left the yard.

🔥

A high pedestal had been placed at the edge of the square. Barak led Deborah there and helped her step up.

There they stood shoulder to shoulder facing the square, which by this time was filled to capacity by the masses of Israel. The people in the crowd were all noisily jostling each other like sheep at a watering trough, so as to obtain a better view of the handsome couple before them.

Then Barak's warriors blew their ram horns, and a hush fell on the crowd. Deborah opened a scroll. And, reading from it together, Deborah and Barak, in voices that carried across the square and beyond, chanted this song:

> *I will sing to the Lord, the God of Israel . . .*
>> *The earth trembled; heaven quaked . . . There was*
> *war in the gates . . .*
>> *The stars fought from heaven, the stars from*
> *their courses battled Sisra . . .*
>> *So may all your enemies perish, O Lord! But may*
> *those who love you be like the sun as it rises in*
> *its might.*

Deborah and Barak went on to praise the tribes that had heeded their call and rallied to the banner for the war, and to castigate those who had remained behind to tarry among the sheepfolds and the ships. This part of the poem was greeted with gloomy silence. It was followed by praise for Jael for the deed she had perpetrated on Sisra, and by further glorification of the Lord. When the couple had completed the entire hymn, the crowd broke into mighty cheers.

Then several poets stepped up to the pedestal. They recited their own psalms in honor of the Lord, and in honor of Barak and Deborah and the redemption they had brought to the people of Israel.

Thereafter, hundreds of women, all dressed in pale pink, entered the

square. Deborah took hold of a drum that was handed to her and, swing-
ing it in the air, she led the women in a procession. Her flowing scarlet
dress formed a splendid contrast to their pink ones. Together they danced
around the square and sang in jubilation:

I will sing to the Lord, the God of Israel . . .

After that, as Deborah had planned, the assembly turned into a feast.
Loaves of bread and flagons of wine in large numbers were distributed to
the crowd. The people sat down on the ground to eat and drink and bless
the Lord and Deborah and Barak for their good fortune.

Later, as Deborah and Barak left the square on their horses, followed
by their retinue, the people once more lined the streets and paid homage to
them as their saviors.

Yet Deborah was left with a vague feeling that the celebration she had
arranged did not elicit favor from the Lord. Perhaps this was because,
though it had been planned for his glorification, it had aggrandized her
and Barak as well. Or perhaps it was because the Lord was not pleased at
the people's celebrating the downfall of their enemies. This was strictly
forbidden by Torah law, which states:

When your enemy falls you shall not rejoice.

She had not planned it so, but inadvertently this was the manner in
which it had emerged. She felt deep guilt on both counts.

Whatever it was, she knew with certainty that unlike what she had
previously hoped for, this celebration would not serve to make the Lord
prevent the Canaanite army from being resuscitated and mounting a new,
possibly victorious attack on them. The memory of the dream she'd had of
Sisra's brother celebrating victory in the wake of such an attack came back
to plague her.

When she and Barak sat down for the evening meal together, she asked
him whether he knew anything about Sisra's having had a brother. Barak
looked at her in some surprise. After straining his memory, he divulged
that when he sent out spies in preparation for his attack on Jabin's castle,

they had in fact mentioned in passing that he was survived by three brothers, though he could not surmise what bearing this had on anything.

A tremor ran through Deborah. She had no wish to share her gloomy
dream with Barak, but continued to brood on it on her own. She was overcome with the conviction that the celebration the Lord expected her to
bring about was much different from the one she had just instigated. Yet
she had no inkling as to how she was to do that and what its nature was to
be. A thousand doubts quivered in her mind, and she could only hope that
in time she would be enlightened.

❦

The next morning, when Deborah had barely arisen from her bed, six
elderly men requested admittance into Barak's fortress. They were the same
elders who had come to see her before, those in charge of the tribes that had
not participated in the war, whom Deborah had taken to task in her song.

Advised of their arrival, Barak hurried to the gate and politely ushered them into his house. But they declined, saying that they wished for a
word with the prophetess, who usually received guests under the open sky.
So Barak had grape juice sent to them in the yard, and Deborah, having
dressed in a hurry, came out to greet them.

After they sat down on the ground and she had positioned herself facing them, the elder of Reuben, who had previously been appointed as their
spokesman, took up their cause and laid their renewed grievance before
her. "Illustrious lady," he opened his speech in a plaintive voice. "You
have castigated us in the hearing of all of Israel."

The prophetess surveyed him and the other elders for a moment, then
replied, "Have I done so unjustly?"

The rising sun reflected in Deborah's black eyes endowed them with a yellow gleam, which intimidated the elders into lowering their eyes before hers.

"No, we have been gravely at fault," conceded the elder begrudgingly.
"But you have shamed us before our people to no purpose. How will we
ever be able to raise our heads again in their sight? Besides, have we not
been punished enough? The vermin are still devastating the grain now ripening in the fields. Soon our crops will shrivel to nothing. And our ewes
continue dropping their young from their wombs before their days are full;

and the Great Sea is still as stormy as if the Lord's wrath were blowing at it.
We are on the verge of facing famine."

"No wonder. The silver you have pledged yourself to hand over to the
elders of the tribes whose sons jeopardized their lives in this war has not
been forthcoming," she retorted sternly. "It is you who are bringing shame
and hunger down on your own heads."

"It is not easy to collect. Many in our midst are so poor, they cannot afford to pay a tenth of the proceeds of last year's crops or of their earnings."

"Then let those who are well off pay in their stead."

"We have ordered them do so, but have not been able to make them
comply with our edict."

"You will not else gain forgiveness from the Lord." With these words,
Deborah was about to rise to her feet to signify that the meeting was over.
But the head elder of Dan hastily intervened.

"Exalted prophetess, on behalf of all the tribes that have been remiss
in their duty, I hereby make a solemn promise: The silver comprising the
required restitution in full will be weighed into the hands of the elders of
the tribes who went to war within thirty days. Only have mercy on us in
these days of our affliction and intercede with the Lord on our behalf so
that he may remove this plague from our land."

Deborah scanned the other elders' faces with a piercing look and waited
for them to speak. "As the Lord lives," they swore each in his turn, "the
compensation will be paid within a month."

"Then I will do all that lies in my power to sway the Lord in your favor.
There is no certainty of this, but perhaps he may relent."

On the following morning Deborah took reluctant leave of Barak,
gathered her escorts, and rode back to the hill country of Efraim.

There she prostrated herself to the ground and supplicated the Lord
for the sake of the errant tribes. "Pray, grant the people forgiveness in the
vastness of your mercy."

She repeated her prayer over and over, until she heard the Lord's response inside her: "I have forgiven as you say."

The plague and storms did not cease all at once, but little by little they
abated. The silver was paid when it was due, and hunger no longer stared
the six tribes in the face.

Chapter Nine

No sooner had Deborah terminated her stay than Barak was surprised by another visit from the elders. Only this time the visitors comprised the head elders of all the tribes of Israel, and they had an entirely different purpose in mind. As he was about to leave for his day's work, a maid came and announced their arrival.

Barak instructed her to show them into his reception hall and to have choice refreshments of honey-sweetened cakes and date nectar served to them. He entered the room and bowed to them, and they bowed to him. He begged them to be seated on the soft chairs that stood in a circle, inquired whether they were well, and waited in some puzzlement to hear what they had to say.

After rasping his throat and coughing impressively, the head of the elders explained that they were a delegation assembled from all the tribes of Israel, and that they had come to speak to him on a matter of the utmost importance.

Barak replied in the formal words he deemed proper for the occasion. "Speak, for I am listening."

The head of the elders then proceeded to recite the speech he had prepared. "Barak, the son of Abinoam. In the recent war against Sisra and Jabin, you have redeemed us from long-standing oppression."

The commander replied politely, "It is magnanimous of you to say so, but it was God's risen arm that saved us."

"You are too modest. It would not have eventuated without your outstanding capabilities on the battlefield. We have a high regard for you and we think of you as our leader."

Barak was beginning to get impatient, and he felt that it was time for them to come to the matter that had brought them to him. So he said, "Be blessed for your kind words. But what is your request of me now?"

The head of the delegation, enunciating his words slowly and carefully, as if each of them was worth its weight in gold, announced, "We have selected you to be anointed as our king and reign over us."

Barak was stunned. But it did not take him long to turn this flattering offer over in his mind, and the obvious reply came to his lips. "The Lord is our king, and he reigns over us."

"He reigns in heaven. The sky is his throne and his kingdom spans the sun, and the moon, and the stars. We need a king here on earth, as the nations around us have."

"We have been commanded not to fall into the ways of the nations."

"We will remain different from them in other ways," proclaimed the elder.

"You know well that the path we are treading is not a good one. We are as a flock without a shepherd. There is constant disorder in our midst, and each man does as is right in his eyes. Had there been a king before the war, he would have ensured that none of the tribes eschewed their duty to come out in defense of our country. We need a king to unite us and forge us into one mighty people. And if our enemies attack once more, we need a king to lead us to victory."

"If it becomes necessary," Barak responded, "I will lead the battle against them. But since there is peace now, I want to provide for my own household. I want to sow my fields and reap their harvest. I intend to plant vineyards and eat their fruit. I wish to take a wife and beget sons and daughters and raise them in the ways of the Torah. I will not be king."

"If you are anointed king, you can hold on to the one and not let go of the other," the head of the elders persisted. "As a king the entire land will be your property, for you will be able to exact tribute from the people who till it, and benefit from its bounty. Thus will you be able to afford not merely one, but several wives, and sire multitudes of sons and daughters."

Barak remained firm. "I have no desire to collect tribute from the people. Let each man eat the fruit of his own fields. I am content with the abundance of mine."

Then a notion came to him. "Go to Deborah, whom you saw here at the convocation, who judges the people in the hill country of Efraim with wisdom and a discerning heart. She is a hallowed leader. You can anoint her your queen."

"We are content to accept her as an exalted judge and prophetess. But it was not she who won the battles. We want you to reign over us."

Barak was flattered, but his mind was irrevocably made up. "I regret having to disoblige you, but I am merely one of the people. You will have to look for a king elsewhere."

After some more futile attempts to convince him, they left, disappointed.

🦁

So, when she learned of this occurrence, was Asherah.

Barak had said that he would soon make her his wife, and if he were a king it would have been easier for her to resign herself to her lot. As queen, it would have been less irksome for her to live among a foreign people in their alien country, as her grandmother—who came to Canaan from the land of the Hittites— had done. Yet Barak had not considered her plight, nor had he consulted her, before he had sent the elders on their way. She was incensed and even less disposed to become his wife than she had been before.

But when word of Barak's rejection of the elders' offer reached Nogah, she honored him, and he became even dearer to her than he had been before. When next he summoned her to his room, she told him so, adding, "For me you are a king as it is."

His eyes lit up, and she perceived a new tenderness in them, one she had not seen there before. He kissed her softly and murmured, "I am glad that I am good in your eyes."

She would have liked to tell him that even though he had no wish to be king, he was nonetheless a leader in Israel. Hence it was incumbent upon him to act in his people's name and reach a covenant with the people of Canaan, for the benefit of both. Since the elders of all the tribes had shown their admiration for him, it would not be difficult for him to convince them to allow him to forge such a treaty. But she recoiled from giving voice to her thoughts, for she thought that he would think it presumptuous if she, a mere maid in his household, were to interfere in his affairs. Perhaps one day she would be courageous enough to raise the matter with him, but not yet.

🦅

After the elders of all of Israel dispersed, the elders of Kedesh decided that it was their time to act. They issued orders for Jael, the wife of Hever the Kenite, to be brought forth from her prison to stand trial before them.

It took place at the town gate, where the crowd assembled to view the spectacle. The white-robed elders were seated on chairs set up on a high place especially for the occasion.

Jael was hauled before them in handcuffs. She stumbled on the way, but when she stood before them she did not bend her head humbly as prescribed by custom, and she was anything but penitent. When the chief elder questioned her, she readily admitted killing Sisra. But when he asked if she was aware that the commandment that prohibited murder applied equally to people who were not Israelites, she replied that she had not committed murder. She had only meted out the punishment that the fiendish killer of thousands deserved, before he had been able to escape and mount another murderous attack on Israel.

Thereupon Jael's husband, Hever, rose to his feet. Instead of pleading Jael's cause, though, he held up a little scroll. From it, he read a portion from the Song of Deborah, which Deborah and Barak had chanted together a few days earlier:

> *Most blessed of women be Jael . . .*
>   *She struck Sisra a blow, she crushed his head . . .*
> *he sank, he fell, he lay still between her legs . . .*
> *where he sank, there he fell dead . . .*
>   *So may all your enemies perish, O Lord!*

The elders had listened to this message themselves when Deborah and Barak had delivered it in the town square. They were thankful that Deborah had pronounced this favorable judgment, thereby preempting the decision they had postponed for so long. For after the highest judge in Israel had pressed her seal of approval on Jael's deed, there was nothing for the elders to do but to acquit her. Accordingly they announced that she was free to return to her home.

Barak, who watched the proceedings, had hardly noticed the words lavishing praise on Jael that Deborah had written, which he had voiced with her at the assembly. Nor had it entered his mind that they would have any consequences. He was displeased with the verdict, but was unable to alter it. That evening, when he came to Asherah's room, he was forced to apprise her of Jael's exoneration.

Sisra's widow was appalled. "You have failed yet again in the pursuit of justice," she complained bitterly. "You have been faulty in handling this from the beginning to the end. Were it not for you, Sisra would still be alive today. And had you pursued the matter properly after his death, his murderess would not have eschewed justice."

She added with disdain, "If only you had accepted the elders' offer to become king, you could have judged Jael yourself. You could have brought down a verdict of her guilt and condemned her to death by stoning, in the execution of which I would gladly have participated."

After a brief pause, she resumed her ranting. "At least go over to her tent now and stab her to death, as she deserves."

"Only our elders and judges are entitled to mete out justice. I am neither."

"Then give me a dagger and let me go there and do what needs to be done," she continued to rave.

Barak could not keep himself from smiling at her presumption. He attempted to reason with her. "After the trial a group of Jael's well-wishers gathered around her and her husband. They cautioned him never to leave her alone, lest vengeance such as you are contemplating overtake her. He vowed to have two of their grown sons, armed with swords, guard her at all times. Even if I let you approach her, they would kill you before you had a chance to bat your eyelids."

This reasonable argument merely fanned Asherah's wrath to new strength. She rounded on him and clenched her hands into fists and pounded them on his broad chest.

Barak divined that any attempt to calm her would be as futile as trying to stem the tide of the sea. So he clamped down his temper, stepped out of her room, and left her to revel in her fury.

It was then that the first shadow of a doubt assailed him. For the first time since his eyes had alighted on her, he asked himself whether she was truly the right woman to be his wife, bear his sons and daughters, and raise them in the spirit of the Torah. But when he remembered her stunning looks, such as no other woman even remotely approached, he laid his doubts to rest.

🦁

Nogah had never been at a wedding, and she had not anticipated that the first one to which she would be invited would be that of her own mother.

On the day of Jael's trial she obtained leave from the woman in charge to abandon her work early. Having changed her dress, she went on foot to the home of her mother's cousin in Hamon. She found the house in a flurry of excitement, and her mother in her room, struggling with the heavy, colorful wedding dress that had been passed down from bride to bride in her family for generations. Nogah helped her pull it on, and clasp to her neck and arms and ankles the countless sparkling jewels of her kinswomen that always adorned the family's brides.

Two of those kinswomen came in and pinned flowers in Reumah's hair, to signify that she would flourish in her husband's home. The wedding was to take place in his front yard, and while she was being borne there in a wooden litter, her relatives beat drums and played flutes and lavishly sprayed wine around her as a sign that she would gladden her husband's heart. When she alighted from her litter, young maidens strew mandrakes in her path for her to tread on, to show that she would bear her husband plentiful fruit of the womb.

The bridegroom came out to meet his bride. He covered her face with a veil woven with golden threads, and they strode toward the wedding canopy together, trailed by Nogah.

The ceremony took place before the sun set over the hills of Nafthali. Nogah stood at her mother's side under the canopy, and when Yair gazed at Reumah lovingly while placing the ring on her finger, her tears gushed down her face like a waterfall at the sight of the happiness that had fallen to her mother's lot.

Afterward the two hundred guests, preening in their finery, lined up to bless Yair and Reumah in these words:

> May the Lord make the woman who is coming
> into your home like Rachel and Leah, who
> together built the house of Israel.
>   And may you both prosper in Hamon, and be
> renowned in Nafthali.

Then they turned to Nogah and blessed her as well:

> May you soon follow in your mother's footsteps
> and may you build a house of your own in Israel.

When the blessings were concluded, the feast began. The tables were set up all around the yard, and baked meats, sweet raisin cakes, and flagons of wine spiced with cinnamon and strong spirits were served. The guests ate and drank abundantly. And they burst into song, chanting moving love songs in honor of the bride and bridegroom.

While this was going on, Nogah sat at the table with Yair and Reumah. They talked to her quietly, trying to persuade her to move in with them without delay.

"You will be like my own daughter, and you will lack for nothing in my house," promised Yair.

"Your kindness, sir, is beyond what I deserve," Nogah responded politely. "Yet my entire life is at stake, and I beg that you favor me by granting me a few days to think this over."

But her mother, conveying a silent message by quizzing her with her eyes, said, "It is foolish of you to vacillate. I will come over to Kedesh in a few days' time to collect you and your belongings."

By then dusk was shading over into evening, and Nogah announced that it was time for her to leave, since she still had some distance to traverse on foot. But Yair would not hear of it. He had a donkey saddled for her and appointed two men who worked for him to accompany her.

When Nogah arrived at Barak's house, night had fallen. The crescent moon was but a sliver in the sky, and all was silent and dark. Nogah slipped into her room, in which the two other maids lay asleep, as noiselessly as she could and slid down onto her pallet. There she lay immersed in melancholy thoughts till late into the night. She was joyous at her mother's well-deserved happiness. But her heart was heavy with the reflection that, despite the guests' blessings on her, she would not follow in Reumah's footsteps for a while yet. Perhaps it would not happen at all.

Chapter Ten

While Deborah had visited with Barak, he had been occupied with her, and Asherah's wish for a Canaanite-speaking maid had slipped his mind. But after Deborah's departure he recalled it, and he instructed the woman in charge to select an appropriate girl for her.

Perceiving that Barak had not summoned Nogah to his room for a while, the overseer concluded that he had lost interest in her. Hence she appointed her to be Asherah's new maid. Nogah was not keen on this task, but she could not refuse.

The morning after the wedding, she came to Asherah's room bearing a tray with her morning meal on it. She proclaimed her name and placed the tray, laden with freshly baked bread and butter and honey-flavored milk, on the table. She told Asherah that she would be back later to tidy the room and prepared to withdraw.

Asherah was disgruntled. "You did not bow to me, as you should have."

Nogah bowed but not deeply, and Asherah was nettled again. "You are slighting me."

"I am not doing so. I have been charged to be your maid, not your slave."

Asherah sat down at the table, and while she began her meal, she regarded her new maid and felt that there was something puzzling about her. So when Nogah once more approached the door in an attempt to leave, she called her back. She bade her approach and stand still in front of her.

After inspecting her, she said, "You look familiar to me."

"You have seen me at the castle on the night of the invasion."

"I recall that. But there is another reason."

"Yes?"

"Your eyes resemble mine. They bear the same color. Could it be . . . ? No."

"Yes. I am your sister."

As Asherah had been vaguely aware of her father's deeds with the slaves, she could hardly doubt the veracity of Nogah's announcement. Nonetheless she, who regarded herself as a noble princess, was not keen to have a menial slave's daughter foisted on her as her sister. Hence, she protested unreasonably, "You're my maid, not my sister."

"I am your maid *and* your sister," Nogah retorted in a soothing voice.

"Apart from your eyes, is there any other sign you can give me in proof of your claim?"

"It would be easier to talk if I could sit down."

Asherah gave permission and Nogah sat next to her, then said, "Look at my earlobes."

Asherah regarded them in wonder. Resigning herself to the inevitable, she reluctantly admitted, "They are precisely like mine and like those of my grandmother."

"The grandmother we shared."

The two girls laughingly fingered each other's earlobes.

Their laughter faded, though, when Nogah reminisced, "On that hor-rifying night, the king had us all brought to the room at the back of the castle for our protection." Then she continued, "Did this not give you thought? Did not the similarity in our eyes strike you then?"

"The light was dim, and being scared for our lives, I did not look at you properly. So, like my mother, I thought that he cherished you in another manner. It did not disturb me."

Remembering that almost the last thought her father had harbored be-fore he died was to ensure her safety, Nogah burst into tears. This brought forth Asherah's as well. But each of the young women nursed her sorrow on her own. They found no pathways for sharing it.

After they had dried their cheeks, Asherah asked, "Did the king recog-nize you as his daughter, then?"

"Not before others. But in secret, he did. I was fifteen years old when he was apprised about me, and since then I was given all the comforts I could have wished for. I was deeply grateful to him for lifting me out of my previous drudgery as a slave, and for spreading the mantle of his protection over me."

Asherah was struck by Nogah's last words and they gave rise to a new notion in her mind. "And now you are doing the same menial work that you used to do when you were still a slave. Wouldn't we be like two bright stars rising in the night sky if we returned to Hazor to build up a new life for ourselves there?"

"Hazor lies in ruins. It no longer exists."

"But it will be rebuilt. As the king's daughters, we will be much revered there," Asherah maintained.

"You would be, but I would be as superfluous in the rebuilt town as a third wing on a bird, if ever it does get rebuilt, which is not certain."

"You are a Canaanite princess, and there will always be a place for you there," Asherah persisted.

Nogah did not wish to argue with her sister, so she replied, "In any case, we will not get there. You are a prisoner and I have no wish to go."

"If you help me," Asherah whispered eagerly, "I will find a way to escape. You will come with me, and I will make you part of our family. You will have a better life in Canaan than you have here."

"How can I help you?"

"I don't know yet," Asherah replied thoughtfully, "but I will devise a plan."

Nogah saw that the sun was much advanced in the sky. She exclaimed, "It is late, and I should have come back by now to do your room. I must start immediately, or else the supervisor will be greatly displeased with me."

"I'll lend you a hand," Asherah responded reassuringly.

The two girls began making up the bed together. But Nogah soon realized that Asherah had no notion of how to perform this task. She begged her to desist and let her work on her own. She rubbed the furniture to a glossy sheen with a damp mop and scrubbed the floor clean. The two sisters embraced stiffly, and Nogah left.

That evening, as Asherah sat in the front room eating her meal with Barak, she was overcome with excitement, which she tried to conceal. Barak realized that it must have sprung from her hope that her Canaanite-speaking maid would help her escape, and he was amused. As the meal progressed, her excitement called forth his. He refilled their goblets of wine and drank deeply.

After the meal, he escorted her to her room and reminded her that there were only a few more days left before the month of her mourning was complete. Then he sat down on a chair, and though she struggled to prevent it, made her sit down on his lap, facing him. He lifted her breasts from the front of her dress and began stroking and kissing them. She strained to pull her dress back up and keep her breasts primly covered, but could not. She mustered all her strength to fend him off, but her exertions had as much effect as if she were attempting to dislodge a rock. His flesh rose in excitement, and he murmured thickly, "I cannot wait any longer. I will take you now."

"You promised to delay for thirty days."

Barak pushed her up from his lap, shot a last hungry glance at her rosy blossoms, and stormed out of the room.

When Asherah was left alone, as she straightened her dress with relief, her thoughts shifted from Barak to her talk with Nogah. For the first time since she had arrived in his home, she did not feel numbed by hopelessness. She nursed the encouraging thought that her newfound sister might deliver to her the key to her freedom. Barak probably regarded her as an Israelite, hence she would be allowed to roam around his house at will. Perhaps she could convince Nogah to procure a carving knife for her.

She decided that she would not raise this with her immediately, but gain Nogah's confidence first. Then she would speak to her, as one sister to another, and try to enlist her assistance.

🦁

When Barak left Asherah's room, he called the overseer and instructed her to summon Nogah to him. As she lay in his bed with his arms around her, it seemed to her that he was even more agitated than usual, and this enhanced her own rapture.

After their desire had been fed, a ferocious thunderstorm broke the evening's silence. The wind howled through the courtyard, dislodging anything that was not securely fastened down. There was a stupendous flash of lightning, followed by a roar of thunder. It sounded as if the sky was crashing down on their heads, and it caused a tremor of fear to run through Nogah.

Barak sensed that the storm was an ordeal to her, and tenderness flooded through him. He murmured softly, "My child, are you frightened of lightning and thunder?"

"A little," Nogah admitted. "In Hazor, I lived with my mother in a tent for many years. There thunderstorms were terrifying to me, because they always threatened to topple our tent, and sometimes they did."

"This house is sturdy. There is no such danger here."

"The night on which you destroyed the castle was also the night of a tempest. It is because of this, too, that the thunderstorm raises a nagging fear in my heart."

"Fear of what?"

"That there will be more wars, and more houses will be destroyed and more people will be killed."

Nogah's words caused an odd, unfathomable twist inside him, and he said, "I will hold you tight, so you'll know that when you are with me you are completely safe."

He made her turn around, so that they both faced the window, and she lay with her back against his chest. He placed his left arm under her and his right arm around her waist, and cradled her. She nestled her head against his shoulder, her hair tickling his face, and snuggled her body into his, molding herself to him.

Thus they lay for some time, gazing out into the thunderstorm together, the sense of his power settling over her like balm. The fire crackled in the hearth, in which logs of wood were smoldering, and it rendered the room warm and cozy. Nogah sighed with contentment.

Later, Barak broke the silence. "I was born on a night of lightning and thunder like this one. It is for this reason that I was named Barak."

"The name 'Lightning' suits you, but it is the thunder in you that I love most."

At hearing her words of love, Barak's hands began roaming over her body, traveling to her breasts, their bulge swelling in his hands. He turned her around and came to her again. Afterward, when she prepared to go back to her room, he would not let her. He told her that he wanted her to feel safe in his arms for as long as the thunderstorm lasted, and they fell asleep together.

🙟

For the next two days, Nogah continued to serve as Asherah's maid. Each day, Asherah made her sit down next to her and they chatted with each other as only sisters could.

They shared memories of their father, of his dignity and wisdom, of his love for his people and his children—sweet memories turned bitter by his death. They showed each other the presents he had given them, necklaces and bracelets and fine scents, to be used only sparingly on special occasions. They also showed each other the decorative knives, useless as weapons but beautifully carved by the same craftsman, virtually identical to each other, which the king had bestowed on each of them in memory of a successful battle, an ornament they both cherished as a memory of him.

They whispered to each other secrets about their mothers, so different from each other, yet both beloved by their daughters. Asherah gossiped with zest about their sisters and about their brothers, the pranks they had perpetrated as boys, the girls whom, unbeknownst their father, they had loved and known in their youth—about all of which Nogah had known hardly anything at all.

On the second day, Asherah brought up the memory of Sisra. She recounted how gentle he had been with her, and how much she had loved him. When Asherah revealed how devastated she had been by his death, Nogah hugged her, and when she perceived Asherah's tears wetting her cheeks, she dried them off with her own dress. But their ostensible closeness was to be short-lived.

While Nogah, recollecting her duties, made up the bed and wiped off the furniture, Asherah watched her in silence. But when these tasks were completed, she spoke to her again. "Now you understand why I am so unhappy here, and why I am so eager to go home."

"Certainly."

"Then help me to do so."

"Have you devised a plan yet?"

"Yes, but it depends on you. We are sisters in flesh and sisters in the trouble that has befallen us. When I escape, you will come with me."

"I will not come with you, but I want to help you. What must I do?"

Dropping her voice to a whisper, Asherah said, "You must go into the cooking room, and when no one is watching you, slip a sharp, pointed knife into your dress. Then bring it to me."

It took some time for the meaning of these words to penetrate Nogah's mind. But when they did, she was stunned, and she flopped down onto the bed, staring at her sister in silence.

Finally Asherah broke it. "Are you shocked?"

"You are out of your mind," Nogah breathed at her.

"I am not crazy, only crazed with despair. Desperate to go home."

"You are willing to kill another human being for this purpose?" Nogah's voice rose, brittle with wrath.

"Barak killed my beloved husband."

"There is no truth in this," said Nogah, now speaking mildly. "Your husband fell victim to a woman and Barak was deeply repelled by her deed."

"He murdered our father and brothers."

"That, too, is not the truth," retorted Nogah vehemently. "He called to them, promising that if they came out without their swords they would not be harmed, but instead they burst out from the rear and began cutting down Barak's men. Then they retreated into their room and fell on their own swords."

"You are determined to take his side."

"You cannot deny my words, for they bear the mark of truth."

"Barak has fed you this stew and you are regurgitating it. Whatever may have transpired, I don't want to remain as his captive. I swear to you by all the gods and goddesses of Canaan that if you smuggle the knife out to me I will not harm him."

"For what purpose do you require the knife, then?"

"Sometimes Barak takes me from this dungeon to walk with him outside the walls of his house. He is not armed on those occasions. If I have the knife with me, I can wave it at him. This will frighten him, and he will let me go. You will await me at a designated spot in the valley, where we will hide until night falls, then walk to Hazor together."

"You know that it would not frighten him. He would come after you, and you would stab him, and he might be wounded or killed. I will have no part in this."

Asherah was dismayed by her sister's response. She surveyed her for a long time, then finally announced, "Do you know what I think?"

"No."

"That you love him."

"It has nothing to do with that. I would not let you kill any other child of Adam, either."

"So you do love him. And he has probably come to you already."

Nogah made no response.

"If you have let him have his way with you, you are not as clever as I thought. You should have known that, although I don't wish for it, he loves me, not you."

"I am aware of this."

"And still you let him?"

Nogah hung her head and regarded her own hands, which lay limply in her lap.

Asherah laughed. "He only comes to you because he is obliged by a silly Torah commandment to refrain from knowing me for thirty days."

"I understand this."

"And don't you realize that he gets excited by playing with me, and then comes to you to find release?"

Nogah admitted in embarrassment, "I did not know."

"So now that you do, will you still let him use you in this despicable manner?"

"The thirty days of mourning will be over very soon now, so it will stop in any case."

"But now that you see what a repugnant man he is, would you not rather help me flee, and join me, and find a Canaanite man who will be good to you and love you?"

"I will turn it over in my mind."

"And you will not destroy our only hope of escape by denouncing me to Barak?"

"I will have to think about this, too."

When Nogah left her room, Asherah was deeply troubled. The girl had been insufferable. Not only was she unwilling to help her, she might well traduce her to Barak. If so, his retribution would be swift and ominous, though she could not imagine what shape it would take. It clearly behooved her to be rid of her sister's presence in the house. There were obstacles in the way of achieving this, but they were not insuperable. She would have to devise a plan for removing them.

Chapter Eleven

This incident occurred during the first month of the year, the month of spring, shortly before the holiday of Passover. On the day after, Barak ordered the maids to remove all leavened bread from the house, as laid down in the Torah, and he burned it before their eyes. Then, leaving behind a large supply of unleavened bread for them to eat, and a small contingent of men to guard them, he assembled the other men who worked for him.

They set out on a pilgrimage to the temple of the Lord, which had recently been constructed in Shiloh, in the domain of Efraim. Even Uriel, who was frail, would not forgo the holy pilgrimage. He, too, wished to share in the joy of offering the Passover sacrifice at the altar of the Lord, in commemoration of the Israelites' exodus from Egypt.

Barak and his men stayed away for eleven days. While they were gone, Asherah and Nogah's month of mourning came to an end. Nogah asked one of the maids who shared her room to trim her hair. Then she arrayed herself in a fine linen dress with blue and red stripes on it and adorned herself with a golden necklace her father had given her.

She took special pains with her appearance, for she planned to go and see Barak as soon as he returned, in order to alert him to danger. She hoped that he would take note of her hair and of her attire, and that he would find them becoming. Then she went out to keep up a vigil in the house's entrance, intending to intercept him as soon as he arrived.

But when he returned, he treated her as if she were one of the trees growing there. Striding past her, he climbed the stairs two at a time and headed straight for Asherah's room.

Nogah was left to swallow her shame.

🜨

While Barak was away, Nogah had relinquished her post as Asherah's maid. She had begged the overseer to assign her to a different task, and another Canaanite-speaking maid was sent to her sister. Asherah, fretting and disgusted because of Nogah's response to her request, had no inclination to talk with the new maid. She spent those days in disgruntled silence.

When Barak entered the yard on his return, she looked out of her window and observed Nogah standing there, waiting for him. She divined Noah's intent of intercepting him and apprising him of the knife she had asked her to provide. She grew apprehensive, while also fuming with wrath.

As she observed Barak totally ignoring her, a smile of satisfaction spread over her face. She quickly realized, though, that Nogah would be seeking another opportunity to convey her tidings to him, that she would not let off until he listened to her. The smile vanished from her face.

Ever since Barak's departure, Asherah had been living in dread over the misdeeds Barak would perpetrate on her upon his return. She was overtaken with anxiety again as she heard Barak's determined steps approaching her room. Beforehand, she had resolved to repel him. But he had made it patently clear that unless she yielded to him, he would keep her confined to her room. She was worn out from her month of isolation, and she no longer had the strength to bear her tedium.

So it came about that when Barak entered her room, his design clearly set out in his face, Asherah succumbed after only a perfunctory show of resistance. She stood still while he hurriedly released her from the robe she was wearing, and heard its rustle as it slid to the floor. This persuaded Barak that he had subdued not only her milky white body but also her recalcitrant soul.

Beyond that, he had no illusions. Many women loved him, but he was forced to admit that the only one he truly wanted was not among them. His attempts to awaken her love had come to naught, but he was so eager for her that he made do with her surrender.

Asherah did not enjoy Barak's deeds upon her as she had enjoyed her lovemaking with Sisra. That would always remain unequaled. But neither did she feel the revulsion Barak had aroused in her initially. She was not left totally untouched by the act, and neither was she left dissatisfied.

Afterward, he announced, "This was worth waiting for. I relished my victory over you more than that over your husband."

Sisra's widow greatly resented Barak's mentioning her beloved husband at that time. She said in a brittle voice, "Are you so sure that this was your triumph?"

"It was one for both of us," murmured Barak, as he lay next to her contentedly, stringing strands of her hair—whose color reminded him of the wheat that was ripening in the fields—around his fingers.

Barak did not emerge from Asherah's room until the next morning. He went to his own room to change his clothing and then immediately left for the fields. When he returned in the late afternoon, Nogah decided that her errand to him was too urgent to suffer any further delay.

🦂

She had never entered Barak's room unless she was summoned to do so. But she now deviated from her usual practice. When she saw him enter it, she followed him and asked if she might come in.

Barak opened the door to her, but when she stepped in he made no attempt to conceal his displeasure. He showed it by regarding her sternly with his bushy eyebrows knit.

Nogah bowed to him. When she straightened herself and saw the disapproval on his face, her courage melted. She cringed before him, wary of incurring his wrath, and could not find it in her heart to say anything.

Barak perceived that she was trembling, in doubt as to the propriety of her conduct. He relented and his heart went out to her. His hard look softened, and relief trickled through her.

He came forward and cupped her face in the palm of his right hand and wrapped his left arm around her and said softly, "What is it, my child?"

Barak's kindness threw Nogah into even greater disarray. She extricated herself from his arm and began to speak disjointed words. "Sir . . . I . . . there is something . . . I don't know if I should have . . . " Her voice tapered off.

He tried to alleviate her agitation. "Say what you have come to say, although I think I already know what it is."

Nogah looked dubious. "How is this, when I have not spoken yet?"

His eyebrows shot up, and his voice was edged with annoyance. "You seem to think me rather dumb. Did she demand that you connive with her and supply her with a knife?"

Nogah nodded her head mutely.

Barak laughed again. "I thank you for your disclosure, but you need not fear. I am well able to foil her designs."

Nogah felt that he was being too offhand, that she had failed in her purpose of warning him of the threat that Asherah posed to his safety. But there was a note of finality in his words, and she took them to be her dismissal. She bowed and withdrew.

🦅

Asherah had no knowledge of this occurrence, but she fully expected Nogah to renew her efforts to traduce her to Barak. She guessed that her sister not only worried for him but was also keen to besmirch her in his eyes, for her own purpose. So Nogah became like smoke to her eyes and vinegar to her tongue.

When Barak came to her room that night, she made her first attempt to have Nogah expelled from the house. "The Canaanite-speaking maid your overseer sent me, Nogah, has been sluggish in the performance of her tasks," she complained. "Even worse: To forestall a well-deserved rebuke, she covered up her fault by resorting to various lame excuses, and argued that I myself was keeping her from completing her work. You would do well to send her off to make her livelihood elsewhere."

"The matter requires looking into," responded Barak gravely. Yet he recognized Asherah's tirade as an attempt to extricate herself from the trouble Nogah might cause her by revealing to him her request for a knife. He promptly dismissed it from his mind.

🦅

For the next week Barak was closeted with Asherah every night, from the moment he came home from the fields until the next morning when he left again. At the close of the week, Barak advised Asherah that he would now wed her. She hoped that afterward he would not be able to keep her a prisoner.

Barak, too, realized that he would not be able to have Asherah as his wife and his captive at the same time. Hence he promised that if she became his wife and swore that she would not try to escape from him, he would let her move about freely.

Asherah took the oath he required.

As she had not been a virgin but a widow, Barak saw no need to pay a hefty bride price for her, even had there been anyone to receive it. But in honor of their betrothal, he gave her a crown of gold studded with diamonds, the value of which was far beyond that of the bride price owing to a princess. He did so because, as he told her, she was the shining crown of his life.

Then he advised her that, much as he loved her, he had a condition that he required her to fulfill before the wedding: that she alter her name, for as his wife, she could not well bear the name of a Canaanite goddess.

Barak saw a smile drift across Asherah's face, as she retorted that she would be willing to assume the name of the Lord, the God of Israel, instead.

He made it plain to her that although he liked laughter, he could not condone levity about the Lord. Besides, he had already selected a new name for her: Oshrah, the feminine version of the word "happiness." He had chosen this name because it resembled her previous one, and because she was the happiness of his life.

She replied meekly that henceforward she would think of herself as Oshrah. Barak was gratified, and the preparations for the wedding began. He wished for a huge feast to show off his bride's beauty to all his relatives and acquaintances. But Oshrah told him that in her heart she was still in mourning. Since she could not invite her own people to the celebration, she would prefer it to be small and simple.

As Oshrah had yielded to his other demand, Barak decided to give in to her on this. Thus, in the presence of only his nearest kinsmen and friends and the maids—who peered out of the mansion's windows—a priest performed the ceremony under a canopy in the courtyard, and they became husband and wife.

Chapter Twelve

Although Nogah had anticipated her sister's wedding with her master, when she witnessed it from a second-story window, she fell into deep dejection again.

Reumah had visited her daughter after her own marriage, insistently urging her to make her home with her and her husband; but Nogah had found several excuses for postponing her decision. Now she weighed her mother's invitation more seriously. Yet she could not find it in her heart to make the move.

Forgoing his work in the fields, Barak spent another week in seclusion with Oshrah, and this time he devoted not only the nights, but the days, too, to his new wife. But a few days later, the overseer summoned Nogah to the master's bathing room to prepare his bath. When he came in, he helped her pour out the pitchers of water that she had ready for him. After that, she wished to go, but he detained her. He shed his garments and ordered her to wash him, as she had done once before. He had not come to her for several weeks, and he was aroused by the touch of her fingers on his body, he lifted her up in his arms and carried her to his bed.

When he began to undress her, she protested. "Now that you have taken a wife, sir, you cannot continue doing this with me."

He was surprised but decided to be patient. "Why not?" he inquired.

"It would distress her."

"She is used to it from her own home. Her father the king used to lie with all the pretty female slaves in his castle." Suddenly he grabbed Nogah's shoulders and shook her. Looking fiercely into her eyes, he shouted, "Did Jabin lie with you as well? Tell me the truth."

She laughed in embarrassment and retorted, "No, sir. Don't you recall that when you came to me for the first time I was a virgin?"

He released her and admitted, "Yes. Why did he not lie with you?"

Nogah was about to reveal the truth to him. But she pressed her upper teeth down on her lower lip and left the words she had been about to utter locked inside her. She felt a strange reticence to reveal to him her kinship with Oshrah, for thus would she prompt him to compare her unfavorably with her beautiful sister. So she voiced the first excuse that came to her mind. "He had no duty to lie with everyone."

Barak laughed in astonishment. "You are prettier than most of the other female slaves he had in his castle. He was a strange man."

"He was a man of noble spirit." The words slipped from her mouth before she could halt them.

She was not surprised at Barak's reaction. "You cannot be serious," he said, his eyebrows drawn together. "He bore the mark of Cain, the archmurderer, on his forehead. Also, he was guilty of turning thousands of our women into slaves."

"Still, he was devoted to his people. He was tireless in distributing charity among the poor."

By that time Barak's thoughts had reverted to what had concerned him before their talk took this turn. Gently, he pushed Nogah's head down onto the pillow and murmured into her ear, "I'm glad that your garden was locked and that I was the first to enter it. And I will continue to do it. I may have a king's daughter for my wife, but I want you and I will lie with you."

She forgot her sister and, with a moan of surrender, opened herself to his invasion.

On the following day, Nogah was appointed to a new task: cleaning and tidying Barak's room every morning. She formed the habit of coming there early, even before he dressed. She would collect the clutter of cups and bowls and clothing she found strewn around the room, and lay out freshly laundered garments on his bed for him to put on. After he donned them, she would crouch down and smooth out his rumpled shirt and his tangled fringe for him.

A few days after she had begun this task, Barak looked down at her laughingly and said, "My child, I know that you want me to be tidy. But you are wasting your labor. It's not in my nature, and I will soon look sloppy again."

"I know it, sir. But if you permit it, I would still like to straighten out your fringe."

"Why?"

She looked up at him with a touch of embarrassment on her face. "Uriel explained to me that the fringes are there to keep Israelite men from straying. If yours is tangled you can no longer see what it is, and it does not fulfill its purpose."

He laughed. "In this, too, you are wasting your efforts."

"I don't mind that," she said, a shy smile lurking in her eyes. Then she murmured almost inaudibly, "Perhaps it is because I love so much to touch you."

This response sparked a smile in his eyes, and he did not demur when she went on fumbling with his fringe. The gentle touch of her fingers, together with her tender words, made Barak eager for her. When his heat mounted, he slid his hands into the front of her dress and began playing with her breasts. He heard the gasp of pleasure he had come to know so well, and the next instant he had her on his bed. Before long he felt the passage to her womb contract rhythmically around him, as she called out her love for him, a call he had never heard at this moment from any other woman, least of all his wife.

After becoming Barak's wife, Oshrah no longer feared that Nogah's squealing on her about the knife she'd asked her to procure would prompt him to punish her. Clearly the tale had already reached his ears, and in his love for her he had decided to overlook it.

Her new husband made no secret of the fact that he did not consider their wedding a bar to his having Nogah as well. As Oshrah felt no love for him, this did not unduly disconcert her. But the conviction was shaping in her mind that her sister was not merely another maid whom Barak used for his pleasure. In some nebulous manner, she gained the sense that he had a decided partiality for her, and that he might well take her for his second wife.

Since fate had decreed that Oshrah be tied to a man for whom she felt no affection, and that she live with him amid his inferior people, the least she considered her due was to be the sole and undisputed mistress of his mansion. Yet Nogah was clearly evolving into a threat to that position. Oshrah made it her object to prevent her from gaining a foothold—even if only in the lesser position of a second wife—in the house she had come to consider her own.

So, not long after the wedding, Oshrah reminded Barak of Nogah's being remiss in her duties. His face once again assuming a serious expression, Barak said, "This is a weighty matter that cannot be dealt with hastily."

Oshrah correctly gauged that he had no intention of dealing with it at all. This increased her animosity toward Nogah, and she hatched a new plan for faulting her and thereby ridding the house of her presence. She could not realize it immediately, though, and had to wait for the right moment to carry it out.

🜨

A fortnight after Barak's wedding, Deborah arrived for an unannounced visit. He was eating his morning meal when, leaving her retinue in the courtyard, she entered his front room.

He rose up in surprise, bowed to her, and exclaimed, "Deborah! You look magnificent. How did you get here so early in the morning?"

"The elders of Hamon wished to consult with me about a particularly pernicious quarrel between two neighbors. They wanted to come to me, but I needed to see the disputed borderline between their two properties before I could form a judgment, so I came to them instead. One of the elders and his family hosted me in their house for the night. I arose early so that I could find you before you went out into the fields."

Barak bade her join him for his meal, and when the maid who served the food had left, he inquired, "Did you come to bring me yet another reward? This time I have done nothing to earn it."

"I've come to get one for myself," she replied in a subdued voice.

He arched a bushy brow. "How do you mean?"

"The strangest thing has happened," she said reluctantly. "I have come to harbor an unsought love for you."

"This is an undeserved honor."

"I know well that honor is of little importance to you. What are your own sentiments?"

He hesitated, scanned her face, then replied, "I adore you."

She was not deceived. "So you don't love me."

"Hear me, Deborah," he said with some asperity. "I have just married the woman I love. I am not capable of loving more than one woman at a time."

Deborah's previous visit to Barak had not encouraged her to expect a more favorable response. But mind and heart were not always congruent with each other, and words failed her.

He consoled her by adding bracingly, "But I can know more than one."

Although Barak was now married, Deborah was not, so their coming together would not form adultery under Torah law. Nor was it forbidden by the Holy Scripture under any other law. So she had no cause to be simpering or ashamed or anything but straightforward about her yearning for him. "Do you wish for it?"

There was a spark in his eyes as he said, "Yes, and immediately."

So Barak did not go out into the fields that day. When he entered his bedroom in Deborah's company, Nogah was still there, scrubbing the floor. Barak instructed her to leave the floor as it was and come back at noontime, with two meals on a tray.

After they had come together for the first time, Deborah said, "And now, my beloved, I will teach you something in the way of a man with a woman," and she did. She taught him to hold back his delight until she had reached hers no less than three times.

Barak, who had never been overly concerned with the pleasure of the women in his bed, let her lesson slip his memory. Little did he know that it would stand him in good stead at a critical moment in the future.

At the appointed time, Nogah came in with a tray laden with quails' eggs, dried fish, and grape juice. She placed it on a table and bowed. As she

did so, her eyes alighted on Deborah, clad in the flimsiest of shifts, comb-
ing her curls in front of a metal mirror.

Deborah, who was able to gaze into people's hearts by glancing into
their eyes, did so with Nogah. She perceived the hurt in them, before the
maid turned and made a silent exit.

After they had eaten their midday meal and come together once more,
Barak recollected some work that remained to be done in the fields. He
prepared to get up, but Deborah drew him back into her arms and whispered, "Will there still be a place for me in your life?"

"What would you have me do?"

"I was hoping that you would come to visit me."

"I will do so, but not immediately. I am busy right now."

"I can see that you are. And not with only one woman, either."

"Yes."

"The hill country of Efraim is entrancing at this time of the year."

"I will come to see you, but I don't know when," he reiterated with
finality. Deborah realized that she would not be able to squeeze any further
promises from him.

🦁

Since Deborah's previous visit, when Oshrah had observed her casting
longing glances at Barak, she had anticipated that the woman judge would
come again. After she had learned of Deborah's responsibility for Jael's
exoneration at her trial, she felt nothing but enmity for her. Nonetheless,
even before Deborah appeared again, she had already plotted to turn her
next visit to good account. Now was the time to realize her notion.

On the third day after her arrival, after Barak had left for his work,
Oshrah sent a maid to Deborah's room, respectfully requesting to be
brought into the judge's presence, as she had a complaint to lay before
her.

It was Deborah's practice to make herself available to anyone who
sought her out, no matter what the circumstances, so that no one would
be denied recourse to justice. Thus she instructed the maid to have Oshrah
meet her in Barak's reception hall shortly. She commissioned another
maid, who was engaged in cleaning floors, to bring to the hall one of her

clerks, who also acted as scribe, and who always accompanied her on her travels. She had her judge's attire with her, and now hastily donned it and briskly made her way there as well.

The hall was empty, save for Oshrah, clad in a modest dress of indistinct color that she considered suitable for the occasion, impatiently awaiting her. Deborah was soon followed by the stocky clerk, who came in bearing a clay tablet and an iron pen. He sat down unobtrusively on a chair near the window, preparing to record the proceedings.

"Revered judge," said the princess, "I have a complaint to lodge against a maid named Nogah."

"Let her be summoned to hear your complaint," said Deborah, charging yet another maid with the task.

When Nogah, somewhat flustered by surprise, came in, Deborah sat down on a chair that was slightly elevated above the others and bade the two young women to sit on chairs facing her.

Then she proclaimed ceremoniously, "The trial hereby begins."

Once the two young women had recited their names, Deborah turned to Oshrah. "Pray voice your complaint," she said.

"Revered judge, it pains me, yet I have to make it known that the maid Nogah is a thief. She was appointed to clean my room, and while there, she stole my most prized possession—a knife—from me."

"Why would she take a knife from you, when she can easily obtain one from the cooking room?" Deborah's voice was low but penetrating, bearing the mark of her stature and power.

"It is not an ordinary knife one uses for cutting food, but a very unusual one, serving for the embellishment of a room. It is of pure ivory and artfully crafted. My father, King Jabin, gave it to me as a keepsake. He had it made to mark an especially successful nocturnal incursion into enemy territory. It portrays a celebration in honor of this expedition, in which I participated: The king is seen seated on his throne, while my mother the queen presents him with a sunflower. I am behind her, playing the harp. One can also see a triumphal procession headed by a soldier, who is followed by two captives. If you search Nogah's room, you are sure to find the knife there."

At hearing this description, something tugged at Deborah's memory, but she decided to ignore this for the time being. She looked inquiringly at Nogah. "Is this true?"

"No, honored judge. I have taken nothing that does not belong to me," said Nogah in a chagrined voice.

Deborah sifted through the girls' words and considered them. Nogah would have had little to gain from stealing the knife and much to lose from having her theft come to light, for she would be summarily sent away from the house in shame. Oshrah, on the other hand, had much to gain by making it appear that a theft had occurred, for thus would she be rid of one who was vying with her for Barak's favor.

The judge observed the two young women's faces, but both of them seemed calm. Then her gaze fell on Oshrah's hands. They were resting on her lap, balled convulsively into tight fists, until her knuckles stood out, white and shiny. She had seen such protruding knuckles before in the people who had come to her for judgment, and they almost invariably belonged to those whose conscience was weighed down by a guilty transgression.

With narrowed eyes, Deborah looked back and forth between the two women. Suddenly she realized something that had escaped her notice before: Their blue-green eyes were as strikingly similar to each other as two drops of water in the Great Sea. She was jolted into a new awareness.

"You are sisters," she declared.

"We are both the king's daughters," admitted Oshrah, reluctantly. "But her mother was merely a slave in his house, while mine was the queen."

"Nogah is nonetheless your sister. Could the king have given a similar knife to her as well?"

"Why would he give her a knife with an engraving of my mother and myself on it?"

Here Nogah broke in. "He gave it to all his children as a token of his affection."

"It would be easy to discover the truth by having both your rooms searched," remarked Deborah.

Oshrah blushed deeply. "Not so, revered judge, for my father gave me two knives, one of which is still in my possession."

Deborah looked at her skeptically. "I doubt this. Your sister has most likely shown you the knife her father gave her, which you are now accusing her of stealing from you. Why did you bear false witness against her? Your own flesh and blood?"

The princess bit her lip. She saw no sense in denying what was so patently clear. "Because she dealt deceitfully with me," she said, justifying herself. "She besmirched me before Barak, out of sheer jealousy because he loves me and not her. She falsely claimed that I demanded that she bring me a knife so that I could murder him, which I would never have done."

Deborah turned to look at Nogah.

"There is not a grain of truth in this," averred the girl. "I did not falsely malign her to Barak or anyone else. She had in fact demanded that I deliver her a knife. When Barak asked if this were so, I merely nodded my head."

The judge looked straight into the beauty's eyes, until Oshrah lowered them in ill-concealed shame.

"Truth has its own voice, and it has just spoken," decreed Deborah crisply. "This, therefore, is my verdict. As the charges against Nogah are false, I declare them void and all accusations against her are hereby erased. You, Oshrah, the complainant, are also the culprit. Since you have dealt vilely with your sister, you shall compensate her for the shame and anguish you have caused her by handing over to her the knife you have accused her of stealing from you. Let it so be recorded."

Nogah, who had been listening to the verdict with mounting relief, now intervened. "My father has given me a knife of my own to remember him by. I have no need of hers and will not accept it."

"Are you willing to forgive Oshrah even without her compensating you?"

"I am, if she promises to let off harassing me."

Oshrah scoffed. "Certainly. Henceforward I want to have nothing to do with her."

"You have had a stroke of good fortune, Oshrah," noted Deborah. "Your sister is willing to forgo the compensation due to her from you. May this also be noted down.

"And now, what is this about another knife as a murder weapon? Were you, indeed, plotting to kill Barak?"

"No. At that time I was still a captive. I merely wanted the knife in order to brandish it in his face so as to frighten him into granting me my freedom."

"As your intent to cause death or harm cannot be proved, you are both free to leave. And so ends this trial," proclaimed Deborah ceremoniously. "Let the record of it be stored in the archive room near my judge's chair in the mountains of Efraim, together with all the other records there."

After the two young women had each gone her separate way, Deborah remained seated in the reception hall. She remembered Barak insisting that Nogah was no more than a maid to him. Thus, the girl had not apprised him of being Jabin's daughter. And neither had Oshrah, who likely feared that if he knew Nogah for the princess she was, she would be a more formidable rival than she was now.

Whatever their reasons for concealing Nogah's descent, Deborah was not going to meddle and be the one to reveal a secret not meant for his ears.

Deborah had a kindness for Nogah. She was content to have had the opportunity to come to her aid in the frivolous complaint laid against her. Yet she had not the power to blot out the sorrow she saw mirrored in her eyes. She pitied the girl, but reflected that there was no less pain inside her own self. For soon she would have to leave Barak's home to resume her work as a judge, possibly not to set eyes on him again for a long time.

🦁

Then Deborah's reflections turned to the ivory knife that had been at the heart of the contention between the two sisters. She thought it might be worth her while to rest her eyes on it. She asked a maid who happened to pass through the reception hall to find Nogah and request that she let Deborah see the ivory knife she had in her possession.

Shortly afterward Nogah appeared. She bowed and handed the judge the knife, which was wrapped up in a piece of linen. Deborah promised to have it returned to her later, and Nogah nodded and left.

Deborah unwrapped it. The picture on it was as Oshrah had described it, and Deborah looked at it raptly, astounded that an object she had never seen before should look so familiar.

Suddenly a vision flashed before her eyes, in which the scene depicted on the knife came to life, and it was much like what she had previously visualized in her dream. The royal hall in which the celebration took place was flooded with the same bluish light that had been cast over it in that dream. The king on the throne was still the man who resembled the accursed Sisra, most likely his brother, and facing him still stood his wife the queen. But unlike in her dream, the queen she now beheld was Oshrah, and what she held in her hand was no longer a sunflower but a dagger dripping in blood. And Deborah knew with certainty that it was that of Israelites.

The princess playing the harp and the dancing noblemen and women who had appeared in her dream were also there, but slowly they retreated into the background. The soldier and the two Israelite prisoners moved forward, to where they had been engraved on the knife. Yet now there were tears streaming down their cheeks, as they rocked to and fro, chanting woeful lamentations.

The vision vanished as suddenly as it had appeared, but it left Deborah shaken and distraught. It demonstrated even more clearly than had the dream that the deceased Sisra's brother was set to become king. Perhaps he would be king and army commander all in one, as several Canaanite kings had been before him.

Could Oshrah be poised to become his wife, the queen? As she was the wife of Barak, albeit unwillingly, this was unlikely. Yet, as Deborah well knew, a wife could be divorced. Thus it was not wholly impossible. When the Canaanite princess did become the king's consort, she would join her husband in celebrating an evidently murderous attack on the people of Israel.

In the evening, after she'd had the knife restored to Nogah, Deborah asked Barak if he knew whether the Canaanites they had defeated had yet chosen a new king, and whether they were rebuilding their army.

"I can reassure you on both counts," he replied. "I have recently sent out spies to the Canaanite territory. They have thoroughly explored the land and reported that neither of these events has come to pass."

Yet when Deborah returned to her palm tree, the memory of the vision she had been privy to frequently arose before her eyes anew. It was incumbent on her to prevent it from turning into gruesome reality, but still she had no notion of how this might be accomplished.

Chapter Thirteen

After Deborah had departed, on that same night, a thunderstorm broke out and a torrential rain lashed at the ground. The spring rains had begun to give way to summer dryness, and Barak welcomed the rain because it raised his hopes for an abundant harvest and rich pastures for his flock. But he remembered how childishly frightened Nogah had been during the previous thunderstorm, and he knew an urge to shield her from it. He headed for the maids' quarters, intending to calm her fear.

His unprecedented appearance there raised a stir among the maids, who were milling around or standing in little groups and chatting along the corridor. At his inquiry, they directed him to Nogah's room. Ignoring their stares, he made his way to her door and opened it, while they continued to line the corridor in amazement.

In the dim light of a single oil lamp, he saw her sitting at the table, her knees hugged to her chest, curled up into herself. On the table sat a cup of water, untouched, though her lips were parched. She was engrossed in the perusal of a scroll, her hands absently plucking at the folds of a woolen blanket that covered her legs. She was evidently attempting to shut out the noise of the thunder, the wind, and the rain from her ears.

When Barak entered, she rose to her feet in agitation and bowed to him, and the blanket slid to the floor. As she straightened herself she swayed a little, and he could scarcely fail to see how forlorn she looked, and how heavy-lidded were her eyes. His heart wrung for her. "Nogah, my child, are you afraid of the thunderstorm? I came to protect you."

"Thank you, sir. It is thoughtful of you, but—"

Although there was no one else in the room, Barak felt that this was not the right place for an affecting scene. He tucked Nogah's hand in his, leaned her against him, covered her with his garment, and led her through the rain-battered yard to his room.

Upon their arrival, he asked her whether it was something even heavier than the storm that was weighing on her. She remained silent, and as he scrutinized her keenly, it seemed to him that she was distraught and unable to speak.

It is then that, for the first time, Barak was moved to ponder Nogah's state of mind. It dawned on him that although she was always eager for him, she was deeply injured by his conduct.

He was upset because, as he argued to himself, she had no right to be. It was even impertinent of her to grieve so much. He had hired her to be his maid and was paying her generous wages. He had singled her out for some special attention, as he had done with other maids before. She had simply read too much into this.

He took pleasure in their passionate encounters, and at times his heart melted at her sight and touch. But this did not give her the right to expect more from him, as she seemed to do, or to make him feel guilty.

Her misery spelled nothing but trouble for him. She seemed to have forgotten that there were other maids who were equally obliging and not nearly as much of a nuisance as she was. His temper began to rise. He turned to her sharply and was about to speak harsh words of censure. Yet when he faced her, he felt a flutter in his heart and realized that he did not want her to be hurt. Instead of scolding her, he sat down on a chair and drew her onto his lap, where she curled up. He rocked her like an infant until her eyelids closed and her even breathing reached his ears.

Strangely, this stirred his body to hardness. He brushed back her tumbling hair from her face, and tilted it up and kissed her. As she awoke, her love for him welled up, as did her ever-ready surge of lust. He rose up and gathered her in his arms and bore her to his bed, and there he comforted her in the only manner in which he knew to comfort a woman.

In the morning, though, after Nogah had left his room, Barak reverted to his previous reflections. Wrath at her sitting as desolate as an orphan in her room the night before bubbled up in him again. She was spinning a web of love and sorrow around him, and unless he was careful he would get entangled in it like a fly in a spiderweb.

While he laced his shoes, he frowned darkly to himself and decided that there was no other remedy but to make Nogah comprehend clearly, leaving no place for doubt, what her position in his household was. The sooner she understood this and came to terms with it, the better it would be.

Thus Nogah's grief prompted Barak to follow the very course that Oshrah desired, something her own false complaints did not have the power to do.

🙣

That evening, when Nogah prepared Barak's bath, as she had done many times before, he led Oshrah into his room. He ordered Nogah to bring in a decanter of wine and two goblets.

When she returned, she found Barak and Oshrah sitting nude in the bath together, facing each other, leisurely reclining in the warm water of the tub, their legs entwined. Barak ordered Nogah to pour out the wine into the goblets and hand one to Oshrah and one to him. And when she looked at her sister, she could not fail to notice a smug smile on her face.

Nogah went rigid and felt as if she had been struck across the face with a lash. She felt her body shrinking, being swallowed up by her anguished soul. For a moment she stood motionless. But unable to think of any excuse to refuse, she did as she was bid.

Then she left the room. Crushed by Barak's senseless cruelty, like a dog beaten by its master, she crept into her own room, where she sat in silent grief late into the night.

Three agonizing days later, she removed Barak's yoke from her shoulders and left his house for good.

🙣

The day Nogah had designated for her departure was a stiflingly sultry day, which added to the oppression of her spirit.

When she finished her work, she dug out the bags in which her belongings had been stowed when she brought them over from Hazor and packed all she owned on this earth into them. After she had carried them into the courtyard, she went to Barak's room to take leave of him.

She requested permission to enter, and Barak, who had just returned from the fields, was surprised to hear her voice. Nogah had only once come to his room without being summoned, and he could not imagine what had prompted her to do so now.

"Nogah," he said teasingly when she came in, "did you come to prepare my bath? It is diligent of you, but I am not ready yet. I must confer with Uriel first."

She made no reply, and Barak now noticed how pale and haggard her face was. A few days ago he had been steadfast in his resolution to show her her place. Now, when he perceived the oppression of her spirit, he felt as if birds' wings were flapping in his chest. He stepped forward and, his eyes betraying his concern, he asked, "My child, what is amiss this time?"

Swallowing with difficulty, Nogah replied, "Sir, I have come to tell you that I am leaving, and to wish you peace."

Her words were as perplexing to him as a hail on a clear summer day. He had taken for granted that she was glued to him by her love, and he was baffled.

"This is nothing but foolishness," he said sullenly. "You belong to me. You cannot go without my permission, and I am not granting it."

Nogah's resolution began to waver, and she harbored the vague hope that he would refuse to let her go. She concealed this and answered, "When you brought us over from the land of Canaan, you assured us that we were free to leave at any time."

"I've changed my mind," he replied petulantly.

Regaining some of her previous determination, Nogah argued, "You cannot go back on your word."

Barak disregarded her claim. "Why do you want to go?"

Driving her recent degradation at his hands to the back of her mind, she said, "If I stay, sooner or later I will become pregnant. And I will bear a child without having a husband, as happened to my mother. I don't want it to be so with me. I have just had the way of women, so I am sure that I am not with child. It is a good time for me to embark on my new life."

"If you become pregnant, I will take you for my second wife," he said gruffly.

"It is generous of you, but I doubt that Oshrah would be made happy by that."

"I will marry you nevertheless."

"It would make for much strife between you. Besides, I don't want to be your second wife. I prefer to find another man. A simple man. One who is neither a military commander nor a leader. A man who has never in his life received an offer to become a king, but one who will love me as much as I love him, and with whom I will be happy."

"I was sure that you loved me," he said, in a voice like that of a cranky child about to be deprived of his favorite toy.

"You know that I do. But I must go so that, in time, my love for you may be extinguished."

Once more, he was disgruntled. "I don't want your love for me to be extinguished. I need you."

"You are building your house in Israel. Let me build mine."

Gradually, he came to grips with her departure. He resolved to retain all that had passed between them in his memory, yet he recognized that he could not block her way to a life of her own. Presently he inquired, "Where do you intend to go?"

"My mother has become a man's wife. She and her husband have invited me to live with them."

"Who is your mother's husband and where does he live?"

"It is better if I do not tell you. If you knew where I was going, I would always live with the illusion that one day you would come for me. This would make it excessively difficult for me to forget you and love another man. My link with you must be severed."

"At least I will lie with you one last time. Come." He approached her, encircled her waist with his arm, and attempted to lead her to the bed.

But for the first time ever, she stood her ground, unyielding. She held out a restraining hand to ward him off, saying, "It would give me much pleasure, but I will not."

Her rejection of him was as unexpected as her wish to leave, and he was annoyed. "Why not?" he queried.

"As I told you, I might become pregnant, and this would destroy the life I am trying to begin."

He took her in his arms, kissed her roughly, and whispered, "I want to kiss your breasts. I want to feel myself inside you."

Her legs melted like wax with desire for him, and she was on the verge of surrender. But she took hold of herself, aware that all she was hoping for might depend on her remaining firm. "Let me go," she demanded in a suffocating voice.

He released her and stood there, with an inscrutable dark look in his eyes. He said curtly, "Go in peace."

Her eyes mourning her impending loss, she responded, "May the Lord be with you," and bowed to him. Then, forcing herself to move, she stepped out of his room and descended the stairs.

She made her way to the scroll room to take leave of Uriel. He praised her decision to leave, but they both cried with the pain of losing each other. They hugged each other convulsively for a long time, and their tears mingled.

Barak, who came in with a lingering hope of still finding Nogah there, witnessed the dispiriting sight of the scribe and Nogah locked in each other's embrace.

They released each other and bowed to him, and a wan smile came to his face. "I know that you don't mind abandoning me," he disparaged her with bitterness creeping into his voice, "but how can you be so cruel as to leave Uriel, who will be deeply grieved when you are gone? You can still change your mind."

Nogah merely shook her head. She stepped outside to where her belongings were waiting for her. She tried to lift them up, but they were too bulky for her to carry on her shoulders for any great distance.

Barak saw this and came out. "Wait," he said. "I will provide you with a donkey for you to ride on and to carry your bags."

Her shoulders straightened up as she said, "This is generous, sir, but I cannot accept it."

He insisted, saying, "You have earned it with your labor."

"I drew my full wages yesterday. You owe me nothing. Tomorrow I will send a messenger to bring it back."

"I have no need of this donkey. I have more than enough without it."

Nogah made no reply, but she was adamant not to accept this present from him.

He summoned one of the stable boys and instructed him to saddle an ass. While they were waiting for it, he turned to her. "Nogah, my child, you are venturing forth on your own and I wish you well. But remember that if matters do not turn out as you hope they will, you may return here. There will always be a place for you in my household."

"Thank you, sir."

Barak continued to stand there, regarding her sulkily. When the stable boy returned with the animal, he hung her bags on the hooks that were attached to its saddle.

Then he kissed Nogah, and she clung to him. He felt the wetness of her tears against his face and tasted their salt in his mouth. There were no more words between them. He hoisted her up onto the saddle and watched her ride out of the yard. Then he followed her, and stood staring after her, his gaze trailing her retreating figure until, rounding a bend in the road, she disappeared from his view.

As soon as she had vanished, he knew that he had made a grievous error in letting her go. He felt an almost uncontrollable urge to chase after her and plead with her to turn back. But this would make him look foolish in her eyes, and in his own. He was no longer a child, and he would not demean himself by acting like one.

No matter. He would find out where she had gone. He would let a few days go by, until she became aware of how much she missed him. Then he would follow her on a horse and carry her back to his home. She would be mounted on it sidewise in front of him, while he kissed her hair, her eyes, her neck. Then straight from his horse to his bed, where she belonged.

🦂

As Nogah proceeded along the path that wound its way like a serpent down from Barak's house, her tears gushed forth, blinding her to the world sliding past. At first she was aware of nothing but the donkey's hooves pounding the ground underneath her. But the stagnant air had given way to a light breeze blowing past her, and it dried her tears. She had told no one where she was going, and as she plodded ahead, she resolved to warn the messenger who would bring the donkey to Barak tomorrow not to reveal where he had come from. She would pay him additional silver in return for his silence.

Thus, there would be no one who would be able, or willing, to divulge her whereabouts to him.

Part Four

In Search of the Light

Chapter One

It was the fifth day of the week, Deborah's day to visit her sons, and she spent a good part of the afternoon with them. As had happened once before, she emerged from their quarters into the yard to the sight of Lapidoth's young concubine, Naavah, retching and being sick at its edge. Only now the girl's pregnancy was well advanced, her belly large and round, and the period of her nausea and sickness should have been long over.

As she had done then, Deborah stood by and waited for her bout of vomiting to subside. When it did, the girl turned toward her and Deborah observed that the blood had drained from her face, before she slid to the ground in a near faint.

Deborah sat down next to her and called out to one of the maids, who was sweeping the yard, to fetch a cup of water. She held up the girl's head on her arm and when the cup arrived, brought it to her mouth and made her drink a few sips from it.

After a while Naavah was resuscitated, and Deborah noted that under her black skin the fresh color of youth had returned to her face. She made her sit up and said, "Although you are feeling better, it would be well to call for a healer."

Deborah's sons had stepped out into the yard, and she motioned to her eldest to set out on the errand. But Naavah objected. "Revered lady, I have no need of a healer. I know what my sickness stems from."

A question in Deborah's eyes prompted the girl to explain, "It is this concoction I have been drinking."

"What does it contain?"

"My friend, who gave it to me, said that it was made from the saliva and semen of various male creatures known to excel in fertility."

"What is your purpose in drinking it?"

"It is said to lead to the delivery of a male child."

Deborah could not help smiling. "We must each of us accept what the Lord sees fit to bestow on us. In any case, whether you have a boy or a girl was determined long ago, when the seed was first implanted in your womb."

"If I try hard enough, it may still change," insisted the young one. "The potion wrought a miracle for my friend. She felt it in her bones that she was carrying a girl inside her, yet after she drank the potion day after day for an entire month, when her time came she gave birth to a boy."

"Why are you so keen on having a boy?" Deborah inquired.

"My friend was a slave as I used to be, and was then taken to be a man's concubine. When she gave birth to a son, whom he had craved for a long time, he made her his wife. I thought that perhaps it would be so with me as well." Remembering who she was talking to, Naavah blushed and fell silent.

Once again, Deborah could not keep herself from smiling. "Lapidoth already has five sons. He likely craves for a daughter."

Naavah did not seem to be convinced. "I have been told that men always glory in sons."

"Which male creatures were used to prepare this nauseating concoction?"

"Rabbits, fish, snakes . . . perhaps others, too. I cannot tell."

"Vipers' saliva may contain venom," Deborah admonished her.

"Perhaps just a tiny bit to render the whole more powerful," admitted Naavah unhappily. "But my friend assured me that it was not poisonous enough to cause real harm," she added on a more hopeful note.

"Poisonous enough to make you spew the juices of life out of you, and then you will bear neither a son nor a daughter. You must never touch this vile preparation again."

She was not confident that she had been able to bring Naavah around to her way of thinking and was afraid that the girl might continue to drink the useless potion that might indeed endanger her life. She charged the maid who had brought the water, and was still standing nearby, to lead Naavah to her bed. She decided to wait for Lapidoth's return from the fields and warn him of the danger.

For a while she sat with her sons again, explaining to them the Torah commandment

You must exceedingly heed your souls,

which prohibited persons needlessly putting their lives at risk.

When Lapidoth entered the yard, she asked her sons to leave and stepped forward to meet him.

After recounting to him what had come to pass, she added, "You had better watch out, lest she poison herself in her futile attempt to bring forth a son for you, so that you might take her for your wife."

"I will see to it," replied Lapidoth as he was about to enter the house.

Before he could, she added, "Since she is your woman, you might as well make her happy by taking her to be your wife."

Lapidoth looked into her eyes, as he had not done for a long time. "I yearn for the woman who was my wife, before she became ensnared in the wiles of her ignoble lover. That woman no longer exists. But I still mourn for her, and I will never wed another."

Deborah was incensed by the manner in which he saw what had passed between them, so different from how she perceived matters. "You sent me away before I had a lover."

"When I saw how luminous your eyes were after you had conferred with that man, I was seized with a fiendish demon of jealousy. It blurred the distinction in my mind between what you had done and what you might do."

"You complained that even previously you were not content because of being cast into the shade by my . . . my . . ."

"I could have overcome this, had I truly wanted to. Despite everything, fate was benign to us in our life together," he said wistfully.

It was the first time he had admitted that much. "But it can never be restored," replied Deborah.

"No," he concurred, then crossed the threshold of the door that led into the house.

Deborah mounted her white she-donkey, which the stable boy had just brought out for her. She urged the animal into a canter, then whispered softly into its ear, "At least we two will not separate. We shall remain together for as long as we both live."

The winter had long passed; the rain was over and done with. Even the spring had drawn to its close and the heat was gathering in the land. But on this day the sun's wrath had been spent. The shadows cast by the branches of the palm tree under which Deborah dispensed justice and advice had lengthened, and those seeking it had dispersed. Yet Deborah remained, wearily reclining on her judge's chair.

During the day, she had shown the men and women who came before her nothing but determined strength and maternal benevolence. But now she was overcome with weariness. She looked at the landscape around her, which to her was more beautiful than any other place on earth. Watered abundantly by the winter and spring rains, it was still covered with grass interspersed with yellow flowers, which had barely begun to wither in the mounting heat. It was dotted with little jagged rocks of odd shapes, which looked as if they had been strewn about by the Lord himself, for her to cast her eyes on.

For a while she did so, with her mind a blank. Then her thoughts reverted to Lapidoth and his concubine. He had apparently succeeded in convincing her that he would as soon have a daughter as a son. Having ceased gorging herself on the poisonous essence, she was blooming, and her belly with her. Deborah begrudged her neither her youth nor her pregnancy, nor yet Lapidoth's favors.

Instead, Barak's image began springing forth in her mind. When he had promised to visit her, he had not told her how much time would elapse before he did. Soon it would be so scalding hot that even a hardy man as he was would hesitate to brave such a lengthy, arduous trip unless propelled by dire necessity. When, then, would she see him?

For a few moments she pursued the notion of dispatching a message to him, under one subterfuge or another, and subtly reminding him of his promise. Then she discarded it: Barak would not forget his promise, but neither was he a man who could be pressed into doing what he had no wish to do. She would have to wait patiently for his desire to see her to sprout.

Deborah had invariably taken up the cause of the poor and the oppressed and the strangers in their midst, and took special pains in making sure they were not deprived of justice or charity. There were always loaves of freshly baked bread ready in baskets, and kettles with barley stews simmering on the cooking stones next to her palm tree, to feed the needy; the air was thick with the rich smell wafting from them.

The silver required to buy those provisions came from the litigants, who were required to pay for the privilege of her judgment. Deborah's aides exacted the same payments from all who came and could afford it, and registered them, so that no suspicion of bribery could be attached to her verdicts. And she saw to it that the proceedings of her trials were also meticulously recorded.

The silver nonetheless accumulated, and it more than sufficed for her charity and for the wages of those in her employ, and whatever else she might require.

This day, for the first time, she weighed the possibility of using what she had saved up to make the stretch behind her palm tree her permanent abode. Years ago, she'd had little houses built for her people on the slope of the hill. But so far, even after Lapidoth had sent her away, she herself had preferred to dwell in her tent, which she had richly decorated with colorful hangings.

She knew that it behooved her, now, to have a stone house constructed also for herself, and she could well afford to do so. Yet she drew back from this decisive step, which would solidify her life as a woman without a man.

Now that she was known to be on her own, there were several men who followed in the wake of the widowed Menahem and were prepared to take her husband's place at her side. But none had succeeded in laying siege to her heart, let alone conquering it. Yet neither could she envision herself living by herself all the days of her life.

As the stew-filled kettles still simmered on the cooking stones outside, so did doubts simmer inside her. In the end, she decided to hold off building her house for a while longer, to see what fate might mete out to her.

A breeze skipped over the branches of her tree, tossing them lightly back and forth. A shepherd's whistle could be heard in the distance and was answered by a dog's bark. When the lights of the first stars burned through the darkening sky, she arose from the chair and walked to her tent.

Chapter Two

After Nogah had faded from Barak's sight, he turned back, still shaken by her departure. He entered the scroll room, where Uriel was sitting at the table, bent over some documents. "Where did she go?" Barak asked him.

Uriel rose to his feet and bowed to his master, then sat down again. "I don't know, sir. She would not tell me her destination."

"But she will write to you. I am sure of it."

Uriel's smile enhanced the creases around his sunken mouth. "From what does your certainty derive?"

"She loves you. And she does not abandon the people she loves."

"She has abandoned *you*."

"I don't believe that she has. She will return. If she does not, I will make her.

When the messenger with her missive arrives, you will ask him where he came from. Then you will tell me."

The old man made no reply, but his wrinkled face showed an odd determination that made Barak's temper run short. "You will do it, Uriel. You will withhold nothing from me."

There was no answer.

"I will not let you fob me off with silence. You must promise."

Uriel's tongue seemed to be glued to his palate.

Fury at the old man's surprising stubbornness flared up in Barak, and his hand tightened to a fist. He slammed it down on the table and shouted, "You will do it! Or else, I'll . . . I'll . . ."

Uriel looked up, with a glint in his eyes like that of an unruly child who has outsmarted his father, and smiled his toothless smile. Barak realized that there was nothing he could do to bend the old man to his will. Seething with wrath, his teeth clenched, he stalked out of the room.

The next day, a stranger brought back the donkey Barak had lent Nogah. But he came at noon, when Barak was out in the fields. He had charged the guard at the gate to ask whoever brought the donkey where he had come from. But the sentinel could only report that the man had failed to reply, had silently handed over the animal, and by now must have returned to wherever he came from.

When five days had passed and no clue to Nogah's whereabouts had yet emerged, Barak began fuming at her lack of consideration for him. Her love for him had nourished his soul and brought him comfort. He had leaned on it as a lame man leans on a cane, and she had withdrawn its support from him. He felt a rampant desire to punish her for the suffering she was inflicting on him.

In his impatience to do so, he came home early from the fields. As he entered the gate, he saw Uriel sitting on a large stone in front of his room, soaking up the rays of the late afternoon sun. He approached, and when Uriel prepared to rise in his honor, Barak placed his hand on the old man's shoulder and prevented his getting up. "I have told you many times over to stop this foolishness."

Uriel remained seated. "Sir," he objected, "we finished the accounts of the lambs' sale and the salaries a few days ago. There is nothing left to be done."

Barak sat down next to him. "You know well that I did not come to do any accounts," he replied. "Did she write to you?"

"No. She has forgotten me."

There was so much sadness in Uriel's voice and in his faded eyes that Barak did not doubt he was speaking the truth. He left the old man without speaking another word.

He tried to devise other ways in which he might unearth Nogah, but he could not think of anything. He knew that her mother was from the tribe of Nafthali, and he presumed that she had married a man from that same tribe. But the domain of Nafthali had many towns and villages in it. She, and Nogah with her, might have settled in any one of them, disappearing into the multitudes of this tribe like a stalk of grass in a meadow.

A few days later, as he came back from his day's work, Barak again saw Uriel sitting outside, basking in the setting sun. This time Uriel did not rise, nor did he look at him; his gaze remained riveted to the ground.

Barak realized that the old man had something to hide. Sitting down at his side, he began hammering him with questions. When Uriel made no reply, he said impatiently, "Tell me the whole."

"There is nothing to tell."

"She has written to you."

"Yes."

"I was sure that she would. Where did the messenger come from?"

"I have no notion," replied Uriel. Then he added resolutely, "But I would not tell you even if I did."

"I need to know. The next time a messenger arrives you will ask him."

"Sir, you will not find out Nogah's dwelling place through me," said Uriel as firmly as before. "You have harmed her enough."

"Who has set you up over me, to censure my conduct?"

"I am not reprimanding you. I am keeping you from hurting my girl more than you have already done."

Barak laughed in derision. "She is not yours."

"Not in the crude sense, which seems to be the only thing on your mind. She is nevertheless mine, because she is as my daughter's daughter to me. More so than my real granddaughters, who, not having visited me in years, are like strangers to me, as if they belonged to the peoples dwelling across the Great Sea. I will do the best I can to keep her away from the evil you have done and may still do to her."

"I have made her enjoy . . . taught her to enjoy . . . There is nothing bad in that."

"You used her to satisfy your own needs without giving her a thought. There is much wrong in it."

"It is not so. We both shared in the gladness of what we did together."

"You loved another woman, and you lay with others, too, and so you made her suffer. And now she is unhappy, because she cannot get over what has happened between you. Because of you, she cannot find her way."

"I don't want her to. I want her back."

"She was one of many for you. But for her you were the only one. Leave her in peace now, so that she can revive the strength in her soul."

"I realize now that she is like her name: She has a radiance that shines from inside her. When she came here she brought this light with her, and now that she has gone, it has vanished. If she does not come back, I will search for her and bring it back into my life."

"If she is downtrodden, as she will be if she returns, she will not bring much radiance into your life."

"It will not be so. I will make her my second wife."

"I will not let you; it would make her more miserable than ever."

"When I get her back, I will make her do whatever is right in my eyes."

Uriel laughed a mirthless laugh, which made his face crinkle even more than usual. "Sir, I am so much older than you are that I may even call you Barak."

"I have told you to do so many times."

"Hear me, then, Barak. You have chosen to marry another woman. Had you sought my counsel, I would have advised you against it. I would have told you that although she is as beautiful as the spring, she is as cold as the frost that covers the ground on winter nights. I would have warned you that you would not see happiness with her, nor would she be content with you. But you did not value the advice I could have given you enough to ask for it, and now you are reaping what you have sown. Even if it were not for your wife, there are still the others you lie with. What have you got to offer my Nogah but misery? Leave her alone."

His words put Barak in a boiling rage. Even an ass knows the owner who feeds him, and an ox knows the trough of his master. But Uriel's wits had dulled. He had forgotten that he had to look to Barak, who gave him bread to eat and a garment to wear, for his survival. If he defied him, he might throw him out of his house, snuffing out his life like a candle. But Barak did not have it in his heart to harm the old man. He rose to his feet and stormed into the house.

He went to his room and sat on a chair, his muscles tight from the tension inside him. Upon reflection, he was forced to admit to himself that the scribe's words were irrefutable, and he turned the fury he had previously aimed at Nogah on himself.

This led him to recall how unbridled her passion had been, astonishing in one with so dignified a bearing. During the peaks of her pleasure she had cried out her love for him. When he had questioned her about this, she had said that her pleasure came not only from his penetration of her garden but also from his invasion of her heart. And this was the woman whom he, in his stupidity, had virtually chased away from his house like a stray dog.

Overwhelmed with remorse, he resolved that when he found her, he would never again treat her in this humiliating manner. He would open his heart to her, so that she would never dream of leaving him again. To carry out this resolution, though, he needed to find her. He sat for what seemed an interminable time, cudgeling his brain for a way to do so. Finally, a notion came to him.

Barak stepped out to the thick wall that ran around his house, and entered a small room that was carved in it. There he found the head of the guards eating his evening meal. The man began to rise from the table, but Barak motioned to him to remain seated. He told him that later, when he had finished his meal, he would like to see him in his own room. He returned there to await the guard.

Soon he heard the man's quick strides, and he rose up to open the door for him. He made him sit down and poured wine into two goblets and offered him one. After they drank, Barak explained his wishes. "My request is that you charge the guards at the gate with the task of looking out for anyone who comes with a letter for Uriel. Once the messenger has carried out his errand, they are to offer him food and wine. While they eat and drink together, they must ask him, as if by chance, where he has come from. If he refuses to reveal this, they ought to offer him silver pieces in exchange for the knowledge." Barak handed him a pouch of silver that was to be used for the bribe.

"I will carry out your instructions in all their details," the head guard promised, then bowed and left.

Confident that his plan could not fail, Barak felt his muscles relax. He called for his bath to be prepared, and once he had bathed and changed his garments, he went to the front room to wait for Oshrah.

Soon the door swung open and she swept in. She was clad in a sumptuous blue-green dress that precisely matched her eyes and swished softly around her ankles. Her light hair was pulled up into a crown on top of her head, showing off her slim, ivory neck. Her head was held regally aloft, and she moved with the flawless grace that bespoke her descent from a long line of kings.

Barak was unable to tear his eyes off her during their entire meal. As soon as it was over he led her to her room and to her bed, and during his moments of exultation Nogah's memory receded.

Yet it was not erased, and on the next day it came back to torment him. Before she left, his life had been just as he had wanted it to be. He had enjoyed Oshrah as his wife, and whenever he had a letch for Nogah he summoned her, who had always done his bidding. From time to time his existence had been enlivened by Deborah's visits and by the rich rewards she continued to offer him. He had failed to perceive that with Nogah this could not go on.

Even before she left, Barak had become aware of her pain. But he had been so sure of her love for him that it had not occurred to him that she would rebel by leaving his house. He repented his insensitivity to her; yet he could not think of any better life to offer her. This did not detract from his determination to set his hands on her. Perhaps when he found her, he would think of some way to make her happy.

Each day on his way back from the fields, he asked the head guard whether any runner had arrived, and each day he was disappointed. Finally, a week later, he received a different reply to his question. But it left him even more cast down.

"A messenger has arrived," reported the head guard, "and we have eaten and drunk with him. We offered him not only wine, but strong spirits as well. Then, as you instructed, we attempted to bribe him. But it was to no avail: The messenger, though affable, refused to reveal anything at all about himself."

His master frowned in silence. Then he told the head guard, "The next time a messenger for Uriel comes, pray appoint one of your men to follow him stealthily back to his town. When he returns ask him to come and report to me."

"I have thought of this ruse already," retorted the head guard, "but unfortunately it would not serve its purpose: Those carrying messages make a living by traveling from one town to another. Upon completion of his task, the man is apt to sit at the town's gates until he obtains a new missive to deliver, and that may take him anywhere in the land."

The head guard was right. Barak no longer knew what else he might do to find the woman who, as he now realized, was his beloved.

Three more days passed, and the head guard once again intercepted Barak. He reported that another messenger had arrived. "Although he did not come to see Uriel, my men nevertheless surmised that you may wish to know where he came from. So they drank with him, and found that he had come from the Canaanite town Harosheth."

This was the town in which Oshrah's mother and mother-in-law had settled after the destruction of Hazor. So Barak was not surprised when the head guard divulged that the man had come to deliver a letter to the lady, his wife.

He had permitted Oshrah to receive letters from her family, and he saw no reason why she should not. But when she did not mention the letter during the evening meal as had been her custom before, this alerted him to danger.

As they ate, Barak inquired, "Have you heard from your relatives lately?"

"I have received a letter from my mother-in-law today."

"And what did it contain?"

"It did not convey any special tidings," she maintained. But he had the distinct impression that she was hiding something.

For the head guard had reported that Oshrah had detained the messenger for a while, so that he could carry with him her reply.

Two days later, the man came to him with the tidings that another letter from Harosheth had arrived. Barak's suspicions were now truly aroused.

Barak had been sure that he had succeeded in eradicating Oshrah's hatred for him. She seemed to have resigned herself to being his wife and no longer found him repellent. As he realized that this was the best that he could hope for, he gradually began to trust her and no longer had her under surveillance. But now, he decided that new measures were called for.

There were two men who guarded Barak whom he utterly trusted. While he was out in the fields the next day, he sent for them. He took them into the shed in which the plowshares were stored and, in a low tone that could not be overheard outside, issued his instructions to them.

Chapter Three

After Oshrah became Barak's wife, her life underwent a thorough change. Overnight, she was transformed from a prisoner into the mistress of a large mansion. She was not a queen, as she felt herself entitled to be, and Barak's house was not a palace. Nevertheless, it was a large fortress. If it was not as elegantly furnished as her father's castle had been, Oshrah could easily mend that. Barak gave her the silver necessary to purchase whatever new ornaments she desired, and she began to do so, thus introducing visible improvements.

Oshrah also was not averse to having numerous maids and stable boys at her beck and call. The sister, who had brought nothing but mortification to her, was no longer one of them. She had no regrets about that. Nogah's departure, which she had witnessed from her window, had called forth nothing but relief.

The other maids treated Oshrah with all the deference she could have desired. When they came into her presence, they bowed deeply and carried out her orders speedily, thoroughly, and without complaint. Oshrah would have had to be better than human not to take pleasure in their submissive behavior.

When she came to inspect the cooking room for the first time, she met with an unwelcome surprise. A maid whom she had not previously encountered came forward, bowed to her, and remained at her side for as long as she stayed in the room. At the rear of the house there was a locked room, probably Barak's armory, that none of the maids could, or would, open for her. But apart from these limitations Barak had imposed on her, she was at liberty to roam around the house.

She was also free to leave it at any time. Among Barak's looted horses, she recognized the young gray mare that had been hers, and Barak had readily given it back to her. She was free to take her out and ride around the countryside at will.

She could, of course, buy a knife in the town's bazaar. But her appearance there would be widely noticed and occasion comment. Word of it would be sure to reach Barak faster than an eagle crossed the sky.

The bazaar was not far removed from the Kenite neighborhood, and she could go there after she bought the knife. There she might attempt to bring about a fitting end to the existence of that woman, whose name, she now knew, was Jael, as she had long yearned to do. But she was also aware that Jael was constantly guarded by her armed sons. So they would be likely to kill Oshrah before she had the opportunity to carry out her mission. Slowly, by imperceptible degrees, her own life had become more valuable to her than it had been ever since her beloved's death. Sadly, she conceded to herself that this design would have to be abandoned.

Oshrah had asked Barak's leave to visit her mother in Harosheth. He had flatly refused, although he promised that in the fullness of time he would escort her there himself. She could easily ride to this town and be back before he returned from the fields. She decided against this as well, because she knew that Barak would brook no disobedience. When he discovered what she had done, he would have no qualms about confining her to her room again. If she failed to return, he would follow her to her mother's house, abduct her, and visit an even harsher punishment on her. Oshrah decided not to endanger her newly achieved freedom and wealth by taking a clandestine trip to her land.

Yet this new life, which had been going on for more than five weeks and little by little had become bearable to her, was rudely shattered by a seemingly harmless letter.

🦅

The letter from Oshrah's mother-in-law advised that Mishma, her eldest son after Sisra, wanted to see her.

Oshrah retained but a vague memory of Mishma, whom she had seen once only, at her wedding celebration. She remembered that he resembled his brother. But at that time her entire being had been riveted on her beloved and she had been oblivious to anyone else.

She managed to retrieve from her memory that Mishma had left Hazor immediately after the first evening's banquet; after which, and with all the trouble that had befallen her since then, his very existence had slipped her mind. But now she was keen to meet him, for it would be a little like seeing Sisra himself.

She answered her mother-in-law immediately, expressing her eagerness to meet her brother-in-law. She added, though, that she could not think how it might be contrived, since it was unlikely that Barak would welcome Mishma in his house.

Sisra's mother sent word that in two days' time her second son would visit a Kenite friend on the outskirts of Kedesh, who had agreed to let him meet Oshrah secretly in his house.

On the appointed day, she rode in a roundabout way to the bottom of the hill, then to the east, where the Kenites' dwellings were located.

The rains around Kedesh had been abundant that year, the clouds sending out showers even in the early summer. So the meadows were awash with sparkling droplets of water and still carpeted by multitudes of brightly colored wildflowers that had not yet succumbed to the heat. From the treetops there came the chirping of birds on their way from the hot countries in the south to the cold ones in the north.

But her eyes were blind to these colors, and her ears were deaf to these sounds, for they were overpowered by the memory of Sisra. In recent weeks, by almost imperceptible degrees, it had begun to pale; but now that she was about to meet his brother it had regained its previous intensity. Her heart ached for him as strongly as his, she knew, still ached for her from his grave.

She puzzled over why Mishma found it necessary to confer with her, and worried that he had come to remonstrate with her for becoming the wife of the man responsible for his brother's death, and to try and convince her to escape from the murderer's clutches.

Nogah's first days in Yair and her mother's house brought the dryness of the desert to her soul. In the morning and afternoon she would help Reumah with caring for Yair's children and whatever else was needed. But in the evening she would sit at the window in her room, her hands slack in her lap, her shoulders sagging, gazing into the darkness outside and inside her.

She remembered all that had passed between her and Barak. She had hoped that when she left Barak's house these memories would fade. This had not come to pass: They continued to weigh heavily on her soul like a massive stone covering the mouth of a well, impossible to dislodge.

Her fertile imagination conjured up tormenting images of Barak in the bath, then in bed, with her sister. She pondered her own bed, as empty as his was full, and her barren life. He had left the door open for her to return; yet her wayward heart remained proud and obstinate and defiant. She would sit at the window until drowsiness sent her to bed and delivered her into a fitful sleep.

Reumah began to arrange it so that Nogah encountered young men. She and Yair were invited to a wedding, and then to a feast in honor of a newborn boy's circumcision. Each time, she made Nogah wear one of her elegant dresses and accompany them. And on the Sabbath she took Nogah with her to the town square, where people came to listen to portions of the Torah being read and to chat to one another.

Nogah was grateful to her mother, but in truth she existed in isolation and took little pleasure in the people she met. Because she was not outgoing, they did not show much zest for her either. There was an air of mystery about her, and they surmised that it derived from some harrowing experiences in Hazor, where her life must have been hell. But since Reumah had cast the bitter reminiscences of her slavery behind her, they could not comprehend why Nogah was not able to do the same.

When she arrived to wherever her mother had dragged her, young men sought her out and asked her about herself and told her about themselves. She kept a smile on her face, as her mother had instructed her to do. It was not the beguiling smile her mother had hoped for, though. The men sensed that she had little interest in them, and before long they drifted away and did not come back to talk to her a second time.

Reumah berated her daughter for her sullenness but kept up her hope that when the man who was for Nogah came along, her spirits would revive.

🜲

Nogah sought for a way to fill the void in her life. She realized that the only thing that was truly of value to her was Barak's scroll, which relayed the tale of the recent war. She cherished it because it formed her only link with him, and her thoughts frequently reverted to it. She began to sit at the table in her room when the evening fell, and read her copy of it, as she had done when she was still in Barak's house.

The report had been written while the impression of the events it described were fresh in Barak's mind. But because it had been composed in haste, it was also disjointed. Besides, all was told as Barak saw the events. But she herself had witnessed some, which, being unknown to Barak, had not been recorded.

The notion took shape in her mind that she would rewrite and improve what he had written. She would find fulfillment in doing so, but it would be too difficult for her to accomplish on her own. She decided to seek out a scribe to assist her, in return for silver shekels that she would pay him from her earnings in Barak's house.

During the evening meal she asked Yair where such a scribe might be found. He directed her to the only one in Hamon. With a twinkle in his eye, he told her that this man was not only skillful but also kind, young, and handsome, and would no doubt be eager to help her.

Chapter Four

When Oshrah rode out to meet Mishma, Barak's men of trust were trailing her. They saw her enter the Kenite neighborhood and make inquiries from someone who lived there. Then she dismounted her horse in front of one of the houses and entered it.

They could not ride back and forth in front of it without attracting attention. They decided that it would be best for one of them to ride out into the fields and apprise Barak of what had come to pass, while the other waited a little way up the hill, from which vantage point he would be able to sight Oshrah when she left the Kenite neighborhood and made her way back to Barak's house.

Barak's fields were extensive, and it took some time for his man to locate him. But he finally found him conferring with a group of his workingmen who were constructing a cistern for the accumulation of rainwater. He bowed to Barak and requested a word with him alone.

As soon as they were out of earshot of the others, the man poured out the story into his master's ears. Barak thanked him for having carried out his mission so well, and rewarded him with silver. Then he sat down in the shade of a tree and weighed in his mind what he should do.

Oshrah had evidently gone to the Kenite's house for a secret meeting in some way connected to the letters she had received. But whom had she gone to meet, and how was he to find out? While he was weighing various possibilities, he was surprised by another visitor: Jael, the wife of Hever the Kenite.

Barak had not seen her since her trial, after which he had blotted her out of his mind. Now, as he watched her approach, it was not difficult for him to guess that she had witnessed something she was in a hurry to report to him. He felt nothing but contempt for one who was intent on wreaking mischief between a husband and his wife. Yet because it was crucial for him to obtain the knowledge she had come to convey to him, he welcomed her in a friendly manner. He helped her dismount her donkey, invited her to sit down next to him in the shade of the tree, and offered her his skin of grape juice to drink from.

After they sat down, he asked, "Was it wise of you to leave your home without your sons to guard you?"

Jael ignored his question. "I have tidings to convey to you," she breathed in an ingratiating voice.

Barak looked at her expectantly.

She moved to sit closer to him, until their arms touched. Barak was wary of insulting her by moving away, as he would have wished to do, and she embarked upon her story.

"Sitting at the entrance of my tent, as I am wont to do, I saw your wife enter the house of a neighbor. A while later, a man on horseback came by and asked me, in my own language, to point him to that same house. When I responded in Hebrew, he failed to comprehend me, so I repeated my words in the Canaanite tongue, which he easily understood.

"This was out of the way in itself. But what was truly stunning about the man was his uncanny resemblance to Sisra, whom I had closely observed before I felt compelled to drive my peg into him. The man I have seen now has the same hair the color of sand, and the same gray eyes and severe features as Sisra. Had he known who I was, he would have stabbed me with the sword he carried on his thigh. But since he did not, he thanked me for my assistance with a smile in his face.

"It is then that I perceived the softness in this smile that I had observed in Sisra also. The man must be Sisra's brother, for he is too young to be his father and too old to be his son. After he had entered the appointed house, I set out straightaway to advise you of what has come to pass."

Barak thanked Jael solemnly for conveying all this to him. But she, who was still smitten with Barak, rejected his words. "I don't want your thanks, sir, but something different." Before Barak could stem the tide of suggestions he had no wish to hear, she continued. "For years I have dreamed of spending just one night in your arms. Or even just an afternoon."

"Be blessed for making me these enticing offers, but unfortunately I cannot accept them."

Jael was stung by the snub. "Why not?" she asked vehemently. "You lie with many women, why not me?"

Barak could not well reveal to her the true reason for his refusal, which was that he was not attracted to her. He did not wish her to feel scorned, so he cast about in his mind for an excuse. "I have a high regard for your husband, Hever, and I cannot demean him in this manner."

"I don't believe you," she said forcefully. "Since the war, he can no longer mend tools for the Canaanites, who detest us. Yet you have not even given him any work to do and he is deeply resentful."

"It was ill done of me. I assure you that, henceforward, I will steer all the work that requires a smith to your husband. In time, this will make you both well-to-do, and enable you to replace that dilapidated tent of yours with a stone structure. Go in peace, and tell this to Hever and he will be content."

"Just kiss me on the mouth, then."

Since Barak felt himself to be in Jael's debt, he led her into a narrow opening between two dense bushes and acceded to her request. She pressed her body to his and prolonged the kiss for as long as she could. Then, abruptly, she left.

To his embarrassment, Barak realized that the kiss had aroused him. He was overcome with a craving—not for Jael, but for Nogah. As he sank down under the tree again, he cursed himself for having preferred Oshrah to her. He wondered how he had not realized before that although Oshrah's features were more beautiful, Nogah's were softer and warmer. It struck him with the force of a blow that although Oshrah's beauty was blinding, it was on the outside, as if it reflected the light of the sun, while Nogah's, though not dazzling, emanated from a glow that shone from inside her.

Then, too, although Oshrah's body was ravishing in its milky color, it was angular, while Nogah's body was slim where it should be slim and round where it should be round. Her breasts were like two heavy clusters of grapes. Her thighs were curved like skillfully crafted sculptures. Her legs were round at the calves but slim at the ankles, and her feet were tiny, as if they had been shaped expressly to fit into his own large hands. It was the body that he wanted to hold and to kiss until the end of his life. He knew a strong urge to do so right now. His inability to bring this about threw him into a burning but futile rage, for there was no one on whom he could pour it out but himself.

Barak sat sweating in the heat of the day, forcing his brain into devising a new way to realize his wish, and also to handle the surprise Oshrah had sprung on him, in such a manner that sweetness may yet emerge from bitterness.

🦁

The young scribe Nogah went to see made his living copying Torah scrolls, which elders of nearby towns and villages bought from him to read on the Sabbath in their squares. He also wrote letters for the many people who could not read and write, yet who had the means to pay silver pieces for his services.

His scroll room was located in a stone house surrounded by thick trees and bushes. When Nogah entered it, she found four people there. One of them was the scribe, who was sitting with a pen in his hand and an inkwell in front of him, writing on a piece of parchment for an elderly woman sitting opposite him. The other two people were an even older white-haired man and his wife. They were reclining on a stone bench against a wall, at some distance from the heavy table at the center of the room, waiting their turn.

The scribe came forward to meet Nogah and told her that his name was Gilad, the son of Amos. After she told him her name and the nature of her request, he offered her some grape juice and invited her to be seated on the stone bench, so that he could complete his other tasks and then be free to help her.

She sat down and looked around her. Three of the room's walls supported shelves laden with all manner of scrolls. Its fourth wall held the stone bench and a large window. This was hung with a light blue curtain, designed to protect the writings from the strong sun. The light that filtered through it was pleasantly subdued, endowing the room with an air of dignified calm.

Nogah turned her attention to the room's owner and she liked what she saw. She judged him to be twenty-two or twenty-three years of age, and she noted that he was tall and slim, with wide shoulders. He had a friendly look in his dark eyes, and refined features. His nose, though long, was straight and well shaped, and his mouth and chin had an air of quiet determination about them.

When he finally escorted the old couple to the door, she noticed that his gray shirt had an unusually large fringe attached to its corners. Nogah compared it favorably with Barak's fringes, which had been sloppily tangled. She smiled sadly at the memory of how her hands had always been eager to rearrange them, and of how at times she had done it, with tempestuous results.

Gilad made her sit down at the table opposite him, and he regarded her with interest. He inquired more closely about the scroll. After she explained its contents, he was intrigued and asked how she had come into possession of it. Nogah recounted her story, leaving out only the identity of her father and her closeness with Barak.

The scribe listened attentively and weighed her words gravely. Then he offered her his advice. "Take with you a blank scroll to your home, and sit down each evening and rewrite a small part of Barak's words, weaving your own tale into them. Each day, bring me the fruit of your labor, so that I may correct what you have written. Only then will you copy the whole into another book."

The girl thanked him for his willingness to assist her, but when she extracted silver from her belt to pay for the scroll he had given her, he refused to accept it. "For," he said, "I will like working together as much as you will; there is no need to reward me." But Nogah insisted, and finally he accepted half a silver piece, which, she guessed, constituted but a small part of the scroll's true price.

Gilad escorted Nogah a little way. "I am eager for your visit tomorrow," Gilad told her. Gazing into her eyes, he added, "Writing with you is not the only part of your visit I will enjoy."

Nogah responded with a smile, for she was encouraged by Gilad's words. As she made her way through the town of Hamon to her mother's house, she reflected that she, too, was looking forward to her next visit with Gilad in pleasurable anticipation.

Chapter Five

Upon entering the designated house in the Kenite neighborhood, Oshrah met with a friendly welcome from her host and hostess. They informed her that Mishma had not arrived yet, and showed her into a back room. There they made her sit down at a small table, offered her dried figs and water mixed with honey for refreshment, and left her on her own.

The room in which she found herself was run-down and sparsely furnished. Apart from the table at which she sat, and two chairs, it contained only a low couch made up of several layers of blankets and topped by cushions. Having taken stock of the room, there was nothing left for Oshrah to do but aimlessly drum her fingers on the table.

Finally she heard steps approaching and rose to her feet. When the door was flung ajar and Mishma confronted her, she pressed her hand to her mouth to keep herself from screaming. He resembled Sisra so closely that, for a moment, she thought that the man she saw was really her husband, resurrected from the domain of the dead to claim her.

Mishma laughed at her discomfiture and then, invoking his right as a kinsman, took her into his arms and kissed her. Oshrah was overcome with a strange haze. She was cast back in time to the night of her wedding, when Sisra had kissed her in the same gentle manner. All that had happened since then was momentarily erased from her soul, and she was Sisra's bride once more.

While her eyes remained riveted to her brother-in-law as if she were in a trance, Mishma took her hand and gently led her to sit down next to him at the table. Then he rattled her again. He opened a bag he had with him, extracted a short dagger, and stuck it out at her with its blade facing her. The blade was sleek and finely honed and dangerous. She drew back from it and, watching it in fright, was recalled to the present.

But her fear at having a deadly weapon thrust at her quickly abated. It did not take her long to realize that Mishma had no intent to harm her. He had proffered the dagger with a different purpose in mind, which he now clarified. "Asherah—for me you will always remain Asherah—the memory of the man we both loved is in the dust, from which you can salvage it and reinstate it to its rightful position. You have it in your power to use this weapon against the man who is responsible for Sisra's death, and thus to avenge his honor. Thereby will you fulfill your duty to your dead husband, to your family, and to your people."

After mulling over Mishma's words for a while, Oshrah shuffled worriedly in her seat and replied with some hesitation, "If I did what you require of me, I would be caught and killed immediately."

"No," said Mishma with strong determination. "Banish your fear. It is not my intent to expose you to mortal peril."

"How can it be avoided?" inquired Oshrah with some curiosity, though with a marked lack of zest.

"You must convince Barak to take you on a journey to the Lebanon, or to any other place that you fancy. There you must camp down for the night. Once in your tent, entice him to lie with you. Bring a skin of wine, and another of strong spirits, along with you, and make him drink deeply. This will lead him to fall into a heavy stupor. As soon as you are sure that he is over the edge of consciousness, pull out this dagger from its hiding place and aim for his heart.

"Once you have carried out your task, walk away stealthily. If the sentinels who will no doubt stand guard over you notice you, tell them that you are merely stepping out of the camp to attend to your needs. I will be waiting for you at an agreed spot, and take you with me to Harosheth where I live and where you will be totally safe."

Oshrah was not appalled by this plan, but neither was she enthralled with it. "At the beginning of my captivity at Barak's house, I used to hatch designs of this nature myself. But since then I have had nothing but love and kindness from him. By now, I don't think that I can do it anymore."

"Do you call it love and kindness to kill your husband and your father and brothers?" With these words, Mishma slid the weapon back into the bag and held it out to her. "Take it at least and think about it."

She plucked the bag from his hand, but warned him, "I promise nothing."

"There is one more thing that I will say to you," continued Mishma. "Regardless of whether you decide to use the dagger, don't remain in our enemy's house. Can he kill your husband and inherit you, too? Leave him, and return to the land of Canaan and become my wife. I love you and I will make you love me. We will see happiness together.

"I have loved you since I first saw you, at your wedding," he revealed. "My eyes were glued to you throughout the evening's celebration. While the other guests became drunk on wine, I became drunk on your beauty. Secretly I was wishing that I, not Sisra, were your bridegroom. Then, because I could not sustain the pain of watching you walk to the bridal chamber with Sisra's arm around you, I hastily departed.

"As long as Sisra was alive, I would not have dreamed of approaching you. But now that he is dead, there is no reason why I should not proclaim my sentiments to you and make you my wife. It will not dishonor my brother's memory. On the contrary. It will ensure that your womb bears children that resemble him as closely as if he had begotten them himself. They will be a memorial to him, and carry forth his name from generation to generation."

Oshrah could not deny that she felt close to Mishma, because of his remarkable resemblance to Sisra. Still, she was not sure what she should do. She stalled for time. "If you love me so much, why did you not let me hear from you until this day?"

"I reckoned that during the first few months after Sisra's death you would still be mourning him deeply in your heart. After that, you were a captive in Barak's house, and there was no way I could have met you. I had to wait for the right time."

"I don't know what to say. For a few dizzy moments I felt that you were Sisra. But of course you are not, and the truth is that I hardly know you."

Mishma put his arm around Oshrah and whispered, "My darling, my dove. Since you loved him, you will also love me, if only because I look so much like him."

Oshrah could not decide what her response to him should be. Her existence with Barak was not one of bliss, but it was one of opulence. If she abandoned him she would have to forgo this comfort. Her previous notion of returning to the land of Canaan was no longer as appealing as it had been, for she had become more fully aware that it, together with its people, was in shambles. How would she fare if she became Mishma's wife?

Aware of her misgivings, Mishma reassured her. "Before the war I was a merchant and accumulated great wealth through my trading. Afterward I also inherited a large part of Sisra's lands, which bring heaps of silver into my coffers.

"Moreover, I have taken over my brother's post as chief military commander. I have begun the laborious process of rebuilding the defeated Canaanite army, and have already sent out my men to collect tribute from the people for this purpose. Some of this will be set aside for me as a reward for my efforts."

Still, her doubts were not laid to rest. "If I became your wife, where would we reside?"

Mishma began stroking her hair. "Don't be in a worry, my beauty. I have begun to build a large house for us, atop a mountain overlooking Harosheth. Soon, a part of it will be ready and we may move into it.

"If we wed, I stand a good chance of being anointed king, and you will be queen. It would be otherwise if your brothers were still alive. But because of Barak's crimes, they are not. Another man of the king's family will need to be selected. As the eldest surviving brother of Sisra, who is also the husband of the king's daughter, I would be that man. When we are king and queen, we will enlarge our house and turn it into a castle that will exceed even your father's in splendor."

He waited for these words to sink in and added, "Once the army is rebuilt and my reign is established, I will avenge our defeat at the Israelites' hands. I will tread on those worms, crimson with our blood. When this happens, you must not be in Barak's house to meet your death among the vanquished, but in my house, to safeguard your life among the victors."

Despite Mishma's promises, Oshrah could not see her way clearly before her. She told him that she would have to think the matter over, and then they would meet again.

❦

After her visit to Gilad, Nogah sat down to write a letter to Uriel. As was her practice, she did not hand it to one of the envoys that sat at the city gates, but to one of the men who worked for Yair, with whom she had become friendly. Once again, she made him swear not to tell anyone where he had come from, and she paid him additional silver to keep his lips sealed.

When night descended, she began her first attempt to rewrite Barak's document. For this purpose she read it again. As she had done many times before, she noticed not only what was in it but also what was missing from it: There was nothing concerning any attempt on his part to seek peace.

Her fear of war surfaced, and with it a nagging question: Why did Barak, whom she had thought so clever, not foresee the horrors that the future held in store unless he intervened in the course of events? She deeply regretted not having discussed this with him when she'd still had the opportunity.

She turned over in her mind the possibility of writing him a letter, in which she set out her worries. But he would interpret it as an attempt on her part to renew her ties with him, and she could not bring herself to do it.

Eventually she managed to tear herself away from her forebodings of a war yet to come, and set to work. The task was more cumbersome than she had anticipated, and she accomplished less than she had hoped. Yet she looked forward to the next afternoon, when she would sit with Gilad again and present the still unripe result of her toil for his inspection.

The next day, upon completion of her household duties, Nogah collected her scroll and set out for Gilad's house. He welcomed her with his friendly smile, and when he had finished his other work, he sat down with her to examine what she had written and introduce some corrections to it. Then he invited her to come out with him for a stroll on the hill near his house.

The town of Hamon was spread out over three rolling hills interspersed by valleys. Beyond them there were more hills with pastures, still fairly lush and green from the past winter's rains. One of these Nogah and Gilad now ascended, clambering over stones and tree roots, until they reached the top. While they enjoyed the view of the town and its surroundings,

Gilad told her the tale of how the area had been conquered from the Canaanites and settled by the tribe of Nafthali some hundred years ago.

At home again, Nogah made more headway with the scroll, and on the next afternoon, after she and Gilad had worked on it together, they went out for a walk again.

This time Gilad told her about his own life. "I am one of a numerous lot of brothers and sisters. Since my father's property is not large enough to provide sustenance for us all, I traveled to the home of a renowned scribe in another town, and studied with him. It soon transpired that I had an aptitude for this work, and since my return home, I have been blessed with the large amount of silver it brings in."

Gilad and Nogah's working and then walking together was repeated daily. When she came to his house, his father and brothers were out in the fields, but she met his mother and his sisters. She liked them and they seemed to reciprocate her feelings. More important, she felt strongly drawn to Gilad and sensed that he was attracted to her, too. Thus the void in her heart began to shrink.

Reumah noticed this and rejoiced in her daughter's good fortune. She warned her not to do with Gilad what she had done with Barak, before she became his wife. For if he found out that she was no longer a virgin, he might make her pregnant, then refuse to wed her. But Nogah made light of her worries.

She wrote to Uriel again, telling him of Gilad, who was like what he himself must have been in his youth, and of the consolation he had brought into her life. She also mentioned her expectation that, sooner or later, he would express his wish to take her for his wife.

Chapter Six

When Jael left him, Barak continued to sit under the tree, immersed in his grim reflections. Nogah's image arose vividly before him. In his imagination, he inhaled the subtle scent of zesty leaves and musky flowers that always clung to her. He recalled the night of the thunderstorm, on which she had snuggled herself into his body for protection, and how much he had reveled in this gesture of trust. Yet he had failed her.

She had always welcomed his caresses, even after he had humbled her by marrying another woman in preference to her, in front of her very eyes. But when he had made her serve him and Oshrah while they were sitting nude in the bath, she had reached the limit of her endurance. He must have been out of his mind to injure her so deeply and then let her go with the pain he had caused her still in her heart.

Remembering her stricken face on that occasion, he blamed himself bitterly; yet his odious deed could not be revoked. He was overcome with an urge to gather her up in his arms and kiss every part of her face until he had smoothed away the look of dejection he had seen there and replaced it with one of bliss.

But his hope of being able to do so faded into the hazy distance. Even if he did find her in the course of time, by then the humiliation she had suffered at his hands might well have pushed her into the arms of another man, and with a jolt of pain he realized that she might be lost to him already.

Eva Etzioni-Halevy

Barak was raised out of his reverie by the appearance of the second man he had appointed to watch Oshrah. He reported that the lady, his wife, had now left the Kenite neighborhood and was on her way back to his house. Barak praised the man and rewarded him with silver.

He lifted his eyes to the sky and saw that the sun had reached its midpoint. Thus, quite some time had elapsed between Jael's alerting him to Sisra's brother entering the Kenite neighborhood and his man apprising him of Oshrah's leaving. It would have sufficed for them to engage in more than a friendly family meeting.

If Sisra's brother bore such similarity to her dead husband, he would have had no difficulty in convincing her that he, and not Barak, was the proper man to succeed Sisra as her husband. Barak was fully aware that her love for himself equaled that of Lot's wife for her man after she had turned into a pillar of salt. The woman who loved him had gone. And he was left with the one who reserved her love for a man whose existence was reduced to a memory and now probably for his brother, who had made this memory wear flesh and bones again.

To his surprise, he did not care about her feelings, any more than he cared about the wind that rustled the leaves on the tree under which he sat. She had moved out of his heart, leaving no traces behind.

Barak knew that the brother would be bound to seek to avenge Sisra's blood by bringing about his own death. There was no more expedient a tool for the avenger to employ for this purpose than the woman who had such easy access to him. He would have to avert this danger.

Since the day was still long before him, he once again embarked on work in his property. But he came home earlier than usual and went to confer with his two men of trust. He was fortunate to find them in their room.

Despite his reluctance to do so, he explained, "I have reason to fear that my wife is concealing a weapon in her room. Pray, wait until she sits down with me for the evening meal," he instructed them, "then enter and search it thoroughly and remove whatever harmful objects you may discover. But be careful to restore all you displace to its previous position, so that your search will not be noticed. Then step into my own bedroom and send a maid to fetch me."

The two men were so loyal to Barak that they refrained from embarrassing him. If they thought that his order was out of the way, they did not show it by as much as a flicker of their eyelids. They merely bowed to Barak respectfully, and he left their room in silence.

※

As Oshrah came, gliding into the front room in her customary regal splendor, Barak was careful not to reveal to her by his demeanor what was going on in his mind. She, too, acted as if nothing special had happened, though she kept her hands hidden under the table, where she was stealthily wringing them.

Barak deliberately asked her, "What have you done this day?".

With seeming unconcern, she replied, "I rode to the dwelling of my seamstress to order some new dresses."

It did not escape Barak that in this manner Oshrah had preempted any questions that he might have asked her about whether she had gone into the town and what she had done there. Grudgingly, he admired her for her cunning.

Flicking an inscrutable glance at her, he lifted the decanter of wine that was perched on the table and poured the red liquid into two goblets. He offered her one, while he himself drank from the other, and regarded her intently over its rim. He had to admit to himself that her lovely face reflected nothing but calm friendliness.

He called for a container of strong spirits. Oshrah declined the cup he offered her, but he himself drank deeply, until he felt the heat of the liquid soar its way down his throat, then radiate to his stomach, where it turned bitter. With his head spinning, he drew out the meal further by dragging from his hazy mind tales about his property, about the grains he planned to sow in the next season, about the vineyards he intended to plant, and much more besides. He refilled her goblet of wine whenever she drank from it, until her eyes became bleary. Still, her seemingly innocent face gave away no more than it had done before.

Time dragged by and still the maid for whom he was anxiously waiting did not appear. Barak asked his wife how she was progressing with refurbishing the house. She reported in some detail about what rugs and tapestries she had purchased already, and what she still planned to buy, and he listened with feigned attention to her words. Even so, the meal was inevitably drawing to an end, and still the maid had not arrived. Barak began to be fidgety, because he could not think of a ruse by which to prolong it further.

Finally Oshrah rose to her feet and left him no choice but to do the same. "Come, let us sit outside for a while to enjoy the crisp evening breeze together," he suggested. She declined, on the ground that she was tired and wished to go to sleep early that night.

Barak no longer had any urge for carnal knowledge of her. But because he was casting about for a way to keep her from entering her room, he invited her into his.

Since she had become his wife, Oshrah had never repulsed him. But this time she felt a need for solitude, so as to gaze into her own soul and feel her way into the future. Hence she said with seemingly genuine regret, "I prefer to postpone our togetherness until tomorrow, because I am, indeed, very tired."

At this moment, the maid made her appearance and announced that two men wished to have speech with him, so Barak released Oshrah and headed for his room.

When he heard what the men had to say, a muscle jumped in his cheek. He had long stopped suspecting that the woman on whom he had showered the best of all he possessed would go to such extremes to be rid of him. He had been mistaken.

After the men left, he paced back and forth in his room, weighing his forthcoming steps in his mind.

The next time Gilad and Nogah walked on the hill, the young man declared his love for her. "Since the day I met you, my love has been sprouting and blossoming and growing by the day. If you reciprocate my love and agree, I wish to press the seal of matrimony on it."

Nogah bent her head and made no response.

"Since your father is no longer alive," he added, "it will be proper for me to seek permission to marry you from you mother, and offer her the bride price that would have been due to your father."

"Pray, sir," begged Nogah, "delay your visit to her for a little while, for I am not sure yet of my own heart."

"Are you in concern about our residence and livelihood?" he queried. "If so, abandon it. Through my work, I have accumulated a sufficient amount of silver to purchase a spacious house for us. We will not have to live in my father's house, as my brothers do. We will live in affluence and you may appoint a woman to oversee our household, while you work with me on writing letters for people, which I think you may find to your liking."

In truth, the life Gilad sketched out for her attracted Nogah strongly. Still, she hesitated, for her love for Barak had not diminished and she could not imagine herself lying in any other man's arms. She had experienced the ultimate in love and pleasure with Barak. Hence she could not contemplate becoming a man's wife before she explored how she felt when he came to her. Her mother had warned her not to let Gilad do so before the wedding, but Nogah was no longer sure that she should heed her warning.

🦂

Although the task of rewriting Barak's scroll was arduous, Nogah worked night after night, and before two weeks were completed, the scroll was. After copying the whole, she gave it to Gilad to read, and on the next day came back to inquire how he had liked the outcome of their common effort.

"It is not only well written," he replied, "but it also forms a highly important account of a crucial chapter in the trials and tribulations of the people of Israel."

He reflected for a while. Then he proposed, "Let us travel together to the house of the Lord in the town of Shiloh, in the mountains of Efraim. There the most important scrolls recounting the tales of the people of Israel are stored, and this one is worthy of finding a place among them."

"We cannot well travel together to such a distant location," objected Nogah, "since we would have to spend a few nights on the way, thus making it look as if we lived together as husband and wife."

"By that time we could be," urged Gilad. "Indeed, let us be wed as soon as possible."

Still Nogah was divided inside. She recalled how Barak had over-

whelmed her with the desire burning in his loins almost as soon as he set
eyes on her. Yet Gilad had let almost two weeks pass without even touching her. Through his reticence he had honored her. But she would have
preferred it had he replaced some of this honor with passion.

She had no doubt that Gilad was a man under whose wings she would
be safe. He would shelter her from adversity, and his eyes would not rove
to other women. But she began to wonder whether they would enjoy the
pleasure of the flesh together. After much agonizing, she decided that she
could not become his wife without putting this to the test first.

Besides, Gilad might not wish for a wife whose secret garden was no
longer locked. Her mother had warned her not to let him discover this
until she was safely ensconced in his home. But Nogah had no wish to be
tied to a husband who regretted having taken her for his wife.

During their next walk, she interlaced her fingers with his and steered
him toward a remote spot, where there were no other people walking, nor
any flocks grazing.

Gilad sensed what her aim was, and responded as she had hoped he
would: He slung his arms around her and kissed her. They were overcome
with the magic of the moment, and with each other's youthful bodies.
Finding some bushes where they could be concealed from view, they lay
down on the grass. The rest followed in accordance with the time-honored
ritual of the way of a man with a woman. Nogah felt no urge to wail out
her love for Gilad as she had with Barak. Still, she was hungry for what he
had to offer.

The young man noticed with disappointment that the barrier he should
have met inside Nogah had been pried open by another. After their act was
completed, he questioned her about this gently, and she unhesitantly admitted that this had not been her first time with a man. The young scribe
was by no means feebleminded or obtuse, and he was quick to realize who
his predecessor must have been.

Because of his constantly strengthening love for Nogah, he was willing
to overlook her previously going astray. He had no intention of giving her
up. Nonetheless, he decided to make sure that she was not pregnant. So the
first question he asked after they dressed pertained to the length of time
since she had left Barak's home.

With a wry smile, in complete understanding of his concern, Nogah disclosed that she had left that house almost a month ago, and that since then she'd had the way of women. Gilad was reassured, and during the next week, they climbed the same hill every day, and there their passion mingled and was followed by the calm they found in each other's arms.

Even so, Gilad began to view the scroll on which they had been working in a different light. He no longer regarded it as an important testimony of crucial events in the history of Israel, but as an attempt by a young woman to glorify her erstwhile lover. His eagerness to pursue the matter all the way to the house of the Lord abated, and he no longer mentioned his willingness to do so.

Still, he urged Nogah to let him approach her mother. Nogah requested one more night to think his offer over.

That night, Nogah found no peace for her soul. Her thoughts chased each other in rapid succession, yet time crawled. She knew it to be the most fateful time of her life, and she was afraid of making the wrong decision. And when the morning dawned, her eyes were red with sleeplessness.

Chapter Seven

A short while after Barak met the men who'd searched Oshrah's room, he entered it himself. He shut the door behind him and leaned against the doorpost, regarding his wife.

She was sitting on a stool in front of the harp he had given her. But instead of stringing tunes, as she was wont to do, she was absently running her fingers over its strings. She sat there dreamily, evidently searching her heart. She was still as lovely as she had been before; but her beauty had lost its allure for him.

When she noticed Barak, she jumped up in surprise and looked at him inquiringly, waiting for him to speak.

He did so, with a smile that curved his lips but left his eyes hard as marble. "I am glad, Oshrah, that at least it is difficult for you to make up your mind."

She strove to appear calm and asked haughtily, "What is it that you are talking about?"

"This," he replied, proffering the dagger his men had found, watching her grow pale.

She swayed to a chair and fell into it sidewise, her fingers curled around its back. Sweat gathered in her armpits, her eyes had palpable fear written in them, and her lips were trembling. But after a short while she recuperated and took an oath. "I swear to you, sir, by all the gods of Canaan and also by the God of Israel, that I never would have used it."

"Only the Lord can judge a human being by what is in his heart. I can merely judge by what I see before my eyes. And what I see is a deadly weapon that, until a short while ago, was concealed among the dainty garments in your sideboard."

"But you know that I would not have harmed you."

Barak gave her a chilly look. "I cannot look into your heart, but I can look into mine. And I see that something that previously flooded it has ebbed: my love for you. Or perhaps it was never there, and it was admiration for your undeniable beauty that I mistook for love."

His admission stung like a snake's bite. "So it is not the dagger. That is merely an excuse."

"Perhaps."

"Then what is it?"

Barak remained silent.

"It is her," she flung at him.

He was about to ridicule her notion but halted himself, for he knew it to be the truth.

"You have professed your love for me and made me your wife. You cannot fling me away as if I were nothing but a fly on your sleeve," Oshrah persisted. "In any case it will do you no good, for you will never find her."

"I will," he said, concealing his doubts from her.

"How?"

"I propose that you leave this for me to deal with," he replied in a subdued voice.

There was a long pause, during which Oshrah sat so still that she might have frozen into a statue. She realized that she did not want Barak to banish her. A short while ago she had been weighing the possibility of leaving him in favor of Mishma, but she wanted to be the one to make the decision, and not to be thrown out as a woman scorned by her husband.

She had expected an eruption of anger from him, even violence, but he had remained frighteningly calm. It was this, more than anything else, that convinced her that no matter what she said or did, she would not be able to recapture her position with him. Finally she spoke, with a tremor in her voice. "I see that you want me to be gone. But what if it transpires that I am pregnant?"

"If you bear my child, bring him to me and I will raise him."

"*She* may not be willing to burden herself with your child from another woman."

"I assure you that she will."

"How do you know?"

"Because, unlike you, she loves me."

A shiver, such as that of a fever, ran through Oshrah. She rose up from her chair and stood facing Barak, and the renewed silence between them dragged on, becoming more daunting by the moment. Finally Barak announced, "I will instruct Uriel to prepare a book of divorcement, which I will hand to you tomorrow morning before you leave, as is our law."

"From now on, I am no longer Oshrah, but Asherah again. You had better tell this to Uriel, before he writes that book."

"I will do as you say, Asherah, and also send you a maid to help you prepare for your trip. There will be a cart for your belongings, and your mare, ready for you, so that you may set out early in the morning."

"Thank you."

"I will also give you a pouch of gold shekels, to help you build your house in Canaan with your new husband. A contingent of my men will escort you on the way."

Once again, the silence was thick between them. Then Barak turned and strode out of her room, his tall frame disappearing behind its door for the last time. She heard his footsteps in the passage outside, hastily retreating from her life.

❦

On the next morning, the maids, all of whom were peering out the mansion's windows into the courtyard, were privy to an unprecedented spectacle: their master, with his two men of trust at his side as witnesses, handing their mistress a book of divorcement. They heard Barak declare, "You are no longer my wife, and I am not your husband."

Those who were close by could later report to the others that he gave her a pouch that contained gold shekels, then handed her a lump of gold and said, "You can have it molded into a statue of Asherah again. That should make you happy."

Then Barak blessed the woman who was no longer their mistress, with these words: "Go in peace, and may you find happiness in your life."

They heard her respond in the proper Israelite fashion: "May the Lord be with you."

He lifted her onto her horse's saddle and she rode out of the gate, followed by her belongings and her guards.

And the maids wondered which one of them Barak would select to console him that night.

On the following night Barak had a dream that was as vivid as if it had truly transpired. In his dream he lay in his bed, with Nogah next to him. He reached out for her softness under the blanket, but just then he woke up and there was only the empty space and the painful arousal of his lust for her.

At first, he was not entirely bereft of female company, but his encounters with his maids were joyless. They slipped easily into his bed and as easily slipped out, also out of his memory. Little by little those deeds petered out and ceased altogether. For the first time since his boyhood, he spent his nights in solitude. He would lie on his back, racking his brain in the futile endeavor of uncovering a mere trace of a clue to where Nogah might be. Each day that passed without a sign of her, another speck of hope drained away from him.

It was two and a half weeks after Barak had given Asherah the book of divorcement that the head guard approached him with tidings about Nogah, whereupon he was stunned by disbelief.

❦

During the night in which Nogah could find no sleep, a stillness, as thick as a cloud, pervaded the air. As she lay on her bed staring up at the heavily planked ceiling, she assured herself over and over again that Gilad was for her, and she for him. But the fact that she had to convince herself strengthened her doubts.

She knew their carnal acts to have been all that a woman could hope for. Yet they had not been what *she* had wished for. For she still retained the memory of something to which they compared as a spring streaming down a gently sloping hill compared to a massive waterfall gushing down a mountain in the north after the snows had melted. Her heart wept inside her with the sorrow of her loss.

Gilad was the man she would have craved had she not previously known Barak. In truth, the only thing amiss with him was that he was not Barak, nor anything like him. The moment she acknowledged this to herself, her decision was made.

What remained of that interminable night passed in her trying to come to terms with the bitter realization that there would never be any man for her but Barak. Since she would never go back to him, and he would never come to claim her, or even be able to find her (if he still wished to do so), she would have to be without a man all the days of her life.

She could meet a man occasionally and come together with him, as she had done with Gilad. But if she did, she would soon come to be known as a woman of easy virtue and this would grieve her mother very much. Besides, she might become pregnant and bear a fatherless child, and this would cause her mother even greater sorrow, on top of shaming her before her tribe and her people.

If she had already become pregnant from Gilad, she would find a distant place to live, hire herself out as a maid, and raise the child on her own. But if, as she hoped, she had escaped that harsh fate, she would never be as reckless as to take that risk again.

Then came the difficult task of apprising Gilad of her decision. Her head throbbing for the pain she would have to cause him, she rose with the sun, washed her body, and set out for his home.

When she arrived, Gilad was arranging his iron pen and inkwell in anticipation of the people who would come to him that day. As soon as he saw how pale and red-eyed Nogah was, he knew her decision, and his heart was wrung for her as much as for himself. He took her into his arms and asked, "My love, why?"

Nogah embarked on the speech she had prepared for herself. "My soul reaches out for you, Gilad, but I cannot be happy with you, hence I will not be able to make you happy."

"It's because of him, is this not the truth?" he stated.

She was flustered but made no reply.

Choosing his words carefully, he continued. "His exploits with women are infamous in the land. You may believe me when I tell you that he is not the man for you. If you went back to him, there would be nothing but suffering for you. You need more time to face this, and for his memory to fade in you. I will not despair. I will come to see you in a few weeks' time."

The words Gilad had uttered contained much sense, which penetrated her mind but not her heart. She smiled a forlorn smile, kissed him on the mouth, and left.

After that, her burden felt lighter. On the way back to her mother's house, she began searching for a way to pick up the fragments of her life and piece them together. The notion of bringing her scroll to be deposited at the house of the Lord in Shiloh had taken strong possession of her mind, and she decided to go there by herself.

It occurred to her, too, that what she had rewritten presented Barak's tale and her own. What was still missing was that of another person who had played a decisive part in the events described in it: Deborah. If Nogah wished her story to depict all as it had truly occurred, it was incumbent on her to weave in what Deborah could tell her. She knew that she judged the people of Israel in the hills of Efraim, at a spot not too far removed from Shiloh. So she resolved to travel there first.

She remembered how much Barak had lusted after this voluptuous woman. But Barak would always lust for one woman or another, and it no longer mattered to her whether it was Deborah or Oshrah or anyone else. Besides, Nogah also remembered how kind the judge had been to her, on the occasion on which she had dismissed the trumped-up charges Oshrah had laid against her. So her resolution to seek her out was strengthened.

When Nogah came home, she found her mother in an unusually cheerful mood, eager to perform the various tasks that awaited her. But when Reumah's radiant eyes alighted on her daughter's wan ones with the dark shadows underneath them, she understood what had come to pass, and hugged her and spilled tears of sorrow with her.

Nogah was aware of how strong her mother's happiness had been before she had spoiled it, and urged her to tell her the cause. When Reumah announced that she was pregnant, Nogah embraced her and shed tears of joy with her. So mother and daughter wept in each other's arms, and their desolation and elation were intermingled.

"Pray, lie down and rest," she begged her mother, "and relinquish your tasks to me. I have come to be fond of Yair's children and can easily care for them in your stead."

But Reumah laughed. "In my happiness I am able to perform the work of three women."

During the evening meal, both she and Yair urged Nogah to reconsider her decision about Gilad. Yair was particularly insistent. "He is not only handsome and well-to-do, but also the most suitable man you could ever hope to find, and quite clearly, he loves you."

Reumah added her voice to Yair's. "I plead with you: Do not let this opportunity slip away, for there might never be another like it."

They invited her to look at them, at how content they were with each other. They told her that she, too, could gain such happiness. They asked her to compare the life of bliss that awaited her with Gilad, with the sad life that would be her lot as a lone woman, without a home that was hers and children of her womb to gladden her days; but it was to no avail.

Two days later, stung into action by her loneliness, Nogah set out on her trip. She wished to travel on her own, but Yair considered this unacceptable. He appointed a man and his wife who worked for him to guard her on the way. After Nogah had packed a few provisions into a bag and put on a simple gray linen dress that would be able to withstand the dust of the road, the three of them mounted their donkeys.

They rode through a morning haze that gave way to a steaming day. This was followed by an even hotter one, in which a dry wind blowing from the desert in the east scalded their faces like fumes from a furnace. But because of Nogah's eagerness to proceed to her destination, she was not deterred by the sweat that poured down her face and her body.

Resting in the heat of the day in the shade of trees at the side of the road, they put up in small towns for the two nights they spent on their way. In each of them the elders at the towns' gates directed them to the houses of hospitable people who offered them food and shelter for the night in exchange for only a few pieces of silver.

On the third day, they reached the town of Bethel, in the hill country of Efraim. There, Nogah found a scribe and purchased a small scroll and two large ones from him. She used the small one to write to Uriel, advising him of her rift with Gilad and of trip. At the town gates she found a messenger who was about to travel to the north with another missive, hence he did not demand an exorbitantly high price for his willingness to deliver hers. The large scrolls she took with her to the palm tree of Deborah.

Only after she had left Bethel, and the bearer of her letter had long been on his way, did Nogah recall that she had failed to enjoin him not to reveal where he had come from. At first this troubled her; then she realized that it need not do so. Even if Barak was still wishful to learn her whereabouts, which was unlikely, the fact that the message had come from Bethel would merely throw sand in his eyes. For by the time the messenger reached his home, she would long have departed from this town, without leaving any traces behind.

Chapter Eight

When the guard told Barak that he had come to impart some knowledge pertaining to a messenger for Uriel, he was overjoyed. But his jubilance was short-lived, for the envoy claimed to have traveled all the way from Bethel, yet Barak could not believe this to be true. Nogah's mother could not have married a man who lived that far away, for where would she have met him? What, then, would Nogah be doing there?

Most likely, the messenger had merely spun a yarn at her behest, to deflect him from her real trail. He should have questioned him himself, but by the time he heard of this, the messenger had departed from the town gates, where Barak went to look for him, and no one knew where he had gone.

Barak wondered whether Nogah might be living elsewhere and had only been visiting Bethel, and while there had written to Uriel to advise him of her trip. But whom could she have been visiting? If she had been a visitor to the remote town, going there to search for her would be as futile as cutting water with a knife. By the time he arrived, she would have left. And apart from the unknown people she had visited, nobody would have been aware of her presence.

In his despair, Barak turned to Uriel again. Sitting opposite him, across the large table, he begged him humbly to reveal Nogah's dwelling place. He reminded him that he had divorced Asherah, and promised to take Nogah to be his only wife, that he would never take another.

It was like talking to a piece of wood. Unmoved by pity, Uriel retorted that even if Barak took no other wife, there would still be the women he would take to his bed. Barak humbled himself even further before the old man, and solemnly swore that as the Lord lives, so would he be faithful to Nogah all his days on this earth.

But Uriel placed no dependence on Barak's oath. His master ranted, snarled, and cajoled him in turn, but Uriel was as stubborn as a mule.

Barak began to be wary, and asked if Nogah had found a new man for herself. When Uriel remained silent, he thought he had the answer to his question, and for the first time since he had become a man, he was utterly miserable.

Yet he nurtured the hope that even if Nogah had found someone, she would not let herself be sullied by him immediately. He was determined to find her before it happened. Then he would snatch her from the clutches of that man and carry her back home with him. Although he himself had despoiled more virgins than he could remember, he wanted Nogah for himself alone. The thought that another man might have penetrated the garden that was only his to enter, and that she might have found pleasure in this, was unbearable, too painful to contemplate.

Even so, he knew that if she had been defiled, he must blame himself. She had loved him with fierce devotion. But he had cast her aside in favor of the shallow-hearted Canaanite. He had been as blind as had been the third father of his people, Jacob, who'd had Leah instead of Rachel thrust at him under the veil of darkness, and had been unaware of it until the next morning, when it was too late.

He was a man and a warrior, not a child who cries when he stumbles to the ground and is hurt. But after nine days of such futile reflections had worn him down, he wished that he had a mother to hold him in her arms, in whose embrace he would have been able to shed the tears that he felt sitting heavily behind his eyes.

These reflections recalled Deborah to his mind. He remembered the first moment after he had met her, when he had regarded her as one in whose presence he would be safe, and with whose wind in his sails he would be capable of sailing forth to defeat his enemies. Perhaps if he saw her now his filial feelings would be revived, and he would be able to sob in her arms and his misery would be eased.

Besides, Deborah judged the people at a spot not far removed from
Bethel. If Nogah had indeed visited that town, she might have proceeded
to see Deborah. Many people came to her to pour out their troubles and
consult her. Perhaps Nogah was of their numbers. Possibly, while there,
she had told Deborah where she lived. It was unlikely, but he had no other
lead and he could not afford to ignore the fragment of hope it offered. So he
decided to pay Deborah the visit he had promised her a while ago.

He made some hasty preparations for his trip, and early the next morning he and his two men rode out of his house's gates.

By then, spring had given way to early summer. The rains had ceased,
and with them, the luscious green color of the meadows had disappeared
as well. The hills of Nafthali were shading over into a yellowish brown that
mirrored the dreariness in his soul. The sun was clinging to stones at the
side of the road, baking them, and his face as well. In this heat, and fraught
with impatience, Barak's way to the hills of Efraim seemed interminable.

When he finally approached his destination, he pondered how best to
elicit from Deborah the knowledge he was seeking. He remembered that
on Mount Tabor and during her visits to his house she had been anything
but motherly toward him. Hence she might resent it if he shed tears in her
arms because of his love for another woman. Out of jealousy, she might
even act with spite and withhold Nogah's dwelling place from him.

So he changed his mind about seeking comfort from her. Instead, he
resolved to keep from her the real purpose of his visit. He would merely
mention Nogah as if by chance, and refrain from raising suspicion in her
mind.

🦂

Nogah with her two escorts reached the palm tree of Deborah in the
heat of the day. She found the place teeming with life. A clerk approached,
registered their names, and demanded to know the nature of their request
of Deborah.

Nogah informed him that she had met Deborah already, and had traveled all the way from the domain of Nafthali to discuss with her a secret
matter of grave importance.

Deborah sat in the shade of her palm tree, listening to a woman's complaint against a merchant, who, she claimed, had delivered to her faulty merchandise, while that same trader periodically interrupted her words with noisy denials.

When the clerk notified Deborah of Nogah's arrival, hope soared within her that Barak's maid had come to her on an errand from her master. So she asked the people who sat before her to wait, and ran some way down the hill to meet her.

After Nogah revealed that she had left Barak's house about a month ago, Deborah was sorely disappointed. But seeing the girl's drawn face, she understood that there was something very wrong with her. Out of pity she embraced her warmly. Then she waited to hear what she had to say.

Nogah explained her aim, which Deborah deemed strange, for she had never heard of anything like it before. But she had no wish to hurt the young woman, who seemed to be sorely injured already. Hence she asked her to wait until she had finished dealing with all the other people, then she would talk to her.

She gave orders for goat milk and dates to be served to her and her guards. Then Nogah was led to Deborah's tent, while her escorts were accommodated in another tent. Nogah was too weary from her trip to notice the colorful tapestries with which Deborah's tent was hung, or the soft rugs covering its floor. What she saw was a low couch in a corner, made up of invitingly soft sheepskin blankets and goat hair cushions. She flopped down on it and immediately sank into a deep sleep.

In this state Deborah found her when she came in that evening. She woke up her guest gently, handing her date nectar to drink, then bade her recount what had happened since she had last seen her in Barak's home.

The girl told her that she had gone to live with her mother, in order to shape a new life for herself. But when Deborah inquired whether she had succeeded in doing so, Nogah's gloomy silence supplied her with the answer to her question.

Barak's erstwhile maid then gave Deborah a detailed account of the scroll she had rewritten, and of her intent to add Deborah's tale to it and then bring the whole to the house of the Lord in Shiloh, to be deposited among the other books that were kept there.

Deborah was dubious of the feasibility of this goal. A record of the war truly ought to be written and deposited in the temple for the benefit of the generations to come, but she doubted that Nogah was the right person to accomplish this. She probably had the events hopelessly mangled, and it would have been preferable if she had not taken on a task that was too cumbersome for her to shoulder. Besides, why would the priests in the temple believe that what she had written was a true account of the events?

Since she wanted to spare Nogah any further disappointment, she warned her, "You must know, Nogah, that not everyone who comes to the temple with whatever he has written can have it deposited there. Most probably, your scroll will be rejected and your entire effort will have been in vain."

Nogah was downcast by Deborah's words, but after she mulled them over for a while, she said, "I still want to try. If you permit me to add your tale to that of Barak, and if you testify to the truth of what I have written, perhaps the Lord may pave my way with success."

Although Deborah did not place much dependence on this, she felt for the girl and did not want to discourage her more than she had done already. So she sat with her during the evening meal, and for a long time afterward, and relayed all she knew about the war—leaving out only the tale of the rewards that Barak had demanded and obtained from her for his prowess in the battlefield. She also gave Nogah the Song of Deborah, which she herself had written in commemoration of the victory, for Nogah to copy onto her scroll.

Later, Deborah continued to question Nogah about her new life. It did not take her long to discover that the young man who had helped her with her writing had been more than merely a scribe to her. Neither was it difficult to find out that her relationship with him had faltered because of her continued love for Barak. Nogah willingly told Deborah all about herself.

Only when Deborah questioned her about the location of her mother's home did she become reticent. She closed up as a flower closes its petals at night, and fell silent. Deborah could not understand the reason for this secrecy, but she had no wish to press the girl.

The traveler spent the night in Deborah's tent, and after she rose up, she worked all that Deborah had told her into her scroll. Then she begged Deborah to cast her eyes over the result of her efforts, and the judge, who had read many scrolls in her time, was pleasantly surprised by its veracity and eloquence. So she wrote a note to the priests in Shiloh testifying that all that was written down was the truth, pressed her own seal upon it, and gave it to Nogah. Nogah spent the following day in Deborah's tent making a copy of the whole, as a keepsake.

By the time she had finished this task, the sun had slid behind the mountains in the west, and it was too late for her to travel on that day. But in the morning she thanked her hostess for her kindness and, with her guards, set out for Shiloh.

Unaware that Barak had sent away his wife, Deborah was left with the sad reflection that despite the many differences between them, she and Nogah had something in common. They loved the same man, who had used them both for his own pleasure. And he had rejected them each in turn by bestowing his own love on another woman, whose proper measure he had failed to take, who was clearly unworthy of it.

Chapter Nine

Thirteen days after Nogah's arrival, Barak ascended Deborah's hill. By then she had thought that in all likelihood he had decided to renege on his promise to visit her. So when she saw him and his men dismount their horses, her heart thumped in her chest like a drum.

She was reluctant, though, to show her buoyancy. She rose from her elaborate judge's chair slowly and, in measured steps befitting her position, came forward to meet him. As she walked, her curls and her blue judge's robe were blown by the wind, and Barak, as always, was struck by the magnificence of her looks and her bearing.

He bowed briefly and presented his guards. Deborah explained that she would not be able to extend her hospitality to him herself now. She led him to her tent, leaving her people to take care of his guards, and asked for refreshments to be brought to them all. Then she resumed her work, but her thoughts were elsewhere—in anticipation of the night, perhaps several nights, of happiness that now awaited her.

The visitor was impatient to attain his goal, but he knew that it would take a while before he could broach the matter that had sent him all the way from the domain of Nafthali to that of Efraim. So after he had refreshed himself, he stretched his body out on the soft blankets that served as her couch and, as Nogah had done before him, fell asleep.

By the time Deborah finally came in, the moon had replaced the sun in the sky. They ate their evening meal in front of her tent, while Barak agonized over when it would be right for him to bring up Nogah. Afraid of spoiling all by doing so prematurely, he resolved to postpone his inquiry until after the meal. When that was completed, Deborah stepped inside the tent, and he followed her and helped her to lower the flaps at its entrance.

Then she sat down on her couch and dragged him down by his hand to sit opposite her. "My lover," she queried, "did you come here from distant parts because you've missed me the way I've pined for you?" She looked at him in the dim moonlight that penetrated the cracks in the tent's curtains, awaiting his response, which was slow to come.

In truth, although he was glad to see her, he had not missed her at all. He was not going to blurt this out. But he did not want to lie to her, either—if only because he knew her to be too shrewd in her dealings with people to be taken in. She would see through flattery as one sees through clear water.

While he cast about in his mind for the proper response, Deborah perceived the guilt fleetingly evident in his face and the worry so clearly etched out on it. She laughed. "You did well in not lying to me. And now, tell me what is truly weighing on your heart." With these words, she drew him to her and placed his head on her shoulder. Then she gently stroked his unkempt hair, which had not known a comb for many a day.

Despite his earlier determination to desist, Barak could not hold back the rush of his feelings. He broke into the guttural sobs that had been locked in his chest for so long. Deborah leaned over him and kissed his hair, while her curls tickled the nape of his neck until he had calmed down sufficiently to be able to speak.

"My adored Deborah, I have destroyed my life with my own hands. I've married the woman I thought I loved, instead of the woman I truly love. And she left me. And when she made off, she tore my heart from my chest. And she would not tell me where she had gone to live. I have no notion of where she is, and I cannot find her. Please help me." He broke into renewed sobs.

So far Deborah had believed him to love the unworthy Asherah, and she had hoped that one day he would sober up and recognize her for what she truly was. But now that she knew him to have bestowed his love on Nogah, who was eminently suitable for him, her jealousy flared up and for a moment it burned like fire in a dry forest.

It took time for Barak's tears to cease, but in the end they did because, as he realized, he had not yet given her an opportunity to respond to his plea for aid, and he still harbored some hope that she would not deny it.

When he calmed down, so, to some extent, did Deborah's resentment, which gave way to the sadness of resignation. At this moment Barak ceased to be her lover, and she knew with the certainty with which autumn follows summer that she had outgrown her desire for him and that they would never lie with each other again.

Reluctantly responding to his renewed need for motherly comfort from her, such as that he had harbored on their first meeting, she bent her head and murmured soft words into his ear, as she used to do with her children when they were little and had bruised themselves and sought comfort in her arms.

Barak waited in trepidation for a more substantial response, but when it came, it was discouraging. "My cherished boy, I would like to help you," she said at last, "but she has not told me her dwelling place either."

Yet her words still held out a glimmer of light. "So she did come to see you."

"Yes, but her visit concerned a matter that you would find unworthy of your notice."

"Tell me."

Deborah sighed wistfully. "I will. But first I want you to know that she still loves you very much. This at least should be of consolation to you."

"I was made to understand that she had found a new man."

"I cannot gossip about her, for it is forbidden by Torah law. I can only repeat that she loves you."

"Is there nothing you can tell me, nothing at all, that may give me a clue to where she is hiding herself?"

"I only know that after she left here she went to Shiloh."

"Shiloh?" Barak repeated blankly. "What could she want there?"

"She went to the temple."

"You are fooling me."

"It is the truth. I'm tired now, but I will tell you the whole tomorrow."

Barak sat up with a start. "Tell me now. I want to leave for Shiloh before the sky begins to pale."

"It can hardly do you any good to go there. Her visit here ended ten days ago, and she must have departed the town by now."

Her words were like a cold shower of rain on his face. Still, there was too much at stake to give up. "I still want to see what I can discover there."

So, with a voice as heavy as her heart, Deborah told him all that she knew, which was more than he had feared, but less than he had hoped for.

By the time her tale came to an end, Barak had realized that in crying in her arms for love of another woman, he had inflicted undeserved pain on Deborah. But the damage had been done and could not be rectified. All that was left for him to do was beg for understanding. "Deborah, my tears before burst out from the depth of my despair. I plead with you, pray, forgive me."

With a smile that barely concealed the sorrow in her fine black eyes, she replied, "Your heart is ever your own. There is nothing to forgive."

"My adoration for you has remained undiminished from the moment I set eyes on you, and so it will remain all the days of my life."

These last words drew another melancholy smile from Deborah, before, in the tiredness from her day's work, she slid down on her couch and began drifting into sleep.

Thus was Barak left on his own to contemplate his next steps. He decided not to delay, and to go on his way while Deborah would still be asleep.

But she arose at almost the same moment he did. They looked at each other wordlessly, and she sensed that he yearned for her to bestow her blessing on his union with Nogah. She nodded to indicate her understanding, and he bent his head before her. Setting aside her own hurt, reluctantly at first, but with an increasingly assured voice as she proceeded, she pronounced these words:

May the Lord make the woman you love come
to your home, and may she be like Rachel and
Leah, and may you build your house in Israel
together.

Beforehand, Barak had feared that his prospects of finding Nogah would be as slim as the last sliver of the moon at the end of the month. But

Deborah's blessing bolstered up his hope that Nogah would indeed come to his home, and he left her with gratitude in his eyes.

He shook his guards into wakefulness, and they swung themselves into their saddles and rode out to the town that housed the temple.

🜨

Barak and his men reached the house of the Lord as the day declined. The shadows had lengthened, and the few clouds floating in the sky had assumed the grayish pink color they usually wore at sunset. He had been there several times before during the festivals, when he, together with the masses of Israel, came on pilgrimage to offer sacrifices to the Lord. But on those occasions he had always known precisely what was required of him. This time, he felt that he was fumbling at the edge of the unknown. He instructed his men to sit down and wait for him while he approached the temple.

It consisted mainly of the Tent of Meeting, which the children of Israel had constructed during their journey in the desert after their exodus from Egypt. Although it was gradually being turned into a large stone building, its ceiling still consisted of only a huge sheet of goat leather. But around it a thick wall had been constructed.

The altar on which the sacrifices were offered stood outside, to the right of the entrance. Thus there had never been any need for him to enter the sanctuary itself, and now he did not know which way to turn.

A young priest stationed at the doorpost inquired as to his request. When Barak announced that he wished to speak to the temple's head scribe, the priest explained that the scroll room was shut down for the night and all the scribes had left for their own quarters. He counseled him to find a place to put up for the night and come back in the morning.

Barak was too impatient to heed the priest's advice. He announced that he was Barak, the son of Abinoam, and that his mission was of the utmost urgency.

The young priest had heard of Barak's feats in the battlefield. When he learned the visitor's name, he retreated a few steps and regarded him in awe. He bowed and invited him to enter the sanctuary while he went in search of the head scribe. Then he hurried away.

Barak entered. He saw the Ark of the Covenant, which was placed on a raised platform against the inner wall with a heavily embroidered curtain separating it, the holiest of holies, from the holy, the rest of the sanctuary. On its left stood a table with two large loaves of bread on it, and on its right stood the big, seven-pronged golden menorah that was always lit in the evening. A large incense burner spread the pleasing odor of holy incense through the entire sanctuary.

In this consecrated place, Barak felt closer to the Eternal One than he ever had before. Walking quietly, he approached the Ark and bowed down until his head touched the ground, and poured out his heart before the Lord:

> *God of hosts. I beg for your merciful help in*
> *finding the woman I love, so that I may build*
> *my house in Israel and fulfill the commandment*
> *to be fruitful and multiply, and beget sons and*
> *daughters together with her, and raise them in*
> *the ways of the Torah.*

When the priest returned, he found Barak prostrated before the Ark, engrossed in prayer. He waited in respectful silence. As soon as Barak rose to his feet, the priest motioned him to follow. They both backed out, so as not to turn their backs on the Ark, then stepped through a back door into a courtyard. They traversed it and reached the scribes' living quarters. The priest led him to one of its rooms, opened the door, bowed, and withdrew.

Barak found himself in a gradually darkening room lit by only a few oil lamps on a table and in recesses in the walls. Next to this table stood an old scribe, whose face was as round as a chariot wheel, and whose head covering could not conceal his shining baldness. His posture was stooped, and upon Barak's entrance it bent even lower as he bowed and invited his guest to be seated. He offered him some cool water to drink, and inquired about the nature of Barak's visit at this late time of the day.

The visitor was well aware how strange his appearance must seem, but he cared little for that. He merely wished to couch his request in terms that would convince the head scribe to accede to it. Speaking in as solemn a voice as he could muster, he said that he had been apprised of a record of his own battles with the Canaanites that had been brought here a few days ago. He asked that it be shown to him, so that he might examine its accuracy.

If the scribe wondered why this inquiry could not have been postponed until the morning, he stood too much in awe of Barak to say so. Instead, he hurried to the scroll room to fetch the book. Soon he returned with the scroll, which Barak noted had been written with a delicate touch, obviously Nogah's.

Barak took the document from the scribe's hand as if it were rich loot from the enemy's camp. He pretended to peruse it, but in truth merely skimmed it, rolling and unrolling it at the greatest possible speed, until he reached its end, where he found these words:

This document is based on the account of Barak, the son of Abinoam, from the town of Kedesh in the domain of Nafthali, and on that of Deborah, the erstwhile wife of Lapidoth, who judges the people in the mountains of Efraim.

It has been written by Nogah, the daughter of Reumah, the wife of Yair, from the town of Hamon in the domain of Nafthali, who hereby testifies to its truth.

When Barak read those last lines, he could hardly contain himself. He felt a strong urge to kiss the book, and the old scribe who had fetched it for him, and the young priest who had admitted him, and the ground in front of the Ark of the Covenant as well. But he concealed his excitement as best he could and asked the old man how he had come into possession of the scroll.

The scribe recounted that a young woman he had never heard of before had brought it, and petitioned him to place it in the temple. He had been skeptical about its content, until he saw Deborah's testimony attached to it, and then he began to treat the young woman with greater respect. After he read the scroll and perceived that it was fairly well written, his esteem increased even further.

Yet he'd had to explain to the girl that it was not for him to decide whether her tale would be deposited at the temple. The Great Council of Elders, composed of seventy old men from all the tribes of Israel, who convened at the temple twice a year, would have to pronounce on this. He promised her that he would have the book copied nine times over, to make it possible for ten elders at a time to read it, before they made their decision.

The girl seemed to be satisfied with this response and prepared to leave. But he detained her, and instructed her to register her own name and dwelling place, in case the elders wished to send for her in order to confirm her written testimony. At first she was reluctant to do so. But when he told her that he would not else submit what she had written to the council, she complied.

After the young woman had departed, though, the scribe had second thoughts about her tale. He deemed it strange that although she had brought Deborah's sealed testimony as to its veracity, she had not attached Barak's. He harbored severe doubts and was no longer sure whether he should show it to the elders. He had planned to consult some of the other scribes about this, but in the following days he had been busy and the matter had slipped his mind. He was glad that Barak himself had come, and hoped that he would now enlighten him as to the truth (or otherwise) of what the young woman had written down.

Barak did not wish to show the scribe how little he valued the scroll, and how impatient he was to leave for Hamon in pursuit of Nogah. Besides, she was evidently eager to have her labor bear fruit, and he did not want her to have done it all in vain. So he told the scribe that he would like to sit for a while and read the account of the war more thoroughly before he expressed his opinion.

The old scribe suggested that he wait until the morning, when he would be able to do so more properly in the light of the day. But this suggestion placed too great a strain on Barak's patience. He retorted that he was in a great hurry, as there were pressing matters requiring his attention, and he would have to depart right away.

So the scribe offered him another drink and let him perform his task while he sipped from his cup. Barak did so as speedily as he could, and introduced two corrections on the sequence of the battle on Mount Tabor into Nogah's words. Then he wrote down his own testimony as to their being faithful to the events as they had occurred, and pressed his seal onto it.

The scribe assured him that the scroll would now receive an entirely different treatment from him. And there was no doubt in his mind that the Great Council of Elders would accept it. It would be copied hundreds of times and be sent to scroll rooms all over the land, and become part of the heritage of the people of Israel for all the generations to come.

Barak thanked the old man with as much pomp as he could infuse into his voice, and took hasty leave of him. On his way out, he once more passed through the sanctuary. Again, he prostrated himself before the Ark of the Covenant, this time in order to bless the Lord for his mercy.

He stepped out into the square, where his men sat waiting for him. He announced that they would set out immediately and would be riding throughout the night. But the men demurred, as not only they, but their horses, too, were weary, and needed food and a night's rest.

Though impatient, Barak recognized the justice of their claim. So they found an appropriate spot in which to pitch their tent. They unpacked their provisions and spent the night there. Barak hardly slept. He woke his men before the rise of the sun, and they rode out of Shiloh as speedily as the children of Israel had fled from Egypt, as if Pharaoh and his entire army were chasing after them.

Chapter Ten

Upon her return to Hamon, Nogah found that her life was even drearier than it had been before. She was pleased with the outcome of her mission: Her scroll had not yet been deposited at the Temple, but she had little doubt that it would be. This did not make her life easier, though, but had the opposite effect. While she had been busy writing, her life had had some purpose. Now there was nothing left but to ponder the years that stretched out before her, shrouded in endless gloom.

Although she shared in her mother's happiness, she realized that her own desolation detracted from it. She was not eager to see the look of compassion mingled with exasperation in her mother's eyes whenever they rested on her. She decided to relieve her as far as possible of her presence. Early each morning she headed off to walk on the nearby hills, remaining there until nightfall.

She left word that if Gilad were to call, her mother was to tell him that she was unable to see him, or anyone. So after he had come to look for her twice, the young scribe gave up and left her alone.

In the evenings, she sought the solitude of her room's window, her ears open to the stillness of the night, her eyes on the dark void in front of them. Her tears had dried, but the ache of Barak's absence had moved into her chest. She found a perverse satisfaction in the almost tangible feeling of her body wilting like a flower that had been torn from the soil that nourished it.

As the nights crept by and weaved together, and no flicker of light blinked into them, it became more and more difficult for her to sleep. One

morning, a week after her return, she decided that she could no longer en-
dure her life. She rose up when the dawn had barely filtered through her
window and the stars had not yet been swallowed up in the morning light.
She washed her body and clad herself in her blue dress from Hazor, which
she still favored. She stepped silently into the cooking room, where she ate
some bread left over from last night, washed down by water.

Then she packed a few belongings into a cloth bag. Long before her
mother emerged from her room, she stepped out of her own. Since it was
her habit to walk on the hills each day, she knew that her mother would not
be worried about her for a while. Later on, she would send word apprising
her of what she intended to do.

As she set out, she looked briefly at the house she was leaving, still
wrapped in the cobwebs of sleep; then she turned her back to it. She slung
her bag over her shoulder and, distractedly kicking little pebbles out of her
path, began walking.

The ground underfoot was moist with the dew of the night. Although
the beginning of the summer was upon them, the early morning air was
still chilly. The breeze was brisk upon her skin, wafting the fresh scent of
the piles of cut hay dotting the meadows, and she gained some comfort
from it. The cheerful twittering of the birds and the flutter of their wings
seemed to float down from the treetops, with the sole purpose of imbuing
her with hope.

Yet the succor she gained from them was short-lived. It was easy for
the birds to chirp merrily, she thought. When they flew high up into the
air, they had their nests to return to. Even donkeys had stables waiting for
them after the toil of the day. But she could only wander with bitterness in
her soul, and nowhere to come back to and rest her head.

By the time she approached her destination the cool of the morning had
given way to the heat of the day. Her dress was heavy with sweat, and her
heart was heavy with what lay ahead.

🦊

Having no knowledge of this, Barak had little doubt of his ability to lay
his hands on Nogah. On the way from Shiloh, he spun plans of what would
happen once he had done so.

He recalled that few words had passed between them in between their lovemaking, and that he knew little about her. She had given him only a few scraps of knowledge about her life in Hazor, and he had no idea of who her father had been. Her mother had clearly been a captive slave there for many years. Hence, as there were no Israelite men there, Nogah's father must have been some Canaanite in that castle, most likely one of the guards. But Nogah had told him that it was painful for her to speak of him because he was dead, so apparently she had loved him. If so, he could not have been one of those whom Barak knew to have been uncouth and cruel.

Whoever her father had been, Barak would not be able to approach him and seek permission to take his daughter for his wife, nor would he be able to pay him a bride price for her. He would approach her mother instead, and gain her consent to marry Nogah, and pay what he owed, to her.

He hoped that the mother would be glad to see her daughter become so wealthy and the mistress of an imposing mansion. And that she would not be averse to receiving the heavy bag of gold he would offer her. If, like Uriel, she worried about the prospect of his being unfaithful to Nogah, he would convince her that he had put his wicked ways behind him. Still, he was impatient to have this obstacle removed from his way.

Barak arrived at the outskirts of Hamon in the late afternoon, and there he met a group of young girls on their way to draw water from a nearby well. They directed him to the house he was looking for, and he arrived there just when the town's men were making their way home from the fields.

Upon entering the front yard, Barak beheld a woman who reminded him of Nogah except in her nose, which was longer, and in her hair and eyes, which were dark. To his surprise, he noted that she was in the early months of pregnancy. She was playing with a group of children, but when she observed his approach, she called upon a maid to take charge of them and came forward to meet him.

He dismounted his horse, bowed to her, and announced, "I am Barak, the son of Abinoam. And you must be Nogah's mother."

Reumah's reception was frosty. "I know well who you are, and I also know who I am. What I do *not* know is why you came here."

"I came to solicit your permission to marry Nogah."

Yair entered the yard and stood next to his wife and said, "I am Yair, Reumah's husband, and I welcome you to our house. Please recline with your men under the tree, so that we may serve you refreshments."

"Be blessed, Yair, for your kindness. What I need right now, though, is not food or drink, but your wife's acceding to my request to take her daughter for my wife."

Reumah wished to make short shrift of it and spoke to him in a determined voice. "Barak, the son of Abinoam, I am well aware that you have raised me from the dust, to dwell among the most generous of my people. I will remain eternally thankful to you for this. Yet I will not allow you to marry my daughter. You already have a wife, and it would not be good for her."

"I shun gratitude and require none from you," Barak said. "I ask to wed your daughter for the sake of her own happiness, for she loves me no less than I love her. As for my first wife, Asherah, you may rest assured. I have given her a book of divorcement and sent her back to her land. I will take Nogah for my only wife. I will never take another."

"It makes little difference. There are still the maids you exploit. Nogah is not the sort of woman who would accept this in silent submission."

Paying no heed to Reumah's words, Barak asked, "Where is Nogah?"

"Leave her alone. She wants to build her house in Israel."

"She will have to build it with me."

"If she became your wife, your coming to the maids would cast her into an agony of hell."

Barak grew impatient. "You know nothing of the matter. From now on I will no longer—"

"I know more than you think," she interrupted him. "Having been a slave in King Jabin's castle for years, I saw what went on there. He lay with any female slave he lusted for; none could refuse him. And you do the same."

Barak stopped still, an arrested look in his eyes, as he queried, "Did he lie with you as well?"

"Who put you in charge over me, that you ask me this question?" Reumah protested, flushing to a deep color in embarrassment.

"So this is how it was," Barak exclaimed triumphantly. "It was stupid of me not to have realized as soon as I laid eyes on her that she was the king's daughter."

Reumah disregarded his words. "Now that you have defeated him, you think that you are an exalted king yourself and that you may do what he was used to do."

"I am not a king, nor do I have any wish to become one. And neither do I keep slaves. From now on, I will no longer approach the maids, or any other women, and I will make Nogah happy. Where is she?" he asked impatiently, "I want to speak to her."

The woman remained steadfast. "I don't believe you. Draw back your hands from her."

Yair intervened mildly. "Reumah, my love, do not determine her life without consulting her. Let us call the girl and ask her."

"Even if I want to I cannot, for I have no notion of where she is. She left the house in the morning before I rose up, and she left no word about where she has gone."

Barak, who had been smiling approvingly at Yair's words, felt the smile fade from his face. "When she comes back, tell her that I have been looking for her. Tell her that I want her to come to me, or else I will return to fetch her."

"She may not come back at all. When I went to her room, I saw that she had taken some of her belongings with her. By now I am in a worry about her myself."

"Nogah will send you word to tell you where she has gone. And I will come and ask you."

"I will not tell you without her consent."

"Then I will come again and again and again, until I find her at home, or until you tell me where she is. Then I will bear her off with me and make her my wife."

He was about to leave, but thought better of it and said, "And I will pay you an enormous bride price for her. You deserve it, for having brought up such an outstanding daughter under such harrowing conditions." After a brief silence, he added, "If this is good in your eyes, we will hold a huge wedding celebration, and you and Yair will be the most honored of all the guests there."

With these words he bowed, and he and his men mounted their horses.

🦌

Barak had manifested much self-assurance in his words. But Deborah's blessing having receded from his memory, he was far from feeling it in his heart. Reumah was determined to shield Nogah from his supposed wiles, as fiercely protective of her as an eagle hovering over its only chick. Even though he had located her home, it would not be easy to find Nogah herself, or to convince Reumah to reveal her whereabouts to him.

His previous elation was swallowed up by dejection as he realized that, once again, Nogah had slipped out of his grasp.

Part Five

Deborah's Unsought Glory

Chapter One

By the time Barak reached his home, he was thoroughly exhausted. He yearned for nothing but his bed. Before he went to lay his head on his pillow, though, he decided to visit Uriel and ask whether he had any inkling of where Nogah had fled this time.

It was unnecessary.

As soon as Barak crossed the scroll room's threshold he halted abruptly, dumbfounded at the sight of Nogah sitting there, clasping the hand of the old man, who was dozing at her side. Deborah's blessing had been realized: The woman he loved had come to his house.

When Nogah saw him, her face lit up. She sprang to her feet and bowed to him. Uriel woke up with a start and slipped noiselessly through the back door.

Barak stared at Nogah and felt his heart leap inside him. Vast relief flooded through him. But he resolved not to show his exultation yet. First, he wanted to mete out to her a small portion of the punishment she deserved for driving him to near despair. For forcing him to traverse a large part of the land in search of her before she came back to him, as she should have done long ago. Wearing a severe look in his eyes, he spoke to her sternly. "What are you doing in this house, Nogah?"

Gazing at the ground, she answered in a subdued voice, "I came to ask you, sir, if you would be willing to take me back as your maid."

His weariness vanished like the dryness of the summer at the advent of the first rain. Nogah's submissiveness aroused him, but he decided not to let her notice his excitement and declared, "Most certainly not."

In a dejected whisper, her voice barely audible, she said, "When I left, you promised that there would always be a place for me in your household."

"I've changed my mind," he said. "I've hired a new maid in your stead and now I have as many as I need."

These words made Nogah wince and her ears ring, as she saw the little that was left of her life collapse. She dipped her head, her hunched posture proclaiming her consternation.

Though she had followed the voice of her heart by returning to Barak's house, she had been plagued with worry on her way there. She would be humiliating herself before him, who would now be her master again. But since her existence without him had been even more miserable than her previous life as his maid, this was something for which she had braced herself ahead of time. She had believed herself to be inured to further smug looks from her sister's eyes as well.

What had tormented her was the fear of what he would do when he found out about Gilad. Despite his own ventures with women, he would tolerate no disloyalty on her part. He might well debase her even further by summarily rejecting her, even in her menial position as his maid. Hence she had weighed the possibility of keeping silent about her encounter with the young scribe. If he were to ask her outright whether another man had come to her, she would not lie to him. But she had vacillated on whether to offer the tale of her own accord.

As it transpired, all her hedging had been superfluous: He did not want her back in any case. This was mortification so deep that she could not find the strength to grapple with it. To conceal her despondency, Nogah averted her face from Barak. She flung her hand out in front of her as if to steady herself, and lurched forward to the door.

Barak let her proceed until she reached it. Then, with a few long strides, he closed the distance between them. He encircled her waist from behind and murmured into her ear: "I will not take you back as my maid, but only as my wife."

For a brief instant Nogah's heart bubbled over with delight. Then she remembered her resolution not to become his second wife. When he whirled her around in his arms to make her face him, she said glumly, "You already have a wife."

"No more."

Nogah was bewildered. "How is that?"

"I have sent her away. Did Uriel not write you or tell you now?"

"No. He is unwell and was dozing all day. Why did you banish her?"

"I'll tell you later; the main thing is that she is no longer here. Even more important: While you were away, I realized something of which I was not conscious before."

"What is this?"

"That you are like your name, Nogah: a light. My light. I was stupidly oblivious of it at first. But it shines from deep inside you and has penetrated deep within me. When you left, it went out of my life. Now it is shining on me again. Do you know where I've been just now?"

"No."

"At your mother's home to search for you. Are you aware of where I was before that?"

"No."

"In Shiloh, to look for you there. And has it come to your ears where I was before that?"

She shook her head.

"I went to see Deborah, to enlist her help."

"Was it worth your while to go to all those faraway places for my sake?"

"I would have gone to the four corners of the earth to find you, if only I knew where they were."

To her amazement, Nogah saw tears of joy in his eyes. She clung to him and shed tears of her own in his embrace, and they wet each other's cheeks.

Barak then lifted her up in his arms and cradled her there, while she wrapped hers around his neck. Kissing her savagely as he walked, he bore her outside and up the stairway. Thus the maids were privy to another astonishing spectacle: their master carrying one who had previously been of their number, but was about to become their next mistress. As they watched him take Nogah to his room, they could only hope that she would be kind and not punish those among them who had shared her husband's bed.

After Barak laid Nogah on his bed, he removed her dress impatiently, and it was not long before he was deep inside her. Yet they were too eager for each other to prolong their enjoyment, and their pleasure erupted too soon.

Barak then recalled to his mind something that had previously faded from it, which, he hoped, might stave off her disappointment. So he said, "Nogah, my beloved, I will teach you something that I myself learned not long ago."

"What is it?"

"You'll see."

When they came together the second time, he proceeded slowly, lighting a fire inside her before he penetrated her. Once Nogah had called out her love for him, Barak delayed until this was repeated twice. Only then did he follow her into delight.

When he perceived her exuberance, he promised himself that she would enjoy this feat of his every single night of their lives.

Afterward, Nogah's face resting snugly against Barak's neck, she murmured into his ear, "After I left you, I withered like a vine in a drought. Your love has revived me, and now I am like a vine on the bank of a brook, bursting into bloom."

"I will love you always, and you will blossom all the days of our lives."

"Where did you learn your new feat?"

"Do you truly want to know?"

"Would I have asked if I did not?"

"Deborah was my teacher."

Nogah reeled from his words. "She is very resourceful, and not merely as a judge. When did she impart this beneficial lesson on you? On the occasion of your last visit with her? While you were looking for me?"

"No. By that time I no longer lusted for her. It was on the occasion of her last visit here."

After speaking these words, Barak fell silent, watching to ascertain how they had affected her. She thought that since he had just mentioned his deed with another woman to her, this was the right moment to reveal to him her meeting of the flesh with another man. But she could not find the courage to do so; hence she remained silent.

Nogah's tribulations left no mark on her face, thus Barak had no inkling of them. Having satisfied himself that she was not unduly upset, he showed her his previously neglected proficiency again, after which they both fell into a heavy sleep of satiation.

The next morning the maids trod around their master's bedroom softly, leaving the couple inside it to sleep until the sun was high in the sky.

When she woke up, Nogah's misgivings overtook her again. The night before, in Barak's arms, she had been able to lay them aside. But now her worry was nagging at her with double its strength.

Barak went out into the fields because, as he explained, he had been away for too long already. The wheat harvest was nearing completion and he needed to make sure that all was proceeding as it should.

Nogah was left alone for the day, and it was a day of shivers periodically running down her spine. Now that Barak had declared his love for her, happiness beyond her wildest dreams lay within her reach. All this might be destroyed in the flicker of an eyelid if she revealed her misdeeds to him. Yet a dark secret clamped inside her would not bode well for their life together. She was wary of building her house on such a shaky foundation. She vacillated throughout the day.

She went to consult Uriel and was reassured when she perceived that he had recuperated from his illness. But his counsel did not make her recover from her own doubts. Stroking her hair fondly, he advised her to leave Barak altogether, immediately. Even though he had sent away her sister, she would always be doomed to suffer the hell of jealousy in his home.

Although Nogah had no intention of following Uriel's advice, it made her spirits flag. And when Barak entered his house, she still wavered over what she should or should not tell him about the young scribe.

W hen Barak entered his quarters, he found Nogah amid pitchers of water, waiting for him in his bathing room. They bathed together, their hands roving over each other's bodies. Even as she reveled in that pleasure, Nogah was not at peace with herself. The soothing warm water, which should have soaked away the stiffness of her shoulders, only heightened it.

Twice she hovered on the verge of spilling out her secret, and twice she choked back the words she was about to utter. She knew Barak to be impetuous, quick to flare up in anger, and he would not take kindly to this slight on his honor.

As he faced her in the bath, Barak recalled their discussion the night before. "I hope you don't hold it against me that before becoming aware of my love for you, I sought pleasure with other women. I assure you that it was all but a pale shadow of our acts."

It dawned upon Nogah that this was the last opportunity she would ever have to reveal her straying to him. If she did not do it now, she would not be able to do it later; for then Barak would condemn her not only for what she had done but also for the tardiness of her revelation.

Suddenly she found the strength within her to say shakily, "No, sir. For it is precisely what I sought with another man."

"What is it that you just said?" Barak shouted, his voice loud enough to awaken the birds sleeping in the nearby trees.

In his wrath, he lifted Nogah to her feet and shook her, as the water from her body splashed onto the floor. "I had surmised already that you had met another man. But I did not imagine that you would let him come to you so soon, while you loved me. I am more furious at you than I can put in words."

Nogah had expected recriminations, but that did not make it easier to bear them. Her face paled, her head spun, and sweat trickled down her brow. For a moment she was unable to speak.

"You have broken faith with me," he accused her, continuing his tirade.

In the certainty that right was on her side, Nogah now found her voice. "Was I to keep faith with you who were faithless?" she retorted indignantly. "Was I to nurse my loneliness while you goaded yourself in bath and bed with Deborah and Asherah, and most probably other women as well?"

"I gave that up even before I knew that I would ever find you. Neither did you have any right to whore," he persisted.

"This is unreasonable, sir," she said as calmly as she could. "I moved out of here in order to find happiness with another man. It was my purpose in leaving. I told you so, and you did not prevent my departure, as you could have done."

Barak wrapped Nogah up in a large towel, carried her to his bed, and none too gently shoved her onto it. He bore down on top of her and with a thunderous expression on his face continued to rave. "I was not aware then of how much I loved you!"

Almost suffocating under his weight, Nogah gasped, "And now that you are, can you not find it in your heart to forgive me?"

"Who is the man with whom you committed this abomination?"

Nogah eased herself from under him. "You have never heard of him, and his name would have no meaning for you," she replied in what she hoped was a soothing voice.

"But who is he? How did he cross your path? Don't dare to conceal anything from me."

"He is a young scribe, and I went to him to seek his help in rewriting your scroll."

"I'll go to Hamon and murder him."

Nogah's courage now returned. She even found the strength to smile at Barak's words. "He did nothing wrong. It was my fault. I let him come to me with a willing soul. If you feel the need to kill anyone, sir, it should be me."

"I love you too much. I'll stab him to death instead," Barak fumed.

His love imbued her with a confidence she had not felt in her dealing with him before. "You will not raise your hand to him, nor will you make even one of his hairs fall to the ground," she said adamantly. "He dealt honorably with me. He offered to make me his wife."

"For that alone he deserves to be put to death. He had no right to take you as his wife. Only I have that right."

"You are talking wildly, sir," she berated him. "Pray, forget him. I have done so already."

"You seem to have a decided preference for scribes. Perhaps I should become one myself." At first Nogah thought he was mocking her. But he spoke with a new humility she had never thought to hear in his voice.

She had no wish to humble him, so she said, "I have a decided preference for *you,* and I don't want you to be other than what you are."

Barak's next words were so soft, she could hardly make out what he said. "My darling, I don't want you to have been sullied by another man."

This response, milder than she had expected, and even more so his docile demeanor, endowed her with the temerity to say, "It's too late to tell me that now. I have done it already. Besides, I am glad that I did, because, like you, I learned something from it."

"I want you to learn things only from me."

"He taught me an important lesson that I could not have gained from you."

Barak's wrath flared up again and he was anything but pleased with this disrespectful response. Brusquely, he asked, "What was that?"

"That I cannot enjoy the act of love with anyone but you. So I will never, for as long as I live, be tempted to try again."

Barak was mollified and regained his good temper, and when next he spoke, his voice was neither humble nor overbearing. "I, on the other hand, may be tempted at times," he confessed. "But I will resist temptation because of my love for you. Because I don't want you to suffer as you have done before."

Nogah tasted relief at Barak's letting her off so lightly. As to the promise he had just made, she hoped that he would keep it, but she was not certain of it. She would have to devise ways of ensuring that he did.

🦂

Later on, when they lay in each other's arms, Barak reverted to the topic of her going astray. "I will not reprimand you again, Nogah, because it was my fault more than yours," he admitted. "But I want to know when it took place."

Nogah reassured him, "There is no cause for concern, sir. It happened only a few times, some weeks ago, and I have just had the way of women. I would not have returned to you unless I was sure that I was not carrying another man's seed in my womb."

Barak surprised her by saying, "I would have taken you for my wife even if you were, but I am glad that it is not so. I hope that we will soon put a halt to this way of women of yours, for nine months. And then again and again and again, until we have a house full of children."

"It will be a great happiness to me. But although you may not have noticed it, I am not your wife yet."

"I *have* noticed it. I have already sought your mother's permission to marry you. She has not granted it yet, but I have her husband's support. If you add your entreaties to mine, I am sure that we will gain it."

"When you saw her, you could not have known yet that I would consent to become your wife," she protested jokingly.

"It did not concern me very much," said Barak, looking gravely into her upturned face. "Having no doubts about your love for me, I would have taken you to be my wife with or without your consent."

Once again, Nogah's eyes sparkled with tears of happiness, and, quite incredibly, she saw them reflected in his.

Soon after, Barak gave Nogah a present. He found a jeweler who showed him a set of large shimmering sapphires, the deep blue of the Sea of Kinereth with the sunlight mirrored in it, which were the closest he could come to the color of her eyes. He commissioned the jeweler to craft a golden necklace studded with these stones. This he fastened around her neck, as he said before two witnesses, "You are betrothed to me forever."

It was not long before Nogah's mother resigned herself to the inevitable. After they had gained her reluctant permission, the preparations for the wedding began.

🦎

Barak and Nogah's wedding was the most lavish feast the tribe of Nafthali had ever witnessed. People from all parts of the land, invited and uninvited, came clad in the most colorful of garments they could procure. The crowd was flowing over, and those who found no place in the mansion's courtyard camped down outside the walls, and food and drink were brought out to them there.

Barak wanted the wedding to be memorable not only for its size but also for the manner of its celebration. After the ceremony, he had a rich fare ready for the guests' delectation. The tables were weighed down with birds baked in cumin, a rare spice from a faraway country; crisp green cucumbers; and little round cakes prepared from crushed carobs. They also boasted pink juicy melons dripping with the sweetness of honey, brought in from the south, which none of the guests, nor he himself, had ever tasted before. The guests pronounced them to be exceedingly pleasing to the palate, a veritable wonder. Choice wines, strong spirits, and sweet pomegranate nectars were poured out freely.

He also summoned a troupe of flute and lyre players and singers to entertain the guests, throngs of whom had stationed themselves on top of his mansion's wall, from which lofty position they gained a better view of the proceedings. But more awe inspiring than anything were the dancers. Accompanied by the beating of drums, they performed a dance in which some of them, dressed as Israelite warriors, leapt into the air and whirled about with drawn swords, while others, dressed as Canaanite charioteers, fell vanquished at their feet. Thus they playfully reenacted Barak's resounding victory over Sisra and the Canaanites in the Valley of Jezreel. Then a swell of singing rose into the air, followed by dancing that lasted far into the night.

Nogah, arrayed in a shining bridal dress the color of gold, trimmed with ribbons in all the colors of the rainbow, and adorned with Barak's sapphire necklace, was in raptures. Nogah's mother, with her husband and some other guests chosen by her, were seated at a special table, perched on a high place. She admitted that she had never witnessed anything to equal this feast.

Yet during the following days, when Nogah reflected on the wedding, she was troubled by the dancers' playful imitation of Barak's battle against the Canaanites. It had been enchantingly beautiful, and there was no reason why he should not revel in his victory, which had brought deliverance to the people of Israel, on this day of joy. But she would have preferred it had he instructed the dancers to choose another tale for their presentation.

𝔅

After the manner in which Asherah had dealt with her, Nogah felt no urge to have contact with her, or even to inquire what fate had befallen her after leaving Barak's house. Yet eight days after Nogah and Barak's wedding, an envoy bearing a letter from her arrived, and this was its content:

> *Hear me, Nogah. There has been much strife between us; but we are still sisters of the blood, so we ought not to remain lost to each other forever.*
>
> *It has come to my ears that you are now the wife of Barak. My erstwhile husband has become my brother-in-law and I welcome him as such. I wish you happiness with him.*
>
> *As for me, I live in Harosheth, where I have become the wife of Mishma, brother of Sisra, who resembles him as one ray of sunshine resembles another. I have been reunited with my mother and my family, all of whom live in this town as well.*
>
> *Perhaps one day, we may also see each other again. So speaks your sister Asherah.*

Having read the missive, Nogah retained the feeling that Asherah must have some ulterior intent in conveying the tidings about her life to her, although she could not fathom what it might be.

In the evening, when she showed the letter to Barak, he laughed. "During Asherah's short stay here, I became familiar with her nature. She did not write to you because she was seized with a sudden outburst of sisterly affection. Clearly, she needs you, us, for some purpose of her own. She did not divulge what it might be, but I am sure that in the course of time she will bare it to us."

However that might be, to Nogah's mind, the letter gave evidence of her sister's willingness to mend the rift between them. So she decided not to shun her, either, and responded in kind:

Hear me, Asherah. Be blessed for writing to me and giving me an account of your new life.

I rejoice with you in your wedding. As we have mourned our father together, so may we share in the gladness of our new marriages and in the hope that the bliss of motherhood will also fall to our lot.

Like you, I cherish the hope that we may meet again. So speaks your sister Nogah.

Asherah's letter, though, was not followed by another one. Thus, being engrossed in each other, Nogah and Barak soon gave up wondering what her intent in writing to them might have been.

🦁

Yet the letter from Harosheth in Canaan, coming on top of the wedding dance glorifying Barak's battle against the Canaanites, recalled to Nogah's mind her previous consternation over his failure to seek peace. After she became his wife, she gained assurance in her dealings with him. She decided that she would try to convince him to do what called out to heaven to be done. But the rumor reached her that the Canaanites had not yet chosen a new king to lead them.

According to that rumor, Mishma, the brother of Sisra, who had become Asherah's new husband, regarded himself the most proper man for this exalted position. But there were other contenders, and he had not as yet gained enough support from the noblemen and dignitaries of Canaan to be established in it. Thus, it would be premature to try to forge a peace treaty with him just yet. Nogah decided to keep her own counsel for the time being; but she anticipated that it would not be long before she would have to speak her mind. She could only hope that she would be able to win Barak over to her way of thinking before the next devastating war broke out.

Chapter Three

Deborah's disconcerting meeting with Barak wrought a transformation in her soul. She still felt injured by his manifesting his love for another while seeking motherly comfort from her. But she no longer hankered after him in the manner that a woman yearns for a man. At least Lapidoth, whatever else he had done, had never harbored filial sentiments toward her, for which she had no use in her man.

Nonetheless her way back to her erstwhile husband was blocked, as she found on the next occasion when she visited her sons. Although she set her visits so that they would take place before Lapidoth's return from the fields, this time he was nonetheless there. She entered the yard at the front of his house, to meet the sight of him sitting in the shade of a fig tree, rocking a yelping infant in his arms, his face as radiant as a river in the sun.

At his side sat his concubine, Naavah, who must have given birth after Deborah's previous visit a mere three days ago. She seemed to have all but forgotten her previous wish for a son. And having made a swift recovery after her delivery, her eyes were shining with the elation of her new motherhood. Deborah felt that she was intruding on a domestic scene in which she had no part; a spectacle that was not palatable to her.

As she came often, Deborah had seen the belly of the young mother-to-be bulge from week to week. So it should not have been a surprise that her pregnancy would engender life, which had now sprung forth from her womb. Yet somehow it was, and it hit Deborah in the face like icy water on a hot summer day. The tiny being in Lapidoth's arms, more than all else, had rendered his divorcing her irrevocable and had brought home to her her own state as a woman on her own.

"It's a girl," announced the deliriously happy father—who after five sons had long pined for a daughter—in a festive voice.

Deborah's sons were sitting nearby, looking bemused at the little creature they had been told was their new sister. They turned their eyes to their mother, seeking guidance from her.

She did not relish the state into which she had been cast. Yet, holding the baby entirely blameless, she felt nothing but kindness for her. She approached, bent down, and placed her hand, like a blessing, on the infant's head. "She is a joy to behold," she said with a benign smile.

As Deborah had now pressed her stamp of approval on the little one, the boys broke into hearty smiles as well and, one by one, crouched beside the child and kissed her. Then Deborah bore them off with her to the backyard, where she sat talking to them until the sun approached the crest of the hills.

Later, when she walked around the house to its front, Lapidoth caught up with her. "It was gracious of you to show benevolence to the infant," he said softly. "The boys would not else have accepted her as their sister."

"May she be a comfort to you and to her mother."

"You have never lacked in generosity."

Since divorcing Deborah, Lapidoth had only rarely addressed her. Even the few words he had uttered now seemed to have cost him an effort. He hovered around her for a little while, as if he had it in his mind to say more.

Deborah waited.

But after some moments had passed, he merely shook his head, as if to indicate that any talk between them would be futile.

The baby's wails could be heard from inside the house, and the new father seemed to be irresistibly drawn to her.

"Go to the child," said Deborah briefly and left.

By the time she had returned to her palm tree, she felt that she had traversed a distance much greater than the one between Lapidoth's home and that tree. The justice seekers having been seen to earlier, there was no one around. For a while she sat on her judge's chair, straight-backed, in solitary splendor, much in the manner of the lone Mount Tabor in the Valley of Jezreel.

Then she arose and walked to her tent. When she reached it, the fatigue of her day's work and the strain of what she had witnessed this day caught up with her. She looked at herself in the bronze mirror that stood on a little case and was anything but pleased with her image. The skin of her face was as cracked as used parchment, her shoulders had rounded, and even her proud breasts seemed to have sagged. She averted her face from her reflection in distaste.

Her maids had prepared a large repast for her, which they had laid out on a cloth on top of a little table at the foot of her couch. But she ate little, and wrapped the rest in the cloth and laid it on the ground outside her tent, thereby indicating her wish to be left alone.

When the lengthening shadows blended with the cooling darkness of the night, she let down her tent's flaps and lay on her couch, sprawled on her back. She flung her arms wide, until they took up its width, abandoning herself to her loneliness.

Bit by bit she began delving into reminiscences of Lapidoth. Of the tenderness between them, spanning many years; of moments of merriment and laughter they had shared; of familiar gestures, well-known whispers and caresses; so repetitive, so dear. Yet he had been willing to forgo all this on the spur of the moment, propelled by a momentary, groundless wrath. And now the way back was blocked by an insuperable barrier: a curly-haired, innocent little infant and its shiny-eyed, no less innocent, youthful mother. The future assumed the shape of an empty path through a deserted wilderness.

Deborah's eyelids closed partway, as her wakefulness slowly diminished. She entered the realm in which memories and fears and hopes intermingle. They melted into a nebulous cloud, which eased her into a tormented sleep.

The next morning she did what she had shrunk from doing for so long: She summoned a builder and, with a heavy sigh of resignation, charged him with constructing a four-room stone house to replace her tent.

While Nogah bided her time, waiting for the right moment to bring the urgency of peace to Barak's attention, she concerned herself with other matters that troubled her. Barak had promised to resist the lure of other women, and she believed that he was, in fact, staunchly determined to do so. But since she was familiar with his lustful disposition, she reckoned it best if he did not have to face temptation.

So she spoke to Barak in these words: "Sir, from now on, I want to be the only one to prepare your bath and bring drinks to your bedchamber."

He laughed in delight. "You don't seem to place your trust in me."

"I do, of course. Only . . . only . . . it will be good for my peace of mind."

"Those pitchers of water are too heavy for a delicate king's daughter to carry."

Nogah's gaze flew to his face as she queried, "How did you discover this?"

"I have long been asking myself why you found these pitchers heavy, when other maids had no trouble with them. But I did not know the answer until I understood it from something your mother said. Why did you conceal it all this time?"

"I did not want you to compare me unfavorably with my beautiful sister. My descent no longer matters. I loved my father very much, and I am still grieving for him in my heart, but nothing will bring him back to life." After a brief pause, she came back to what weighed on her mind. "What concerns me now is that the maids no longer prepare your bath."

"The pitchers of water are still too heavy for you. And I have no inclination to carry them myself after a long day of toil in the fields."

Nogah's face showed a flicker of disappointment. Barak folded her in his arms and added, "But we can call in some stable boys to bring them." And this was what they did.

Barak had to face the reality that Nogah was a different wife from the one Asherah had been. She was wild in her love and passion for him, as Asherah had not been, and he was rapturous. But her stance on managing the household was not always to his liking.

His first wife had improved the appearance of the house out of all recognition. Nogah praised her sister for what she had accomplished, but left it at that. While Asherah had always seen to it that the stews set before him were seasoned to his taste, Nogah had to be prodded to do so. Nogah relied for this on the woman in charge of the household, while she busied herself with other matters, first and foremost the maids.

By then, the women Barak had brought in from Hazor who were not in his employ had found shelter elsewhere. But the maids were a constant presence in the house. Although Nogah did not want them near her husband, she was nevertheless concerned with their welfare.

She implored Barak to supply them with beds to sleep on. And also that these beds be covered with soft pallets and clean sheets, which were to be changed and laundered, as were their own. Barak believed this to be a superfluous expense, but he did not wish to disappoint Nogah, so he acceded to her request.

Then she confronted him with another demand: The girls were no longer to work from dawn until nightfall. Those who rose up early to clean the house and grind flour and bake bread, and cook the morning and midday meals, would conclude their work when the sun stood high in the sky. They would then be replaced by others, who would launder and mend the garments and the bedding and prepare the evening meals.

Barak thought this a strange notion, for he had never heard of anything like it. But Nogah insisted that the maids' workload was too heavy, and that she knew the lot of the maid because she had been one herself. So they would have to engage several more maids and pay their wages. But because of his love for Nogah, Barak let her have her way in this, too.

After that, Nogah enlarged her view. She put it to Barak that although he was rich, he was not giving away much to the poor, the widows, the orphans, and the strangers in their midst.

Barak demurred, saying that he already let them roam around his fields and collect all the grain and olives and grapes the reapers left behind, as was the Torah commandment. But Nogah maintained that this was far from enough, that he could afford to give more. She reminded him that opening one's hand to the poor was among the most important Torah injunctions.

So Barak gave in to her on this as well and allowed her to dip her hand into his coffers to distribute charity as she saw fit. But he admonished her by saying that if she kept on squandering his wealth, they would soon be poor themselves, and then they would not be able to give away anything.

She was unperturbed and retorted, "But think, sir, of how much silver we will save when you no longer have to purchase pieces of land for the husbands you used to find for the maids you made pregnant."

Barak did not know that Nogah had been aware of this practice of his and he laughed in embarrassment as he said, "Who told you?"

"I will not reveal this."

"It is not necessary. I know that he did it in order to warn you and keep you away from me. But I will not punish him, because he has failed in his evil design." He added, "I see that you are determined to make a faithful husband of me."

"I thought that you intended to mend your ways."

"Yes, certainly. I will do it, because of my love for you. From now on, the only woman I will ever make pregnant, my beloved, is you. And I will do it often."

One evening, as they were eating their evening meal, Barak told her that Uriel's eyesight had dimmed and that he was no longer able to do the accounts and write letters for him, as he had done before. Hence he had decided to replace him with a young clerk, who would also be his scribe.

Nogah grew pale with shock. "My beloved husband, Uriel will be devastated."

"He cannot see what is before his eyes, and he makes errors with the accounts, which cause us much damage. I will buy him a nice house, and I will continue to pay his wages as before. He will be able to bask in the sun as he likes to do, and he will be content."

"He will feel as useless as an old mule sent off to graze in the meadow because no one wants to ride him anymore. I have another notion, one that will also save us much silver. I will sit with him and help him with the accounts and the letters and lighten his burden."

"It will weigh heavily on you."

"I will enjoy it immensely. I will help Uriel, and I will also copy scrolls and write some myself. I want to explore the beauty of words through my eyes by reading them and through my hand by writing them."

Barak also had a notion of his own. He had the room adjacent to his set up as Nogah's bedchamber and an adjoining door built between them. Thus they slept close to each other and they did not have to step out into the passage, which would be cold in the winter, to seek each other, as they did each night.

Chapter Four

W hen Nogah found that she was pregnant, she felt a stab of pride in her husband and in their love for each other, which she immediately shared with him. No sooner had the first bout of nausea heralding her pregnancy subsided than she rode over to her mother to advise her of the glad tidings.

By that time, Reumah's belly was as round as a mound of wheat with the child inside her, and it was difficult for mother and daughter to hug each other. But somehow they managed it and, as they had done before, they shed tears in each other's arms. Only this time they were tears of joy, no longer marred by sorrow.

Afterward, while they sat chatting, Reumah asked if Barak was keeping his promise to be faithful to her. Nogah answered with a twinkle in her eye. "My mother, he is faithful and intends to remain so in the future. But I do not rely solely on his noble commitment. I take good care that he upholds it."

When Reumah asked how she achieved this, she replied shyly, "I keep the maids away from him. I have brought all the maids who worked for him in the fields to work for us at home, where I can supervise them; and I see to it that he employs only men in the fields. But mainly, I keep him too exhausted with our love to have any power left for other women."

These words, and the glow of bliss she perceived in Nogah's face, made Reumah even happier than her daughter's pregnancy.

For three months, mother and daughter were both pregnant. Then

Reumah gave birth to a daughter, while Nogah began bearing her swelling belly proudly before her.

Some nine months after the wedding, she went into labor. When her pains blotted out all else and she melted into them, they were somewhat alleviated by the ministrations of the most skillful midwife to be found in Kedesh. And by her mother supporting her back with her knees as she crouched on the birthing stones, mitigating her sharp screams of anguish with soft whispers that were like balm in her ears.

An eternity later, after the child tore its way out of her body, the memory of her harrowing pains gave way to the delight of seeing her husband's radiant face. He hugged and kissed their firstborn son, his little face a perfect blend between his father's dark-skinned countenance and his mother's blue-green eyes.

It was a custom in the tribe of Nafthali to hold a celebration in honor of a boy's circumcision equal in size to a wedding, and Barak and Nogah eagerly honored it. They invited all their relatives and friends, and people from near and far came of their own accord.

They did not invite Mishma and Asherah. But rumors of the celebration having reached Barak's former wife, she nonetheless came. She arrived with an infant daughter in her arms and a wet nurse at her heels. As neither Nogah nor Barak had had any tidings from her since the one letter she had sent them almost nine months before, they were greatly surprised at the sight. Nogah realized that what had transpired before no longer mattered, and that it behooved her to show her willingness for a full reconciliation by according her a warmer welcome than she deserved. Thus she rushed forward and the two sisters embraced each other and blessed each other on the birth of their infants.

Then Asherah sprung a further surprise on them. She stated that—as everyone must realize by looking at her two-month-old daughter—she was, without doubt, the issue of Barak's loins. Hence Mishma had refused to accept her as his own, stating that it was not the custom in Canaan for a man to raise another man's child. She reminded Barak of his promise that if she gave birth to his child, he would raise it.

The infant girl's marked resemblance to Barak could not be denied: She had his dark curls and large dark eyes and thick eyebrows, which looked

delightful on her tiny face. Barak took the baby, who was diligently suck-
ing her little fingers, into his arms and kissed her face and her hair. Then
he lifted his eyes from his daughter to his wife, and a silent message passed
between them. He told Asherah that he and Nogah would bring up the girl
together with their son.

Asherah expelled an audible sigh of relief. She revealed that she had
not yet chosen a name for her daughter. She had thought that since Barak
and Nogah would raise her, they should have a voice in its selection.

Thus, after a brief consultation between the three of them, Barak and
Nogah stepped onto the high place that had been built especially for the
performance of the circumcision. They announced that their son would
be called Shlomi, and that Barak and Asherah's daughter would be named
Shlomith. They had chosen those names, two variations on the word "sha-
lom," so that the children would serve as signs of peace between Israel and
Canaan. The guests broke into loud cheers.

Then the priest who performed the circumcision announced that the
boy had now been entered into the covenant of our father Abraham, and
his name in Israel would be Shlomi. The guests clapped their hands to
welcome the squalling infant into the congregation of Israel, and Nogah
calmed him down by laying him to her breast.

Asherah stayed the night, and on the next morning, as she sat with
Nogah in her bedchamber, expressed some worries about her child's
welfare.

Nogah reassured her by telling her that the house was open for her to
come and visit her daughter anytime she wished to do so. She told Asherah,
"She is a lovely child. Besides, she is the daughter of the man I love and of
my sister. Could I be anything but kind and loving toward my own niece?"

"I want her to grow up as a Canaanite."

"Then you should not have brought her to me. I can only raise her in
the spirit of the Torah, as I will raise my own child and the others that, I
hope, will come in his wake."

"You are part Canaanite yourself."

"I was. But that part of me has gone up in smoke with my father. I have
struck roots here, and I am an Israelite like all the others you see around us."

Asherah nodded in acceptance of the inevitable.

🐾

Nogah cared for Shlomi and Shlomith with devotion and love, as her mother had cared for her. In time, she almost forgot that Shlomith had not made her way into the world out of her own womb.

Each evening, after she had assured herself that both infants were soundly asleep in their cradles, Nogah and Barak would sit on two chairs at the back of the mansion under their window, so that they could hear them if they woke up. They savored the calm of the evening, and the beauty of the distant hills in the silvery light of the moon and the stars, and the gentle rustle of the wind in the treetops, and the joy of being together.

The night's balmy silence hovered above them; all around them was at peace, yet Nogah could find no peace inside her. One evening, she gained the fortitude to speak to Barak of her longtime anxiety. "Sir, although I have no right to do so, pray, allow me to speak to you about something that causes me deep worry."

Barak was startled "You know, my child, that you can speak to me of anything that is in heaven above and on the earth below. What is it?"

"It concerns your people, our people. You have refused to be king, and I honor you greatly for it. But you still have the people's welfare on your shoulders."

Barak adamantly rebutted her words. "I am merely a warrior. Forced into war against my will, released from it with utter relief. Now that the war is over, I am not in charge of anything. I am like everybody else."

"You have led the people into war," Nogah insisted vehemently. "You must also lead them into peace."

"There is peace in the land now."

"But it will not last, unless you do something to preserve it."

"The Canaanites have been decimated and pose no menace to us. They are so devastated from their last defeat that they cannot do battle against us for many years."

"As time goes by they are regaining their strength, and they are probably building up their army by now. It will not be long before they are ready to attack. You have to prevent this."

"Nogah, my beloved, I will not incite them to war by raiding their land as I have done before. What else can I do?"

"Mishma is on the path to becoming king in my father's place, the most powerful of all the Canaanite kings. You must approach him and speak peace with him."

Barak wrapped himself in a long, worrying silence. Then he delivered Nogah a severe reproof. "So far I have acceded to all your demands and denied you nothing. I have let you tamper in whatever way you saw fit with that scroll of mine. I have granted your wishes where the welfare of the maids and the poor is concerned, although this drains out our silver, as if it rested in a pouch riddled with holes. I have let you retain Uriel as my clerk, even though he can no longer see what lies in front of his eyes. I have let you prevail in all this, because my love for you is as wide and deep as the Great Sea.

"Yet even the mighty waves of the sea are bounded by the shore. But you have overstepped the boundaries. I will not permit you to interfere in my dealing with Mishma. Even for your sake I will not humble myself before my mortal enemy, a man of blood and deceit.

"You will do well to abandon this and shift your efforts back to the welfare of the maids and the poor, to the scrolls you like to write with Uriel, or to whatever else may capture your fancy, except this. You will never raise this with me again."

Barak's words blew like a cold wind over Nogah. She bent her head, strands of her thick wavy hair tumbled down her cheeks, and tears of mortification brimmed over in her eyes. "I regret having spoken those words," she faltered. "Forgive me, sir."

At the sight of her, Barak's heart melted like honey in boiling milk. He lifted her face to meet his kiss, rose and scooped her up in his arms, and, cuddling her like an infant, carried her up the stairway to his bedroom. In the exultation of his knowing her, Nogah forgot Mishma, and the Canaanites, and all that prevailed between the four edges of the earth except her love for him.

Yet later, as Barak lay in peaceful slumber, sleep would not come to her. She lay awake for a good part of the night, deeply troubled in her soul.

It took six months for Deborah's house to be erected on its sturdy stone foundations, and then to be furnished and decorated in accordance with her fastidious taste.

When all was ready and she had settled in it, she took a degree of pleasure in all the comforts it offered, which she'd had to forgo while she lived in the tent. She enjoyed its spaciousness, the coolness its thick walls provided in the summer, and the warmth from the fire burning in the hearth, which they retained in the winter. She liked the ornate table and matching chairs that took up a large part of the front room. She feasted her eyes on the vividly patterned tapestries that decorated its walls, on the intricately knotted rugs that were spread on the bed and the floors, and on the elaborately crafted pottery that covered its other surfaces.

She found only one fault with it: As she had rejected all her suitors, there was no one to share it with her. To her, the manifold colors of its decorations were but an artifice to conceal its emptiness.

Still, as it had been before, so it was also after the house's completion: No one watching Deborah as she sat on her judge's chair could have guessed that she was anything but totally satisfied with her life on her own. She looked every bit the self-assured prophetess and judge that she was, incessantly dispensing justice and wisdom, as indeed she had been doing for as far back as she could remember.

Five months after she had moved into her new abode, those ascending her hill, surprisingly, included Jael, her husband, Hever, and their three sons. One of her clerks advised her of their arrival, adding, "They have not come to seek justice, but to pay obeisance to you."

"Obeisance is due only to the Lord, but, pray, bring them to my house so that I may greet them there."

When it was time for her noontime rest, they were already sitting at the table, waiting for her. They rose up and meant to bow down before her, but she forestalled their gesture by rushing forward and embracing Jael. "Most blessed of women be Jael," she said, repeating the part of the song pertaining to her that she had chanted at the assembly in Kedesh, which had led to Jael's exoneration.

Once she had made them sit again and share her midday meal, she asked, "What has brought you all the way from the north to these parts?"

Speaking for them all, Hever replied, "We are on our way to return to our people, who dwell far to the south of this land. We are using this opportunity to thank you for your kindness to Jael, to us."

"Thanks are superfluous," she responded. "But what made you decide to leave our land? Have the Israelites not been hospitable to you?"

"They are our friends. It is the Canaanites that we fear."

"How so?"

"Mishma, the brother of the notorious and happily deceased Sisra, who dwells in Harosheth, has placed himself in charge of rebuilding the army. And having married King Jabin's daughter, he is also coveting the throne vacated by the king's death. My fellow smiths, who repair tools for the Canaanites in that town, have heard rumors that he is hatching a most sinister plot. Before all else, he means to mount a raid on our house in the thick of night and kill all five of us in our sleep."

"You did well not to sit by idly and wait for calamity to overtake you. But I hereby invite you to settle here, in the hill country of Efraim, where you will be both welcome and safe."

Jael now spoke for the first time. "Exalted judge, your goodness is renowned far and wide and rightly so. We bless you for offering us hospitality in the heart of your land. But there are no other Kenites here, and we would feel out of place, like fish on dry land. We prefer to brave the dry heat of the southern desert, if only we can be among our people."

Later in the day, after having sent the visitors on their way with more hugs and blessings, Deborah pondered the knowledge she had gleaned from them. It was the first solid proof she had obtained of Sisra's brother having set himself up as commander of the army, with an eye to the throne and Asherah as his queen-to-be. The dream and vision she had been privy to were clearly on the way to being realized.

Once again, the vision brought forth by the ivory knife, of Mishma on the throne, with Asherah handing him a sword dripping with Israelite blood, seemed to come to life. In her spirit, she saw the Israelite prisoners shedding more tears and rocking in even greater despair and chanting ever more pitiful lamentations.

By showing her that vision, the Holy One had laid at her door the task of turning their sorrow into laughter and their lamentations into hymns of joy. Was it a task too heavy for her to shoulder? She could not believe it to be so. If the Almighty had charged her with it, he would also grant her the ability to carry it out. She would have to rise to the challenge. But how?

She could, of course, alert Barak to the danger and entrust him with the task of building up an army of his own. Yet, as two major battles had failed to bring a coveted rest to the land, she was convinced that a third one would merely serve to unleash a fourth. Perhaps reverting to her first notion of seeking a peace alliance with the Canaanites would better serve her purpose.

After the humiliation Sisra had meted out to her, she could hardly approach his brother, the budding Canaanite leader, herself. The most proper one to make the attempt was obviously Barak.

Before the commander's last visit, Deborah had purposely refrained from writing to him, lest he interpret her missive as a subtle attempt to put him in mind of his promise for such a visit. Now that they were no longer lovers, she had no qualms on that count.

So on that same evening, by the light of two oil lamps that had been set up for her on the sides of the front room table, she sat and composed a letter to him.

Chapter Five

A week after he had rebuked Nogah for meddling in his dealings with the Canaanites, Barak was surprised to receive a missive from Deborah, the content of which was even more astounding than its arrival:

Hear me, Barak. My life of solitude has given me leisure to ruminate more deeply than I have done before. My thoughts have led me to lay before you a matter of the gravest importance.

You have shown our people that you are skilled at waging war. You must now demonstrate that you are equally accomplished at making peace.

Will the sword devour forever and never let off?

I call on you to travel to the home of Mishma, the brother of the man you so gloriously defeated, the man who is on his way to becoming the mightiest king of Canaan, and seek to forge a covenant with him.

I would make a pilgrimage to his dwelling myself were it not for the fact that I am a woman, and that his brother had already sneeringly rejected my advances in this respect. There would be no advantage in debasing myself a second time.

You would not be liable to such humiliation. You have already made a name for yourself in all of Israel. Mishma cannot deprive you of it. But he is still struggling for his position. If you help him by honoring him in the sight of his noblemen, he will be indebted to you, and most likely will not scorn your offer.

So speaks Deborah, whose prayers to the Guardian of Israel will accompany you on your mission.

When Barak raised his eyes from Deborah's letter, his thoughts were not kindly. She had been the one to spur him on to war with the Canaanites. How could she have had such a complete change of heart?

Nogah had been standing at his side, reading together with him, and he looked at her suspiciously. He asked if she had written to Deborah to engage her as an ally for her design. But Nogah assured him that she had not. She added ruefully that she would have done it had it entered her mind, but it never had.

At first, Barak decided to brush aside Deborah's words as if they were dust blown in by the wind, and deign to make no reply. But he was aware that he had been insensitive to her, and he had no wish to inflict any further wounds on her soul. So he sat down in the scroll room and composed a convoluted reply, the gist of which was that he placed the greatest reliance on her judgment and would give her proposal the utmost consideration.

He sent off his letter by a runner and deposited Deborah's in a remote corner on the highest shelf. He also wished to shelve its contents in a remote corner of his mind, yet he could not and her request kept buzzing in his head like a persistent bug.

A month later, a second, more insistent missive from Deborah went the way of the first. Like its predecessor, it kept tugging at his mind. It struck him that it would be easier for him to stride to war proudly at the head of his troops than to beg peace humbly from his enemy. He could not bring himself to do it.

🦁

Another month passed, and Asherah, surrounded by six guards, came to visit her daughter. Having spent a day and a night with her, she went to see Nogah in her room before she left. She sat with her head bent forward, twisting the skirt of her dress and gazing at the aimless movements of her fingers.

Nogah, sitting opposite her, waited for her to speak.

Finally Asherah said in a distraught voice: "The names that you and

Barak have chosen for our children are very well, but they are meaningless. Useless. Worse than that: ridiculous."

At her sister's disquieting words, Nogah felt a chill run through her. "What are you intimating?"

"What is the advantage of naming our two children 'Peace' and 'Peace,' when there is no peace? When only war can prevail between our peoples?"

Dragging her chair close to that of her sister, Nogah took hold of Asherah's restless hands, folded them against each other, and pressed them between her own. "What is it that you know?" she whispered.

Asherah pulled her hands out of Nogah's grip and began pleating her skirt again. "Nothing, nothing," she said, but her words lacked conviction.

"This is not the truth. Is Mishma building up the army? Tell me. Perhaps it is not too late to avert disaster for both our peoples."

But no matter how strongly Nogah pleaded with her sister, she could not extract anything from her.

Asherah had sworn an oath to her husband, by all the Canaanite gods, which she intended to keep. Hence she had no intention of revealing to Nogah that Mishma no longer supervised the cultivation of his vast lands, that instead, he devoted his days to the army, of which he was the supreme commander. Neither did she apprise her sister of the fact that Mishma held lengthy meetings with his officers, who came to see him almost daily.

Nor did she mention the occasion on which those officers had taken their evening meal with her and Mishma, and after they had gorged themselves with wine and strong spirits, they'd called out cheerfully that the day of reckoning was drawing near. That soon the slimy worms would perish, trampled under their chariots' wheels.

But Nogah had gleaned more from Asherah's words than her sister had intended to reveal. The fears that she had long harbored of her own accord were distilled into new strength.

She took hold of her sister's hands again and said in a tremulous voice, "Do you believe that when Mishma ascends the throne, he will be willing to make peace with Barak, and thereby with the people of Israel?"

"Knowing both men closely as I do, I have to say truthfully that peace between them is as likely as catching the water of the sea in a fisherman's net. Both are men of war and they cannot speak peace with each other. A blood feud pitches them against one another. There is too much pride, too much hatred, too much desire for vengeance." Then she withdrew her hands again and said, "I have talked too much already. I must go."

🏃

When Deborah perceived that her dispatches to Barak had borne no fruit other than friendly responses, she decided to take further action, by engaging the elders as her allies. She did not content herself with gaining the support of one head elder from each tribe. Instead, she sent out edicts to the Council of Elders of all the tribes of Israel, comprising no less than seventy elders, and summoned them to assemble at her palm tree, in ten days' time, for a consultation.

They all responded, to a man. When they arrived, and after her aides had seen to their sustenance and accommodation, she made them sit on mats in front of her judge's chair. Then, in her fiery voice, which carried from one side of the hill to the other, she outlined to them her new notion of seeking peace with the Canaanites, by approaching the man Mishma, who was set to become their most powerful king.

The elders listened intently but demurred. After much whispering among themselves, the head elder of Judah spoke in all their names. "What has overcome us? After such glorious victories over our foes, have we become as timid as rabbits, trembling at the sight of our own shadows?"

Reddish flames leapt from Deborah's black eyes. "We are not invincible. And even if we win, there will be casualties again and we may be among them. The dead cannot praise the Lord. But if there is peace, we will live and extol his glory."

"Hallelujah!" exclaimed the elders in unison and obediently raised their faces heavenward.

After many flowery speeches had been delivered, a majority among them concurred that the plan of the prophetess had merit. When Deborah began blessing them at length for their decision, the head elder of Efraim interjected, "Who can we send on this crucial mission?"

Deborah had anticipated this question. "As there is no king in Israel," she responded, "the only man who can bring it to fruition is Barak, the son of Abinoam. For only he can speak to Mishma as one military officer to another. Furthermore, he is also related to him by ties of kinship, which should make it difficult for the Canaanite to deny him access to his home."

Another head elder, the one from Barak's own tribe, Nafthali, raised an objection. "The man is a valiant warrior and will not quake before an enemy he has twice vanquished."

Deborah, who had been resolute with the elders, felt herself on less solid ground with Barak, who had all but ignored her two previous exhortations to him. Yet she replied assertively, "If you join me in seeking peace and send him your decree, he will have to bow to it."

"Hardly," persisted the elder from Nafthali. "As he has not bowed to Sisra and Jabin, is he likely to bow to us?"

"We will prevail over Barak," she insisted.

In the face of such staunch determination from the prophetess, the elders capitulated. "As you say, so shall it be," they called out, one after the other.

Thus they wrote a dispatch, charging Barak to begin negotiations for peace in their name. After they had all pressed their seals on it, they entrusted it to a courier, whom they sped on his way with silver, bidding him make all possible haste to reach his destination. This accomplished, they dispersed to their homes, there to await Barak's response.

When the rolled-up and impressively sealed parchment reached Barak, he wrote a lengthy reply that reiterated much of what he had previously written to Deborah, committing himself to bestow his undivided attention on their decree. He instructed Uriel, who was aided by Nogah, to prepare seventy copies of it. He pressed his seal on each of them and sent them all off by messengers. After that, the elders' message to him found its place next to Deborah's on the highest shelf in his scroll room.

For a while, Barak continued turning the contents of the message over in his mind. In the end, he concluded that he had done all that could have been expected of him. He had won the war, which now made peace possible. Let another man be the one to seek it.

He wrote as much in a letter to Deborah and intended to make copies of it for the elders as well. But he hesitated, and in the end he could not bring himself to send it off.

Chapter Six

Ⓞne autumn morning some two months later, Asherah, escorted by her guards, came again. After a fine drizzle had ceased, and the sun had emerged from behind the clouds, the two sisters sat chatting under a large vine whose branches had been trained to form a shady canopy over their heads. Then Asherah surprised Nogah again.

She revealed that she had come to retrieve her little daughter and take her back to her own home.

Nogah was flabbergasted. She doted on both the children, carried them both on her hips, dandled them both on her knees, and sang sweet lullabies in both their ears. And here was Asherah, slighting all she had done, putting her to shame. "What is wrong?" she gasped. "Have you any reason to believe that I am not treating her well? That I am not lavishing love and care on her as I do on my own son?"

"No, no," Asherah retorted in an effort to appease her. "I am not casting any aspersions on you. I have no doubt that you are as kind and loving to her as I would be myself."

"Then what is it?"

To Nogah's annoyance, Asherah made no reply.

"Besides," continued Nogah, "you have told me yourself that Mishma is not keen to accept her."

"Because he loves me he will have to."

"But why?"

There was only silence.

Finally Nogah felt compelled to say, "Barak is Shlomith's father, and he holds her in deep affection. Unless you bring forth a very good reason for wanting her back, I don't believe that he will relinquish her."

"In truth," responded Asherah, casting down her eyes, "I was planning to bear her off before he comes home from the fields."

Once more, Nogah was taken aback. "You cannot truly believe that I would let you take the child without her father's consent. And why? Just tell me, why?"

Finally Asherah relented. "I will reveal my reason to you. It is that Mishma has overcome the other contenders, and he is shortly to ascend the throne and reign over the northern part of Canaan. I will be the queen."

Nogah embraced her sister warmly and blessed her for her good fortune. Before long, though, the inevitable question rose to her lips. "What has this got to do with your desire to take your daughter back?"

Once more, Asherah was mute; but Nogah had her own thoughts, which made her head throb.

Afterward, Nogah left Asherah to play with her little daughter. But she took up a vigil close to the gate, to foil any possible attempt on her part to whisk away Shlomith without Barak's permission.

Asherah did not try. But as they ate their evening meal together, she reiterated her request to take charge of the child, repeating also her revelation about her husband's impending anointment as a Canaanite king. Barak extended his blessings to her for being about to become a queen, as she had always wished to be. But he flatly refused to hand over their daughter to her. He told her that a child was not a pebble that could carelessly be cast back and forth at will. Having appointed him and Nogah to raise her, Asherah must now leave Shlomith with them until the girl was married and moved into her husband's house.

Shlomith's mother seemed genuinely and deeply distressed. Her beautiful face was overcome with a deathly pallor, and her delicate white hands, resting on the table, were shaking uncontrollably. Yet she could not be persuaded to utter a word about the reason for this. The next morning, before the rising of the sun, she and her escorts rode back to Harosheth empty-handed. And Nogah knew with grim certainty what her sister's words of the day before had implied.

Later, after a rainy day had given way to a clear evening, Barak and Nogah left the children in their nurses' charge and took a stroll around the walls of the mansion. They looked down upon the valley below, in which the rays of the moon were reflected on the wet meadows, as a gentle breeze blew their hair and cooled the nape of their necks. While they walked, Barak pronounced the manner in which Asherah had acted the evening before to be greatly puzzling.

When Nogah made no response, he regarded her sidewise, and demanded that she tell him whether she knew anything that she was keeping from him. She replied that she knew nothing, but that she might guess. He prompted her to do so, but she insisted that she could not because Barak, whom she would never dream of defying, had ordered her never to bring up the topic again.

Barak smiled in appreciation of her ruse. "I retract my hasty words. Say what is on your mind."

"It seems to me, sir, that Mishma is now completing the reconstruction of his army. The ceremony to anoint him as king will probably take place within a few weeks. Asherah is aware that as soon as he assumes his position, and has the power to do as he sees fit, he will mount a surprise attack on our stronghold, which is but sparsely guarded. Asherah fears that, in the chaos of battle, her daughter may be killed together with us. Hence her wish to remove the infant from this house.

"You must not judge her harshly. It is what any mother in her place would want. She has even done us a favor, for inadvertently she has alerted us to danger."

Barak strode on beside Nogah with a dark look on his face.

🔆

Although he did not admit it, this time Barak's talk with Nogah, coming alongside Deborah's and the elders' advice, left its mark on him. Prodded by her words, he sent out spies into the Canaanite domain. They confirmed that Mishma was rebuilding his army of charioteers.

In consequence, Barak took stock of his own forces. Since his army assembled only when a war was imminent, there was not much that needed rebuilding. But he began surveying the armories where the swords and shields were kept, and he ordered the swords to be honed and the shields polished for possible use.

As he was once again walking with Nogah in the vicinity of their home a few days later, he admitted this to her, adding, "If the Canaanites attack, they will walk into the fire they themselves have kindled, into the furnace of their own affliction. I will show them the might of my arm until they no longer will be able to tell their right hand from their left. And I will teach Mishma himself a lesson. When the scoundrel finds himself at the edge of my sword, he will follow his brother into the grave, where his flesh will rot together with his name."

Barak's words did nothing to allay Nogah's fears, but they gave her the opportunity she had been looking for to lay her own thoughts before him. "Pray, sir, let me speak to you but this one time," she said with a pleading note in her voice. "It is too crucial a matter for you to stifle me into silence."

Barak sighed his resignation. "Speak."

"My beloved husband, you may be able to slay the Canaanites, as you have done before. But what will be the purpose of it? After a while, they will come back to do battle against us again. There will be another war, and then another one and another one. Our young men will have to be mustered. Then those who are still boys now will have to be called up. And later on, our son, who is now an infant sleeping peacefully in his cradle, and the ones I hope will still be born to us, will have to go into battle, too. Perhaps they will not come back."

"What is your proposal?" Barak asked, wary of her next words.

"As I said, you must appear before Mishma, with words of peace in your mouth."

"Despite Deborah's and the elders' edict, I am not the people's leader. I cannot speak in their name."

"Sir, if a war breaks out, and they have need for it, they will come to you for help. It is better that you help them now, so that the need will never arise. You could talk to Mishma honorably, and he would honor you in return."

"Then let Mishma approach me in that manner. His brother and his people are the ones who have been defeated."

"It is precisely for that reason that he will never turn to you. He would find it too humiliating."

"So will I be humbled if I come to him. It would look as if I cowered before him, as frightened as a deer at the approach of a fox. It would be a slur on my name forever."

"You are the victor in the last war and you can afford to be generous. By doing away with conceit, you would exhibit not fear but courage."

"He tried to persuade Asherah to thrust a dagger through my heart. His treachery is still etched in my memory."

"When you accept hospitality in his home, he will not deal with you in this manner."

"Will a leopard alter his spots?"

"You will not become loving friends. It is for the sake of our children and theirs."

Barak reached out his hand and tousled her hair, then ran his hand through his own and said, "I will give the matter some more thought."

Perceiving cracks in Barak's wall of resistance, Nogah was hopeful. Yet four weeks passed, and nothing happened. Nogah's trepidation increased.

Chapter Seven

Then came a thunderstorm, as fateful as any Nogah had ever lived through. The clouds were heavy in the sky, shoving and colliding with each other, suddenly torn apart by lightning, which scorched an enormous slit in them. This was followed by thunder and a torrent of rain that drenched Barak and Nogah, who were in the courtyard, to the skin before they found shelter inside the house.

As soon as they had reached Barak's room and shed their wet clothes and dried their bodies with soft towels, Barak took Nogah to his bed. "Do you know, my love, what my true reason for marrying you was?" he asked.

His wife shook her head.

"So that I could weather all the storms of my life with you."

Nogah made no reply, but with his arms around her, Barak felt little tremors of fear running through her. "What is this, my child?" he asked. "You cannot still be frightened of thunderstorms when our house is sturdy and you have me to protect you."

If he thought that these words would sweep away her fears, he was mistaken. "The truth is, sir, that the lightning is tearing not only the sky but also my heart, and the thunder is pounding within my head. For the storm of war can bring down the sturdiest of houses, and you are not protecting me and our children as I had hoped that you would."

Barak understood what her words implied, and said wearily, "By Torah injunction, a wife should be ruled by her husband. You should be in my hands as clay in the hands of the potter, but instead your neck is as stiff as a pillar of marble. Worse than that: You are trying to bend me to your will by your unceasing pestering."

Yet he was secretly shaken by her words, and they burned themselves into his mind. He now also admitted to himself that there might be more to Deborah's and the elders' exhortations to him to seek peace with Mishma than he had gleaned at first.

He promised Nogah to let Deborah's and the elders' and her view override his, on condition that she turn around so that they could both face the window and look out at the thunderstorm together, and inhale the damp smell that hung on the bark of the trees until they fell asleep. She willingly complied.

Following his promise, Barak did not postpone what needed to be done. Having advised Deborah and all the elders of what, at their decree, he was bent on doing, and intent upon getting the unpleasant task out of his way as soon as possible, Barak wished to set out for Harosheth immediately.

To his dismay, Nogah would not let him. And he bowed to her better knowledge of the Canaanites, as he had not done before.

🦎

In her determination to ensure the success of Barak's mission, Nogah resolved to tread cautiously. Mishma must not be taken by surprise, for its sheer jolt might cause him to spurn Barak's offer and send him shamefacedly away from his house. Such a slight on Barak's honor would bring the looming war even closer.

Thus she sent word to Asherah, asking her to visit. When she came, Nogah implored her to speak to her husband's heart and soften it in anticipation of Barak's visit.

At first Asherah put Nogah off. "My husband's heart is so hard with his hatred of Barak that nothing can affect it," she argued. "I know, too, of a certainty that he would resent it very much if I interfered in the affairs of what is soon to become his kingdom, which he believes no woman, not even an impending queen, has a right to do."

Nogah was discouraged but tenacious. "The blood of both people courses in your infant daughter's veins," she reminded her sister. "The time has come for you to show not only the beauty of your face, but also that of your soul."

Yet still Asherah refused to intervene. "Apart from all else, I am with child again," she argued, with just a hint of whining in her voice. "My sickness is upon me morning after morning. I cannot be burdened with this troublesome task as well."

Nogah blessed her profusely on having conceived again. But she did not accept Asherah's new pregnancy as a valid excuse for eschewing her duty. Thus she spoke to her in these words:

"If you think that when the war rages around you, you and your family will find refuge in your husband's fortress, as Noah and his family took refuge in the ark at the time of the flood, you are mistaken. When everything else descends into chaos, you and your little daughter and your family and the infant in your womb will also be destroyed. Who knows if the Lord has not designated you to be queen at this time, that you may ensure peace for the land?"

This harsh speech gave Asherah pause. "I will have to seek counsel from my own goddess," she replied, but Nogah knew that she had already relented in her heart. She charged her with reiterating as many times as possible in Mishma's ears that Barak had had no part in murdering his brother, so that Mishma was not in honor bound to avenge his blood by killing him.

An interminable week passed before a messenger from Asherah arrived. By that time Nogah had almost given up hope of her sister's petition to Mishma bearing fruit, and her heart was heavy with the failure of her scheme.

When she caught sight of the messenger at the gate, she raced to him at the speed with which clouds cross the sky on a windy day, and fairly tore the little rolled-up scroll he bore out of his hand. But when she read it, she was deeply disconcerted. It advised her that in spite of her repeated pleading, Mishma was not disposed to lend an ear to Barak's proposal.

Nogah perceived that her efforts had been in vain. The prospect for peace had collapsed around her like a house built on sand foundations. Her interference had brought nothing but shame on her husband, who now looked like a poor man who had come to glean the grain left over from the harvest in Mishma's fields, and had been chased away in contempt.

Repenting her futile interference in what was not her concern, Nogah wished the earth would open its mouth and swallow her into its depth. Fortunately, when Barak saw how downcast she was, he did not berate her for her stupidity. She was profoundly grateful to him for sparing her any homilies on this count.

🜲

Three weeks later, Mishma was installed as king. But no sooner had he ascended his throne than an unexpected event took place. It transpired that the husband of one of King Jabin's other daughters, who had long been trying to undermine him secretly and unsuccessfully, now suddenly gained added support and came out into the open with his challenge. He even had the temerity to change his name to Jabin, to signify that he was to be the next king.

This newly named Jabin assembled the noblemen of Harosheth and its vicinity in his own home with great fanfare. There he proclaimed fearlessly that the brother of the commander who had brought nothing but a crushing defeat to Canaan's warriors was not fit to reign. As Sisra had done, he was heading for another war, and was bent on bringing down yet another disaster on a people already weary of slaughter.

Some of the noblemen kept faith with Mishma, but most did not hesitate to turn their backs on him and transfer their allegiance to his brother-in-law.

In the face of this conspiracy, which was on the verge of turning into a revolt, Mishma was in dire need of greater support from the noblemen and dignitaries. He realized that it was incumbent upon him to perform a memorable deed to bolster it up.

Thus, he reluctantly charged Asherah to learn from her sister whether Barak's offer of peace negotiations still stood. To Nogah's relief, although Mishma promised nothing, he was at least willing to receive Barak into his house and hear what he had to say.

In order to make his appearance before Mishma as ceremonious as pos-

344 *Eva Etzioni-Halevy*

sible, Barak sent word to the elders of all tribes and requested that they each send their head to join him in his mission.

When they arrived, Barak, accompanied by a delegation of those twelve elders, with only a small contingent of men to guard them, rode over to Harosheth. Unlike Hazor, this town had not been devastated in the war. It had a solid wall around it, and many elegant stone houses in it. The most impressive of these was Mishma's new castle, built on a mountain, which Barak and the elders and the guards now climbed.

In order to refrain from injuring Mishma's pride, they were not riding the horses they had looted from the Canaanites. Instead, they rode donkeys, and this endowed them with a humble demeanor that favorably impressed their host. He responded to this gesture by stepping out to meet them and graciously inviting them into his reception hall. In this room, which Mishma had already endowed with a throne and all the trappings of royal power, Barak fleetingly saw Asherah. She was visibly pregnant and seemed to be deeply content with her husband.

Barak bore pricey gifts for Mishma and all his family. Although the very thought of it made him cringe, he also proffered a sealed container. When opened, it was found to contain some of the gold and silver that he and his men had looted from the Hazor castle. Mishma accepted the gifts with a bow of his head and words of kindness on his lips.

After the guests had been served food and drink, Mishma took Barak to his office. After listening to Barak's proposal, he spoke to him sternly. "Peace is as precious to us as it is to you. But you have trampled our honor under your feet long enough. We have suffered sufficient humiliation at your hands."

The Israelite commander took this as a rejection of the offer he had barely made, and, testily, he hovered on the verge of rising to his feet and leaving. But Mishma added, "In order to reinstate our honor, I stipulate it as a condition for a covenant between us that the overbearing woman who put my deceased brother to shame by demanding that he negotiate with her as if she were a man, or he a mere woman, come here to pay homage to me. She must declare her fealty to me in the hearing of all my noblemen."

Barak reeled from Mishma's words."That would be tantamount to her proclaiming you king of Israel," he said, exasperated. "It is not possible."

After some thought, he added placatingly, "But I may be able to persuade her to bestow her blessing on you as the head of all the kings of Canaan. Deborah is the most highly regarded and widely adored leader in all of Israel and her words would reverberate throughout the land. They would greatly enhance your stature among Israelites and Canaanites alike."

As Mishma voiced no objection, a courier bearing Barak's proposal to Deborah was sent on his way.

They all knew that it would be no less than a week before Deborah's reply, or she herself, could be expected to arrive. There was little that they could do to while away the time in Harosheth. The elders were content to laze about during the day and be regaled with sumptuous banquets night after night. As Asherah knew precisely what they were and were not allowed to eat under Torah law, their food was prepared under her strict supervision, to the elders' approval.

But Barak became restless. "My lord king, I crave your indulgence, for I miss my wife," he admitted to Mishma with a smile of embarrassment on his face.

"My sister-in-law is always welcome in my home," replied Mishma graciously. "Let her come here."

"She is seeing to the little ones," Barak persisted. "I beg your permission to absent myself for a few days."

Mishma, who had become as tame as a lamb, did not withhold it.

Barak had invested all his persuasive powers in his missive to Deborah. Moreover, she herself had prompted him to seek peace with Mishma. But when she had written to him earlier, she had stressed that she saw no purpose in humiliating herself before Mishma. Hence, as Barak made his way to his home, it was anything but clear to him what her response to his rather far-reaching suggestion would be.

Chapter Eight

When Barak's missive arrived, Deborah was sitting under her palm tree, in the midst of listening to the voluble complaints of two priests from the temple in Shiloh against each other. Once they had both been appeased and left, it was time for her to repair to her house for her noontime rest. There she reread the document and was thrown into a quandary.

She had not foreseen that Barak's attempt to reach peace, into which she had urged him, would entail her debasing herself once again before a Canaanite rascal. She was not swayed by Barak's conviction that this would serve the cause of peace. But neither could she entirely dismiss the possibility.

If Mishma closely resembled Sisra, as she had gleaned in her vision, would he not deal shamefully with her, as his deceased brother had done before him? What would she do if, like Sisra, he humbled her by intimating that women's assets lay in their availability to men? Would she not feel compelled to retaliate by bursting into another prophecy foretelling his demise at the hands of a woman, as she had done with Sisra? And would such mutual denigration not hasten the advent of yet another war, precisely what she wished to prevent?

Then again, if she did not respond to Barak's call and if his efforts to reach peace came to naught because of her failure to lend him countenance, how would she ever be able to face herself? Would she not spit at her own image as it was reflected at her in her bronze mirror?

Thus, she struggled with herself, unable to find answers to her nagging questions.

Once again, the fate of the people hung in the balance, and she was the one who would tilt it in one direction or the other. But this time she was searching for a path unseeingly, like a blind man.

With the strength of the Lord coursing in her veins, she had never faltered before. Now, for the first time in her life, she was in dire need of counsel, which failed to materialize. Despite her silent pleading, the gates of heaven remained resolutely shut. The voice of the Lord, which had so often been audible inside her, was muted, strangely indistinct. It showed the way neither to Harosheth nor away from it. Instead, it seemed to point her toward Lapidoth's home. Or was it her own prompting that directed her there?

She returned to her palm tree, there to deal with more disputes. As soon as the last seeker of justice had left, she mounted her white donkey and rode over to that house.

🦗

Unlike her custom since Lapidoth had banished her from his home, Deborah did not immediately seek out her sons, but looked for him, instead.

Lapidoth had already returned from the fields, and she found him standing in front of the house, regarding her from afar.

Having stabled her donkey, she approached him, and words she had not thought she would ever utter struggled to make their way from her mouth. "I came to seek counsel from you."

"The last time I offered it, it was not palatable to you," he retorted stiffly, showing that his hurt at her hands still lay buried inside him and had not diminished over time.

"Now I am floundering in the dark. I will be guided by you," she said in a subdued voice.

They stood face-to-face with each other. "Tell me your trouble."

She explained what had come to pass, then hung on his words, awaiting his verdict. He turned her words over in his mind for a while. Then he pronounced his approval of her endeavor. "Go in peace, and may the Lord be with you."

Deborah found the courage to say, "I was hoping that you would be with me."

Lapidoth let the silence linger longer than she would have thought possible, until she felt it gripping her chest. At last he said brusquely, "I will not deprive you of this opportunity to be alone with your lover."

"He is not my lover; he has not been for a long time. I am a field that has lain fallow for over two years."

"Why did you not tell me as much before?"

She felt a sob rising up in her, which she speedily swallowed before it became noticeable. "It would have made no odds. You have another woman now, and I will not cling to your neck."

"There was never any love between us. I took her because I was alone in body and soul and overwhelmed by need, and she submitted for lack of choice."

"She has presented you with the daughter I was unable to give you, and by now my womb is no more capable of sustaining life than the Sea of Salt."

"True," conceded Lapidoth. "But you have borne me five sons, each a jewel more precious than rubies in the crown of my life. No husband could ask for more."

Deborah raised a further objection: "The chisel of time is beginning to carve furrows around my eyes."

Lapidoth regarded her with a soft smile in his eyes. "I yearn to press my kisses on each one of them, no less than on the crevice between your breasts."

"And Naavah?" she asked, dreading his reply, for she had no wish to share him with a concubine, especially one young enough to be her daughter.

"She has found a man closer to her own age, the overseer of our fields. Yesterday I wished them a long and happy life together, as they stood under the wedding canopy."

It was as if the sun and the moon and the stars had come down from the sky to share her elation. "So do I wish them happiness, from the depth of my being."

"Where is the book of divorcement with which I have foolishly granted you your freedom?"

"In my house."

"Send one of our maids to retrieve it," he said urgently, and Deborah instructed one of the girls who worked in the household as to where the book was to be found.

The last beams of sunlight filtered through the branches of the trees. There was a soft, balmy breeze and Lapidoth's gaze upon her, gently caressing her face. The spirit of peace that had previously departed from their home had returned, filling it and the yard in which they stood to capacity.

By the time the maid reappeared, Lapidoth had collected some rushes and lit a fire and called in two of his day laborers to serve as witnesses. He drew the document from the girl's hand and announced ceremoniously, "This book is void, as if it never was." Then he consigned it to the fire and watched the flames licking it until it blackened and gave off acrid smoke, before it was eaten up by them.

The sound of the fire crackling as it consumed the scroll was like a sweet melody in Deborah's ears. The smoke stung her eyes, yet soothed them like balsam. Its thick smell was like the perfume of myrrh in her nostrils.

"On the impulse of a moment I forsook you, but with love beyond measure I bring you home again," declared Lapidoth. "I acknowledge you as my wife once more, now and forever."

"Though mountains may shift," she responded with a quiver in her voice, "and hills may shake, my love for you shall be immovable. Henceforward the covenant between us will never fail." With these words on her lips, and her face streaked with tears of contrition, she walked into his open arms and buried her face in his neck.

For the first time in more than two years they sat down together for the evening meal, attended also by their astounded sons, whose babbling voices spoke their rapture.

That night they were joined in love, sharing moans of pleasure and sighs of contentment and the calm of satiation. There were tender words of affection between them that no longer needed to be said. And they reveled in the knowledge that they had found new pathways to each other's hearts. That henceforward each evening would carry the promise of the night to come. And that only death would ever pry them apart again.

卐

On the way back to Harosheth from his home, before entering the gate of Mishma's castle, Barak encountered Deborah and Lapidoth and their entourage, bent on the same destination.

After greetings were exchanged, he perceived from the glow in her eyes and the new bloom in her cheeks that Deborah had been reconciled with her husband, and he rejoiced in her joy.

Although Lapidoth had never been favorably disposed toward Barak, he knew that this was not the time to bear grudges. Thus he praised the erstwhile warrior for his attempt to cut his sword into a plowshare. Then, leaving their people behind, the three of them mounted the stairs to Mishma's throne room.

Having learned a lesson from her meeting with Sisra, Deborah purposely let her husband precede her up the stairs. As Mishma set great store by such signs of wifely servility, the gesture found favor in his eyes. Thus, quite unexpectedly, he broke into a smile of welcome.

The next day, the other kings of Canaan and the noblemen of Mishma's domain assembled in his courtyard, where benches had been set up for them in the shade of the trees.

Once they had been offered refreshment, the head elders of Israel took up their position on the top of the stairs at the entrance of the castle, high above the ground. The one they had appointed as their spokesman stepped forward and announced with great pomp that he was conferring on King Mishma the blessing of all the elders and the people of Israel.

Then Barak joined him and called out that he had come to convey to the king greetings and a message from his warriors. It was that they would all be happy to lay down their weapons and do war no more.

Finally, Deborah, flanked by Lapidoth, appeared. She was resplendent in her scarlet dress, overlaid with a yellow shift, the one she donned only on the most festive occasions. At the sight of her regal stature and demeanor, a hush fell on all those present. With her fiery voice, which was renowned even in Canaan, she chanted this poem:

Hear me, you kings, you noblemen, give ear!
I will speak the praise of Mishma, the greatest king
of Canaan. You, who have answered his call, be proud
of your champion.
He is triumphant in war, even mightier in peace.
He resembles the sun in the morning, as it rises in all
its might.
May the Lord make his countenance shine upon him!

Her words flowed smoothly from her mouth, like water down a slope. The kings and noblemen of Canaan broke into loud cheers.

Deborah had unashamedly bent the truth. She had showered profuse and undeserved flattery on Mishma, in the hope that it would further peace. And indeed, as soon as the guests had dispersed, the head of the elders, together with Barak and Mishma, sat down in the seclusion of the host's office and negotiated until late into the night.

The next day they were joined in the reception hall by the noblemen of Canaan and the elders of Israel. In their presence, they proclaimed a covenant in which the border between Israel and Canaan was clearly set out. In evidence of this, they wrote the words of the treaty onto a scroll, of which the head of the elders and Barak and Mishma obtained copies, and they pressed their seals on those scrolls.

Together they and their men rode to a designated place. There they had seven finely chiseled large stones brought to them on which they engraved the words of the treaty, and which they set up to mark the boundary between their two lands.

In the time-honored tradition, they placed their hands under each other's thighs, and before the noblemen and elders, they swore an oath never to cross these boundaries except when bearing the banner of peace, and never to wage war on each other again.

In the meantime, Mishma's workmen had dug a well, from which they drew water. They sealed the alliance between them by drinking this water from the same cup, and by eating from the same loaf of bread.

This ceremonial meal was followed by their return to Mishma's castle. There, a grand feast had been laid out for them. In recognition of Deborah's share in bringing about the alliance, Barak was about to lead her and her husband to the head of the huge set table that awaited them. But Deborah, still mindful of the lesson that had been imparted to her by Sisra, modestly took her place at the foot of the table, where Asherah and other queens and noblewomen of Canaan joined her, to Mishma's nod of approval. Then began the sumptuous meal, in which all those present gorged themselves with spiced fish of all the varied species the Great Sea had to offer and fruit and wine and laughter.

Early the next morning, Deborah and Lapidoth and Barak and all the Israelites mounted their donkeys and left Harosheth together.

Before they parted to return to their homes, Barak made Deborah privy to his doubts as to whether Mishma would abide by the treaty they had forged.

But she reassured him by saying that Mishma now owed them a debt of gratitude for glorifying him in front of his noblemen, and also for adding so much gold and silver to his coffers, all of which he badly needed to fortify his position. Besides, having forged a covenant in meticulous adherence to ancient Canaanite law, and having sworn an oath in the presence of his noblemen, Mishma would be in honor bound to keep it.

🦂

Deborah considered that the alliance was the Lord's doing, and it was marvelous in her eyes. She exulted in the knowledge that she, alongside Barak and Nogah and Asherah, had been the Lord's vessel in bringing it about. And she recognized the feast in celebration of this alliance to be her greatest accomplishment. She had not planned it so, had merely groped her way toward it. But though she had humbled herself, it was her real triumph, the crowning glory of her life.

Nogah, too, acknowledged to herself that it had been Deborah's wisdom and foresight that had been steering the fate of Israel. It had guided the people to war when the necessity arose, but also to peace when the possibility emerged. Nogah also blessed her sister for surpassing herself in the service of peace. And she thanked the Lord for arranging it so that her own labor in assisting them had been rewarded.

More than anything, she felt a thrill of pride in her husband, whose thunder and lightning had mellowed into the soft light rising at the dawn of a new day.

Epilogue

Deborah continued to judge the people of Israel under her palm tree in the mountains of Efraim. Her time apart from Lapidoth eventually receded into the nether regions of her soul, and she hardly remembered it. She was highly revered by the people all the days of her life.

Mishma became the mightiest of all the kings of Canaan. He dealt summarily with his rebellious brother-in-law. Because he was his kinsman, he did not have him executed or incarcerated. Instead, he exiled him and his family, putting them all on a merchant ship that set out to the far side of the Great Sea, and they were never heard of again.

Asherah bore Mishma three sons and three daughters. And she came to be known as the most beautiful queen of Canaan ever.

Apart from their firstborn son, Shlomi, Nogah bore Barak four more sons and two daughters. They lived to see their children's children, and their children, too. Nogah continued to enjoy the companionship of her mother, who endowed her with twin brothers before her womb ceased bearing fruit.

Uriel lay down with his fathers at a ripe old age, surrounded by Nogah, Barak, and their children, who were as a loving family to him, gladdening the last years of his life.

The scroll depicting Barak's war with Sisra and Jabin, which Nogah had rewritten, was accepted by the Council of Elders to be deposited at the house of the Lord. It was copied many times over and dispatched by messengers to scroll rooms across the land. It became part of the heritage of the people of Israel, which was passed down from generation to generation, until this very day.

Those who had been killed in the war, both Israelites and Canaanites, could not be brought back to life. But those who survived lived a life of contentment, with each man sitting under his vine and his fig tree.

And the land was at peace for forty years.

Historical Note

This novel is set in ancient Israel, an agricultural-pastoral society, in the era of the Judges. By biblical account this period (widely dated as spanning from the twelfth to the mid eleventh centuries BCE) followed shortly after the initial occupation of the land of Canaan by the Israelites. As described in the biblical book of Judges, it was marked by domestic turbulence and fraught with bloody battles against various enemies, including the Canaanites and the Philistines.

However, hostilities were intermittent: The book of Judges states that warfare was interspersed with periods of peace. One of these came about at the conclusion of the war between the Israelites and the Cannaanites led by Deborah and Barak, and it lasted for forty years (Judges 5:31), and so it is described in this novel.

In those days, the tribes of Israel formed a loose confederacy, with a large degree of tribal autonomy, under the traditional, patriarchal authority of the "elders." In moments of crisis, all or part of the tribes rallied behind sporadic leaders, referred to as judges. Some of these served as political figures, dispensers of justice, and military heroes or commanders at one and the same time. Some, most prominently Deborah and later Samuel, were prophets as well.

Their multifaceted leadership apparently did not derive from any coercive power they might have wielded. Rather, it stemmed from their widely renowned charismatic personalities and from the high esteem they enjoyed among the people. It was also based on the fact that the political structure was close to what today we would refer to as a theocracy, which rendered it legitimate for the prophet, the representative of the Almighty, to rule, as also depicted in this book.

During this era, the tribes were beginning to aspire to a permanent national head ruling with the aid of a central administration. In other words, they wished for a king, who would unite the unruly tribes and confront the menace of old and new enemies, as also illustrated here. However, this aspiration did not come to fruition until the later years of the Prophet Samuel (widely dated to the late eleventh century BCE), who anointed two kings in his lifetime.

It was rare, but not unheard of, for women to achieve elevated positions as the Lord's prophets. Apart from Deborah there were Miriam, the sister of Moses (Exodus 15:20), and Huldah (Kings 22:14), and there might have been others whose memories have been lost in the mist of time. Deborah was arguably the most eminent of these, as well as the most prominent woman leader in the Bible and in ancient Israel. As such, she might well serve as a role model to women aspiring to leadership today.

I tried to show that apart from her unique public standing, she also had a rich and complex private life. In this aspect of her existence, she was very much a woman, in both her strengths and her weaknesses, and this did not detract from her stature as national leader. This is also something from which women harboring political ambitions may derive inspiration: From antiquity to the present, power and femininity have not stood in contradiction to each other.

In the period covered in the novel, literacy was not yet widespread, and scribes acted as teachers to limited circles. Even so, there is indirect evidence for some literacy among women, especially those of high social standing: The Bible ascribes to Hannah (the mother of the Prophet Samuel) an important literary work, "The Song of Hannah." In the same vein, it ascribes to Deborah the major share in composing the unique, beautiful poem known as "The Song of Deborah."

Women's literacy is also attested to by archeological evidence: Some seals belonging to women have been discovered, with their owners' name inscribed on them. Since seals were used to confirm the authenticity of written documents, it may be presumed that the owners could read the documents on which they pressed their seals. The seals unearthed are mainly from the ninth to the seventh centuries BCE. But it is possible that similar ones existed in the twelfth century. Hence it is not anachronistic to present Deborah and the two other heroines of this novel, both of high social stature as king's daughters, as versed in the art of reading and writing.

There is no substantial evidence as to who wrote the various books of the Bible that followed the Torah, the Five Books of Moses. Some commentators have raised the possibility that women participated in writing those books, a possibility I have also taken up in this novel.

Acknowledgments

This is to express my deepest gratitude to the people who have generously devoted their precious time and effort to reading previous versions of this book. Each of them has made an invaluable contribution to its improvement. They are (in the chronological order of reading it): Tamar Fox, Tamar Halevy, Maria Antoniou, and Jane Cavolina (who read the manuscript twice and corrected numerous flaws in both content and style). I greatly benefited not only from these persons' comments but also from their personal encouragement.

Special thanks go to my agent, Judith Riven, whose excellent comments on the manuscript, and whose support, have been far above and beyond the call of duty.

I am deeply indebted to Ali Bothwell Mancini, the book's editor, for her encouragement, her brilliant remarks, and her detailed guidance, which saved me from many pitfalls, helped me through the final stages of writing, and improved the book's quality beyond recognition.

Finally, hearty thanks to my husband, Zvi, and the rest of my family, for their unfailing patience and understanding.

It is not a figure of speech, but the plain truth, that without the practical and emotional assistance of these persons, *The Triumph of Deborah* would not have come into existence.